CATHERINE HART
BETINA KRAHN
LINDA LADD
BARBARA DAWSON SMITH
KATHERINE SUTCLIFFE

The romance authors you enjoy all year long present five very special tales of love and reunion, rekindled romance, and family celebration. As a seasonal special, here are the best in romantic fiction from these outstanding authors, stories to be treasured now and for many years to come.

Avon Books Presents:

CHRISTMAS ROMANCE

D1319892

**If You Enjoy These Stories,
Be Sure To Look For—**

TEMPEST
by Catherine Hart

CAUGHT IN THE ACT
by Betina Krahn

FROSTFIRE
by Linda Ladd

DREAMSPINNER
by Barbara Dawson Smith

FIRE IN THE HEART
by Katherine Sutcliffe

Avon Books Presents:

CHRISTMAS ROMANCE

Love Stories from

CATHERINE HART
BETINA KRAHN · LINDA LADD
BARBARA DAWSON SMITH
KATHERINE SUTCLIFFE

AVON BOOKS ◆ NEW YORK

AVON BOOKS PRESENTS: CHRISTMAS ROMANCE is an original publication of Avon Books. This work, as well as each individual story, has never before appeared in print. This work is a collection of fiction. Any similarity to actual persons or events is purely coincidental.

AVON BOOKS
A division of
The Hearst Corporation
1350 Avenue of the Americas
New York, New York 10019

Published by arrangement with the authors
Library of Congress Catalog Card Number: 90-93386
ISBN: 0-380-76205-6

First Avon Books Printing: December 1990

AVON TRADEMARK REG. U.S. PAT. OFF. AND IN OTHER COUNTRIES, MARCA REGISTRADA, HECHO EN U.S.A.

Printed in the U.S.A.

RA 10 9 8 7 6 5 4 3 2

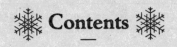 Contents

A Christmas Melodie

Catherine Hart

1

Abilene, Kansas
Mid-December 1867

MELODIE stepped carefully down from the train and looked about in uncertainty. What was she supposed to do now? She'd never traveled before, and had no one to advise her. To her vast relief, she spotted a porter just a few steps away.

"Sir!" she called over the roar of the locomotive. "Sir!"

"Yes, ma'am?"

"Can you please aid me in locating my luggage and having it transferred to the local stagecoach station? I must confess I am at a loss as to how to accomplish this myself."

Unlike Kansas City, Abilene boasted no cabs for hire at the train station. The best help the porter could find was a pimple-faced fourteen-year-old boy and a wobbly-wheeled pushcart as transport for her bags. Melodie was forced to walk the entire way to the hotel where the stage made its scheduled stops, carrying Ming's traveling cage herself when the grouchy little dog refused to ride atop the precarious pile of luggage.

By the time she was finally shown to a small, dreary room on the second floor, her shoes were wet through

3

with snow, and her feet were almost numb from the cold—and not for the first time, Melodie was beginning to have second thoughts about this venture. Sitting on the edge of the bed, her head drooping wearily, she wondered when and why her life had taken the turns that had landed her in her present situation. Here she was, a withering rose upon the vine, a twenty-six-year-old spinster on her way to Denver to catch herself a husband.

What would happen if she and Mr. Mortimer Schnickelgruber did not suit each other well enough for marriage? Melodie didn't even want to think about that! Her prospective groom could very well be her final opportunity to become a bride, her last chance at security and peace of mind.

Oh, certainly there were other men out there looking for wives, but most of them wanted women younger than Melodie. That or they were widowers looking for cheap caretakers for their homes and their motherless children, and Melodie was convinced that she would rather endure the solitude of spinsterhood than the havoc of raising a brood of noisy children. As the only child of older, rather fussy parents, who were themselves without siblings, she hadn't been around children much and, frankly, they made her nervous. Melodie knew her shortcomings as well as her merits. While she might still adjust to having a husband underfoot, she knew she was much too impatient and set in her ways to cope with small children.

This, in itself, made Mr. Schnickelgruber an excellent choice for her. He had no children and little likelihood of fathering any at his advanced age of fifty-seven, or so Melodie hoped. A miner who had made his fortune in Colorado's gold mines, Mortimer had lived a rollicking and merry existence until recently. Now, his excesses had caught up with him, and he wished to spend his gout-slowed latter years in the pleasant company of a gentlewoman.

At least, this is what Melodie had been led to believe

in her brief correspondence with the man. Unfortunately, she'd not yet met him; thus the trip to Denver to do so now. Her sole knowledge of him came from a small advertisement in the *Kansas City Star* and his reply to her inquiry for further information. To his credit, he'd sent her the necessary fare for her trip to Denver, and Melodie could only hope he would be just as generous in providing her return fare if the two of them decided not to wed. If he refused, she would undoubtedly be stuck in Denver, like it or not, and seeking whatever decent employment was to be had there for a lady of her genteel upbringing.

Melodie sighed, eyed her drenched shoes and stockings with a baleful eye, and debated forgoing her supper in favor of dry feet. Venturing out into the snowy street in search of supper—the hotel did not offer dining facilities to its customers—did not appeal greatly, but her stomach was even now rumbling in loud complaint. She'd eaten nothing since breakfast but a cheese and butter sandwich and an apple on the train, and it was now past six o'clock in the evening. Ming needed feeding too, or he might keep the entire hotel awake tonight, or get them both booted out into the snow.

If she did not stir herself soon, the eating establishments would undoubtedly stop serving supper before she could order a meal, and she would go hungry until morning, or longer. Who could know if she would be able to find some place to eat before the stage left in the morning?

As she tugged her wet shoes over clammy stockings, Melodie allowed herself yet another moment of self-pity. That she, Melodie Kern, had been brought to this! A pitiful mail-order bride with a pug-nosed dog!

It was all Great-aunt Gertie's fault, blast the hateful old bat! If she hadn't begged and wheedled, and promised to bequeath all her worldly goods to Melodie in return for Melodie's nursing during the best years of her youth, Melodie would undoubtedly have married long ago. She'd had several promising prospects at the time, handsome young swains eager to take her to wife.

If she had it all to do over again, Melodie felt sure she'd choose to marry rather than look after Gertie—but perhaps not. Great-aunt Gertie, Melodie's father's youngest aunt, had been left with no one else to care for her. If Melodie had refused, the elderly woman would have had to hire strangers to aid her in her declining years. For some reason that Melodie still did not entirely understand, she had felt a moral obligation to take care of her great-aunt, knowing that if she didn't and anything happened to hasten Gertie's demise, Melodie would never forgive herself.

Surprising everyone, most of all Melodie, Gertie had lingered for eight long and exasperating years. In that time, the old woman had seemed determined to make Melodie's life a living hell, and in the end Gertie had certainly had the last laugh. Upon her death, she had, indeed, bequeathed everything to Melodie—all of her debts, of which there were so many that even the small house had to be sold to cover them, leaving Melodie with a total inheritance of two hundred and thirty-one dollars and one snippish Pekingese dog.

Melodie glared at the dog, and Ming growled back at her.

"Oh, hush up, you sassy little beast, before I give in to the last remnants of sanity and send you to the nearest glue factory!"

Morning brought little to cheer her. A cold wind was howling down from the north. The weak wintry sun of the day before had disappeared behind threatening gray clouds. The stage was early; Melodie was running late; and Ming decided to take his own sweet time with his after-breakfast constitutional. Breakfast for Melodie was a half-cup of coffee and a sweet roll, quickly gulped.

While her bags were being loaded atop the coach, Melodie climbed aboard and placed Ming's cage on the floor at her feet. Let the rotten animal play foot-warmer for a while! After all, he'd gotten *his* breakfast!

Much to her surprise, late though she was, Melodie was still the first person to board the stage. With any luck, there would not be a full coach going to Denver. Perhaps with Christmas little more than a week away, and the constant threat of snow, especially in the mountains, there would be fewer travelers.

Her wishes were in vain. No sooner had she settled herself as comfortably as possible on the hard, worn seat than the door of the coach opened and in popped a little girl approximately seven or eight years of age. She was followed in short order by another little girl, this one barely out of babyhood, perhaps three years old. Both were dressed in woolen capes and matching green bonnets. Blonde ringlets framed their delicate faces as they hugged their dolls and smiled shyly at Melodie.

"Bets, you sit here, next to the lady," the older girl said, doing her best to pick up her sister and hoist her onto the seat next to Melodie. "And I'll sit next to you."

In his cage, Ming snarled, drawing the girls' attention. From her perch next to Melodie, Bets leaned down and peered at the furry animal. "Doth your dog bite, lady?" she lisped, raising huge blue eyes to Melodie's.

"Occasionally," Melodie responded dryly, "which is why he is confined. I would suggest that you keep your fingers away from the cage, just to be safe."

Melodie was beginning to wonder where the girls' parents were, and what was taking them so long to board, when a mop of red hair and a face full of bold freckles appeared over the step. The boy grinned, revealing a large empty space where his two front teeth should have been, and Melodie knew instinctively that she was looking at pure, raw orneriness. The stout little lad clambered into the coach and onto the seat opposite her. Still eyeing him warily, Melodie was only half-aware of another small person entering, until she turned her head and stared in mute despair. Twins!

Saints alive! Two pint-size devils with cowlicks and freckles!

"Hi! I'm Tommy!" one piped up cheerfully.

"And I'm Timmy!" the other added. "Who're you?"

"Are you goin' to Denver, too?"

"Timmy! Tommy! Behave yourselves, or Pa will have your hides." This from the older girl, leading Melodie to the conclusion that all four children belonged to the same family.

Before Melodie could gather her wits enough to respond, a man climbed into the coach, swinging the door shut after himself. He seated himself next to the boys, removed his hat, and settled his long legs before him. A lock of blond hair fell over his forehead, and he brushed it back as his turquoise gaze swept the occupants of the coach.

Nodding politely to Melodie, he spoke to the children. "Everybody ready? None of you forgot anything, did you? Anyone have to do anything important before we leave? The driver can't stop every time one of you thinks you have to go, you know, so speak now or hold it."

There were nods all around, which the man seemed pleased to note. Melodie was still wondering where the man's wife was, if perhaps the mother was the main thing that had been forgotten and left behind, when the driver cracked his whip, shouted to the horses, and they were on their way.

Melodie was doing her best to ignore the young family, garnering all of her courage to endure a week of being cramped into this small coach with all these energetic children, when the man spoke to her.

"Ma'am? Is this your glove? It was lyin' here on the floor of the carriage."

Melodie turned her head and gazed straight into the most beautiful eyes she'd ever beheld. They were the color of a tropic sea, or what she imagined a tropic sea to be, a perfect blending of blue and green, with sparkles of sunlight caught in their depths. For a moment she simply stared, completely forgetting herself.

"Ma'am?"

His voice recalled her to herself. Her glove dangled from his extended fingertips. "Oh! Yes! Thank you, sir!" She reached for her glove, but the man did not immediately release it to her.

"David Cooper, ma'am. And these are my children: Jennifer, Betsy, Tommy, and Timmy."

It would have been extremely rude not to respond to the friendly introduction, and she would have felt even more of a fool by withholding her name. "Melodie Kern, Mr. Cooper," she answered with a stiff smile, determinedly tugging her glove from his grasp.

The twinkle in his eyes told her he knew she had deliberately omitted designating her marital status, and was amused by her tactics. "Are you travelin' all the way to Denver with us, Miss Kern?" Was there a slight emphasis on the *Miss*, or was she imagining it?

"It would appear so, Mr. Cooper."

"Visitin' relatives for the Christmas holidays, perhaps?"

"Perhaps." It wasn't really a lie. After all, Mr. Schnickelgruber was a prospective relative.

"I've always admired a woman of few words. Rare thing these days, you know?" His lips curved into a smile guaranteed to melt icebergs. "Almost as unusual as your name. Melodie. Makes you think of bird songs, doesn't it, girls?"

By the time he turned his fascinating gaze from her to his daughters, Melodie could scarcely breathe. Land sake, but the man had more than his fair share of charm! No wonder he already had four children. Why, his poor wife probably stood no chance of ignoring his amorous attentions.

She shook her head at such fanciful thinking and tuned an ear to the conversation at hand. David Cooper was chatting easily with his daughters. At the same time, he reached out and grabbed Tommy's leg, which had been swinging rhythmically closer and closer to

Ming's cage, then adroitly popped Timmy's licorice ball back into his mouth while Melodie watched in amazement.

"Bluebird songs?"

Cooper nodded in agreement with Jenny's suggestion.

"No." The little one, Betsy, pulled her thumb from her mouth and grinned, a fair imitation of her father's dazzling smile. " 'Nary thongth."

Melodie caught herself wondering what the child was trying to say. Her curiosity was satisfied when Cooper nodded again. "I like that, Bets. Canary songs. Yes, that's exactly what the name Melodie sounds like."

Once more, he caught Melodie's eye, then winked! Melodie was immediately aghast. The scoundrel! How dare he flirt with her! And he, a married man! Perhaps she'd best remind him of that fact right off. Melodie's nose came up several notches as she speared him with a righteous look. "Will your *wife* be meeting you and the children in Denver, sir?"

His smile dissolved, replaced by an expression that spoke of regret, sorrow, and anger. "My wife died a year ago this past fall," he informed her tersely.

🔔 2 🔔

NEVER in her life had Melodie felt so small, so mean. She wished she could simply disappear, melt into the seat and be gone. She settled on an apology, hoping it would soothe the sting of her hurtful words. "I apologize, Mr. Cooper. Please forgive me for being so waspish. Traveling does not agree with me, it seems."

Cooper gave her a grudging nod. "Are you sick?" he asked gruffly. "I can ask the driver to stop for a few minutes if you are."

"No, but thank you for your concern, sir. I'm tired, cold, irritable, and nervous, but other than that, I'm fine." She ventured a small, tentative smile. "This is the first time I have traveled, you see, and I'm afraid I was not very well prepared for the rigors."

David returned her smile, and Melodie felt something soft bloom inside her. She was inordinately glad he was no longer angry with her.

"Well, we'll have to see what we can do to make your journey more pleasant," he said, then frowned as his breath crystallized before him. A quick glance at his sons proved why it was rapidly becoming colder inside the coach. Tommy and Timmy were on their knees tugging at the loosened leather flaps that tied down over the windows of the coach to keep out as much of the cold weather as possible. The twins were fast defeating this purpose.

With a sigh and a shake of his head, David grabbed each of the boys by the back of the britches and hauled them into their seats. "Sit and behave!" he ordered quietly but firmly. "And leave those window ties alone. We have a long way to go, boys, and we don't need you freezin' us along the way."

From behind his back, David pulled out a thick wool lap robe. He shook it out and offered it to Melodie. "Fold this around your legs and tuck your feet under it." As she did as he suggested, David helped his daughters do the same.

"Now, settle back and take a nice little nap," he said to Melodie, "and before you know it, all your problems will be solved. When you wake you'll be rested, warmer, and things will look a lot better."

Once more he grinned at her, and, ridiculous though it was, Melodie felt warmer already. She nodded off, listening to the pleasant sound of his deep voice as he played a quiet word game with his children, easily engaging their agile young minds.

Meanwhile, David wasn't really concentrating on the silly game he and his offspring played; his thoughts were drawn to all the worries that plagued him these days. Little more than a year ago, things had been wonderful. Ann had been alive then, and David's world had been filled with the sunshine of her love. She'd been their anchor, keeping them all firmly in place. Under her wing, even the twins had behaved better, though not by much, it was true. But now she was gone, and they were adrift in a sea of confusion, without direction.

For a while, they'd muddled through. While David had tended to his work around the ranch, their housekeeper had watched the children, just as she'd helped do when Ann had been there. Now, however, the chore was doubly hard, even though Jenny, at the tender age of seven, tried desperately to fill her mother's empty shoes. They'd managed somehow until a month ago, when the housekeeper had suddenly and unexpectedly run off with a traveling shoe salesman, leaving David and the children floundering once more.

He'd tried. He'd truly tried to keep things going smoothly, to hold his little family together through sheer determination and devotion, but there just weren't enough hours in the day, or enough hands to do all the work required. Try as he might, he could not be both mother and father to four children without some kind of help. He could not run a ranch, keep house, and raise the children by himself, or with the inadequate help of his hired men.

He'd hired another housekeeper, but she'd promptly quit when Tommy threw her eyeglasses down the outhouse hole. David couldn't blame her, and he'd paid for new spectacles, but she'd left him in the lurch once more. Even his foreman's wife refused, after two days, to watch "those little hooligans" for more than a few minutes at a time, and then only if it were truly necessary.

Now, just a week before Christmas, they were headed for David's older sister's house in Denver. The children thought they were going just for the holidays, but David knew differently. He'd written to Lisa, explaining his problem, and she'd told him to bring the children to her. Though she and Jarod had two young boys of their own a few years older than Jenny, they offered to keep David's four until he could make other arrangements. Unspoken lay the thought that it might be some time, perhaps years, before David could manage to have his little family together again under their own roof, maybe not until they were old enough not to need so much constant tending and could fend fairly well for themselves.

Meanwhile, Lisa and Jarod would raise them with love and proper guidance, David was certain, and Lisa would especially dote on the girls. But David's heart was breaking at the thought of being separated from his children. First Ann, and now the children. What would he do without them? What would he do?

The stagecoach skidded slightly and rocked to a halt, the motion bouncing Melodie's head against the side of the coach, waking her abruptly.

Moments later, their driver, Sam Nichols, appeared at the door, his beard white with crusted snow beneath his wind-ruddied cheeks. "Folks, I sure do hate to say this, but we're gonna hafta skip the noon stop if we're to have any hope of reachin' our evening rest station. This snow's startin' to get deep, and it's already driftin' a foot high in places. I'm gonna take a shorter route, one that's a little rougher, but it'll get us there quicker."

For the first time Melodie realized that the threatening clouds had begun to disperse their heavy burden. Peering past the driver's bulk, she saw the snow glistening white and blowing in the wind like a sheer white curtain. Beside her, the girls squealed in delight, and the boys wriggled with the urge to have a good romp in the stuff.

"You folks might as well get out and stretch your legs while you've got the chance," the driver suggested. With a look at David, he asked, "If you'd be willin' to lend a hand, sir, I'd be obliged. I think it's time to turn this old pony wagon into fit transportation for all this snow."

Before they could decipher this last comment, he moved away, and they could hear him talking cheerfully to the horses, as if the snow and the cold were no real inconvenience, as if the bitter wind bothered him not at all. Melodie and the Cooper family tumbled from the coach. All about them, snow blanketed the rolling land, covering all its imperfections and making everything appear clean and white and deceptively safe.

No sooner had Betsy's feet touched ground than she was hopping from one foot to the other, her pixie face scrunched into an awful grimace. "Pa, I gotta go wee-wee!" she announced none too quietly, tugging urgently at David's coat sleeve.

"Jenny, you take Betsy with you and follow Miss Melodie. Take care now, not to step in a hole or wander too far from the coach. This looks like it's buildin' into a blizzard, and it'd be real easy to lose your way. Stay close, you hear?"

His turquoise gaze swept up to meet Melodie's, and her protest died on her lips. Obviously, his admonishments included her, and just for a moment she bristled, feeling twelve years old again; but the warm caress in his eyes made her feel things no twelve-year-old ever felt. Her heart lurched into her throat, and her face began to burn with a quick blush.

Jenny saved her from appearing a complete fool by replying to her father's query. "Sure, Pa. We'll find a private spot in callin' distance." The girl's bright eyes, so like her father's, leveled a warning look at her brothers. "You just keep an eye on the boys, 'cause if I catch 'em trying to peek at us, I'm gonna ask Miss Melodie to set her dog on 'em, and that critter looks as mean as a badger!"

By the time they'd all relieved themselves and walked the kinks out, including Ming, who didn't care for the snow at all and growled incessantly, the stage-coach was ready to travel once more. With David's help, Sam Nichols had folded down two long runners which were hinged to the underside of the carriage. Once locked into place, they rode just beneath the wheels, effectively turning the stage into a sleigh.

Standing back and admiring their handiwork, David gave a slow whistle. "Well, I'll be! If that isn't something! When did the stage line finally get smart and think of this?"

"Like it, do ya?" Sam asked with a chuckle. His blue eyes sparkled with merriment. "It's my own idea, and right clever, if I do say so myself." Casting a look toward the dismal skies and the blowing snow, he added, "Still, we'd better get a move on, while we can still see two feet in front of us."

While Sam checked the horses one last time, David helped Melodie and the children into the coach. Once more they were off, this time with runners skimming over the snow like skate blades on a frozen pond. David passed around beef sandwiches from the basket at his feet, deliberately handing one to Melodie. "Don't be shy, Miss Melodie. We have plenty and are more than willing to share with you."

"But how did you know to bring food?" she questioned.

He laughed. "I didn't, but with four youngsters, I've learned to be prepared for anything. Here, have a potato." He tossed it to her, chuckling as she juggled frantically, half-smashing her sandwich as she caught it. The children giggled, each catching his or her own potato in turn.

"Oh!" she squealed, half-laughing with them.

"Why, it's still warm!" she exclaimed in surprise and delight.

"They were well-wrapped. If I'd thought about it, we could have put them in our pockets while we were out of the carriage. They'd have kept our hands warm."

"I'll have to remember that the next time I'm out in cold weather," Melodie commented. "I hear winters in Denver can be very harsh."

"You're not from Denver, then?" David asked.

Her mouth full of bread and beef, Melodie shook her head. "No," she said, when she could again speak. When he continued to give her that speculative look, she felt compelled to explain. "I am going to Denver to be married, Mr. Cooper. My intended husband lives there."

"I see." Was it disappointment she saw flicker briefly in those wondrous eyes, dimming them for a moment, or was she imagining it?

For reasons beyond his own understanding, David was disappointed to hear that pretty little Melodie, with the songbird name and the violet eyes, was engaged to be married. Not that David had actually considered the idea of remarrying just yet, and he certainly hadn't considered Melodie Kern with that thought in mind. So why did it bother him that she was traveling to Denver to marry someone else?

"I suppose I should wish you happiness, then," he told her in a flat voice that carried little enthusiasm. "Who is the lucky fella? I've visited my sister enough times to know some of the townspeople. Maybe I've met him."

Color flooded her cheeks, though why she should be embarrassed to impart this information, Melodie did not know. "His name is Mortimer Schnickelgruber," she stated softly, rather reluctantly.

Across from her the twins burst into wild guffaws, sputtering and spewing half-chewed mouthfuls of potato over the interior of the coach as they nudged each other with their elbows. The girls were little better, twittering behind their hands and trying to hide their faces. David's own face was nearly as red as Melodie's now, as he tried to contain his own mirth.

"I . . . uh . . . I don't believe I've had the pleasure of meeting him," he said from between compressed lips, his voice quavering suspiciously. "I'm sure I'd have recalled the name." With that, hilarity won out, erupting from deep within his chest.

"This is not at all funny," Melodie objected frostily, her mouth pursed in disapproval. "A person should not be ridiculed for his name, since he cannot help what that name might be. I am quite sure that Mr. Schnickelgruber is very proud of his ancestry and his parents, who undoubtedly had more say in naming him than he did himself."

"No doubt," David conceded, holding his aching sides. "But any man worth his weight in salt would change his name before going through life with a name like Schnickelgoober, for God's sake! Can you imagine the torment he must have suffered, the teasing he took from everyone? Old Morty must have been mortified!" This set off another round of laughter.

"That's Schnickelgruber, and I must assume, as I pointed out to you just a moment ago, that Mr. Schnickelgruber takes pride in his heritage and his name. The crude comments and laughter of others must not concern him overmuch, or he would have changed his name long ago. Perhaps he has more worth than to let petty harassments plague him."

"That or he's too stupid to notice," David muttered, wiping the tears from his cheeks. "So, tell me, Miss Melodie, what is it about Mortimer Snickergruber that attracts you?"

Melodie's chin rose in defiance. "Schnickelgruber," she corrected irritably. "And I don't consider that any of your business, Mr. Cooper. Feeding me one small meal hardly entitles you to know any more about me than I wish to tell."

"Is he handsome?" David persisted in that particularly wheedling tone that boys seem to perfect even before they can walk upright. "Do you have a likeness of him? A tintype, a drawing?"

In fact, Melodie did have a tintype of Mortimer, but she was not about to confide such information to David, let alone show it to him. The beast would only ridicule Mortimer all the more, since the image was not altogether complimentary. Oh, it wasn't awful, either, but it did show the man's age. Her prospective groom had a receding hairline, and there were deep grooves etched into the flesh of his face, which Melodie suspected were an accurate indication of the iniquitous life he had formerly led.

There was no other way to describe his nose other than to say it was bulbous. Certainly, it dominated his face, while his thin lips were all but nonexistent. He did have nice teeth, so unblemished for his age in fact, that Melodie couldn't help wondering if they were real or store-purchased. His eyes were his sole redeeming feature, large and soulful, like a lost fawn's. This guileless look had convinced Melodie that she could believe the man's story about changing his ways and settling into a sedate way of life. Besides, at his age what else could he do?

"Melodie?" David prompted, drawing her from her reverie.

"What? Oh! What was it you said?"

"I asked if Schnickelgroper is handsome?"

"Schnickelgruber, Mr. Cooper! Schnickelgruber! And no, he is not overly handsome. He is passable, however."

"Passable, huh?" David's smile was a tad smug. "What does he do?"

"Do?"

"For a living? To make his way in the world? To earn his keep?"

"Oh!" She blinked, as if the question were an odd thing to ask, then said slowly, "Why, nothing that I know of."

"Nothing? That you know of?" David echoed. "What kind of answer is that? Just how well do you know this man, Miss Kern? How did you meet?"

She frowned at him. "We haven't met. That is the purpose of this trip, you see, to see if we suit each other."

"No, I don't see. If you've never met, how did you become acquainted? Is he a friend of your family?"

Her frown deepened, and she pulled herself up straight in her seat. "Mr. Cooper, your questions are becoming quite personal, don't you think? Why on earth should I account to you for what I'm doing?"

"Why on earth would you be going to all the way to Denver to marry some man you've never even met?" he countered smoothly. "Good Lord, woman! Do you realize the grief you could come to? The danger you might be walking into? The man could be a thief, a murderer, the Bluebeard of 1867, for cryin' out loud! You can't just sashay into Denver and marry a man sight unseen!"

"I can if I want to!" she huffed, her voice rising.

"Why would you want to?" he yelled back, glowering at her. "Are you really that stupid?"

"Papa," Betsy piped up, only to be ignored.

"I'm not stupid! And Mr. Schnickelgruber is not dangerous!"

"Papa!" Jenny joined her sister's plea for attention, receiving only an impatient wave of David's hand that signaled for her to wait.

"Then what is he, since you know so awfully much about him, my dear?" David sneered.

"He's rich, he's old, and he doesn't have children!" she shouted angrily in reply. "He's also the man I'm going to marry!"

"Papa!" both girls chorused urgently.

"What?" he barked. Then, more calmly, taking a deep breath and concentrating all his efforts to regain his composure, he asked, "What is it you want, girls?"

"We've been trying to tell you, Papa," Jenny explained in that very grown-up way she had recently adopted. "Timmy unlaced the window covering again, after you told him not to, and he's thrown his boot out of the carriage!"

"He *what!*" David stared in horror at his five-year-old son, wondering if he could control his urge to strangle the little scamp. Would the boy ever live to the ripe old age of six? Timmy sat there, looking for all the world like a freckled angel, watching serenely as his twin brother, not to be outdone, proceeded to throw his own boot out the window. As David rapped on the roof of the coach, signaling the driver to stop, and muttered obscenities under his breath, it was Melodie's turn to laugh.

"As I was saying, Mr. Cooper," she said mockingly, "one of Mortimer's drawing points is the fact that he is childless. Additionally, he has no other living relatives to meddle in our lives. Doesn't that sound perfectly serene?"

"Yeah," David snarled back. "Almost as nice as Mortimer and Melodie Snickelgoofer! Remind me to order a platter with your names engraved on it as a wedding present." Then he hurled himself from the coach, into the swirling snow.

3

A FEW minutes later, it was David's turn to apologize, and he did so humbly, if slightly more grudgingly than Melodie had done. "I'm sorry. I have no right to poke my nose into your personal plans—but I still think you're making a big mistake. I know you don't care beans for my opinion right now, but do yourself a favor, Melodie. Spend the time to get to know him first, before you take those vows. Will you do that? Will you at least think about what I've said?"

She agreed to that much, not wanting dissension between them, and didn't even mention the fact that he had used her name in much too familiar a manner for such short acquaintance. Still, she savored the small thrill that had shot through her as he had said her name, his voice seeming to vibrate around the syllables, making them quiver to life like a harp's strings beneath a master's touch.

Perhaps the sound was inspired by her thoughts of music, but a few seconds later, Melodie tilted her head, listening intently. "Pray tell me I haven't lost my wits entirely—but do I hear bells?"

David's smile lit his entire face. "I wondered when you'd notice," he admitted. "Sam seems to have taken Christmas and all this snow to heart. While I was retrieving my sons' boots, he was tying bells to the horses' harness. Sort of makes it seem all the more like a regular sleigh ride, doesn't it?"

"I don't know," Melodie answered breathlessly, enchanted by David's smile and suddenly feeling light-hearted and giddy. "I've never been on a sleigh ride before that I remember. But I do like it. Yes, I like the bells very much."

"You've never been on a sleigh ride before?" David questioned. "Well then, we'll just have to show you how it's done properly, won't we, kids?" he suggested, winking at his youngsters as if including them in some grand scheme.

"Now, a sleigh ride just isn't up to snuff without a few carols, is it?" He raised a brow comically, making everyone laugh.

"Are we gonna thing, Papa?" Betsy lisped hopefully, wriggling in her seat like an anxious puppy.

"That we are, pumpkin," he assured her, his eyes shining like exotic jewels. "Name your favorite tune, little darlin'—a Christmas melody for our Christmas Melodie," he quipped with a roguish grin in Melodie's direction. "And the rule is that we all have to join in the singing."

Melodie groaned, and blushed, and grinned like an idiot, as Betsy listed "Thilent Night" as her first request. Jenny then requested "Away in a Manger," and the twins wanted to sing "Deck the Halls," which ended up decked with "balls" of holly, rather than the traditional boughs; but the boys insisted this was the way it was supposed to be sung. When Melodie's turn came, she led them in singing "What Child Is This?" to the tune of the old English song "Greensleeves." By this time their voices were all primed for several rousing choruses of "The Twelve Days of Christmas," David's choice, of course.

On and on it went, their singing accompanied by the jingling bells and the steady plod of the horses' hooves, until they had sung every Christmas song they could think of and their voices were almost hoarse. Their harmonizing was off-key most of the time, with many a sour note, but how they enjoyed themselves! And how the time seemed to fly with something to occupy their minds! Even the twins were good, which was amazing in itself, and everyone seemed to forget how cold it was and how uncomfortable the coach's seats were. Cramped became cozy, crowded became snug; the sway and bounce of the carriage were fit accompaniment to the music. It was the most fun Melodie could remember having in a long, long time.

It was after the children had fallen asleep (baby Betsy had put up a small fuss and but had finally succumbed with her trusty thumb in her mouth and her small body snuggled up tight against Melodie's side) that Melodie realized that the regular rhythm of the horses' strides had changed. "We're traveling more slowly now," she commented softly, not wanting to wake the children. She found herself squinting to see David's face, then realized that it was also becoming dark quite fast.

David's frown matched hers. "Yes," he agreed, then went on to explain while he lit the lantern fixed inside the coach door. "The horses are probably exhausted about now. Most of the time stage teams don't have to pull this long at a stretch. If we'd stopped at the noon station, Sam would have exchanged these horses for fresh ones."

"The difficulty of pulling the coach in the snowstorm must be taking its toll on them as well," Melodie surmised.

"Right." David peeked outside the coach, where it was barely light enough to see that the snow was still coming down, driven in blinding sheets by the ever-building wind. He shook his head in a worried gesture. "It doesn't look as if it's getting any better out there, either. I don't know how much longer the horses can continue to pull a coach like this, runners or not. They need shelter and food and rest, probably more so right now than we do."

As if to emphasize his point, a strong gust of wind buffeted the coach, making it sway even more. Despite the leather flaps tied securely over the windows, frigid air rushed in, making Melodie shiver. Reflexively, she pulled Betsy closer into the shelter of her body.

"We should be there soon, shouldn't we?" she asked, gnawing at her lower lip. "At the way station, where Mr. Nichols said we'd be spending the night?"

"I don't know, Melodie. I suppose so; I hope so."

"But you're worried, aren't you? You think perhaps we might be lost or something, that our driver should have stayed on the regular route."

"It's not that I don't believe Sam knows a shorter way." David ran agitated fingers through his hair, mussing it without noticing or caring. "It's just that it's so damned easy to lose your way in a storm! All your familiar landmarks suddenly look the same, if you can even see anything through the blowing snow. Before you know it, everything looks white and strange, and you don't know up from down, let alone north from south. At least if we'd kept to the original route, supposing we didn't inadvertently stray from it even then, someone would have known where to look for us."

A gasp escaped her, making David suddenly aware of what he'd said, and how he'd frightened her. "Melodie, I didn't mean that the way it sounded. Honestly. We're gonna be fine. You'll see. Old Sam has more tricks up his sleeve than a Chinese magician. He'll get us there safe and sound. I can almost promise it."

He was vastly relieved to see color return to her ghost-pale face. "I'm going to hold you to that 'almost' promise," she told him weakly, swallowing hard on her fear. For a terrifying moment she had allowed herself to envision their frozen bodies being discovered by searchers. It was not a pretty picture, and she could only hope that it would not soon become a reality.

"Please don't disappoint me, David Cooper," she whispered, her lips quivering. Her wide violet gaze pleaded as eloquently as her softly shaking voice. "I don't think I'd like being lost in this storm, even with someone as nice as you."

It seemed one moment they were moving slowly through the dark, stormy night; the next, David was herding Melodie and the children into the blessed warmth of the large main room of the way station. Though it was still early evening as near as Melodie could determine, the room was empty of other people and the coals on the grate in the huge open fireplace were cold.

While David lugged in their bags, which Sam had left in a snowy pile just outside, and shut the door behind them, Melodie and the children wandered further into the room. It was a large, welcoming space with a divan and several comfortable chairs grouped upon a colorful rag rug before the fireplace. Numerous sets of dining tables and chairs were scattered about the room, and along the back wall a polished oak bar invited patrons to tip a mug of beer or a shot of whiskey. To one side, near the foot of a set of stairs, stood a small desk with what seemed to be a registry book open upon it.

Since no one seemed to have noted their arrival, Melodie walked to the desk, picked up the small bell there, and gave it a brisk shake. For a small bell, its peal was enough to bring an army on the run, yet no one appeared to welcome them. In fact, the place seemed to be strangely deserted. Even with the storm keeping any local customers tucked away at home, there should have been someone around—the owners, a bartender, a few stranded travelers. The smells of supper should still be lingering in the air, along with the odor of cigar smoke and wet wool socks drying by the fire. Instead, there was only silence and an eerie emptiness.

"Where is everyone?" Though she was almost whispering, Melodie's words seemed to bounce loudly off the walls, or so it appeared to her as she fought off a shiver of apprehension.

Stamping the snow from his boots, David glanced around and shook his head. "I don't know, and right this minute I don't really care. All I want is to get the children out of their coats and settle them before the fire, where they can get warm."

He set words to action as he crouched down and pulled a groggy Betsy to him. "Come on, sugar plum. Take your thumb out of your mouth so Papa can get your arm out of your coat sleeve."

Taking her cue from him, Melodie aided Jenny, who was too tired and cold to play her "little mama" role just now. For all their previous energy, even the twins offered no protest as the adults helped rid them of the heavy coats and boots.

"Your turn, Melodie," David said as she stood and faced him, only scant inches separating them. His long, lean fingers reached for the buttons of her cape-coat.

"I can't just yet." Was that her voice sounding so

breathless and fluttery? Deliberately, she took a step backward, away from him. "I have to take Ming out for his walk."

His wondrous turquoise eyes, with their thick fringe of brown lashes, were laughing at her now. "Somehow, I had the impression you weren't all that fond of the critter. Now you can't wait to tend to him?" David teased.

"He was Aunt Gertie's dog. She willed him to me when she died, and since Ming knows me, and I can't think of another living soul who would be willing to put up with his nastiness, we're sort of stuck with each other. Whether I like him or not, I can't let him suffer." She was rambling on like an idiot, but David was still standing so close, and it was making her nervous, and she didn't quite know what to do about it.

"Why don't you just open the door and let the little mutt out to fend for himself for a few minutes, Melodie?" David suggested softly. "If the blasted ball of fluff has an ounce of sense, he'll do his business and come right back in, and you won't have to get wet feet in the process. No reasoning creature would willingly stay out in this storm."

A smile flirted at her lips. "Yes, but I'm not so sure that Ming is a reasoning creature, you see? More often than not, he's just pure dumb dog."

David's eyes, his smile, caressed her face, warming it. "Just throw him out in the snow and see what happens," he said. "Meanwhile, you get out of that coat, and I'll stoke up the fire. Then, if the owners of this place still haven't shown their faces, we'll raid the kitchen and forage for supper. Maybe we'll even get lucky and find some cocoa in the cupboards."

All the while he was speaking, his eyes kept straying to her lips, and Melodie's knees were fast melting beneath her. Never had a man's gaze affected her this way, setting her heart to racing fitfully and sending hot waves quivering through her veins until her toes wanted to curl inside her shoes. It felt as if baby bunnies were running amok in her tummy, hopping about in wild abandon.

"Melodie?" David said her name softly, and her tongue snaked out to wet her dry lips.

"What?" she croaked, her voice all but gone.

"Stop looking at me like that, or I'm bound to kiss you; and once I start, I don't think I'll be able to stop." His grin turned wry. "Then the fire wouldn't get tended and we'd all freeze, the children would starve, and Ming's eyeballs would bulge out twice as far as they do now."

He sent her mouth one last, regretful look, then sighed mightily and turned away. "Go let the dog out, Melodie, before we shock the children and anyone else who might wander in here."

David was right about Ming. Regardless of how stupid the dog might seem on occasion, he wasn't dumb enough to stay out in this storm. He dashed back in between Sam's legs as the driver stomped stiffly in from the stables. "Got the horses fed and bedded down for the night," he announced in a satisfied voice. "You folks gettin' settled in all right?"

"We'll manage, Sam, but where are the people who run this place?" David asked. "I think it spooked Melodie to find the place deserted, and I have to admit it seems odd to me, too."

"Oh, don't you worry about the Johnsons none. Every Christmas, they spend a week or so with their son down in Tucson, if they can. They probably saw signs of the storm movin' in and left a couple of days early, that's all, so they wouldn't get stuck here tendin' to the likes of us." Sam chuckled. "Nothin' to fret over, as long as there's food in the pantry and dry wood for the fire. We'll do just fine, for as long as it takes."

It wasn't so much what Sam said as what he didn't that had David frowning. "Sounds like you think we might be stuck here a while."

"Yep. Hope you folks didn't have any real important plans, 'cause unless I miss my guess, we won't be goin' nowhere for several day—probably not till after Christmas."

♌ 4 ♌

SOMETHING woke her: some small sound, some minuscule movement, drawing Melodie from the comforting depths of sleep. Then she felt it. Before she'd even opened her eyes, she knew someone was staring at her. Someone—or something! There it was again, that slight shuffling sound, and just a waft of air, as if something had just breathed on her.

Melodie tried to swallow and almost choked on the panic that threatened to overwhelm her. Oh, God! What if it were some kind of animal that had gotten into the house? What it if were a slavering, beady-eyed rat? Or a hungry badger? Or even a half-starved wolf?

Dare she look? How long could she just lie here, motionless, willing the thing to go away? How long before it smelled her fear, or sensed how badly she was beginning to tremble beneath the mound of blankets covering her? How long before it decided to attack anyway, whether she moved or not, whether she lay there or leapt from the bed and tried to escape? Dare she try to outmaneuver it? To outrun it? To try to scream for help, always supposing her voice wasn't already frozen with fear?

Pearls of cold sweat had formed on her brow before she gathered enough courage to peek out between the veil of her quivering lashes. What she saw made her eyes fly wide open, her mouth doing likewise, as she stared at the creature in mute horror. It was sitting on her chest, its tiny, beady eyes trained unblinkingly on her face!

Her hysterical screams bounced off the walls and threatened to rattle the windows loose from their casings.

One floor below, in the station kitchen, David Cooper was attempting to prepare breakfast for his hungry brood. At Melodie's first ear-piercing shriek, the bowl of hotcake batter flew from the crook of his arm and shattered in a gooey mess across the floor. He and his two young daughters shared a startled look, then exclaimed as one, "The twins!"

Tearing the towel from his waist, David tossed it onto the counter, already running for the stairs. Behind him, he called, "You girls watch the pancakes!"

Betsy and Jenny shared another look between them, then shrugged. Together they pulled a chair up to the stove to watch the pancakes that were already bubbling on the cast-iron griddle.

David's heart was pounding in his ears as he raced into Melodie's bedroom and skidded to a stop. She was hunched up against the headboard, the covers pulled to her chin, panting and whimpering and pointing to an object atop the blankets. She was trembling so violently that the entire bed was shaking, and her eyes resembled two giant pansies. Standing at the foot of her bed were Timmy and Tommy, hopping about and waving their arms and having almost as much of a fit as Melodie.

In the center of the bed lay a small brown glob of fur, not much bigger than David's thumb.

In spite of his best efforts not to, David felt a smile tug insistently at the corners of his mouth. A chuckle was already rumbling within his chest, threatening to burst forth. Stepping forward, he took a closer look at the tiny creature on Melodie's bed, his suspicions confirmed. It was a mouse—a little bitty baby field mouse causing all this commotion.

However, this was obviously no ordinary mouse. Nor had it wandered up on Melodie's bed of its own accord. About its teensy neck was tied a string, the length of which formed a leash, and David would have bet his last dollar that his sons were the guilty culprits in this prank. Just now, though, they were wailing something that sounded like, "She killed Buster!" and behaving as if they were the injured party. Melodie was no longer screaming; she was merely staring glassy-eyed at the mouse, her mouth working soundlessly.

With no further delay, David retrieved the mouse, noting that the little thing did, indeed, seem to have expired—most likely from fright when Melodie screamed, if the boys were to be believed. Dumping the furry corpse into Tommy's outstretched palms, he ushered both boys out of the room. "Go on now. I'll deal with you two in a few minutes. Right now, you've scared Miss Melodie out of her wits, and if we're real lucky, she won't go the same route as poor Buster here, no thanks to you two."

"But Pa..." they intoned as one, sounding truly distressed.

"I said we'll discuss it later," David repeated. His gaze slid to the deceased rodent and he softened slightly. "If it will make you feel any better, we'll hold a funeral service later. Why don't you go try to find a little box that's the right size?" That would keep them busy for a few minutes, at least, while he tried to calm Melodie.

She was sitting on the bed with her eyes closed, still quivering. Her color was coming back quickly, however, so he assumed she was recovering from her fright.

"Have you ever envisioned those two staked over an anthill?" she queried sharply, irritation lacing her voice. Her eyes popped open to meet his as he chuckled softly.

"No," he answered, "but the idea definitely has merit. Personally, I was waiting for a band of gypsies to happen by, so I could make a decent trade, maybe even a profit on the deal."

Melodie snorted inelegantly. "Humph! I'll wager they'd have them two days, at most, and they'd pay you to take them back!"

David was laughing outright now. "You're probably right. They are more of a handful than most folks want to cope with, I guess."

He paused slightly, grinning down at her, and said, "You know, I don't think I've seen anyone react quite that drastically to a tiny little mouse before. Are you all right now?"

"I think so. I . . ."

Melodie was interrupted by Jenny, who called anxiously up the stairs, "Pa? Pancakes aren't supposed to catch fire, are they?"

David's eyes flew wide. His mouth flapped open. "Oh, Lord! The pancakes. I forgot about the pancakes!" Like a madman, he dashed from the room, and Melodie heard him taking the steps at a bound.

"Sliding down the banister would be faster!" she called after him. "Ask the twins! I'll bet they've already shined it a time or two this morning!"

By the time Melodie dressed and came down to the kitchen, David had put out the fire, aired out most of the smoke, and managed to clean up the evidence of the morning's burnt offering. Sam had discovered the henhouse and gathered fresh eggs. He'd also milked the two milch cows that shared the stable with the horses—a chore, he told them, the stage drivers performed each year when the Johnsons left to visit their son. Then Melodie and David began anew. This time, working together, they managed to put a decent breakfast on the table without mishap.

Afterward the children went off to prepare for Buster the Mouse's funeral, and Sam returned to the stable to tend his beloved horses. David and Melodie were lingering over a last cup of coffee when David suddenly asked, "Who's Aunt Gertie?"

Melodie rattled her cup against the saucer, so unexpected was his question. "I beg your pardon?"

"Aunt Gertie," David repeated patiently. "You mentioned her earlier, remember? You said she willed her dog to you."

"And little else," Melodie agreed with a frown.

"You sound bitter," David observed.

"Yes, I suppose I do, but I think, under the circumstances, I have good reason to be." His raised brow urged her to continue with an explanation. "I spent the last eight years nursing that hateful old woman; eight years of frugality and listening to puritanical sermonizing; eight years of fetching and carrying and not being able to go out and spend time with friends of my own. All on the vague promise of inheriting at least a roof over my head and a tidy little nest egg, since my youth was spent and all my suitors long since wed and raising families of their own. More fool I!

"What did I actually get in return? One nasty, hairy little dog and a pile of debts so large that once the house was sold, there was a paltry two hundred dollars left. Hardly fair compensation for eight years of drudgery and devotion, wouldn't you say?"

"Ah, but now the slaves and Miss Melodie Kern are freed," he quipped, saluting her with his coffee cup. "Gertie's gone, and you're off to become a blushing bride after all. And a rich one. Old Stickelgrubber *is* rich, isn't he, Melodie? You *are* sure of your facts this time, aren't you? It would be a shame to marry the old fella and have to put up with his eccentricities for years, only to find yourself an impoverished widow."

This time Melodie didn't even both correcting David's deliberate mispronunciation of Mortimer's surname. Rather, she answered tartly, "I find your comments and your questions beneath contempt, Mr. Cooper. You needn't make me out to be so greedy, simply because I am taking advantage of a rare opportunity, one which suits my needs and might never come my way again. Additionally, I fail to see why you need to ridicule a man you've yet to meet. How can you dislike a man you do not know?"

"It's a darn sight better than marrying him and not knowing him!" David retorted. "Truthfully, Melodie, how did you and Morty become acquainted? Is he a long-lost cousin or something?"

She surprised both of them by answering him. "No. As far as I know, the only living relative I have left is some old great-aunt living in New York, and I have had quite enough of old aunts for a while, thank you."

"And Schnickelgruber?" He said it correctly this time, wanting an answer much worse than he wished to torment her just now.

Blushing, Melodie contemplated the dusting of grounds in her coffee cup. "I answered an advertisement in the *Kansas City Star*."

David immediately forgot his new resolution not to upset her. "You did what?" he roared.

"I was desperate, don't you see?" She faced him earnestly now, imploring his understanding. "I had to sell Aunt Gertie's house, and the new owners wanted possession by the end of this month. I had no place to go, few options open to me, and precious little time to consider them. Then I saw this advertisement in the newspaper, and even though it seemed a bit risky, I decided it was worth an inquiry, at least. Mr. Schnickelgruber replied, and after a brief correspondence, we decided to meet."

Though his eyes were shooting angry sparks, David asked quietly and calmly, "How brief?"

"Pardon?"

He sighed, his patience straining. "Your correspondence with the man, Melodie. How lengthy was it?"

"Six weeks," she admitted sheepishly.

"And what did you discover during this correspondence, other than the man's claim that he is rich? Where does he live? What does he look like? How old is he? Is he kind to children and animals? Has he ever been married before? Did he beat his first wife and rob banks for a living? Does he believe in bigamy? Is he wanted by every lawman in seven states?"

By now he was so exasperated with her, he wanted to shake her until her teeth rattled, or until some good sense filtered into her brain. "Just what, exactly, do you know about this man you say you're going to marry, other than what he has led you to believe? And how do you know that one tenth of all he's telling you is true?"

"Assuming it is, for the moment, Mr. Cooper," Melodie cooed mockingly, "he is fifty-seven years of age. He made his fortune in the gold mines. He is alone in the world, with no wife or children. Does that satisfy your immense curiosity, sir?"

Shrugging, David said thoughtfully, "Partly. What I fail to understand, Melodie, is why it has to be Schnickelgruber. Why not someone else you already know, or a friend of a friend in Kansas City, or even me?"

"You?" she stammered, not altogether certain she'd heard him correctly. After all, there was this silly buzzing in her ears all of a sudden, and she hadn't felt this light-headed since she'd opened her eyes to see that mouse on her chest.

Where the idea had come from, or when it had taken root in the dark recesses of his brain, David didn't know. Until he'd said those words, it hadn't consciously occurred to him to propose, if that's what he'd actually done. Truth be told, David was every bit as surprised as Melodie at this moment. Still, upon quick consideration, he found he was serious. He actually liked the idea of marrying Melodie. Besides the fact that she was a very attractive woman, David had glimpsed a wonderful, warm person beneath that prim exterior. Those wide, innocent violet eyes sparkled with beguiling mischief when she smiled, making her whole face come alive. Even angry, she enchanted him. Once she let her hair down, Melodie would be really something—and David wanted to be the one to show her how!

"Yes, me," he stated. "Why not? After all, at this point you know me better than you know old Stickelgopher. I know I'm not the best catch, but I'm not exactly repulsive, either." He went on to list his good points, hoping to impress her. "I'm still fairly young, with all my hair and my own teeth. I'm healthy and strong, and I've been told I'm not too hard on the eye. I own a ranch outside of Abilene, and while I'm not rich, I'm certainly not poor. I think I can promise to keep you in comfort, Melodie, if not in furs.

"How about it? Doesn't Melodie Cooper have a nicer sound to it than Melodie Sneezelgruber? Besides bein' easier to say?"

Even before he'd finished, she was shaking her head, rejecting his offer. "David, I'm truly flattered, but I can't marry you."

"Why not?" He wasn't going to be put off without a good reason, and the fact that she'd just used his given name led him to believe that she must have secretly thought of him as something other than "Mr. Cooper" at least once before. It was small encouragement, to be sure, but better than nothing.

"I'm practically engaged to marry Mr. Schnickelgruber. Besides, he paid my way out here. It just wouldn't be right."

"I'll give you the money you owe him. You can send it back to him with a polite note of regret."

"I can't do that, and I can't marry you."

"You still haven't given me a good reason."

"Because you have children, and I don't get along well with children." Just thinking about it had her wringing her hands in agitation. "I don't understand them, and they make me nervous. That's one of the primary reasons I'm hoping that Mr. Schnickelgruber and I suit each other. He doesn't have children."

"Doesn't he want any?"

"What has that to do with anything?"

David rolled his eyes heavenward. "Such innocence! Melodie, husbands and wives usually share a bed, and one thing leadin' to another, babies are a normal result. You did know that, didn't you?"

"Of course," she said, her face beet-red. "However, I doubt he'll be . . . uh . . . we'll be . . . well, the man has gout and is getting on in years, you know. He's probably not as . . . uh . . . active as he used to be. Besides, he stated in his letters that he wished to spend his remaining years in gentle companionship with a woman of good repute."

David's loud hoot expressed half disbelief and half amusement. "Oh, come now, Melodie! Even you can't believe that! Hell's bells, woman! Gout or no gout, the man's only fifty-seven, if he's not lying about his age. That's plenty young enough to still bed a pretty young wife—and if you think for one minute that he's too old to father children, then you're in for a rude awakening, my dear. Many a man older than that has seen his seed take root in fertile fields."

Melodie's face paled. She'd truly believed Schnickelgruber would be too old to father children. Now, suddenly, she had to face the possibility that if he considered himself ready to marry, he might also wish to start a family of little Schnookelgrubers; and the mental image of several small versions of Mortimer and his bulbous nose was not the most pleasant to contemplate. Still, after accepting travel expenses, Melodie at least owed him a chance to voice his views—didn't she?

To David, who was waiting and watching, she said, "Are you sure fifty-seven isn't too old? Or are you just saying it to scare me off of Mr. Schnookelgroper?"

As Melodie cringed, mortified at having mangled the man's name, David crowed with triumphant laughter.

On some level Melodie had just rejected Schnickelgruber, and David could not have been more delighted. Whether she knew it or not, whether she was ready to admit it or not, David was increasingly certain that Melodie was destined to become the next Mrs. Cooper.

Now all he had to do was to convince her of that, and to convince her that she wasn't half as nervous or inept around children as she thought; and his four active offspring had plenty of time in which to teach her what was expected of a mother. After all, they were snowbound together. She was literally a captive, with nowhere to run and nowhere to hide to escape their persuasive endeavors. The poor woman didn't stand a chance!

In answer to her last question, David replied, "Melodie, I wouldn't lie to you about something so important. Believe me, the man may have almost thirty years on me, but children are possible, and probable. Most men want children, even if they sometimes don't want to be bothered with the actual rearing of them. They want a living legacy, a small monument to their own lives on this earth, a replica to carry on their name. I truly doubt old Mortimer is any different in that respect than the rest of us."

A frown furrowed her forehead as she considered David's words. "You may be right. I suppose I'll have to give this serious consideration."

With a grin, David reached out. Long, tanned fingers smoothed the wrinkle from her brow. "You do that, sweet lady. And while you're at it, you might reconsider my proposal. After all, if you're gonna have children anyway, why not mine? Besides, old Schnitzelgruber may give you money, but I'll give you laughter, Melodie. I'll make your heart sing with it all the days of your life, and that's something all the gold in the world can't buy."

🔔 5 🔔

MELODIE stared out the window and sighed. It was mid-morning, but the sun was obscured by blowing snow, and the storm showed no signs of lessening. In fact, the snow was coming down so heavily and blowing so hard that a person couldn't see more than a couple of yards ahead. Sam and David had ingeniously strung guide ropes from the house to the stables and the outhouse, so no one would accidentally lose his or her way, since neither building could be seen from the house, though both sat within forty feet of the main building. There was already a foot and a half of snow on the ground, and that in the level areas where the wind hadn't whipped it into drifts well over a man's head.

Again Melodie sighed and turned away from the window. "Do you suppose we truly will be here over Christmas, as Sam has predicted?" she asked David, who was kneeling before the huge fireplace, adding another log to the flames.

"I'd almost bet on it, which creates a problem I hadn't anticipated." He cast a quick look about, noting that his four youngsters were busy playing with the dog, and beyond hearing if he kept his comments low. "The children will be expecting the usual gifts and such, and I'd counted on reaching Denver in time to do some last-minute shopping, though I did pack a couple of items I'd purchased early. I'd really hoped to make this Christmas special for them since the holidays came so shortly after Ann's death last year—and since I'm not really sure how long it will be until I see them all again," he added softly, his expression tender and sad as he observed his little family.

At this new revelation, Melodie's curiosity was piqued. "What do you mean by that? Why wouldn't you see them? Where will you be?"

There was a telltale glimmer in those turquoise eyes, and his voice was gruff as he answered her. "I'll be back at the ranch shortly after the holidays. They don't know it yet, but the kids will be staying on in Denver with my sister, Lisa, and her family."

"Why?"

"Because I can't manage raising them and running the ranch on my own any longer," he admitted with a rueful smile. "I can't put a home over their head and clean it, too. I've tried, believe me, but the laundry piles up while I'm out chasing stray cattle, the house goes to wrack and ruin in no time at all, and supper's more often than not inedible."

"But you said you weren't poor," Melodie said in obvious confusion. "Can't you hire someone to help with the children? Someone to clean and cook?"

David's smile drooped even more about the edges. "I tried that. One disappeared at the first opportunity; she ran off with a traveling shoe salesman. Another quit after four hours." At Melodie's questioning look, he shrugged and admitted, "The twins, of course; they threw her eyeglasses down the outhouse hole. Naturally, I bought her a new pair, and I offered to double her salary, but she refused to even consider stayin'."

"Did you offer to marry her?" Melodie asked stiffly, her words carrying the bite of an arctic wind.

David's head snapped about and he stared at her, dumbfounded. "What did you say?" he asked softly, as if daring her to repeat it.

Melodie glared back, her chin quivering slightly as she asked instead, "Isn't that why you proposed to me, Mr. Cooper? So you would have someone to tend to your children and your home?"

"Actually, Miss Kern," he answered, his eyes flashing, "the thought never occurred to me. I'd been thinking more in terms of someone sweet and feminine to tend to *my* needs."

"In your bed, no doubt, which would only result in more babies in short order. I'm beginning to think your housekeeper had the right idea. At least she'll always be in shoes."

"Meaning, I take it, that you think I'd keep you barefoot and pregnant?"

"Wouldn't you? That would seem to be a favorite activity of yours, if your four small children are any indication."

"Done properly, it's a mutually enjoyed activity, Melodie," he informed her dryly, "though I assume you've never had the opportunity to know its pleasures. I'd be more than willing to demonstrate, my dear, anytime you'd care for a lesson. I can almost guarantee your satisfaction."

By now, Melodie's face was afire with embarrassment, and she could scarcely stammer, "You . . . you beast! You braggart! Oooh! You arrogant ass!"

He laughed. He actually had the temerity to laugh at her! "Ah, Melodie, my naive little darlin'! Marry me, and I'll teach you how to curse properly. I'll teach you how to love and laugh and play; how to let down your hair and have more fun than you've ever imagined. Together we'll cut those hateful stays and laces that make your spine so unnaturally stiff, that make you go all sour and stuffy and starchy. We'll throw away all your corsets and set your funny bone free!"

"The funny bone is located in the elbow, Mr. Cooper, and is not confined by the corset," she advised him imperiously, though even now her lips were beginning to twitch with humor.

"Wrong funny bone, Miss Melodie," he corrected, wagging his eyebrows at her. "This one is in the torso, which explains why, when you wish to tickle someone, you aim for the ribs, not the elbow."

* * *

He promised her laughter; he offered her passion. He hadn't offended her intelligence by declaring himself madly in love with her on such short acquaintance. Nor had David tried to sugar-coat the reality of his four active children and their equally lively imaginations. While he'd told her he was not deliberately seeking her hand for the sole purpose of obtaining a mother for them, neither did he deny that, should she marry him, he would expect her to care for them.

Melodie had to admit that she was tempted, if just for a moment. If it hadn't been for the children, she might have already said yes. After all, the man was absolutely gorgeous! Those eyes made her think of tropic seas and sun-warmed sands, of exotic breezes and forbidden fruit. He had the most beguiling smile, with those flashing white teeth and those tempting, perfectly formed lips; not to mention his thick blond hair with that wayward lock that kept falling over his forehead and that hint of a boyish, barely tamed cowlick.

Aside from his physical attributes, David had a delightful, if slightly wicked, sense of humor, something that Melodie had to admit had been sadly lacking in her life. It felt so good to laugh with someone now, to share the warmth of a smile. Also, if the way he treated his children was any indication of his nature, David was not prone to unwarranted anger, though Melodie knew he did have a healthy temper when unduly provoked. He was patient and gentle and loving with them, and it made Melodie ache to share all that with him, too.

She couldn't help but wonder if he had been as sweet and understanding with his wife, or was it just with the children? Had he been madly in love with Ann? Had she loved him? How long had they been married? How had she died? Was she pretty?

Sooner or later, Melodie knew she would have to ask David, or be eaten alive with curiosity. Besides, if he was serious about wanting her to marry him, he should expect that she would want to know more about him and what his first marriage was like, especially after he'd berated her for how little she knew about Mr. Schnickelgruber. And it wasn't as if she was merely morbidly curious or incurably nosy; after all, a woman had a right to know these things about the man who'd proposed to her, didn't she? Even if she was merely toying with the idea of marriage to him, rather than seriously contemplating the possibility?

True, it was an intriguing fantasy, but unthinkable nonetheless. Lust after David though she might, Melodie needed four children like she needed the plague. Leprosy held more appeal than the thought of a lifetime of malicious mischief from those twins, and was probably a darn sight less painful! No, she couldn't ever actually consider such a thing—could she?

Over lunch, Melodie learned that David had fought for the North in the War Between the States. In fact, until just a couple of years ago, he'd spent precious little time at home, and despite her frequent pregnancies, Ann had almost single-handedly kept the ranch going during those rough years. Upon hearing that, and the echoing love and admiration in David's voice as he spoke of his wife, Melodie experienced her first real twinges of jealousy for the dead woman. Why, he made her sound like some tireless, miracle-working saint!

"I left for the war in June of '61, never guessing that the twins would arrive almost nine months later, practically to the day!" David recalled with a shake of his head. "Then I couldn't manage a furlough until after they were over a year old."

A quick mental calculation told Melodie that history must have repeated itself on David's military leave, resulting in Betsy's birth a year prior to the war's end. She could only wonder how many children they would have had if there had been no war to keep David away from home except for that brief furlough, or how many they would have now if Ann had lived.

David's military background was just the beginning of Melodie's lunchtime discoveries, however. It seemed that David had more than four children along on this trip, though the rest of his relatives were not the normal flesh-and-bones variety. Betsy was prone to fantasy, and had invented two imaginary friends. Even then, they were not your garden-variety imaginary friends. No run-of-the-mill brothers or sisters for Betsy—she had invented a grandmother. To take the place of her mother, Melodie suspected. Her second friend was an invisible bear named Honey.

"And where were Nanny and Honey on the stage, or was I just too tired to notice them?" Melodie asked hesitantly, feeling foolish as she set another place at the table for the vaporous Nanny. Betsy had all but demanded it, and David had nodded his approval that they should humor her.

"Oh, Papa wouldn't allow Honey to wide inthide with uth. Honey wode with the luggage, and Nanny wanted to keep Tham company. Nanny liketh fweth air."

"I see—I think," Melodie replied, still not proficient at deciphering Betsy's lisp. Seating herself once more, she glanced down the table to see David's grin, and wished she were close enough to kick his shins.

"Mith Melodie," Betsy observed with irritation, "You fowgot a plate fo' Honey."

Melodie met this newest demand head-on. "No, I did not. Bears do not eat at my table, Betsy. Honey may eat in the kitchen with Ming when we are finished with our meal."

Betsy puckered up and began to wail. "But Honey alwayth eath with me!"

David, blast his hell-bound soul, just sat there, leaving Melodie to deal with the child. "Then take your plate into the kitchen and eat your meal there, if you must eat with your bear friend, Betsy," Melodie suggested mildly. "But shush that whining, or I'll think you need a nap more than you need your dinner." Inspired, she added, "Besides, all your crying is making your Nanny upset. Old folks have fragile nerves, you know."

Betsy quieted at once. When she rubbed at her eyes with fisted knuckles, Melodie knew she'd been correct in assuming that Betsy's "grumps" were partially from being tired. She would have to try to prepare the noon meal earlier tomorrow, to avoid another cranky episode.

From the head of the table came a suspicious snort, as if David had inadvertently laughed with a mouthful of soup. Immediately, the twins attempted to imitate their father, slurping and slobbering like hogs at a trough.

Melodie ignored it as long as she could, which amounted to all of fifteen seconds, before calling out in a loud voice, "You boys must just adore taking baths, since you are so very fond of making messes of yourselves."

The sputtering noises stopped; it was as if the twins had turned to stone in the blink of an eye. They sat in stunned silence, their blue eyes wide with surprise and suspicion, looking like a pair of toothless elves. Then, ever so carefully, they picked up their spoons and began to eat with extreme care.

With a smothered mumble, his napkin covering half his face, David quickly excused himself from the table and left the room. Sam managed to stay seated, but he, too, hid a wide grin and stifled a guffaw or two.

Never had Melodie heard so much nonsensical chatter, or so many unusual questions. All afternoon, as she sat by the window and tried to read, the children alternately squabbled and quizzed her poor, beleaguered brain. Again, David was little help, seeming to enjoy seeing her stumble over her own tongue as she dealt with his precocious offspring.

He sat there, grinning like a mute fool, as he and the twins played marbles on the wood floor, ingeniously creating their circle with a piece of string. With another length of string, Jenny and Betsy, fresh from her nap and much more pleasant now, played cat in the cradle. Their activities, while fairly quiet, did not occupy their busy minds enough to hinder what seemed like a hundred and one of the oddest questions Melodie had ever been asked to answer.

"Where do mice go when they die?"

"To mouse heaven, I would suppose."

"Even when they get eated by a cat?"

"Yes."

"Can fishes drown?"

"Not that I've ever heard of."

"Why not?"

"Because God doesn't want them to."

"Why do growed-up ladies have bumps on their fronts?" This from Jenny, who thus far had been Melodie's favorite of the four, because she was so well-behaved. Jenny had just lost her favored status. Meanwhile, David's face was going through odd contortions as he struggled not to laugh.

Mustering a falsely sweet smile, Melodie cooed, "Ask your papa, dear, as soon as he stops trying to swallow his own tongue."

"Do you gots any children of your own?"

"No."

"Why not?"

"Because I don't have a husband yet, and a husband must come before the babies."

"Why?"

"Just because that's the way it's supposed to be."

"When you get a husband, will you get some babies then?"

"Perhaps."

Something in Melodie's tone must have alerted them, for Betsy frowned and asked, "Don't you want babieth, Mith Melodie? Don't you like little childrens?"

In his place on the floor, David froze, as if anxiously awaiting Melodie's answer. Melodie chose her words carefully. "I don't know very much about babies, Betsy. I don't know much about little girls and boys, either. I have no idea what they like or don't, what makes them happy or how to play with them. However, I suppose if I learned more about them, I'd like them well enough."

"We can teach you," Jenny ventured shyly, her friendly overture bringing the sting of tears to Melodie's eyes. "Then maybe you'll like us, too."

"Yeah," Tommy agreed, blue eyes agleam. "Timmy an' me can teach you lots of things, like how to climb trees and how to trap snakes."

"And how to pick the best stones for yer slingshot," Timmy added importantly.

Jenny's eyes sparkled just like her father's, with that same unique color. "We'll teach you how to dress dollies and have tea parties."

Betsy ambled over and pulled herself into Melodie's lap, offering to share a suck of her wrinkled thumb. "We'll teach you all about babieth," she said, blinking up at Melodie owlishly. "Then Papa can help you get thom of your own, if you want—but only if you pwomith to alwayth like uth the besth."

While Melodie sat there wanting to die of humiliation, and not knowing what to reply, David put on his most innocent face, which only made him look all the more mischievous, and volunteered, "Oh, yes, Miss Melodie. I'd love to help you get some babies."

"I'm sure you would," she murmured sharply, fanning her flushed cheeks with her hand. "Lord knows, you seem to have a particular talent for it, and you've certainly had enough practice!"

6

THE children were snuggled into their beds, warm and clean and sleeping that special peaceful slumber that comes only to the very young and innocent. Melodie had experienced another first when she had assisted them in getting ready for bed, washing and slipping them into their pajamas. She'd never washed such small, pudgy fingers, or swished a soapy washcloth into such little ears. She'd also never bathed a boy before, never even seen a male baby without his diaper. It was an education of sorts, and it had been an effort to keep the telltale color from flooding her cheeks.

Now, as Melodie sat before the downstairs fire, her knitting needles fell silent as she recalled how sweet and angelic the girls had smelled, how darling they'd looked in their long flannel nightgowns. She'd helped them wash their hair and had spent many minutes brushing the long golden tresses free of tangles and plaiting the baby-fine hair into braids for the night.

The twins, with their missing front teeth and their fire-red hair drying about their heads in devilish spikes, had fallen a bit short of the innocent look, though Melodie had had to chuckle when she spotted one plump white rump peeking out from the drooping rear flap in Timmy's long underwear. Naked, they'd resembled ornery, disheveled, chubby little cherubs—with rosy cheeks and freckles and nary a wing in sight.

They'd talked her into telling them a bedtime story, too, when David failed to return from the stable by the time they were ready to be tucked beneath their quilts.

47

At a loss, Melodie had little idea how to proceed, having forgotten most of the fairy tales she'd heard as a child. Betsy inadvertently came to her rescue by demanding a story about a beautiful princess. The boys wanted tales of witches and animals, and Jenny wanted at least one dashing prince.

With impish imagination, Melodie complied, weaving a tale of a prince who would not eat his green vegetables and thus fell under the spell of a wicked witch. The witch turned the prince into an ugly green frog, decreeing that he could only return to human form if he was kissed by a princess whose favorite food was spinach. Eventually, of course, after many trials and tribulations, such a princess happened along to save him, and they lived happily ever after on her Vegetable Isle. The moral, of course, was that terrible things could happen to you if you refused to eat your vegetables, and that nice things come to those who do eat them.

The children loved her story, giggling with glee when the nasty witch drowned in a lake of asparagus while chasing chocolate butterflies for her own dessert. Melodie, feeling inordinately pleased with herself, had almost died of embarrassment when she turned to find David leaning nonchalantly against the door frame. He was grinning from ear to ear, having obviously heard the entire tale, or most of it.

"Will you tell us another story tomorrow night?" Jenny requested sleepily.

"Of course," Melodie replied oh-so-sweetly, leveling highly irritated, glittering violet eyes at David. "Remind me to tell you the story of the village idiot who simply could not stop grinning, and how all the girls in town wanted to bash him in the head."

Now the children were asleep, and Sam had retired to his own room for the night. Melodie and David were alone in the main room downstairs, and the air was tense between them, rife with a feeling of expectancy.

"Village idiot, huh?" David said softly, finally breaking the long silence between them.

His words startled her, coming from so near, sending gooseflesh skittering over her arms. Melodie raised stunned eyes to find him standing over her, his legs braced apart, his arms crossed over his broad chest as he stared down at her from his superior height. How had he moved so close, so quietly, without her being aware? Why did his eyes suddenly have such a devilish gleam? And that smile seemed a cat-after-the-canary smirk.

A frisson of breathless excitement skipped up Melodie's spine. Standing there backlighted by the flickering firelight, kind, humorous David looked more like a bold pirate about to partake of booty than the patient, understanding man she'd thus far known him to be.

"David?" The quaver in her voice betrayed her nervousness at this sudden change in him. Her large lavender eyes questioned him as he continued to loom over her.

Then he leaned toward her, and his hands came down on either side of her, effectively trapping her in her seat. "Wh . . . what are you doing?"

His face came closer, until her head was forced back against the cushion in order to keep his features from blurring. "I'm going to kiss you, Miss Melodie Kern, and you are going to love it. So close those enormous purple eyes of yours, stop chattering like a magpie, and part your lips just slightly."

With no more warning than that, his mouth swooped down to capture hers. Her lips were already parted, in complete and utter surprise, and now she felt his, warm and firm, moving against hers; teasing, testing. It seemed he stole her very breath, only to replace it with his own. His tongue slid past the barrier of her teeth, and Melodie jerked in shock as it touched hers. Reflexively, she tried to pull away from him, but long fingers clamped gently about her jaw, holding her head steady while his tongue glided alongside hers, learning the hot, silken textures of her mouth.

"Ah, Melodie, you taste like heaven," he murmured against her mouth. "I knew you would." Again, his lips molded hers in tantalizing desire; again his tongue plied hers, until instinct took over and suddenly she was kissing him back, pressing her mouth urgently to his, snaking her tongue into his mouth for a trembling taste of him. Melodie's stomach was doing somersaults, and her head was spinning alarmingly, until she remembered to breathe.

As she gasped for breath, David's deep chuckle vibrated through her. His fingers threaded through her hair, loosening the pins holding it away from her face. It tumbled down in thick, honey-brown tangles as she heard him croon, "Let your hair down for me, Mellie. Like this. No restraints, no holdin' back, all wild and free and sweet." Somehow she knew he wasn't talking about just her hair when he said those things.

Melodie wasn't sure just when she became aware that David was seated on the divan, with her cuddled on his lap. Her head was cradled against his shoulder, and he was peppering her throat with tiny nips and kisses, whispering marvelous things to her as his tongue swirled into the shell of her ear, creating the most delightful shivers.

Vaguely, Melodie knew she should object, should tell him to stop this madness, but then his long, tanned fingers splayed across her breast. Even through her clothing, his thumb found the sensitive crest, brushing lightly back and forth over the burgeoning peak, and every sane thought flew straight out of her head. Instead of a protest, a strangled whimper of yearning escaped her arched throat as she offered herself wantonly to his touch. Hot, molten desire coursed through her, setting her flesh aflame and pooling like lava in her throbbing loins.

The next thing she knew, those warm, work-roughened fingers were caressing bare flesh, and the bodice of her dress lay open. The straps of her chemise had been pushed from her shoulders, and the top tugged down to reveal her breasts. Spirals of intense pleasure and yearning flooded her, making her dizzy with desire. Still, this was wrong . . . "David. David, please!"

He paid her no heed, his head lowering toward her bared chest. As his hot mouth opened over her thrusting breast, Melodie lurched in stunned delight. Her fingers wound into his hair to stop him, then lingered to press his head more firmly to her aching flesh. "Oh, David!" she exclaimed softly, her breath catching in her throat. "David, we can't. We shouldn't. It's sinful!"

Oh, but what splendid sin it was! His lips were tugging gently now, suckling her, and she could feel the pull all the way through her. There was a tightening, a building yearning in her lower body, a need for something more, though Melodie was not yet sure what that something was. Her entire body was quivering, like an archer's bowstring once the arrow is released. His teeth grazed lightly over her nipple, just enough to send a piercing shaft of desire spearing through her veins. Then his tongue was lapping, soothing, arousing all at once, until Melodie thought she would scream with wanting.

Still, when his hand found its way beneath her skirts, lifting them and gliding along her thigh, Melodie stirred enough to object anew. "No, David. No. You must stop."

"Let me, Melodie. Please," he murmured softly, his breath teasing a rosy nipple. "I can make you feel so good, darlin'. I promise. I can show you a piece of heaven you never thought you'd see." His fingers traced intricate patterns on her inner thigh, urging her legs apart. Before she could close them again, he'd found the hot, moist center of her yearning.

"It's wrong," she gasped, already drowning in a strange, sensual need. "It's bad." His fingers slid over her damp feminine flesh, and Melodie arched into his touch with a moan. She couldn't seem to help herself.

"No, Mellie. It's beautiful. You'll see. You'll fly, honey. You'll soar so high, even the birds will envy you. Your heart will sing a song sweeter than angels have ever heard."

She was melting; she was burning alive! She was living, breathing, seething flames, steaming and writhing in his arms, his to command. As his tongue and his teeth coaxed her nipple into a dimpled peak, his talented fingers found her wetness. Gently, tenderly, they sought entrance into the sanctuary of her feminine secrets, that sacred chamber of sweet sensual bliss. Warm and wet, sleek as satin to the touch, enough to drive a man wild. And so very virginally tight, so untouched and untried that it boggled David's mind to know that he was the first to venture here.

She was panting now, her eyes tightly closed, past knowing what she was doing, past caring about anything except fulfilling this immense aching within her, this vast emptiness, this yawning need. Twisting and bucking in his arms, she strove to bring her body close to his touch, pressing into his hand even as his fingers plunged into her again and again. Deeper, wider, his probing fingers tormented even as they sought to give her that ultimate pleasure.

Tiny, wild little whimpers rose from her throat, sounds that almost drove him insane with his own throbbing desire, that threatened to destroy his nearly threadbare self-control. She was so unbelievably responsive, so beautifully sensual, and David wanted her so badly he thought he'd burst—but this time was just for her, to show her how it could be, to tease and taunt and make it impossible for her to resist him or to reject his proposal.

Suddenly she stiffened. Her eyes popped open, wide and glazed with passion, and David felt the first ripples begin to course through her. A high, keening sound started in her throat, and he covered her lips with his to stifle it, taking her cry and making it his own as her body began to convulse in his arms, sucking and pulling at his fingers until he could scarcely contain his own triumphant cries.

Melodie's first emotion following the cataclysm was a sort of awed amazement. Even now, echoes of that wondrous ecstasy shook her, like aftershocks following an earthquake. And that was exactly what she equated this tumultuous rapture with—an earthquake. Then came an embarrassment so severe that she wanted to curl up in a tiny ball and die; failing that, she hid her flaming face in David's shirtfront, not wanting to face him ever again in this lifetime.

His chuckle vibrated through his chest and her cheek. "Come on, sweetheart. I know you're embarrassed, but there's really no need to be." He shook her gently. "Come out, Melodie," he singsonged. "Come out and face the music."

His taunt, as if she were one of his children, was enough to do the trick. Anger overrode humiliation. "Oh, do shut up!" she spat, as she sat up and tugged the front of her dress together. Then to her further mortification, she realized that David's hand still lay very intimately at the delta of her legs. With a cry of fury and dismay, she brushed his arm aside and leapt to her feet—or tried to. Upon finding her feet, she discovered her knees were uncommonly weak, and she almost toppled onto her face before David's helping hand aided her in finding her balance.

"Melodie," he said reasonably, holding her elbow in a firm but gentle grip as she tried to wrench away from him. "What happened was all very natural. You have nothing to be ashamed about, believe me. You were a delight to behold. You have no idea what it did to me to have you come apart like that in my arms. And that's only the start, Mellie. It gets better from here. Next time, I'll share the passion with you fully, my body joined to yours, and you'll truly know what it means to be a woman."

"Next time?" she whispered. "Next time?" Her voice grew stronger as she let her temper show. "What makes you think there will be a next time, David Cooper? While I know I behaved like a mindless idiot, I have no intention of repeating the transgression."

"Are you gonna stand there and try to convince me that you didn't like it?" he asked incredulously, a smile edging his mouth.

She surprised him by replying truthfully. "No, but that has very little to do with anything. You, in all your male arrogance, have ruined me, Mr. Cooper. Now there is no way I can, in good conscience, accept Mr. Schnickelgruber's offer of marriage."

"Then accept mine," David suggested hopefully.

Her accusing gaze snared his, her huge violet eyes swimming with tears, and David relented. "My dear, innocent Melodie. You are not at all ruined. Your precious virginity is still intact, and you can feel free to marry any man you want, with a clear conscience. But I still want to be that man, Mellie. Think about it, and think about what we just shared."

"Why should I?" she muttered, sounding like a belligerent child who really, underneath it all, truly wanted to be convinced.

"For one thing, not every woman is as responsive as you are, Melodie; and not every man would appreciate that in a woman. I do, honey, and that's where we're well-matched. Besides, do you really think you would respond so beautifully to just anyone's touch? Darlin', what we can have together is a rare and wondrous thing. I doubt old Schnickelgruber will take the time to excite you, and even if he tries, that doesn't mean you'll enjoy his touch. You didn't sound overly thrilled with the man's 'passable' looks, or the idea of sharin' his bed or bearing his children. How do you think you'll like his hands caressing you, his mouth upon yours?"

Melodie gave an involuntary shudder, picturing Mortimer's lovemaking in her mind, based on what she'd seen in the tintype. Noting this small sign of revulsion, David pressed his point more graphically.

"While he's not too old to father a child, he's still getting on in years. His skin probably sags a bit here and there. His teeth may be rotting, or maybe he doesn't have many left in his head, or much hair on top, for that matter. Maybe he snores to lift the rafters. Maybe he doesn't bathe regularly and he stinks. Wouldn't that be wonderful to discover a little too late?"

"This is all wild supposition, David," Melodie hastened to point out.

"True," he granted readily, "but you already know that you come alive in my arms, that my kisses and caresses thrill you, and your pleasure gives me pleasure. That means a lot when you're plannin' on livin' together day in and day out, not to mention all those long nights, for years and years."

"Anything else, Mr. Wonderful?" she prompted mockingly.

"Yeah. You've spent enough time around me to know that I'm clean. I don't have any really annoying habits that I can think of. I don't snore. I'm faithful to a fault." He paused dramatically, then added with a devilish grin, "And I really liked your bedtime story, Mellie. Especially the part about the witch chasin' the chocolate butterflies. That shows some wild imagination, lady, and if you're half as inventive in bed as you are with those stories, you're gonna make one hell of a wife."

🔔 7 🔔

THE best thing was to stay busy. Then she wouldn't dwell on how embarrassed she was, or the situation which had prompted all this guilt and humiliation— or all those sinfully delicious things David had made her feel the night before. Blast his handsome hide! Every time the man glanced her way now, she could feel the fires of hell licking at her cheeks and snapping at her heels!

Busy! Keep busy! Melodie reminded herself. Then you won't think about it so much—maybe—if you're lucky.

The children, especially the twins, did their best to help her fill her time. Suddenly, everywhere she went, even to the outhouse, Melodie felt like a mother duck. All she need do to confirm that thought was turn around, and sure enough, there they were, her four little ducklings waddling along in a row behind her, shadowing her every step. Why they weren't pestering the daylights out of their father, she couldn't begin to guess. Perhaps they'd merely decided she made a better victim, a newer challenge.

In self-defense, Melodie figured if she couldn't escape them, she might as well try to involve them in some of her activities. She decided to make Christmas cookies, some to eat and some with which to decorate the tree she planned on having David the Newly Childless find and cut and drag into the main room of the station. Though she could not find any ornamental cookie cutters, Melodie improvised and soon had ginger and sugar cookies in the shapes of balls, bells, snowmen, and angels spread out on baking sheets.

Of course, by now it looked as if a flour bomb had exploded in the kitchen, with her and the children all in the direct line of fire. And the best, or worst, was still to come—icing the baked cookies in several colors of frosting, to make them pretty for the tree. The children were already arguing over who was to have which color, and which cookie design to decorate first.

By the time David poked his head around the kitchen door, Melodie looked like something the cat had dragged in. Her hair was liberally dusted with flour and sticking out in several directions, and she had globs of cookie dough stuck to her apron and herself. She looked tired, and he couldn't help but wonder if his active brood was too much for her to handle. She wasn't used to this sort of thing, and it was rather a trial by fire, being cooped up with all of them, with no escape from their noise and endless squabbling.

Then he saw her smile, a weary smile to be sure but a genuine smile nonetheless. It was like watching the sun come out from behind the clouds. She reached out a dough-coated hand and ruffled Timmy's hair, chuckling at something the lad had said. The others laughed with her.

Even as David watched, unnoticed, Melodie gathered the last of the badly painted cookies and placed them on a tray to one side. Then she handed each of the eager youngsters a small bowl of their choice, keeping one for herself. To David's amusement, she then dipped her fingers into her bowl, swirled them about, and came up with a glob of colored icing which she promptly popped into her mouth, fingers and all. Within seconds the kitchen was filled with the sound of five persons noisily sucking frosting from their fingers, as the children aped Melodie's example.

He had to laugh. They sounded for all the world like piglets suckling hungrily at a sow's teats; they looked like messy little piglets, too. All five of them! "Hey!

Where's mine?'' he asked when his laughter gained their attention.

"Where were you when the work was being done here?" Melodie countered playfully. "No work, no treat."

"Yeah, Papa," her apprentice bakers echoed. "No work, no treat."

"Greedy! That's what you are! All of you! Greedy little piggies!" He went from one to the other, giving each of them a peck on the cheek and a tweak on the nose. When he came to Melodie, he kissed her cheek; then very deliberately, he took her hand and brought her sticky fingers to his mouth. One by one, as she stared at him in speechless shock, he licked the icing from her fingers. His lips suckled, and his tongue played with the sensitized pads, while she gasped and tried to jerk her hand from his. As his teeth kept her finger trapped, his lips curved in a smile, his eyes twinkling into hers.

The children giggled, thinking it great fun to see their father teasing Melodie in much the same way that he always teased them. The redder Melodie's face turned, the harder they laughed, until David finally took pity on her. With one final lick at the palm of her hand, he released it. Still, he couldn't resist a parting wink and a final comment as he sauntered out of the kitchen. "Delicious!" he declared adamantly. "Cookie batter and icing never tasted so good!"

Melodie was pudding! A puddle of pudding! She was absolutely certain that every bone in her body had turned to mush as she'd sat there gaping at David and letting him nibble at her fingertips. Every nerve in her body was tingling, as if she'd held hands with a lightning bolt. Her stomach was all aflutter, her fingers were trembling noticeably, and inside her shoes, her toes were curled into tight, tense rolls, like ten steamed sausages. What *was* that man doing to her?

"Mr. Sam, do you believe in Santa Claus?"

Upon realizing that their presence was more hindrance than help in cleaning the kitchen clear of the cookie mess, Melodie had bundled all four children into their coats and sent them out to the barn to visit with Sam and his horses for a while.

Puffing on his pipe, Sam scratched his gray-white beard and answered gravely. " 'Course I do. Why?"

" 'Cauth we want thomethin' thpethal for Chrithmath," Betsy told him importantly, "an' we gotta tell Thanta right away, tho he'll know in time to do it."

"Somthin' special?" Sam interpreted, his blue eyes sparkling.

Tommy and Timmy nodded in unison, and Tommy added, "Yeah, an' we can't tell Pa, 'cause it's for him, too. A surprise. Sorta."

Jenny explained further. "We sent a letter before, but it's too late to send another one now, isn't it, so he knows about this other special wish?"

"Oh, it's never too late for Santa," Sam told them. "Not if the wish is important enough. Is yours really that important?"

Four heads nodded solemnly. "Yessir," Jenny confirmed. "We want a new mama, and we already have her all picked out, if Santa could fix it somehow so she'd like us an' Pa good enough."

Sam chuckled. "You wouldn't be talkin' about Miss Melodie, now would ya?"

"Uh huh." Again, four heads bobbed in agreement.

"We even decided that if Santa would do this, we wouldn't need nothin' else—no toys or nothin'," Timmy said with a grimace. This was obviously a sacrifice on his behalf, and he didn't care who knew it.

"Well now," Sam drawled, hooking his thumbs into his suspenders and drumming his fingers on his portly middle. "This calls for some drastic measures. Any o' you young'uns know how to write?"

A short while later, a hasty, secret ceremony took place behind the stable. While the Cooper youngsters watched, wide-eyed and hopeful, Sam Nichols burned a special wish letter. "Now, close your eyes and wish as hard as you can, and blow the smoke to Santa."

Eight eyes scrunched tightly shut, four mouths quickly puckered and puffed at the thin stream of smoke, while Sam looked on with a gentle smile. Nothing in the world quite matched a child's simple, innocent belief.

"What do you suppose Schmoozelgripper is going to think when you don't show up in Denver by the time you should?" David asked her.

Melodie dropped a stitch, frowned, and briefly contemplated stabbing David with her knitting needles. "I imagine he will think I have robbed him of his money and have no intention of meeting him at all. That's the first thing I would believe; unless, of course, he realizes that the stage is late and undoubtedly stranded somewhere in the storm."

The storm, thank heavens, had finally blown itself out earlier this evening, and after three days of endless howling, the silence seemed odd. It also seemed strange, but blessedly so, not to hear four piping voices screeching to the limits of their tiny lungs, but again the children were all abed and fast asleep. "What is your sister going to think when you and the children don't show up for Christmas?" Melodie added, not wanting to get into another heated discussion about her fiancé. In fact, right this moment, she didn't want to even think about him. More and more these days, she was wishing she'd never heard of the man, let alone answered that blasted advertisement.

"She'll worry some, but she won't panic right away. She knows I can take care of myself and my family pretty well, in most situations. She'll figure we're holed up somewhere to wait out the storm."

His casual comment about being able to care for his family made her wonder once again about his wife. "How did she die?"

"Who? Ann?"

Melodie hadn't meant to ask the question aloud, but since she had, she nodded. "If you don't want to talk about it, I'll understand."

David answered anyway, his face solemn and his words deliberately void of emotion. "She fell off a ladder. It was outside, and she was trying to fix part of the window frame that had come loose and was rattling. She fell and broke her neck." He paused, and she saw him swallow hard before adding softly, "Doc said she probably died instantly. I hope so. I hate to think of her hurting, trying to call for help that never came."

"Why?" Melodie asked. David looked at her oddly, not understanding her question. "Why was she on the ladder?" Melodie elaborated. "Why didn't she have someone else fix the window? Why didn't she ask you, or one of the men who work there?"

With a heavy sigh, he shook his head. "I've asked myself that same thing a million times. I was out riding fence that day, but there were other men around the place. But Ann was independent, and stubborn. Maybe she thought everyone was too busy with work of their own. I don't know. Maybe she just wanted to do it herself, for whatever reason. It doesn't do any good to wonder why now, though. The answer died with her, and even if we knew, it wouldn't bring her back."

"I'm sorry. You must have loved her very much. It must have hurt you terribly to lose her that way, because of a senseless accident."

Sincerity rang clear in Melodie's voice, and David found he was very grateful for her understanding. He didn't want Melodie feeling jealous of Ann, as a lot of women would under the circumstances; yet, neither was he going to deny the love he'd felt for his wife. He *had* loved Ann dearly. At one point, she'd been his whole life, and her death had brought him to his knees in despair. But a year had passed, and more; and his grief had eased gradually, until thoughts of Ann now brought the pleasant ache of heart-warmed memories.

And there was Melodie, awakening his desire again, making him aware of an entire range of emotions he'd shoved to the back of his mind, bringing him back to life and to dreams he'd thought long-dead. Melodie, his little brown-haired songbird with the velvet-soft eyes and the crazy bedtime stories. She was his. She belonged to him. There was no way on earth he was going to let her marry Schnickelgruber. He'd lost one love, through no fault of his own; he certainly wasn't foolish enough to let this one slip through his fingers without doing everything he could to stop her.

Maybe he should have been surprised to find himself falling in love with her so fast, but he wasn't. If anything, he was grateful to a kind and benevolent God. Not everyone was fortunate enough to love once in a lifetime. He was being blessed twice over. True, it was happening quickly, almost too quickly to be believed, but he was familiar with the heady symptoms even if Melodie was not. He also believed that, with luck and a little more time, she would come to care for his offspring, no matter how much she claimed not to want children. For himself, David was not concerned. He'd already introduced her to passion; eventually, he'd teach her to love.

Just when David wanted to impress Melodie the most, when his very happiness depended upon it, his own children seemed equally determined to undermine all his efforts. Just when he needed them to be on their best behavior, it seemed they were destined to be at their very worst. Of course, David had no way of knowing that he and his youngsters had the same goal in mind, and that they were becoming just as discouraged as he was. Though they tried their best to be good, everything seemed to turn out wrong. No matter what they did, they got into trouble with Melodie.

Melodie had begun a campaign of her own. Since

she was now in charge of this household until the owners returned or until the roads were clear enough for the stage to continue to Denver, she suddenly found herself cooking and cleaning for many more persons than she was used to. Each day, there were several beds to be made, meals to prepare, dishes to wash, rooms to clean and dust, clothing to launder, floors to scrub when snow and frozen mud got tracked in underfoot.

To top it all, the little ones were forever leaving small messes behind, and Melodie was fast tiring as their personal maid. Gathering them together, she told them sternly, shaking her finger at each in turn, "I have no idea how you live at home, or if your father lets you get by with this deplorable behavior there, but I have had a bellyful of it. From now until we leave, there will be new rules for you to follow. Each morning, when you rise, you will gather your dirty clothing and deposit it in a small pile outside your bedroom door, where I can collect it for laundering. Then, before you come down to breakfast, you will make up your beds."

"But we don't know how," Jenny pointed out.

"I'll show you, and then you will do your best from there. I'll also be checking, and if I find that you haven't made your bed, your breakfast will wait until the job is done. If your breakfast grows cold while you're at it, you'll learn not to dally, or to like cold oatmeal and eggs, won't you?"

Four lower lips protruded in various pouts.

"Also, you are all old enough to manage a dishcloth, so you can take turns drying the dishes as I wash them. You will pick up your toys when you are finished playing with them, and you will put them away. I am tired of walking into a room and seeing it a mess. And if I step on one more marble, I'll have someone's bottom over my knee before you can say jackrabbit! Now, do the four of you understand what I have just said, and what I will be expecting you to do?"

Sullen looks met her, but they all reluctantly agreed

to her edicts. Behind Melodie's back they grumbled to themselves, wondering if they hadn't chosen their new mother a little too hastily.

"Maybe we should talk to Sam again," Timmy complained irritably.

Tommy shook his head. "Nah, it's prob'ly too late."

"Well, shucks! Why'd she hafta wait till now to be so mean. If we'd known b'fore..."

"Yeah, but she still makes good cookies, and she can be lots of fun sometimes, and she cooks lots better than Pa," Jenny stressed. "And she sewed the tear in my best dress, and put a new button on the back of Timmy's jammies, and sewed up all the holes in all our socks—even Pa's."

"An' I like her bedtime thtories," Betsy mumbled past her wrinkled thumb. "I like Melodie—even better than Nanny and Honey Bear. I wanna keep 'er."

"Me, too," Jenny voted.

Timmy and Tommy thought about those yummy cookies, and all the other delicious things Melodie could bake, and decided that they, too, could put up with her bossy ways.

Despite any and all hardships, the vote was unanimous. They wanted Melodie. But would she have them? And could they all live through the changes she would bring to their lives?

When David wandered through the kitchen after the noon meal, he stopped dead in his tracks, scarcely believing his eyes. For long, speechless seconds, his mouth gaped open. Then he practically screeched, "What are my sons doing dryin' dishes? Kitchen work is for girls!"

The look Melodie leveled at him should have fried him to a cinder. "And what does that make me, pray tell? Head scullery maid? I'm telling you here and now, David Cooper, that I am not about to do all this extra work by myself. You and your children make most of the work; a few chores aren't going to kill them. In fact, it just might help counter some of your overindulgence of them. They're abominably spoiled, and it's your fault; and drying a few dishes certainly will not make weaklings out of these boys. Now, if you have nothing better to do than complain, kindly remove yourself from my kitchen."

A little while later, David passed through the main room to find each of his four offspring standing in four separate corners, facing the converging walls. Sitting on a chair in the center of the room, rocking and knitting at an amazing speed, Melodie monitored her charges with a glower. David was almost afraid to ask. Gathering his courage, he questioned mildly, "What did they do?"

"What didn't they?" she grumbled in return. With a sigh, she proceeded to enlighten him. "Your darling daughters decided to amuse themselves by trying different coiffures. Pins and combs defied them, but they have acquired amazing dexterity with a pair of scissors. The only blessing is that I caught them before they could turn each other completely bald—and it will grow back, eventually."

David was undecided whether to laugh or cry. Wisely, he did neither. "And the boys?" he asked hesitantly.

"Ah, the boys!" Melodie said with a mocking smile. "The Terrible Twins were having great sport chasing Ming about the house while pelting him with their peashooters. Between the poor animal's howls and your sons' gleeful screams, it's a wonder people in the next county haven't come running to the rescue."

"I see." David decided not to challenge her newfound authority. After all, if things went well, she would be the children's stepmother before long. Besides, Melodie wasn't in the best of moods at the moment. Considering retreat the better alternative, David took himself off to chop firewood.

🔔 8 🔔

THE storm was over. The sun was shining brightly, making the snow-laden land resemble a gigantic meringue-topped pie, its many wind-whipped swirls and dips liberally sprinkled with glistening sugar crystals that caught the sun and reflected it in a million blinding prisms. The trees had donned lace dresses upon their trunks and spreading branches, taking on the look of tall maidens dancing in embroidered white gowns at their debutantes' ball. Above, the sky was a clear cerulean from horizon to horizon, with nary a cloud to clutter its pure beauty.

The children were like prisoners granted unexpected freedom from lifelong sentences. As they cavorted in the snow, their wild shrieks of glee echoed across the miles of pristine white. Melodie was similarly elated, if slightly less exuberant in exhibiting it. It was a relief to be able to send the little urchins outdoors to play and work off some of that abundant energy, even if she did spend half the day afterward wiping running noses.

Bundled into her own coat, with the collar tucked high about her neck, Melodie gathered pinecones and fragrant boughs from a convenient stand of trees within sight of the house. As she worked, she hummed a lively Christmas tune. About her, the air was fresh and crisp, the snow so bright it hurt her eyes to look at it; the children's shrill laughter rang clear in her ears, and she felt ridiculously happy.

Caught up in her own thoughts, Melodie was taken

unawares when a wet, white blob of snow hit her left shoulder. For a moment, she thought it had dropped from one of the laden branches. Then another hit her square in the back, hard and quite deliberate, judging by the laughter accompanying the missile. Swinging about, her mouth open and her hands on her hips, Melodie was the most vulnerable of targets, and she caught the next snowball full in the face.

As she scraped the frosty stuff from her mouth and eyes, silence suddenly reigned, as David and the children awaited her reaction. Was she going to be mad as a wet hen—a cold wet hen? Or would she be a sport about it and join in their game? Eyes narrowed into slits, Melodie stared at them, not saying a single word. Then she promptly turned on her heel and stomped off.

With heavy sighs and hurt looks, David and his troop shared their mutual rejection. Their disappointment was short-lived, however, as several icy spheres came sailing toward them with amazing accuracy. Caught by surprise, David took a snowball smack in the head. Each of the children were hit at least once, and now it was Melodie's delighted laughter that tinkled through the frosty air. "Take that, you dastardly demons!" she exclaimed on a laugh.

"Dastardly demons?" David crowed. Turning to his children, he demanded, "Are we gonna stand for that, troops?"

"No!" the twins chorused, hopping up and down.

"Yeth! Yes!" the girls squealed.

Glowering playfully at them, David roared, "Traitors!" He pointed in Melodie's direction, ordering his daughters, "Be gone with you, you turncoats! Join your general and prepare to fight!"

For the next half hour, they waged war, boys against the girls, pelting one another gleefully. Laughter filled the air, interspersed with squeals and boastful taunts and Ming's excited barking. Breathless and exhausted, they finally called a truce in favor of hot cocoa and dry socks.

Their small frolic set a precedent for days to follow, when David and Melodie would take a few minutes to join the little ones for a time of play. Together, they built snow people and snow animals, erected miniature forts, made snow angels, and took turns pulling the children on a flat sheet of tin Sam had found in the barn and turned into a makeshift sled.

Melodie was having the time of her life. After years of being shackled to her elderly aunt's side, with rarely a moment for a breath of fresh air let alone actual fun, she was relishing this frivolous freedom. Soon the extra outdoor activities began to show additional benefits. Though she'd always had good skin and thick hair, her complexion now glowed with health; her honey-brown mane took on an added sheen and her eyes a special sparkle. Muscles that ached soon became accustomed to regular exercise. She felt alive and wonderful, and her mirror reflected this new, vital woman she was becoming.

Melodie wasn't the only one to delight in these changes. The others, especially David, took note and complimented her lavishly.

"You look weel purty, Melodie."

"Will you fix my hair like yours, Melodie? Please?"

"Your cheeks look like juicy red apples," David told her with that familiar grin. "That's a direct quote from Tommy, but I think so, too. I also think your lips look like ripe strawberries, and since I'm partial to red fruit, I was wondering if you'd mind if I nibbled on you a while." He set words to action and soon had Melodie giggling helplessly, too weak with laughter to escape his amorous advances—and in the middle of the afternoon, too—right out in the barnyard in front of God and everyone!

That wasn't the first time, or the last. David seemed intent on tormenting her with teasing touches and flirtatious kisses. Bit by bit, he was breaching her ramparts, wearing down her resistance with every tantalizing caress. He was deliberately and methodically seducing her! And in the brashest manner!

She'd be stirring a pot of soup on the stove, and he would lean over her shoulder and blow his warm, ticklish breath into her ear, or whisper romantic nonsense to make her blush, causing her to shiver and break out in gooseflesh. Or she'd be setting the table for supper, and he would pat her bottom in the most familiar gesture, making her straighten with a startled shriek and toss silverware hither and yon. His arm would brush her breast in passing; his hands would find a hundred excuses to encircle her waist or stroke her hair or cheek; and the moment she became absorbed in her knitting or reading, his lips would unerringly find that sensitive spot on her nape that always sent immediate waves of desire coursing through her.

It had been years since Melodie had decorated for the holidays. Aunt Gertie had been too sick and too irascible to entertain guests. Besides, Gertie would have put Mr. Dickens's Scrooge to shame with her lack of Christmas spirit. Most years, decorating her aunt's little house hadn't been worth the endless carping it precipitated.

Now, though her supplies were limited, Melodie made up for lost time. The bar top, staircase banister and posts, tables, and fireplace mantel were all festooned with pinecones and boughs of greenery, interspersed with candles and oil lamps. Lacking other materials, Melodie used her imagination and her brightest red yarn to crochet lacy bows and ribbons for further decoration, saving several for the Christmas tree to be erected on Christmas Eve. David had already promised her a tree, and she was as excited and breathless with anticipation as the children.

As an added touch, as per Dr. Moore's poem "The Night Before Christmas," seven stockings hung from the mantel, one for each of them, including Sam, all in a row from largest to smallest. Melodie's stocking hung next to David's, and every time she looked at it, dangling so close to his, she felt a surge of longing that shocked her because of its intensity, and because of the startling fact that the yearning she felt was no longer merely physical. Her desire had grown far beyond that, much to her dual delight and misery.

Melodie was very much afraid she was losing her heart to David Cooper, children and all. With every passing hour she was coming to care more and more deeply for the man and his little brood, and she truly did not know what to do to stop it—or even if she still wanted to. It was like watching her own destiny rush up to greet her, as if she were helpless in the face of her own fate, merely standing there waiting for the final pieces of the puzzle of her life to fall neatly into place, aligning themselves alongside David's and the children's.

If this was love, it was both frightening and exhilarating. It was like walking upon quicksand, where dry land was expected, and feeling as if your next step could very well prove fatal. Half the time, Melodie's heart was in her throat. She went absolutely giddy at his touch, and mushy at a mere smile—but could she trust such topsy-turvy feelings, which were so foreign to her? Could she seriously contemplate accepting his proposal—choosing David and four lively children over Schnickelgruber and his assets? Did she really want to follow her wayward heart instead of her more logical brain? Did she dare take this chance at happiness? Did she dare not?

While she wavered on the brink of making this monumental decision, perhaps she should let David work at convincing her a bit more. After all, she did so enjoy his many and varied tactics to win her, his campaign for possession of her heart. The man had a remarkable talent for innovation and imagination, and far be it from Melodie to stifle his creativity!

* * *

The stockings hanging limply over the fireplace created another problem, but one for which Melodie had a ready remedy. Candy. There was no fresh fruit with which to stuff the stockings, but there were nuts in the pantry and plenty of sugar for making Christmas treats. Her sole problem was finding the time and the solitude to create those sugary delights. Certainly, if it were to be a surprise, she could not do it while the children and David were about. The aroma alone would give her away. She would have to wait until late at night, or very early in the morning, when they were all asleep.

Her strategy worked, up to a point. She was in the process of making hard candy. She'd already managed to boil and flavor and pour a large batch of cinnamon candy and was testing the syrup for the clove-flavored candy when David nipped on the side of her neck.

With a breathless shriek, she leapt into the air, losing her wooden spoon in the bubbling sugar mixture. "You lunatic!" she gasped, clutching her chest in an effort to calm her thumping heart. "Do you always propose, then try to frighten your prospective bride to death before she can accept? One of these days, David Cooper, I'm going to find a way to pay you back for all these years you've scared off of my life!"

"Sounds like you plan on being around a while. Does that mean you've decided to marry me?" he asked hopefully, his eyes dancing. She wasn't about to give him that satisfaction, not just yet, especially after having the wits scared out of her. "I'm still thinking about it," she allowed, fishing the spoon from the steaming goo. "Now, if you're going to stay, please sit down somewhere out of the way until I can find a use for you."

"I can think of several suggestions for ways you and I could put one another to good use," he observed teasingly, wagging his eyebrows at her. "Shall I name a few guaranteed to steam the windows and curl your toes?"

"Save them for a more appropriate time, will you, David?" she asked dryly. "Right now I'm busy steaming some windows of my own with this candy project, and I can't afford the distraction." The smell of clove permeated the kitchen as she instructed, "Now, while I pour, you grab the spoon and help scoop this mixture onto the cookie tray. It's hard to do both at the same time, and as long as you're here, I can use the extra pair of hands."

Working together, they finished the clove candy and made another batch of peppermint-flavored hard candy that cleared their heads and had David's eyes watering. The flavor was so strong that he swore he could taste it by smell alone. "That's what brought me down here in the first place," he admitted sheepishly. "The aroma of cinnamon woke me up."

Melodie grinned and shrugged guiltily. "It's hard to be sneaky when you're cooking something like this. I don't make a habit of cooking in the middle of the night, you know, but this was supposed to be a surprise for the children's Christmas stockings."

He was truly touched that she would go to so much trouble, especially when the children had been such little terrors lately. "That's sweet of you, Mellie. It really is. It'll mean a lot to them, and to me—even more if you fill my stocking with some of it, too."

"I intended to, but you weren't supposed to know anything about it until Christmas morning. Now you've spoiled the surprise, and you've no one to blame but yourself."

As penance, David volunteered to stay awake and help her make a huge batch of popcorn balls, another of molasses candy, and wrap several dozen caramel squares in waxed paper. Periodically he managed to steal a kiss here and a caress there, teasing her outrageously all the while.

When they finally finished the candy, including the kitchen cleanup, it was only a couple of hours until dawn, and they were both silly for lack of sleep. He walked her to her bedroom door, where he stole yet another kiss. "Tell me you love me," he whispered wetly into her ear.

"You love me," she repeated with a girlish giggle.

"I know," he told her softly, his beautiful turquoise eyes promising her the world. "Tell me you'll marry me."

Again she gave his words back to him, but more solemnly this time. "You'll marry me."

"I absolutely will," he agreed, "and I'll do it gladly. After all, it'll accomplish the same purpose, and you'll still be mine. As long as you understand that, Mellie, everything will be just fine." He planted another kiss on the end of her nose. "I hope you know you just promised to marry me; and I hope you don't think you're gonna change your mind in the morning."

"But David—" she started to argue.

"But nothin', lady. You're mine now, come hell or high water." He sauntered down the hall toward his own room, where he stopped and turned to give her a roguish wink. She was still staring after him, a foggy, bemused expression on her face. "Good night, Mellie. Sweet dreams, darlin'."

She'd gotten very little sleep. Her head was pounding, and her eyes felt as if they'd fall out at any given moment. So it was natural that all four of the younger Coopers picked today to try Melodie's patience to the limit. First they were playing cowboys and Indians, whooping and hollering until Melodie wanted to run screaming out the door, pleading for mercy to anyone who would rescue her. This was enough to bear, but when they tied Ming to a chair, pretending he was to be burned at the stake, they went too far. The little dog's frantic yelps, plus the cruelty of the act, were too much.

Within minutes, all four youngsters were sporting half-moons on their reddened bottoms as they ran off to find their father and report to him that Melodie had spanked them with the business end of a wooden spoon. Shortly thereafter, they went tattling again, this time with soap chips coating their teeth and tongues. The girls had gotten into trouble for holding a spitting contest. The twins had gotten caught cursing like drunken sailors. They'd all had their mouths soaped.

By day's end David was ready to tear his hair out, and Melodie was willing to help him do it. The silence that lay between them as they sat before the fire later that evening after the children were in bed was not as congenial as usual.

David's features were a bit mulish as he put the finishing touches on the whistles he was carving for each of his offspring, as well as one for Sam. He'd already fashioned a small wooden kitten for Jenny, a replica of Honey Bear for Betsy, and a carved horse for each of the twins. It wasn't much, but it was all he could manage as additional Christmas gifts for his children. He could only be thankful he'd found such soft, ready wood, since their only other gifts were little music boxes and new dolls for the girls; a cowboy hat and play gun and holster for Tommy; and a pretend Indian headband and bow and arrow trimmed with chicken feathers for Timmy. After today, Melodie was simply going to love those last two gifts!

For her part, Melodie was glad she'd brought an abundance of yarn with her. It looked as if she'd use almost all of it by the time she'd knitted a muffler, mittens, and house slippers for each of the children; blue and green for the boys, and red and yellow for the girls. There was also a pair of slippers for Sam, and a muffler and slippers for David, which she'd managed to keep hidden from his prying eye.

Now, as the fire warmed her, Melodie's eyes grew more and more heavy. Her fingers grew limp, losing their grip on the knitting needles, and her head bobbed as sleep finally claimed her. She didn't stir an eyelash as David gently scooped her into his arms and carried her off to her solitary slumber, promising himself that it would not be many more nights before she shared their marriage bed, and all of its many delights.

🔔 9 🔔

CHRISTMAS Eve day had finally arrived. The big celebration was at hand, and the children were practically wriggling with anticipation. They weren't the only ones. Melodie couldn't remember the last time she'd been so excited about Christmas, or when she'd been so busy or had so much fun.

With a hundred last-minute things still left undone, Melodie was meeting herself coming and going. David, bless his heart, decided to take the twins with him and Sam when they went out to find the "perfect" Christmas tree and bring it back for proper decoration. In their dishcloth aprons, the girls helped Melodie in the kitchen, where she could keep an eye on them and Christmas dinner preparations at the same time.

Already, the house was filling with the tantalizing aromas of cooling pies and pumpkin-nut bread, and the sharp tang of beets and vinegar for pickled eggs. These Melodie was preparing ahead, as well as the butter and rolls. Tomorrow, the smoked turkey Sam had found hanging in the smokehouse would find its way into the oven, stuffed with Melodie's special dressing. There would be gravy and candied carrots to round off the meal, and they were all sure to be as stuffed as the bird by the time they were done.

For tonight, there would be a quick meal of ham slices and sweet potatoes, so they could get to the business of trimming the tree. Of course, there would be eggnog and fudge for snacking, since tree trimming was such hungry work, and popcorn for stringing and eating.

Before long, the tree sat thawing in the corner of the main room, its trunk in a bucket. It was, indeed, the perfect tree, full and green and not too big for the limited number of decorations they would bestow upon its prickly branches. While the tree warmed and spread itself out in the heat of the room, prior to decoration, David sat the children up at the bar and helped them make a few more items with which to trim the tree. Melodie listened, amused, as the twins worked their elfin magic on their father.

"I'll have me a beer, barkeep," Timmy barked out in as deep a voice as he could manage, pounding a pudgy fist atop the bar. "And a whiskey for my pardner."

Tommy nodded, pretending to hitch his gun belt higher as he tried to look tough. "Yep, fightin' outlaws is thirsty work."

"Sorry, fellas," David told them with a chuckle, playing along with them. "I'm fresh out of whiskey. How about a ginger bear and a sarsaparilla?"

Melodie swore their freckles lit up with delight as David surprised them by pouring each of them one of the flavored, nonalcoholic beverages from the stock behind the bar. Not to be left out, the girls clambered onto the high bar stools and promptly ordered two root beers, grinning from ear to ear when David complied.

"I don't ordinarily serve women at the bar, you understand," he told them with a saucy wink, "but seein' as it's a holiday, and you two are such ravishin' beauties, I'll make an exception."

Now it was Melodie who couldn't help but join in. Swinging onto the end bar stool, she tossed her head and batted her long lashes at David, flirting outrageously and making the children giggle. "What about me, mister? Don't I deserve a sarsaparilla, too?"

"Well, now." David pretended to consider her request. "Since you're a tad older than these other ladies, it'll cost you. A quick glimpse of ankle and a kiss ought to cover it, I guess." His grin was comically diabolical as he pretended to twirl the ends of an imaginary mustache between his fingers.

"Well, if I must!" Melodie declared, sighing dramatically. Quickly, she leaned across the bar and gave him a peck on the end of his nose. Then, almost before he could think to look, she flipped the very edge of her skirt up and back down, granting him a peek at her modestly booted ankle.

"That's it?" he complained exaggeratedly.

"Afraid so, fella," she told him smugly. "I'll take that drink now, please."

Still later, while they were busy making intricate paper snowflakes, folding the plain white paper Melodie had found in the pantry and taking turns with the scissors, the boys tried to teach Melodie to whistle. They all howled at the ridiculous faces she made in the attempt, and by the time she gave up in disgust, David was holding his sides in pain.

"Okay, smarties," she challenged. "I'll bet I know how to do something you can't do."

"What?" they chorused.

"Twiddle. I'll bet none of you can twiddle your thumbs properly."

"Oh, that's easy!" Tommy bragged, and proceeded to interlock his fingers and roll his thumbs about in a circular motion.

"No, no!" Melodie declared. "That's not how it's really done. Now, gather 'round, and I'll show you the proper way, like my granddad taught me." They watched in fascination as Melodie laced her fingers together and then managed, with amazing dexterity, to make one thumb rotate in a forward movement, while the other circled in a backward motion, both at the same time, each thumb circling the other in the most dizzying fashion.

"I'll be danged!" David exclaimed in genuine astonishment. "I've never seen anything like it!" The children hadn't either, and were well-occupied for quite some time trying to imitate Melodie's clever feat.

"You're a sneaky lady," David whispered, chuckling at his offspring's clumsy efforts. "Now they'll be bound and determined to learn that, and while they're at it, they're not up to any other mischief."

Melodie smiled, pleased with herself. "And it's quiet and takes lots of concentration," she pointed out. "Good for long stagecoach rides."

The tree looked lovely. A garland of popcorn spiraled about it, from top to bottom, while red bows and white snowflakes danced from its spiked tips. Bright copper pennies with holes punched through for hanging were Sam's generous contribution, while David had fashioned a tin star for the crowning touch at the very top of the tree. The star and pennies sparkled in the light of the few, carefully placed candles Melodie and David had secured to selected branches. A bucket of water stood ready, just in case.

With the tree decorated, it was time for songs and stories before bedtime. Sam produced a mouth harp, proclaiming he was much better with it than at singing. Seeing this, the children immediately bewailed the fact that they had no instruments to play; whereupon, Melodie promptly disappeared into the kitchen, reemerging with spoons, washboard, and waxed paper. An additional foray into the bedrooms produced combs, while David located an empty whiskey jug, claiming it as his personal favorite. Sam even brought in his sleigh bells.

Together, the adults showed the children how to make their own harmonicas by humming through wax paper–covered combs, how to jingle the bells and clank the spoons in time to the music. Melodie manned the washboard, strumming upon it with her infamous wooden spoon. With light hearts and merry voices, they sang and played until they had exhausted their small repertoire of Christmas carols.

Then David opened the Bible, and in solemn tones read the story of the birth of Christ, reminding them all of the true meaning of this joyous holiday. Afterward, much to the children's delight and everyone's amazement, Sam entertained them with a recitation of "The Night Before Christmas," which he had memorized word for word. The children went off to bed willingly after that, with smiles and dreamy thoughts of Christmas morning.

Sam followed close behind, yawning widely and declaring that all the excitement had exhausted him. Melodie suspected he was merely being polite and giving her and David some precious time alone to place the gifts beneath the tree and fill the stockings, which they did, and some time to snuggle down in front of the fire and just relax after such a hectic day.

Pleasantly tired, supremely content, Melodie sat on the rug, her legs tucked beneath her skirts. Leaning back against the divan, she gazed into the dancing flames, letting them soothe her with their flickering rhythms while she sipped from the small glass of wine David had brought her. It was quiet now, serene, and she let the peace filter through her. Beside her on the floor, David did the same, the silence between them warm and comforting.

By the time David turned to her, Melodie was feeling very relaxed. As he dangled a bit of greenery before her, he gently removed the wine goblet from her hand and set it safely aside. "My favorite holiday custom," he told her with a devilish smile.

She managed to frown and smile at the same time. "What are you babbling about now, David Cooper?"

Again he wagged the sprig at her, then dangled it above their heads. "Mistletoe, my dear Melodie. I believe a kiss is the forfeit. And not just a measly peck, either!"

Now she recognized the evergreen leaves with their white berries. "You scamp! Where did you find that?"

He chuckled and waggled those eyebrows at her. "Out in the woods. See what happens when you send me out in the snow and cold to bring you Christmas trees?"

"Lands, yes!" she exclaimed with a soft, teasing laugh. "You turn into a raving madman!"

"Mad for you, my lovely Melodie. Mad for your strawberry lips and your sweet kisses." Only half teasing now, David let his mouth hover over hers. "Kiss me, darlin'," he murmured enticingly. "Put me out of my misery."

Their lips met and clung, moist and sweet. She tasted of berry wine as he sipped at her lips and tongue. His brandy-flavored kisses went to her head faster than any liquor, immediately setting her thoughts and emotions spinning in a euphoric fog. Flames began to lick at her flesh, heating it, sensitizing it to David's special touch, so that when he slid his hands over her, she whimpered in delight. Shyly, she returned his touch, embracing him and caressing him with tentative strokes, loving the way his hair slid through her fingertips as she urged him closer still.

She did not demur as his fingers found the row of buttons down the back of her blouse, releasing them one by one. Neither did she object when he gently tugged the blouse from her shoulders, tossing it aside as his lips found the tender curve of her breast above the lace edge of her chemise. And when that garment, too, was tugged from the loosened waistband of her skirt and discarded, baring her breasts to him, Melodie eagerly offered herself to his searing gaze and his hot, seeking mouth.

Stars exploded in her head as David suckled and teased at her breasts, laving them lovingly with his tongue. Heat curled in her stomach, like a living thing, making her writhe with unfulfilled need. Once more, his lips found hers, tasting of nectar and sweet promises. With slow kisses and warm, wandering hands, David was offering her a glimpse of heaven that Melodie was helpless to resist.

Somehow, the rest of her clothing seemed to disappear, as if by magic. She was so drugged by David's kisses that the house could have tumbled about her ears and she would not have noticed. His clothing went the same route, and it was only when her seeking fingertips met with hot male flesh that she realized that they lay naked in each other's arms.

By all rights, Melodie supposed she should have been embarrassed, perhaps even frightened. Never had she seen a man without his clothing, let alone one as obviously aroused as David was. It crossed her mind that seeing the twins in their bath was vastly different from seeing David now. Yet he was beautiful; strong and proud and so majestically male. Even the scent of him was different, enticing her to nuzzle her nose into the wedge of hair matting his chest.

His fingers found her, seducing her with silken strokes that fanned the fires of her desire to the point of explosion, yet held her just shy of rapture. Pleasure built until it was so great, it was almost painful to experience; Melodie lay quivering in his arms, damp with desire, eager to lay herself upon the altar of womanhood for the first time in her life.

"David, make me a woman, please," she implored softly, her own fingers curling lightly about his prominent manhood, urging him with their own sweet persuasion. "Make me your wife. Here. Now."

He could no more have refused her plea than he could have held the tide from the shore. Tenderly, lovingly, he made her his, turning her small whimper of pain into glad cries of ecstasy. For a short time, heaven belonged to them, to be held in their hands as the sun burst brightly all about them, showering them with golden splendor and drenching them in glorious passion.

Afterward, as he held her in his arms, he vowed his love to her, asking her once more to be his bride. "Please, Melodie. I know I took unfair advantage, and I deserve to be hung by my thumbs rather than rewarded, but I beg you to marry me. I love you, sweetheart. I need you to make me whole, to give my life meaning."

She accepted in her usual pragmatic manner. "All right, but only because I love you beyond all belief, David Cooper. And because your children are running amok without proper guidance. And because I couldn't live without you, since you've stolen my heart and I see no hope of gaining it back."

"I'll give you mine, with all the love it can possibly hold," he promised, sealing his pledge with a warm, sensuous kiss. Melodie's toes immediately curled.

Much later, David tiptoed upstairs and returned with Melodie's nightgown and robe and a pile of blankets and pillows. They made a bed on the floor in front of the fireplace. "I don't want to shock the children, but I'm not about to let you sleep alone after what we've just shared," he told her, his eyes adoring her. "Unless you can think of something better, this is the best arrangement I can come up with."

"This is just fine." Melodie sighed contentedly, nuzzling closer to his big, warm body. "Perfect, in fact." The silly smile that arched her lips refused to be erased; rather, it grew. "I'm happy," she murmured, sounding almost surprised by the fact. "No, more than merely happy. I'm ecstatic and delighted and delirious and ready to burst with joy. I want to shout it to the world!"

"What about Schnickelgruber? Do you think you'll come to regret not choosing him? After all, the man can probably buy you almost anything your heart desires."

"All the money in the world isn't worth as much to me as one of your smiles, David Cooper," she assured him, gazing deeply into those beloved turquoise eyes. "Money could never replace Betsy's lisp, or a hug from Jenny, or the sight of the twins reciting their prayers after a day of mischief. You taught me that, you and the children. You've filled my heart until it's spilling over with love. It's all quite new to me, you know, and scary, too. I don't want to disappoint you, David."

"Just be sure, Melodie, and love will take care of the rest."

"I'm sure. I'm sure I love you. I'm sure I love those four urchins of yours, too, though I'm not sure why. They just sort of tug at your heart when you least expect it, don't they? Sort of like their father."

Too excited to sleep any longer, the children discovered them just past dawn, and were not at all shocked to find their father and Melodie snuggled together in their nightwear. Hadn't they requested Melodie as their mother as their Christmas wish? For the same reason, they were delighted but not particularly surprised to learn that Melodie was going to marry their papa, just as soon as a wedding ceremony could be arranged.

What did surprise them, and David and Melodie as well, was the fact that Sam was nowhere around. However, they didn't actually miss him for a while, being busy unwrapping their Christmas presents. The children were thrilled with their gifts, and thanked Melodie and David over and again. David was well-pleased with his scarf and slippers; and Melodie adored the carved songbird David had made for her.

"When we get to Denver, I know a man there who can mount it on top of a music box, so that it will turn around and play a melody." He laughed at his own choice of words. "How about a Christmas carol, to always remind us of this time when we fell in love? Of course, nothing can ever compare to my own darlin' Melodie, who crept into my heart with her own sweet song."

Their gifts to Sam were no longer beneath the tree, so they had to assume that he had come down earlier and taken.them. His gifts to all of them were fresh apples and oranges stuffed into the tops of their stockings. Where he'd gotten the fruit, Melodie could not imagine.

When Sam did not come down to breakfast, Melodie began to worry. When she sent the children up to wake him, and they reported that he was not in his room, she assumed he was out at the stable, tending to the animals.

David went out to fetch him and returned to say that Sam, the stage, and all eight horses were gone. "Maybe he just hitched them up to give them some exercise," David suggested. "Maybe he wanted to check the route a ways and see if the roads are passable yet."

It was a plausible excuse, one Melodie accepted until Sam missed Christmas dinner. "David," she whispered, not wanting to alarm the children, "something is wrong. Either Sam has deserted us here for some unknown reason, or he has met with trouble along the road. Either way, we are left here with not one horse to our claim."

"Don't fret, honey," he told her. "If need be, I'll walk to the nearest house, or ride the blasted milk cow for help. But I think you're worrying for nothing. Sam can take care of himself, even if it means he's stranded elsewhere; and this is a way station, don't forget. Sooner or later another stagecoach will happen by, and we'll be on our way again. It won't be long, Melodie."

David was right. Sam never did come back, but the day after Christmas, a westbound stage headed for Denver made its noon stop at the way station. Upon hearing their tale, the stagecoach driver shook his head in dumbfounded amazement. To his knowledge, there had been no scheduled run to Denver from Abilene on the day of the storm. Furthermore, he'd never heard of anyone putting runners on a stagecoach and driving it like a sleigh; and as far as he knew, the stage company did not employ a driver meeting the description they gave or answering to the name of Sam Nichols.

Luckily, there was room for all of them in the stage-coach, and shortly after lunch, they were on their way to Denver once more, still shaking their heads in bewilderment. "I just don't understand it, Melodie," David said, still trying to sort things out in his head. "Sam was as real as you and I. I'd stake my sanity on it!"

Melodie agreed, though she, too, was baffled. "I know. Maybe one of these days it will all make sense, but right now I don't mind telling you, I'm awfully confused. If I didn't have those pennies from the Christmas tree in my luggage, I'd doubt my own mind right now."

"You took the pennies?" David asked. "Why?"

"As a memento of our first Christmas together," Melodie admitted sheepishly. "I'm afraid I'm an incurable romantic and terribly sentimental."

"And I love you for it."

While the adults gave up trying to solve the mystery of Sam Nichols, the four Cooper children exchanged delighted grins and nodded their heads in sage agreement. Even if the grown-ups never figured it out, they knew what had happened, and they knew the power of believing in something with all your heart.

Sam Nichols . . . Saint Nicholas—it was all the same to them.

WARMEST HOLIDAY WISHES
from ...
CATHERINE HART

While some people from Ohio enjoy winter sports, CATHERINE HART prefers a cozy fire, spiced tea, and a sizzling book. With loving husband, three children, and ten historical novels to her credit, she believes in fairy-tale romance, mystical fantasies—and Santa! Look for her new romance, *Tempest*, coming soon from Avon Books.

Six Little Angels

Betina Krahn

For
Regina Maynard
*and all the children whose lives
she has touched.*

And in memory of
Lydia Krieg

1

*London's East End
December 12, 1882*

"Noni, you're not dying. Don't even talk like that." Regina Lofton's tear-streaked face leaned closer to the old woman's head as it lay on the pillow. "You can't die." Her fingers trembled as they flitted anxiously over whispy strands of silver hair, smoothing and stroking them back from Nanny Dodd's ashen face. "Your little ones, Noni. What would they do without you?" More tears burned down her reddened cheeks as the old lady's faded eyes fluttered closed. Her gaze fastened on the labored rise and fall of the old lady's chest, and she held her breath.

"Remember what we did ... wi' your old dollies, Gigi?" The old woman strained to produce even a halting whisper. "When they got old an' tired ... we put 'em on a shelf in the nursery ... to rest."

"But Noni—" Regina's throat squeezed shut, and the tears that had collected at her chin dripped onto the dingy ticking of the bed where her old nanny lay dying. She shifted on the edge of the mattress to cast blurry eyes on the huddled figures of several young children who were gathered around a crude metal stove at the far end of the long room. Noni's little ones.

Grief welled in her chest, crowding her breathing so that she had to grit her teeth to keep it from escaping in sobs. Then Nanny Dodd's eyes opened, now luminous and glistening, and Regina felt the old woman's cool, age-thinned hand seeking hers over the quilt. She clasped it tightly and lifted it, rubbing her cheek against its fragile, blue-veined skin.

"It's my time to rest now, Gigi. Didn' think it would come so soon . . . but . . . there's no more time." She swallowed with effort and her eyes closed briefly as she collected strength to speak again. "My little ones, Gigi . . . they're my lambies . . . just as you were." The old lady's careworn fingers moved against Regina's smooth skin, caressing. "My sweet Gigi. Such a good an' true heart. You had th' prettiest curls . . . th' dirtiest knees."

"Noni, please, don't talk. You have to save your strength." Regina bit her lip and blinked to clear her eyes.

The old woman roused and her gaze became lucid and penetrating for a moment, as it had been in those days when she had been the creator and authority of Regina Lofton's girlish world.

"P-promise me, Gigi." Nanny Dodd's other hand reached for Regina's arm and squeezed it tightly as she strained to raise her head from the pillow. Her voice dropped to a raw, pleading whisper. "Promise me you'll help my lambies. Promise me you'll find homes for 'em. Don' let 'em be put out as foundlings again . . . in one of those awful places. *Promise me . . .*"

"I promise, Noni," Regina whispered in choked tones. "I won't let them be sent to a foundling home or orphanage, I swear." The desperate intensity of the old woman's voice sent a quiver through her. Her old nanny was indeed dying. In that tumultuous moment of recognition and loss, she would have promised her very life if it had brought her dear old nurse peace of mind.

Nanny Dodd had been mother and teacher and companion to her for the first fourteen years of her life. Even after the old woman was pensioned by the Lofton family, five years ago, she had remained a force in Regina's life; a touchstone for her fervent heart, a quiet moral anchor in the sea of change and uncertainty that accompanied a young girl's transition to womanhood. The impending loss of that certainty, that selfless, loving presence, filled Regina with quiet anguish.

"I'll find them good homes, Noni . . . loving homes . . . with people who'll care properly for them. I'll see to your lambies."

Nanny Dodd searched Regina's lovely, earnest face, then nodded, as though a great weight had been lifted from her. The spark in her eyes damped and she sagged back against the worn ticking, looking exhausted but strangely at peace. Her eyes closed and she squeezed Regina's hands. A small, angelic smile appeared on her face that remained, unchanged, into eternity.

Regina sat weeping softly by her old nanny's deathbed, lost in memories and a haze of sadness. But soon the rustle and scrape of shoes and bare feet on the wooden floor and the press of little hands and bodies against her skirts brought her back to the present. She dabbed her burning eyes with her lacy handkerchief and focused on the several pairs of rosy cheeks and big trusting eyes that were her nanny's unexpected legacy to her.

Six—there were six of them. The oldest, Jennie, was a pale, delicate-featured girl of eight years, with somber eyes and long brown pigtails. Next in age came five-year-old Jonathan, whose cap of silky brown hair, big hazel eyes, and winsome smile made everyone who saw him reach out to pat or touch him. Then came two-and-a-half-year-old William, with his freckles, upturned nose, and startling blue eyes, and then fifteen-month-old Betty and Ruthie. The youngest, Edward, was Noni's latest rescue from London's mean streets. He was barely six months old.

Regina had come to know the older ones during her occasional visits with Nanny Dodd, and they'd come to know and trust her. Now they were all staring at her like the little lost lambs Nanny Dodd had declared them to be. One by one, their eyes drifted to the still form of their foster mother and then returned expectantly to Regina.

"Be she dead, then?" Jennie asked in a timorous voice.

"She is." Regina straightened on her seat as she watched their frowns of confusion and the tears forming in their eyes. Little blonde Betty, plastered against Regina's right knee, had an oozing, gray-green streak running down her upper lip. Without thinking, Regina reached out with her own lacy lady-handkerchief to give Betty's nose a good wiping. An instant later little blonde Ruthie fairly climbed Regina's left knee while wrinkling her clean nose, sniffing, demanding the same treatment. Regina obliged. Betty and Ruthie were identical twins who demanded everything in equal measure.

"You mustn't worry," Regina heard herself saying, as she looked into Jonathan's luminous eyes. The baby, Edward, was trying to pull himself up by the side of her bustle. She lifted him onto her lap where he nestled in the crook of her arm, drooling on her immaculate sleeve and skirt. "I promised Noni that I'd take care of you. You mustn't be afraid."

She halted, biting the inside of her lip and looking around her at the long, single room that had been their home since Nanny Dodd had taken them in. Canvas cots and blankets were stacked in one corner, near the metal stove, and along the far wall were shelves neatly filled with dishes, salvaged garments, odd-sized mittens, and a few very worn picture books. There was no rug on the floor, and smoky tallow lanterns provided the only light within the yellowed walls, but the room was scrupulously clean. Nanny Dodd could have spent the last years of her life in comfort in a pleasant flat, or at a seaside village, on the pension the Loftons provided. But she had chosen to settle here, in this tenement on the east side of London, rescuing and raising children who had nothing but a name and no one in the world to claim them.

Regina roused and sent Jennie for the neighbor woman, Mrs. Haskins, and was both relieved and saddened to learn that Nanny Dodd had already made provisions with the local undertaker. When they carried the body out, Regina was left with six children, a score of details to tend and a slow-dawning comprehension of the magnitude of the problem she'd just inherited. She prevailed upon the goodly Mrs. Haskins, who had a brood of five children of her own, to provide supervision and care for the children at night, until she could make other arrangements. And until she could find proper supervision or proper homes for them, she realized she would have to come daily, herself, to take care of them.

Added to the grief she felt at her nanny's passing, the responsibility seemed overwhelming. But it was destined to get worse. Even as she calmed and patted and reassured the children, preparing to depart for her own home, the landlord arrived at the door, having been informed of Nanny Dodd's death by the over-eager undertaker. Under Regina's indignant gaze, the ill-kempt Mr. Balthar strode about the room, reeking of tobacco, inspecting the contents with a sneer and a sniff, and poking the furniture with his cane. Then he announced that he already had a new tenant and wanted the "brood of brats" off the premises in three days.

"Three days? Why that's—unconscionable! These children have no place else to go."

"Ain't no skin off'n my nose, missy." Discolored teeth showed behind Balthar's thin lips and patchy, ill-trimmed whiskers. His yellowed eyes slid speculatively over Regina's lustrous auburn hair, womanly shape, and stylishly bustled dress. "I got a bizness to tend. A tenant dies, I move anoth'r'n straight in."

"Then I'll... pay an extra month's rent." Regina took a step forward and felt the children collecting at her back, huddling in her shadow. "Or two months."

"I already got a new tenant. An' I want them brats out." The vile Mr. Balthar jerked a grimy thumb at the door, plainly enjoying Regina's outraged sputters and her blush of ladylike anger.

Soon they stood, scowl to glare, backs rigid, jaws set, neither willing to budge. Mrs. Haskins finally broke the stalemate by mentioning that Nanny Dodd's rent was paid until Christmas Day, like the rest of the tenement's inhabitants. She wasn't foolhardy enough to mention that his reason for collecting rents on the holy day itself was to extort additional payment from his tenants under the guise of "gifts."

Regina cast Mrs. Haskins a grateful glance and demanded use of the lodgings until Christmas Day. She dredged up the names of two magistrates who were friends of her family and would undoubtedly be interested in the plight of her "charges."

"All right, Christmas Day it be," he growled impotently, and punched a furious finger at her on his way out the door. "An' not a minute past!"

Regina watched the way the thin wall vibrated as the door slammed. "Not a minute past," she vowed firmly.

The landlord's visit had deeply disturbed the children. It took a while to reassure them with quiet words and gentle touches. Mrs. Haskins watched the bravely cheerful face Regina presented the little ones and finally spoke up.

"I wish I could take 'em all in, Miz Lofton. But me an' the husband got all we can do to feed our five. I could take Jennie here. She gets on good wi' my brood an' is big enough to be a help."

"Jennie?" Regina sank to her knees beside the girl

and took her hands gently. "Would you like to go and live with Mrs. Haskins and her family?" She held her breath, watching the girl's big brown eyes.

"Can I sleep wi' 'er girls, Dottie an' Celia?"

Jennie and Regina both looked to Mrs. Haskins, who nodded. When the good woman opened her arms, Jennie hurried to her and threw her arms around her new mother with her eyes closed.

"Me, too!" Five-year-old Jonathan hurried to squirm into the embrace and two-year-old William launched himself, head-first, into Mrs. Haskins's skirts, yelling, "Me, me, me!" As Mrs. Haskins struggled to stay upright, she raised a sorrowful look to Regina and shook her head wordlessly.

Regina peeled their little bodies from the woman's skirts, assuring them that they would still see Jennie for a while yet. Her throat tightened so she could hardly speak. "But you'll soon have a new mother and a new home too."

Well-intentioned as it was, it was the worst possible thing to say. Jonathan's lower lip puckered, William burst into sobs, and soon the twins were wailing. Baby Edward, startled by the commotion, began to bawl as well.

Two hours later, Regina dragged her plain woolen cloak over her beleaguered wool jersey dress and wound her way down the four flights of stairs to the street level. Her back ached, her eyes burned, and her arms felt as if they'd been permanently stretched from the children hanging on them. But not even her haze of inner misery could supplant the stark reality of her situation. She was now responsible for the welfare of five active little bodies and their innocent, trusting little hearts.

Where on earth was she going to find homes for five penniless, friendless orphans? Good Lord, she didn't know a single family, whether in society or in service, that might be willing to take in one orphaned child, much less *five*, and all in a matter of two weeks!

Having grown up under Nanny Dodd's influence, Regina had learned to feel strongly about the plight of children who were unlucky enough to be thrust on the public mercy by the death or destitution of their parents. When Noni began to take in foundlings to raise, Regina was determined to help and provided Noni a bit of coin from her own pocket money. But until now, she hadn't fully understood the burden those vulnerable minds and hungry little bodies could lay upon a loving heart.

When she opened the street door, the dank gloom of the London night rolled in on her, taking her by surprise. She hadn't realized how late it was. And when a grizzled, scruffy old fellow pushed past her, knocking her back against the wall as he entered the tenement, she also realized how far she was from the cab stand.

Then a still worse thought struck her. She wouldn't be home for supper! Her parents would know she'd been out and about unescorted, after dark. And if they suspected she had been to visit Nanny Dodd in the rough East End . . .

Sir Charles Standworth Lofton, Regina's shipping magnate father, had made his feelings well-known on the subject of her continuing relations with her old nanny. He disapproved. Strenuously. Regina's mother, Lady Alice, while a bit more sympathetic, was equally adamant that Regina must abandon sentimental ties with the woman who had, after all, been *paid* to nurture her.

Charles and Alice Lofton were united in their view that Regina's continued contact with the old woman put "reformer" ideas about child welfare and unseemly "liberal" notions in her head. And they were positively convinced that Nanny Dodd's influence had something to do with Regina's unthinkable rejection of what they considered "an advantageous offer of marriage" to a wealthy nobleman several months past. If they had the faintest notion of the promise she'd made to her nanny, Regina was certain they would intervene to send the children straight to the closest foundling home—with a generous donation, of course.

Now she had two problems: finding homes for the children before Christmas Day *and* keeping the entire process a secret from her parents! She straightened inside her heavy cloak. By hook or by crook, she'd find a way.

The light of a gas street lamp cast a weak glow from a far corner, illuminating the dingy, unpainted doorways of the tenements that were stacked like so many discarded boxes along the narrow cobbled street. There was little traffic, only huddled forms that hurried here and there, anxious to escape the bone-chilling dampness. Regina swallowed her trepidation, pulled her cloak hood over her head, and stepped out into the London night, reminding herself she'd walked the route before.

Her heart beat faster as the night sounds and her own footfalls combined to fill the gloom around her with unseen menace. She kept to the side of the street, near the battered brick buildings, and walked briskly. One block, then two; she counted them off. When she turned the corner, a horse-drawn cab loomed out of the dimness, filling the greater part of the street. She paused a moment. If the driver had long to wait for his fare, he might be persuaded to carry her to the cab stand, or perhaps even home.

Just as she reached the cab and was about to hail the driver, the door of the nearest tenement slammed open and two black-clad male figures came hurtling out the door, heaving and shoving, locked in furious combat. There were muffled groans and curses and a woman's strangled cry from the doorway behind them. Regina had no time to react beyond turning with a start. That same instant, one combatant bashed into the other, sending him sprawling violently, straight into Regina.

She was slammed into the wheel of the cab, hitting

with such impact that the wind was knocked from her momentarily. Dazed and breathless, she slid down the wheel spokes to her knees, scarcely aware that the man who had hit her was struggling to his feet and charging his opponent again. The thuds of bare knuckles meeting flesh vibrated eerily in the gloom. They wrestled and growled and grunted until there was a final, savage *thud* and one of the men lay crumpled in the street, the other towering over him, panting.

Angry voices penetrated Regina's recovering senses: men shouting nearby and a young woman crying. There was a scuffle, a door slammed, and deep silence descended. As Regina shook her head and tried to rise, she heard a muttered curse and the sound of approaching footsteps. She was abruptly seized by the shoulders and hauled to her feet.

"Dammit!" A ragged baritone assaulted her. "Are you hurt?" She was too surprised to resist when a strong hand invaded her cloak hood to lift her chin forcefully into the light.

"I said, are you . . ." The owner of that hand froze, staring at her face as though it had just turned him to stone.

Regina found herself facing the velvet-rimmed lapels of a black evening coat, a low-cut, white waistcoat, and a very fashionable shirtfront. Her eyes widened with alarm as they traveled up rows of pleated frills to a taut, angular face and an uncompromising glare that were appallingly familiar.

Not him, she groaned silently. *Not here, not now!*

She knew that dark hair, now disheveled and hanging over his forehead, and those piercing eyes, which in better light would be hazel-green and probably narrowed behind a sardonic scowl. Her stunned gaze retreated downward. She knew that patrician nose, that wide, arrogantly chiseled mouth and prominent chin. And in the same moment, she knew she was in trouble.

"You?" His hands tightened on her arm and face, as if testing her reality. She managed to straighten and jerked her chin away at the same instant he relinquished it. But his freed hand went to her other arm, closing on it, pulling her closer.

"What in God's name— Are you injured?"

"I th-think . . . not." She tested her head and shoulder with a trembling hand and found soreness but no swelling.

"That's a small mercy." The gentleman raised his head to toss a quick, scathing look at the dark street around them, then straightened to his more than six feet of height, towering above her. "Where is your carriage, Miss Lofton?"

"I—I didn't bring one, your lordship." Her whisper sounded a little choked to her own ears. She was excruciatingly aware of the strength of his fingers digging into her shoulders and of the trickle of bright crimson at the corner of his swelling lip. His eyes glowed and his chest was heaving. She both saw and felt his panting breaths grazing her cheek in the cold night air. It was the viscount's face and his arrogant, high-handed manner, but the raw anger and intensity belonged to someone else entirely. "I was about to . . . hail a cab."

"A cab?" Disbelief mingled with growing frustration in his face. "There aren't any cabs on these bloody wretched streets at night."

The irritable sweep of his eyes around their surroundings drew hers to follow. Her gaze landed on the crumpled form of the man on the pavement, and the full sense of what had happened dawned in her mind. Maximilian Strand, the aloof and imperial Viscount Lloyd, had been engaged in a brawl—fighting bare-knuckled in the streets of one of London's roughest boroughs! The shock of it left her almost speechless.

The elegantly clad viscount watched her blue eyes light with discovery as her gaze rested on the man lying in the street. He made a low, growling sound that was the verbal essence of frustration, and gritted his teeth, watching her and wrestling visibly with some decision.

"I shall escort you home myself, Miss Lofton," he

announced finally, turning her bodily and nudging her toward the carriage door. "Be so good as to step into my cab."

"No, thank you, your lordship." She resisted both the urge to stare at him and his gentlemanly pressure at her back. She had to get away from him, had to get home as quickly as possible! "I'll walk."

"Not on these streets, alone and unaccompanied," he declared. There was an edge of exasperation to his usually composed tone. When he pushed her toward the door and she refused to budge, his patience snapped. "Get in, Miss Lofton." Still she balked. "Climb in or I'll toss you in!"

"Oh-h-h!"

In scarcely more than a heartbeat Regina found herself lifted by the waist, thrust through the open door of the cab, and plopped on her bottom on the cab floor.

"How d-dare— ohhh!" she sputtered.

"Now *stay!*" He punched a furious finger at her for emphasis and turned on his heel to collect the body that lay senseless in the street. She scrambled up onto the single seat, shocked to her very toes by his unthinkable assault on her person. Through the open door, she could see him straining to haul his victim onto his shoulders. Staggering slightly under the weight, he carried the insensible wretch to the cab and deposited him on the floor with a thud. Then he snarled an order to the cabby and climbed inside, too, just as the cab lurched into motion.

2

THE viscount was tossed against the seat beside her and muttered silently as he righted himself, straightening his evening coat and tugging down his vest with a jerk.

Regina pressed her back against the far side of the cab, staring, feeling unnerved at the way his presence and raw emotion seemed to fill the cab. For some reason, her eyes fastened on his hands as he smoothed his clothing and investigated the damage to his lip. His hands were well-proportioned, long-fingered and supple, and something about the sight of them made her feel a little panicky inside. Then into her mind came a vivid image of those hands coldly grasping what rightfully belonged to others.

"How dare you set hands to me." Embarrassment gave her tone special vehemence.

"I hardly 'set hands to you,' Miss Lofton. I simply helped you into my cab."

"Against my will!"

"In your best interest," he declared firmly. "It is the height of idiocy to be out in these precincts after dark, alone and afoot . . . much less *female* and *unprotected*."

She stiffened and leveled a scathing glare on him. "It would appear I am not the only *idiot* abroad tonight. Stop this cab at once."

"Not before I've squelched whatever scandal is being formed in that maddening little head of yours," he said with astonishing heat. "You came upon me at a most inconvenient time, Miss Lofton, and I intend to see

101

that this unsavory incident goes no further than this cab." Just then the cab hit a hole and bounced, causing the body at his feet to shift. When he rearranged his long legs around it with a snort of contempt, her gaze fell to his victim, whose identity suddenly dawned upon her.

"But that's—" She pointed at the fellow, then pulled her hand back into her lap and stared at the viscount.

"The estimable Jared Strand. My brother." The admission was obviously distasteful to him, and her shocked response and indrawn breath added visibly to his irritation. It was a forerunner of the very reaction that would occur all over London if word of this incident was allowed to spread.

"You were fighting with your own brother?"

"I assure you, there are ample reasons for the drastic action I have taken on his behalf." His angular face reddened as he turned on the seat to face her.

"On his behalf?" she said, experiencing again just how broad his shoulders were. Lord, it was like facing a forbidding black wall. She shivered, alarmed by the same strange, prickling sensations she had experienced in his presence nearly a year ago, just before she rejected his "most advantageous" offer of marriage. "You've knocked him senseless. I fail to see how being bashed senseless could possibly be to his benefit!" Her blue eyes flashed in the dimness. "And since you've taken *my* benefit so to heart, do you intend trouncing me next?"

He looked as though she'd just tossed icy water in his face. His features cooled and hardened before her eyes, solidifying into a rigid mask, purged of feeling. The transformation was so sudden and complete that Regina blinked and looked away, confused. He had assumed a detached air that put both her and the rest of the world an arm's distance from him, or below him. He was again the cold, commanding aristocrat she recognized, but for some reason that fact didn't reassure her.

"My brother has an eye for the ladies, Miss Lofton. If you take my meaning." His attention fastened on the color rising in her cheeks. "Currently, he fancies himself enamored of a mill girl who resides in those tenements. He'd gone to her lodgings tonight with the intention of taking her away with him. It was my duty, as head of the family, to prevent such a reckless and irresponsible act."

A shiver of defiance ran up her spine. "Reckless and irresponsible, is it? To want to marry where the heart leads, instead of where rank and advantage dictate?"

She saw his wide shoulders twitch and his elegantly carved lips tighten into a thin line. "I don't believe I mentioned marriage, Miss Lofton," he said, stingingly. "Nor, I am certain, did my 'honorable' brother. I believe he intended to reap the benefits of nuptial bliss without submitting to bothersome legal requirements. It would have meant a scandal, undoubtedly an expensive one. And I would have been left to sort it all out in the end. I simply chose to sort it out early, before major harm was done."

"How perfectly *efficient* of you," she observed tartly. And how like him to reduce a deep, romantic passion to no more than a financial folly, she thought. It was precisely this impenetrable air of control of everyone and everything around him that had led her to reject his offer of marriage.

He had been totally unknown to her when he approached her father with the idea of marrying her. Her father had been delighted at the prospect of a wealthy and titled son-in-law and considered it as good as done before they were even introduced. But at their first meeting she'd taken one look at his arrogant face and imposing bearing and felt an icy-hot shiver of warning. And after one endless evening in the cold superiority of his company, hearing about his very profitable mills, lucrative mines and estates, and impeccable pedigree, she had flatly declared to her horrified parents that she would rather be boiled in oil than wed him.

The man had a stongbox for a heart, she was convinced. He was the very embodiment of that term the Americans were so fond of: *robber baron*. The vast profits of his mills and estates were undoubtedly obtained at the expense and exploitation of the less fortunate, including *children*.

"A great many things clamor for my time. It pays to be efficient wherever possible." The viscount's bare hands clenched at his sides, and a muscle in his jaw flexed vigorously. For a moment his gaze glided down the front of her cloak, but he scowled and pulled it back to her face. "I must insist upon your discretion, Miss Lofton."

It was a command, she realized, an edict from the autocratic Viscount Lloyd. He wanted it and his wanting was reason enough, he seemed to think, for her to give it to him. A burst of righteous rebellion surged in her veins. He was so accustomed to ordering his world, to wielding influence, that he couldn't imagine someone would—

Influence. The word burst like a rocket in her brain. He knew people, lots of people, probably vast numbers of people. And some of those people, somewhere in the sprawling reaches of his domain, must want . . . *children!* Her thoughts and her heart began to race. It was madness. It was unthinkable. But just now it seemed the only possibility she had. A long moment later, a determined glow crept into her face. If he wanted her to keep quiet, she had just decided, then he would have to pay for it.

"You do have a problem, your lordship. You've an embarrassment on your hands and you want my silence." She paused and fortified herself with a deep breath. "Well, you may have it. For a price."

"A price?" He sounded a bit strangled. She'd caught him completely off guard.

"You have a problem. Well, so do I. Agree to help me with mine and I shall be as quiet as a boneyard about yours."

Dusky color rose from beneath his collar, filling his face, and he looked for all the world as if he might be considering carrying out her taunt: trouncing her bodily. But she was determined to have whatever help she could get from him for Noni's little ones. After all, she reasoned stubbornly, he probably owed London's exploited and impoverished children a debt or two of his own . . .

"A price? Why, that's . . ." His shock-raised brows swooped down to hover like hungry hawks over his eyes. Then the second premise of her demand reached him, and he turned his head to look at her from the corner of a narrowed eye. "Your problem?" The flicker of his eyes betrayed the practiced subordination of emotion to calculation. "Just what is your problem, Miss Lofton?"

He was obviously recalling her circumstances at the time of their meeting: alone and afoot in the rough East End. A man didn't get to be a baron of industry without being fairly quick on his feet.

"Give me your word that you'll help, first," she demanded.

"I'll do nothing of the sort." He leaned toward her, adding the intimidation of his wide shoulders to the cool challenge in his gaze.

"Then I shall have to see this unfortunate 'family situation' of yours spread from pillar to post," she said evenly, forcing herself to meet his glare straight on. She hadn't the foggiest idea how to go about spreading gossip from anywhere to anywhere, but her dainty, elegant mother was reputedly a past master at it. It couldn't be too difficult.

"You're serious." He sounded as though the prospect astonished him.

"Perfectly." She had to make herself sit still as he leaned even closer across the seat. The piercing quality of his eyes and the poised power of his physical presence worked on her nerves as he searched the determined set of her jaw. But even under that scathingly personal scrutiny, she did not flinch or waiver. The children's futures were at stake.

"Dammit. It's blackmail," he declared flatly. When he withdrew to the far side of the seat, she almost melted.

"You'll give me your word, then?" The strained relief in her voice made him look at her. "You'll help me?"

"I seem to have no choice." He sounded disgusted with himself and turned his face away to peer out the cab window. "What is this *problem* of yours?"

"I have to find a home for a baby."

Everything seemed to freeze, even time. An uncountable eternity passed before he turned to look at her, his jaw slack with shock. His eyes flew to the parted front of her cloak.

"Good God." He reddened. "You mean to say—"

"N-no!" Her own face flamed when she realized what he was thinking. "Not th-that." She pulled her cloak closed and wrapped her arms protectively over her narrow waist. "I was given a baby, by a dear old friend."

"Dear old friends give young women babies all the time, Miss Lofton," he said derisively.

"This 'dear old friend' happened to be my old nanny!" She shifted irritably on the seat. "She took the baby in as a foundling and then became quite ill." Her throat clogged so that she had to swallow to continue. "Noni died this afternoon." She looked down at her gloved hands and blinked several times. "I was with her at the end and . . . she made me promise to find a home for the baby."

She could feel his eyes on her as he weighed the truthfulness of her story. Her pang of conscience was brief and relatively painless. It really was the only way, she told herself. And perhaps it would do the cold, impervious viscount good to have to help someone for a change. "I must have help in finding a family or a married couple who want a healthy child."

"And that's to be my task, is it? Locating a home for

this baby of yours?'' His features were hardening once more, constraining his reaction as he watched her softened posture.

"Yes." She lifted her head to behold his face and was startled by the angry intensity of his expression. "You've given your word. You swore to help—"

"Whatever your opinion of me, Miss Lofton," he broke in, "I am generally known for keeping a pledge." The steel of his tone sent an involuntary shiver through her shoulders.

A pall of silence fell between them. Regina settled back into the corner and looked out the coach window, feeling unsettled by his contained anger. She stole a look at him from the corner of her eye and felt her pulse skip a beat. She was probably a bit mad, as well as desperate, to try to coerce such a powerful and unfeeling man. Suddenly there it was again, that odd, prickling feeling just under her skin. It was a bit like dread and a bit like . . . something else.

When they came within two blocks of her home, she asked him to stop the cab, to allow her to walk the rest of the way. He rapped irritably on the roof. When the vehicle slowed and stopped, he leaned past her to jerk the handle and swing the door open, dismissing her. She let herself down from the carriage, then stood with her hand on the door.

"Nanny Dodd's flat is just around the corner from where we met this evening. Twenty-four Channel Street. You'll have to meet me there tomorrow morning."

"I have an appointment tomorrow morning," he said sharply.

"Then you'll have to disappoint someone else," she declared. She gripped the edge of the door, feeling his animosity billowing over her like a physical wave. "We have to find that home by Christmas Day. The landlord is tossing . . . the baby . . . out on Christmas Day. We have less than two weeks, your lordship."

She closed the door before he could react and hurried

down the street toward Lofton House. From inside the closed cab came a virulent "Dammit!" She lifted her skirts and began to run, stopping only when she was well inside the great front doors of home.

"They've been asking for you, Miss Regina," Barnes, the butler, whispered as he took her cloak and gloves. A conspiratorial jerk of his head toward the salon doors on the left of the great marble hall warned her of her parents' location. His scowl was a clue to their current dispositions.

"I'll just slip upstairs," she whispered, trying to catch her breath. The stout, black-clad butler nodded and tiptoed off. But all their stealth went for naught. She was no more than halfway to the sweeping marble staircase when her father's great bass voice boomed out over the wide center hall.

"Regina Elizabeth Lofton!" Sir Charles Lofton was standing in the salon doorway with his spectacles in his hand, a newspaper tucked under his arm, and a forbidding frown on his face. "Your mother and I would have a few words with you. In here, if you please. *Now.*"

She followed her father into the electrically lit salon, with its exquisite Empire furnishings, velvet drapes, Aubusson carpets, and long, gilt-framed mirrors. She stopped a safe distance from her mother's chair and felt them eyeing her appearance. She glanced down at her rumpled and drool-spotted wool jersey and winced.

"I was at Nanny Dodd's today, all day." She seized the initiative, knowing she owed them an explanation and hoping a confession would dilute their ire and their interest. "She sent a note, asking me to come and I went. She'd been ill of late. And today . . ." Her eyes began to fill with tears as the reality of it descended on her anew. Her voice became small and girlish. "She died. I was with her and she . . . just held my hand and . . . died."

She fumbled for her pocket and her handkerchief,

finding neither. Her father's immaculate handkerchief was thrust into her hands. She closed her eyes and nodded mute gratitude as she buried her face in it. She felt her mother's arms close around her shoulders and heard her mother's voice, soft in her ear.

"We know you loved Nanny Dodd very much, Gigi. And we shall always be grateful to her for caring so much about you."

Her father cleared his throat. "Even so. But now it's time—" A vehement shake of the head from his wife stopped him.

"It's time for Gigi to go lie down a while." Alice lifted her daughter's chin and smiled through the moisture in her own eyes. "Shall I help you to your room?"

Regina shook her head and cast a wan smile at her parents. They really did love her, for all their edicts and expectations. It was with no small pang of guilt that she escaped their presence for the privacy of her room.

Charles and Alice Lofton watched their only daughter leave the room and then looked at each other. "It's for the best," Charles declared, settling his spectacles on his nose with a sigh. "Now perhaps she'll get on with her life . . . quit worrying about masses of nameless, faceless children and start worrying about producing a few of her own."

"Charles!" Alice seemed a bit put-out by his remark. But she had to own that her sentiments ran very close to his. "We have to get her married first, Charles," she said, dabbing a remnant of a tear from her eye. She took a deep breath, smoothing the narrow waist of her gown and the draped overskirt that swept back to form an elegant bustle. She took her husband's hands and pulled him to the sofa.

"Now, who do you know who would make a handsome, rich, titled . . . and *patient* husband?"

Rich, titled, and passably handsome Maximilian Strand blew through the doors of his club that night in a royal state. He spoke briefly with the major-domo, then repaired to the half-empty bar to get stinking drunk. He began with brandy, went to Scotch whiskey, then on to fire-breathing cognac. The bartender scratched his head at the usually cool and gentlemanly viscount's unprecedented mood, but he continued to pour.

By the fifth drink, Max found himself hallucinating Regina Lofton's face. His palms began to moisten, as they had in her presence. She appeared in his vision just as she had in the dimly lit cab: her chin tucked as she huddled against the wall so that she looked at him from beneath petulant brows.

It was the very image of her, with her glossy auburn hair and her huge, Dresden-blue eyes, that peered up at him from beneath an indecently long fringe of lashes. His mind conjured every line and curve of her creamy oval face and even the provocative tilt of her nose, which just saved her face from dire prettiness. He imagined those wide, graceful lips the color of sun-blushed peaches and the unconscious habit she had of chewing the inside of them. Her hair had a deep reddish cast, but she didn't have a freckle on her face or throat—his eyes drifted downward over his vision—or on her lovely bosom, which meant she probably didn't have them anywhere on her body. *Her body*. A shiver went through him at that unholy thought. Lord, it was happening to him again, that bewildering melting of his logic and determination and social graces into one unwieldy and humiliating lump of feeling.

Why her? Why tonight? He slammed his eyes shut, trying to blot out the sight of her. In the middle of another of his brother's damned romantic fiascos, he had turned around to find himself facing his own romantic disaster, in the flesh.

From the first time he'd seen Regina Lofton, across a large and crowded ballroom, he'd been struck by the freshness of her beauty and the genuine graciousness of her manner. He'd watched her walk and converse and smile and dance. He'd seen her eyes sparkle and her shoulders move beneath the draped beading of her fashionable bodice, and by the end of the evening he'd been utterly taken with her. He was at an age and of a station in life to marry and establish his nursery, he reasoned, and he decided to approach her father with the idea of a marriage. Things went well with Sir Charles and he soon found himself introduced to the entrancing young thing he had marked as his future bride.

But being near her, feeling her eyes on him, was like being plunged unexpectedly into hot water; it all but took his breath. In his male world of bewigged lawyers and droning contracts, of brandy and cigars, managers and minions, there had never been anything like her. He found himself hot-faced and unexplainably tongue-tied, and retreated into that which he knew best: the impressive tally of his financial achievements and the impeccable lineage of his family and title. Throughout the one excrutiating evening they spent together, he saw the sparkle in her eyes dim and her enchanting shoulders stiffen. He watched her fidget uneasily with her fan and felt a shiver when he set a hand to her waist as they danced. By the end of the evening he didn't have to speak with Sir Charles to know the fate of his suit. It was painfully obvious that Regina Lofton wanted nothing to do with him.

And now that he'd finally convinced himself he wanted nothing to do with her—ever!—she came brazening and blackmailing her way straight into his life again, dragging some other man's baby with her!

Sir Lawrence Trexel, Knight of the Garter and notorious rumor-broker, stood in the hallway watching Maximilian Strand pelting back liquor like a man beset. His eyes lighted with true gossip's fervor, and he hurried into the bar to deposit himself beside Max with a sympathetic smile. His curiosity was soon rewarded and his smile was transformed to pure radiance. After a few sly inquiries into the reason for the bender, Max Strand turned to Sir Lawrence and asked rather drunkenly if he knew anybody who wanted a baby.

Sir Lawrence hurried away, fairly vibrating with gossip's glee. What a morsel! Max Strand had gotten somebody in a family way and now needed a place to stow the results of his indiscretion! By the time he departed the door of the club, Sir Lawrence was laying plans for a "gossip watch" on Maximilian Strand, to learn more, and already had the first recipient of this juicy tidbit firmly in mind.

Lady Alice Lofton, he thought. *Oh, yes. Definitely. Lady Alice simply must be the first to hear this one!*

3

THE next morning Regina rose early and dressed as plainly and sturdily as her wardrobe would allow. Over her stiffest, boniest corset and bustle frame, she donned a white, tuck-fronted blouse with a standing collar, a heavy woolen skirt, and a matching jacket with a layered peplum that was gathered to drape over her bustle. She had Elsie, her maid, button her sturdiest leather boots on her, then stood before her mirror feeling . . . fortified.

She drilled her maid on the "dressmaker" story she'd concocted as an excuse for her day-long absence, and set off for the nearest cab stand, on her way to Noni's children.

She arrived at Noni's flat to find chaos. Mrs. Haskins had just begun to prepare breakfast porridge before being called away to tend a small emergency with her own children. Young William and the twins were crying, and Jennie and Jonathan were arguing over who was to watch baby Edward—who needed fresh nappies in the worst way. The smells, the crying, the arguing and shoving: Regina felt utterly overwhelmed. In desperation, she made herself think what Noni would do, what Noni always did.

Routine, she realized; Noni always insisted on a morning routine for her children. Regina peeled off her cloak and jacket, then pulled Jennie and Jonathan aside and began to sort things out. Within half an hour, the children were all decently clothed and being fed—all but Edward, who, Regina was appalled to learn, had to have goat's milk. As yet, no one had milked the goat Noni had acquired and stabled in a small shed in the alley behind the tenement. As Edward began to fret and cry, her spirits began to sink. She hadn't the foggiest notion of how to go about milking anything!

Max Strand arrived at 24 Channel Street in a cab, having refused to bring his own carriage into such perilous precincts. He brushed his caped greatcoat and adjusted the already perfect knot of his tie, while suppressing the painful reminder of his past night's perfidy that was pounding in his head.

By the time he asked after "Nanny-something's" lodgings and climbed four flights of stairs, his head was ringing like a blacksmith's anvil and his jaw was set like granite. He paused in the hall outside, hearing children's voices and the occasional cry of a baby inside, and glanced about him at the dismal state of the place. It was hard for him to imagine Regina Lofton in such reduced circumstances.

Regina hoisted the fussy Edward onto her shoulder and hurried to answer the door. The viscount loomed in the doorway like a great dark cloud and as he came forward, it seemed that he pushed all of the air out of the room. She was left breathless.

His piercing eyes narrowed as they swept the lodgings and the children, who were staring at him from where they played on the floor and worked at clearing the table. His gaze came to settle on Regina and little Edward, and she felt another of those unnerving shivers that his scrutiny always generated in her.

"I'm here," he announced in a surly tone. "Let's cut to the short of it, shall we? Which one of them is it?"

"A-actually . . ." She backed toward the center of the room. The children watched her wary reaction to the formidable-looking man and began to collect at her back and behind her skirts, as they had when Mr. Balthar came. She squared her shoulders and took a nervous breath.

"Actually, it's any one of them . . . *all of them*."

"All of them?" It took a moment to register. "But they can't possibly *all* be—" He stalked forward, scrutinizing the motley brood hanging onto her skirts and then her features, as if searching for some trace of resemblance. A heartbeat later he was perfectly furious—with her and with his own gullibility.

"Dammit—all of them?" He lurched forward, halting only when the children squealed and hid their faces. "You little liar! *A* home for *a* baby, you said. Not half a dozen!" He paced back and forth, sputtering and fuming, then he stomped closer with his eyes blazing and jabbed a finger at her. "I thought it was— I never agreed to this. I'll have nothing to do with it!"

Regina thrust baby Edward into Jennie's hands and turned to face him. Their eyes met like flint striking steel, showering sparks all around. She was stunned. Not by his anger; she had expected that. But by her own suddenly frantic need to have him stay!

"Then just walk away," she demanded, reacting against that frightening, vulnerable feeling. "There's the door. By all means, leave. Who needs you?"

He wheeled and jerked the door open, then halted halfway through. Something in her taunt made him waver, then turn enough to shoot a burning glare at her. His shoulders flexed and his gloved hands clenched. He suddenly stalked back across the room, seized her arm, and dragged her into the hall with him, slamming the door behind them.

In the dim hallway, his hands closed on her shoulders and pulled her shocked form close to him. She just managed to brace against him, but was too surprised or overwhelmed to summon the strength to push him away. They stood staring at each other with chests heaving and eyes glowing, touching, testing.

He was again that angry, passionate stranger who had tossed her bodily into his carriage the night before.

"Th-there are the stairs, your lordship," she said hoarsely.

He didn't move. His eyes lowered from hers and seemed to fasten on her lips. His own lips parted, sending a trill of panic through her. He felt her violent shiver and straightened with a grim expression.

"Who do those children belong to?" he demanded.

"My old nanny took them in as foundlings. They don't belong to anybody," she said in a choked voice, "except me, I suppose. I swore to Nanny Dodd as she lay dying that I'd find them homes. And I never go back on my word." Her lashes lowered and her blue eyes darkened accusingly before she dragged them away and averted her face. Her stomach was doing crazy turns and her heart was thudding so loudly in her ears that she was sure he must be able to hear it, too. She had to fight the urge to look into his eyes, to stare at his chiseled mouth. What was happening to her?

"It was my promise . . . and it's my problem." She sagged with confusion in his hard grip.

He held her a moment longer, then with a muttered "Dammit," he spun her around and pushed her back through the doorway ahead of him. She turned and found him jerking his kidskin gloves from his hands, finger by irritable finger. The children ran to her, then peeked from behind her skirts to watch him shed his

cashmere greatcoat and lay it carefully over the back
of an unpainted chair by the table.

He turned to them in his charcoal-gray morning coat
and pin-striped trousers and set his fists on his narrow
hips. He was again the cool, imperial Viscount Lloyd,
and his words had the weight of a royal command.
"Just who are these little hooligans?"

Regina watched him with a massive and somewhat
irrational sense of relief. He was staying.

"This is Jennie." She pointed to the girl and reached
to take the crying Edward from her arms. "She's already got a home. Then there's Jonathan; he's five. Say
'Good morning' to the viscount, Jonny." Jonathan
scowled, but at Regina's prodding, moved forward.
Keeping a fistful of Regina's skirt in his left hand, he
offered his right to the viscount. The nobleman's face
tightened oddly as he bent and took that little hand for
a brief shake.

Over Edward's lusty wails, Regina introduced William and the twins and finally the screeching Edward
himself. The viscount's face darkened at the baby's
unholy assault on his hearing. "Whatever is the matter
with him?"

"He's hungry." She jiggled the baby cajolingly. "He
has to have special food and no one's milked Victoria
this morning."

The viscount naturally asked what in heaven's name
"Victoria" was, besides the name of their sovereign
queen.

Shortly Max Strand found himself stalking down the
stairs with a pail in his hand, following young Jonathan
to the makeshift goat byre in the alley. His face was
burning with indignation and outrage, but a few more
piercing shrieks from the starving Edward in his throbbing ears and he would have volunteered to milk a bull
elephant in order to escape! What in God's name had
he gotten himself into?

The goat byre was a cramped, smelly place, and Victoria proved to be every bit as stubborn as her royal

namesake. Jonathan solemnly held the goat's tail and
volunteered that Noni always sang to Victoria when
she milked her. Max raised his head to look at the boy
with a face like carved stone.

"I am not going to *sing* to a damned goat!" He turned
on the stool, tucked his long legs out of the way with
some difficulty, and reached for the goat's teats. But
Victoria apparently objected to the taking of such liberties without a proper bit of wooing first. She kicked
both the bucket and Max's knee, then bucked and
tromped on Jonathan's foot, setting him howling.

Three grudging choruses of "Sur le pont d'Avignon"
later, Victoria relented and let down her milk. Max
managed, through sheer force of will and a passable
baritone, to fill a third of the small pail. Then he un-
crumpled his long legs and followed Jonathan back up
the stairs, admonishing him to never, *never* tell Miss
Lofton that he'd actually sung to that wretched beast.
The boy looked up at him with big hazel eyes full of
puzzlement, then brightened.

"Oh, you mean Gigi. I won't tell." Just then Jonathan's face seemed to contain considerably more than
five years' worth of worldly wisdom. But then, Max
realized, the boy had likely seen a bit more of the world
than most five-year-olds. The thought lodged in a very
vulnerable place in his mind.

Minutes later, Regina desperately tugged a rubber
nipple onto the bottle of warm milk and finally silenced
Edward's cries. When she looked up with relief, she
found the viscount glaring at the children, who were
huddled in a row on the edge of Nanny Dodd's bed,
staring back at him. Her gratitude evaporated. When
he turned to her and spoke, his words had the effect
of fingernails raking a schoolroom slate.

"They look like ragpickers."

Regina's chin came up and her eyes narrowed with
surprised anger. Only a minute before she'd been feeling grateful to him for his help. Was there nothing
human inside the man at all?

"I won't be associated with ragpickers," he declared regally. "Nor will I be accused of foisting guttersnipes on the families of my acquaintance."

"You have a choice, your lordship." She blazed with feral intensity, hurling her gaze at the door.

"Yes, I do." He watched the protective outrage in her eye with perfectly calculated dispassion. He looked the children over again, quite deliberately, then cast her an inscrutable glance over his shoulder. "I can choose to see them rigged-out properly."

Her anger was cut short, truncated by surprise as he turned back to the children and said, "I don't suppose you would happen to have a sewing basket about the place?"

Jonathan, seated on the edge of the bed, nodded and scrambled off to drag a chair to the shelves and root around for Nanny Dodd's sewing kit. He handed it to the viscount without the slightest quailing. With Jonathan looking on, his lordship sorted through the meager implements with an imperious finger. He caught the loop of an old, glazed linen tape measure and lifted it from the basket. Then he addressed Jonathan directly, man to man.

"I don't suppose you could find a bit of paper and something to write with, too?"

Jonathan's face broke into a broad smile and in a moment he was dragging a precious piece of paper and stubby pencil from that same cluttered shelf. He jumped down and carried them proudly to the viscount, who found himself holding a used paper envelope, carefully opened and saved. A muscle in his jaw twitched noticeably.

He beckoned the other children over and when they hung back, he addressed Regina with a clear annoyance. "Tell them to come here and let me measure them. I haven't bitten anyone in years."

Regina pushed to her feet, feeling unnerved by what was happening. With Edward still nursing noisily in one arm, she ushered the children from the bed to the viscount. Jonathan volunteered to be measured first, then surprised the nobleman by asking if he could write down the measurements.

"I know my numbers, and letters," he said proudly. "Noni taught me."

His lordship looked at the five-year-old as if he were considering both the boy and the idea, then nodded gravely. To both adults' surprise, Jonathan wrote not only the numbers, but also the first letters of each child's name beside them, in a neat row down the edge of the old envelope.

One by one, the children released Regina's skirts and allowed the formidable viscount to wrap the tape around their squirming tummies and to measure their bobbling heights and the length of their feet. When at last they came to Jennie, she shrank at Regina's side and shook her head timidly.

"I already got a home," she said.

The viscount looked at the longing in her gray eyes and cleared whatever seemed to be stuck in his throat. "But you don't have a new dress. And I'll not be blamed for you going without," he declared. A wrenching look of hope spread over Jennie's pale face and when Regina nodded, she, too, stepped forward to be measured.

Regina watched the process in a state of disbelief. Her eyes lingered on the viscount's lean, long-fingered hands, which were firm yet gentle as he touched the children. She was baffled by his actions, which were such a stark contrast to his irritable, condescending attitude. In fact, she was so absorbed in watching him that she failed to see Ruthie coming too near the iron stove, then stumbling.

A cry went up and, without thinking, Regina thrust Edward into his lordship's startled hands and rescued the toddler. The mild burn to Ruthie's fingers was quickly soothed with cold water, then butter and kisses. But it left baby Edward perched awkwardly on the viscount's unyielding shoulder, with a very full stomach. Presently, as the furor of the accident died, Edward emitted a giant burp . . . bringing up some of his breakfast, which slid in an unnoticed yellowish ooze down the back of the viscount's immaculate coat.

Regina finally looked up to find him standing rigidly in the middle of the room, holding Edward stiffly out in front of him. She hurried to take the baby, and their hands met briefly in the transfer. The touch brought their gazes together like a glancing blow. The viscount recoiled and straightened his already straight tie and smoothed his already smooth coat. Regina lurched back and buried her attention in the sleepy Edward in her arms, her cheeks pink.

"I can't waste the entire day here," he said gruffly. "I have important matters to attend." He reached for his greatcoat and slipped it over his shoulders, then snatched up his hat and gloves. "I shall send some things around."

With that, he was gone. Regina sank into a chair, feeling wobbly inside and confused by his contradictory behavior. Minutes later, she felt Jonathan pulling on her arm and roused from her disturbing contemplation of the Viscount Lloyd.

"When will his lordship be back?" Jonathan wanted to know. Jennie and William had gathered around her, too, with the same question in their faces. She had to give them an honest answer.

"I haven't the foggiest idea."

Early that afternoon, Sir Lawrence Trexel spotted Maximilian Strand in a fashionable bazaar of shops in the Picadilly. He hurried across the street and into the building to see for himself: the young nobleman with his arms full of knitted baby booties, caps, and linen nappies involved in deep discussion with a matronly clerk, who kept referring nervously to a yellowed bit of paper in her hand.

"Two of everything," the viscount was ordering the

woman. "Have them wrapped and ready by the time I leave the premises."

"Y-yes, your lordship." The plump woman's ruddy complexion grayed. "I'll find the very best smocks. But surely you'd want to pick out the dresses; there's quite a range of price, even in the ready-to-wear."

"Choose whichever you think best, madam." The viscount sounded near the end of his patience. He dumped the things in his arms on the counter and snatched up his greatcoat. "Just be quick about it." When the viscount turned from the counter to put on the garment, he jolted back a step, seeming surprised to see Sir Lawrence standing behind him. Then he lifted his chin and reddened. "Sir Lawrence."

"So good to see you again, Viscount." Sir Lawrence tipped his hat and hurried toward the front doors with the vision of a scandal burning in his mind: Max Strand with an armful of nappies and a streak of soured baby burpings down the back of his ever-so-expensive coat!

Late that afternoon Alice Lofton came breezing into her husband's study with her stylish hat askew and her face flushed. "Charles, you simply won't believe what I've just heard!" she announced, settling her bustle onto a parlor chair. "The most horrible thing, and who would have guessed it of him—he seemed so proper and gentlemanly and decent—"

"Alice!" Charles removed his spectacles from his nose and pinned her with a look. "Just the meat of it, if you please. Who, what, and where."

"The Viscount Lloyd. Has a . . . a . . . 'love child.' Somewhere. Told Sir Lawrence himself only last night. And today he was seen buying nappies and baby buntings in public, bold as brass. Think of it!"

"Lloyd? Are you quite sure?"

She nodded, fanning herself with her hand. "And to think, Charles, that our Gigi might have been married to him by now, and caught up in this sordid business." She closed her eyes, scarcely able to bear the weight of such a possibility.

Sir Charles frowned. "I wouldn't credit it, except for Sir Lawrence's word; he's scrupulous about his news." His frown deepened. "You know, Gigi disliked Lloyd from the first, said there was something not quite right about him. Perhaps she wasn't just being headstrong and overly romantic, after all."

"Our Gigi's really a very sensible girl at heart, Charles," Alice vowed solemnly. "Why, instead of moping about over Nanny Dodd, she's carried her sorrow as a true lady would—straight to her dressmaker's."

It was well past dark that evening when Regina finished tidying the dishes from the stew supper Mrs. Haskins had provided them. She'd had to occupy the children as best she could, with stories and lessons and patting-games. It had seemed the longest day of her entire nineteen years as she watched the door and chided herself for doing so.

When the knock came, she was directing their evening toilette, washing faces and hands and necks. She didn't make it to the door before it opened and the viscount ducked his head and stepped inside. His arms were full of paper-wrapped packages. A driver in smart livery edged in behind him to set a large stack of boxes on the floor, then withdrew.

She stood, dumb with surprise and only dimly aware of the children gathering around her with widened eyes, jumping up and down and declaring, "It's him!"

It was him, Regina realized. Him with his piercing hazel eyes and his dark feathery brows that drooped a bit at the corners. Him with his wall-like shoulders, and long, tapered frame, and firm hands. And his arms were full of clothes to cover and warm Noni's children. Her throat was tight with confusion as she forced the words out.

"You came back."

His customary frown deepened to a scowl. "It seemed easier than explaining to the good merchants of Picadilly why I wanted these things delivered to Channel Street," he declared. His gaze glided over her surprise-pinked cheeks and her rumpled blouse, and lingered a moment too long on the strands of softly curled hair that had escaped her proper bun. She fought an absurd urge to pat and smooth her hair as he turned to the bed and emptied his arms of packages to remove his outer garments. And as he sorted the packages on the bed, Regina's eyes fastened on a dried, yellowish streak down the back of his coat, which simply had to be Edward's work. A trickle of warmth wound its way from her head all the way to her toes.

Jonathan ran to the bed, his eyes shining with excitement. William barreled into the viscount's legs, and the twins followed, squealing. Even Jennie abandoned her usually sober mien to rush to the bed and stand clapping her hands, jiggling with anticipation. The viscount looked down at them from his great height with an air of supreme dispassion.

"You little hooligans. Mob me, will you? Next, I suppose, you'll be wanting to open them." He made it sound like an outrageous offense on their part. He sighed heavily and pushed the packages back so he could sit on the edge of the bed. Then he lifted one parcel after another, peeking inside, seeming surprised by what he saw. Then he actually rolled his eyes.

Regina watched, first with consternation, then with growing fascination. He was drawing it out, she realized. He seemed to be savoring the excitement as much as they were, but with a manner so absurdly controlled that it mocked itself. It was almost a parody of his usual crust and hauteur.

When he couldn't hold out against their curiosity any longer, the viscount thrust the packages into the children's hands with orders to open them. In a frenzy of ripping paper and giddy laughter and cries of discovery, the children uncovered and explored their new clothes. They struggled into their new shifts and smocks and stockings, then twirled and jumped and ran to Regina to let her see. Then they donned their new shoes and stomped around until the people in the room below complained and they were forced to stop.

Regina admired them all, but she had to finally call a halt and insist they set their new things aside and climb into their nightshirts. As they were being tucked into bed, Jonathan caught the viscount's sleeve and asked if he would read a story from one of Noni's books.

"I'm not any good at fairy tales," the viscount replied with muted gruffness. A muscle in his lean jaw worked visibly as the boy's big hazel eyes bored hopefully into him. Jonathan scrambled from his cot, ran to the shelves, then shoved a large, tattered book into the viscount's hands. His worshipful smile made resistance impossible, and the viscount lowered himself stiffly to the edge of Jonathan's cot and opened the book.

Regina sank onto the side of Betty's cot, stroking her hair and watching the viscount's rigid posture and self-conscious rendition of "The Ugly Duckling." He seemed to feel her eyes on him and glanced at her occasionally, scowling, as if daring her to laugh at him. But Regina had never felt less like laughing. His stiffness and the hints of humanity she glimpsed in him caused a strange emptiness in her middle that seemed to spread through her body and limbs. What kind of robber baron let himself be wheedled into reading a bedtime story? And why was she feeling these strange hollow feelings inside from just looking at him?

The story ended and Jonathan looked up at the viscount with boyish expectation in his sleepy face. "Will you find me a home with lots of books? I like books."

The viscount straightened. His face darkened. Across the room, Regina held her breath, wishing she could intercede and warn him, or plead with him, about how fragile a child's hopes could be.

"I shall . . . see what I can do," he said softly.

Regina turned away to tuck the covers around Ruthie with an odd lump in her throat.

4

As the lamp was turned down, Regina felt the viscount's gaze settling on her and hurried for her jacket and cloak. Mrs. Haskins arrived for the night and after a few quiet words with her, Regina turned to find the viscount already buttoned into his greatcoat and asking how she was being carried home. She mumbled something about a cab, and he gave her a dark look and declared he'd see her home, since he'd brought his own carriage this time.

Minutes later, Regina settled against the deeply padded leather seats of the viscount's grand conveyance and suffered a small quiver that had nothing to do with fear or dread. It seemed to be caused by the fact that the viscount was settling onto the seat beside her, and it felt appallingly like . . . anticipation. She clasped her hands sternly in her lap. But her senses stubbornly fastened on the heated presence on the seat beside her, just inches from her knees, from her shoulders, from her—

Her eyes flew wide and she chewed her lips to staunch the shocking itchiness in them. But there was nothing she could do about the way her heart was beginning to pound, or the tightness in her throat, or the light-headed, breathless feeling that was claiming her.

"They call you 'Gigi,'" he said quietly once the carriage was under way. The directness of his words let her know he was looking at her, and the undercurrent of intimacy in his tone made her very conscious of the darkness around them.

"Nanny Dodd called me that from my nursery days. They took it up from her." She swallowed hard, trying not to let her confusion show.

"Gigi. Gigi . . . Gigi." He tried it out, giving it a softer, more sensual sound with each repetition. "It suits you."

She couldn't help the massive shiver; it shook her from the tops of her shoulders to the tips of her toes, raising gooseflesh over every inch of her body. And it seemed to linger, in after-tingles of expectation, in sensitive and embarrassing places in her body. She gasped silently and prayed he hadn't noticed.

But he had. And for the first time Max realized, even as she was realizing, that her shivers might have nothing to do with revulsion or distaste. They seemed to be her body's unique reaction to him, a sensual and all-encompassing response, and somewhat involuntary. His breath stopped in his throat. What would it take to refine that reaction, to make it come willingly? What would it take to make her open herself to him, to make her see him and respond to him as a man?

The intimacy of their time with the children had weakened both his defenses against her and his discretion. Suddenly he had to know, had to touch and experience her. And no amount of gentlemanly restraint or inbred caution could staunch that long-suppressed desire.

"Are you cold?" he asked with a slight huskiness.

Regina glanced once at him, then a second time, and her gaze caught on his hands. He was removing his gloves, slowly, finger by finger, sliding them from his lean, supple hands. Watching him, she forgot to breathe. Then before her helpless eyes, his bare hands reached boldly for hers, separating them and pulling one onto his lap.

He began to pull her glove from her, finger by tantalizing finger, sliding the soft leather over her skin, deliberately massaging the length of each digit as he uncovered it. Then her glove was completely off and her naked hand was captive in his, flesh against bare flesh. He toyed with her fingers, tracing their shape and teasing their sensitive inner surfaces and the pads at their tips. He stroked her palm, exploring its creases and sensitive mounds and valleys as proxy for the rest of her. Then he fitted his big palm against hers and slowly, sinuously, threaded their fingers together, forcing her sensitized skin tightly against his until her fingers began to curl over his hand of their own volition.

She raised her face to him, shocked by the way he'd claimed her hand . . . and made her feel that he'd claimed a great deal more. Her whole body suddenly flushed with embarrassing warmth and that strange emptiness in her middle deepened, becoming focused in her stomach like a hunger. The next moment, her cloak hood slid from her head and she realized he had removed it. His free hand came up slowly to touch her hair, brushing the fashionable tendrils at her temples, stroking the silky upsweep of her coif, then riffling the wayward locks that had worked free and now lay against her neck. His hand moved again and she felt a whole section of her hair uncurl onto her shoulder. Then another slid, and another. He was pulling the pins from her hair, one by one. And all the while he was pulling her gaze into his, capturing her senses in a slow, inescapable spell of sensation and discovery.

His hazel eyes glowed as they delved into hers and his warm breath grazed her upturned face. He turned on the seat, coming closer, and his hand slid fully into her hair, cupping her head. His other hand released hers and rose to touch her cheek. His fingers were warm and gentle as they feathered over her features, just as she somehow knew they would be. He traced her chin, her nose, her forehead, and then her eyes, forcing them to close. Then he rubbed her lips with slow circular motions, setting them afire, making her want to lick them to make the burning stop.

His hand slid from her hair, and the small pearl buttons at the back of her standing collar began to give way. His fingers invaded her collar, rubbing and stroking the nape of her neck. Streams of warmth spread from that contact in all directions, and she felt swirling, liquid sensations in her limbs and lower body. Her very bones seemed to be weakening under that devastating touch. Then somehow her cloak was open, and his hands were warm on her waist and rising up her ribs.

The darkness was like a blanket enfolding her senses, blocking out everything but the discovery of him. He bent to press his lips to the side of her neck, and she tilted her head to allow it. His hands on her shoulders and waist, moving and caressing, all but took her breath. Then suddenly his arms were gliding around her, pulling her hard against his chest, bending her body to his. His mouth was tantalizingly warm on her throat, her ear, her cheek.

As she turned her head, her parted lips brushed his mouth. A heartbeat later, his lips slid over hers and a low moan vibrated between them, part his, part hers. Kissing was both soft and hard, she learned instantly. It was part giving and part taking. A sharing, a stealing, and a savoring. And it was nothing like the chaste pecks she'd experienced in darkened gardens and secluded window seats.

His bold, arrogant mouth moved in tantalizing ways, his lips molding and teasing hers in slow, changing combinations that felt like satin sliding on silk. Each subtle movement of his head brought another heavenly sensation that both incited and pacified her curiosity, evoked and explored her response.

The silence deepened as the motion of the carriage stopped. The change rippled through her senses and she clutched the sides of his coat, trying to blot it out.

He groaned and pulled her closer, sliding his tongue over her lips and finally slipping it between them, seeking the moist satin of her mouth directly. That small invasion, so powerful and so unexpected, shocked her enough to make her pull her mouth away. And like a gathering wave of reality, her senses collected more of her surroundings and her position in his arms.

"Gigi," he murmured into her hair, "let me." He pulled her hard against him and sought her lips again. But she resisted as she came jolting back to full reality.

Her cloak and jacket were hanging on her shoulders, the neck of her blouse was undone, her hair was a shambles, and her lips felt thick and hot from—his kisses! He'd undone her hair and clothes, and he'd touched her, and—oh, Lord—she'd allowed it!

She shoved against him and shrank back on the seat, pulling her cloak together and staring at his swollen lips and heated face in complete horror. Her only thought was escape. She lunged for the door and succeeded in turning the handle before he caught her. He reeled her back partway as he scrambled to find both his wits and his tongue. Unfortunately he found the latter first.

"Gigi, I want you—"

She quivered with humiliation as his words struck. She had let him . . . and now he wanted . . . His eyes were dark and frightening, and his features seemed coarsened with desire. He was again that fierce, passionate stranger who had so unsettled her last night. In that moment, all she could think about was getting away from him. She twisted away and launched herself through the carriage door, stumbling onto the paving stones and away from the carriage.

Only then did she look around. By the garish glow of new electric street lamps, she could see familiar houses—large, well-lit ones that neighbored Lofton House. She was home! She pulled her cloak tightly about her and darted toward her house with his voice at her back.

"Regina—Dammit! Miss Lofton—"

She was gone. Max snarled an order to his driver, then slammed the door as the vehicle began to move. His chest was heaving, his face was burning, and his hands were aching fists. He'd kissed her and put his hands all over her and told her he wanted her as if he expected her to render up her virtue on the very spot! He looked down at his roused and aching lower half and found her glove lying on his lap, across his... Flaming, he snatched the glove away, closed his eyes, and groaned furiously.

"What a horse's arse you are, Max!"

The next evening, Sir Charles Lofton was met by his wife as he returned from his shipping company offices. She pulled him into the salon and closed the door to ensure privacy. Her blue eyes sparkled and her cheeks were flushed from keeping such a monstrous scandal to herself all afternoon.

"Wait until you hear, Charles! It's just too terrible," she breathed, pressing her hand over her bosom. "The Viscount Lloyd's... *tendre*. She lives in the East End, in a tenement! Sir Lawrence said his carriage was seen outside all evening, taking up most of the street, bold as Dancing David. Think of it, Charles..."

She averted her eyes with an exquisite shiver of distaste and Sir Charles wagged his head gravely.

"Probably a girl from one of his mills. Poor thing."

Three days later, Regina stood in the middle of Nanny Dodd's flat with a twin on each hip and little William hanging on her skirt, clamoring to be held too. Her coif, like her patience, was unraveling, and her skirt and blouse were soot-smudged from her attempts at feeding the children and tending the stove over the last two days. The twins were cranky and their noses were runny, Jonathan and Jennie were constantly at odds, her parents were increasingly baffled by her devotion to her dressmaker, and she was running out of friends to supposedly visit for hours on end. She was exhausted, both physically and emotionally, and everywhere she looked she saw the number *eight*... reminding her there were only eight days until Christmas. Eight short days and five homes still wanting. She grew positively ill at the very idea of Christmas.

"Gigi." Jonathan's voice broke through her misery. "When will he come again?"

There was no need to ask who was meant. Regina's eyes filled unexplainably with tears that she just managed to blink away. She looked down to find Jonathan standing beside her with a frown on his face.

"I don't know, Jonny. He may not come again." The bereft feeling that swept over her was followed closely by a wave of anger. There hadn't been a word from him in three long days. He'd waltzed in, bought them a few clothes, raised their hopes, then left them flat. The high-handed wretch. He was probably punishing her for her audacity in blackmailing him... or perhaps for her dismissal of his earlier offer of marriage... or perhaps for her rejection of his advances in the carriage.

She found her fingers touching her suddenly sensitive lips and then sagged. He had a whole list of reasons to despise her and not a single good reason to help her. Robber barons were cold, arrogant, amoral, and greedy. They never did anything without expecting a profit. And she'd made it insultingly clear there wasn't any profit to be had from her in finding homes for her children. The only thing he could reasonably hope to gain from the situation now was a bit of revenge against her.

Unbidden, the image of his hands as they measured the children rose in her mind. She shook it off angrily and carried the twins to Nanny Dodd's bed for a rest. As she turned away, she had a sudden, shocking vision of his face above hers in a darkened carriage and felt a disturbing flush of heat all through her. He was indisputably arrogant, amoral, and greedy, but their shocking encounter of three nights ago suggested that beneath that stony exterior he wasn't entirely *cold*.

She sank into a chair by the table, feeling lonely, powerless, and abandoned. She had to face it: no one was going to help Noni's lambies but her. She struggled to focus her thoughts past the despair that filled her. If she contacted the Children's Home Society and explained the problem, perhaps they would take care of the children until she could find them homes. Then she thought of the orphanage's great barnlike rooms with their cold steel cots and recalled the tattered clothes and pale, listless faces of the children who slept there. What of her promise to Noni . . . and her own love for Noni's little ones?

She was hardly aware that she was crying until she felt Jonathan's hand on her shoulder, patting softly. His words of comfort seemed to come from Noni herself. "Be sure to use your handkerchief and not your sleeve, Gigi."

Max charged up four flights of stairs, only to stop dead at the door to Nanny Dodd's room. He stood recovering his breath, clenching and unclenching his fists, as he searched the unpainted door for clues to what he would find inside. It had been three days since Regina Lofton had bolted from his carriage . . . and his hungry clutches. He'd been so furious with both her and himself that night that he'd vowed not to set eyes on her again until he'd found at least one adoptive family.

But that vow had proven far easier to make than keep. He'd spent two days frantically sorting through his acquaintances, near and far, in search of childless couples and small families who wanted more children. He told himself that his mad pursuit of those elusive homes had nothing to do with her; his pride in his word was at stake. His unnerving reaction to the children themselves, especially the boy Jonathan, probably had something to do with it as well. The little hooligans had an appalling way of getting to one, he decided. If it weren't for them, he'd turn around and walk away—let her spread her wretched gossip from Genesis to Doomsday, if she dared!

Then with a hurried trip down to Ashford in Kent yesterday, he'd finally been successful. He had a sure home for little Edward and word had come this morning of possibilities for at least two of the others. He could return to Channel Street, and *her*, in triumph. Then why was he still standing before her door, filled with an unholy mixture of eagerness and dread?

The knock startled Regina. She slid William from her lap and had just made it to her feet before the door swung wide and the cause of her fears and anger appeared in the opening. Jennie, Jonathan, and William ran to him immediately, jumping up and down and exclaiming that he'd come back. Baby Edward and the twins were awakened by the noise and began to fret. In the midst of the confusion, Regina felt a towering wave of relief course through her at the sight of him.

There he stood in his caped greatcoat and gentlemanly top hat, looking cool and collected and capable. For a moment she forgot feeling abandoned and trifled with. He'd come back! All she could think was that she wasn't alone in her problem anymore. The strength of his presence lifted her spirits and set her heart hammering. Her heart . . . hammering with excitement? The idea was like an electrical jolt to her fatigue-dulled pride.

"Where on earth have you been?" She stalked toward him, realizing with satisfaction that she'd startled him. He ripped his hat from his head and his frown slid into a full glower.

"Where do you think, Miss Lofton?" He bent to usher Jonathan and William further inside and closed the door behind him. "I've been out finding homes for these urchins"—he motioned to them with his hat—"as agreed."

"Without a single word to me—us—for days on end!" she declared hotly. He lifted his cool hazel eyes to her and swept a tight, critical look over her disheveled appearance and around the dingy flat. She became acutely aware of her rumpled skirts and reddened eyes and of the tawdriness of her surroundings. How dare he come back with a sneer and a scoff! A dry pricking at the back of her eyes warned of coming tears and she stiffened, horrified.

"I wasn't aware it was necessary to apprise you of my every movement, Miss Lofton. In point of fact, I wasn't sure you'd wish to hear from me at all, ever again." He watched her recoil from his oblique reminder of their last parting and was suddenly furious with her. "But, as I've pointed out before, I am known for keeping my word. I searched for homes, Miss Lofton, and I found one . . . for the baby."

The shock of the announcement and Edward's piercing wail struck her in the same instant, just saving her from dissolving into tears before him. She hurried to the cradle and lifted Edward out, cuddling him protectively as she turned to face the viscount, her eyes wide and dark with confusion.

"Y-you did? B-but where, w-who . . . ?" Caught off balance and unnerved by her own unreliable emotions, she retreated into the comparative safety of ire. "You can't give a baby like Edward to just anyone; he has special needs. Who are these people?" she demanded, growing more suspicious by the syllable. "What are their names and where do they live?"

"It's couple in a small village near Ashford, in Kent." He planted his fists at his waist, steaming visibly at her challenge to his honor.

"What sort of income do they have? How do you know they're decent, upstanding people?"

"I've known them for years, that's how. He's a physician—who better to care for a child with special needs? They've been married for six years without producing any children of their own." He stomped closer, towering over her, his face dusky with bottled ire. "They've even got a damned paddock for a damned goat or two. Satisfied?"

It set her back on her heels. As she felt his intense gaze searching her face she remembered the smudges she had seen under her eyes in her mirror that morning. Her hair was certainly in ruins and her clothes probably looked like she'd slept in them. He was perfectly groomed and composed and handsome, while she looked and felt like a charwoman—a rather inefficient one at that. He'd managed the impossible task of finding a home for Edward, while she'd scarcely managed to keep Edward full of goat's milk for three days.

"I've made arrangements to take the baby to them tomorrow," he said thickly, stepping back. "You'll have to make him ready by six in the morning. I want to get to Kent and back by—"

"Tomorrow?" She stared at him with dawning horror, then at Edward, who was pulling at a strand of her hair and spitting contented bubbles. She swallowed hard and rubbed his downy cheek, only now coming to grips with the inevitability of giving him up to another's care. Something heavy settled in her chest, making it hard to breathe.

"I'm coming with you."

"You're what?" He cocked his head as if he doubted his hearing.

"I'm coming, too. I want to see these people with my own two eyes."

"What are you afraid of, Miss Lofton?" Anger erupted in him at this new affront. "That I'll dump him off at the nearest foundling home and be done with it? Dammit, that is the limit! The absolute limit!" He paced furiously back and forth, growing more outraged with each step.

"I've just spent three bloody long days ignoring my own business affairs to scour the countryside. And now that I've actually found a decent home for one of your blessed ragamuffins, you won't even trust me to take the child there! What kind of man do you take me for?"

Confusion boiled up in her. She wasn't sure what she thought of him. She only knew he seemed to be keeping his promise to her, one made against his will. And that simple fact threw all the rest of her ideas about him into a tangle. Whatever else she thought of him, she couldn't believe that the viscount would place a baby into an unhealthy situation. She looked down at Edward's vulnerable little face. Neither could she just hand him over to a household of strangers she hadn't even seen. She raised her head.

"I go . . . or Edward doesn't."

Max reached deep into his own stinging pride and played his lowest card. "Who will look after the others if you go?"

Her heightened color drained abruptly. She looked around them at the troubled little faces watching their angry exchange. He had her. There wasn't anybody else to care for them. Despair tightened her throat and her shoulders rounded. She lifted her face to him, eyes brimming with tears of frustration, chin trembling.

God. Tears. Max felt as if someone was tearing him apart, sinew by aching sinew. "Dammit!"

He wheeled and again strode up and down the room, exasperated beyond bearing. She didn't care for him, didn't trust him, didn't even believe him! Yet all she had to do was turn her big blue eyes on him and he melted into a spineless mass of pure longing. He stopped to stare at her and the way she was holding Edward close. That protective embrace, the tears. Then it suddenly dawned on him that there could be more to her resistance than distrust and defiance. Was she finding it hard to let the baby go? Women did that . . . got attached to babies.

Suddenly he had the most powerful and absurd desire to collect her into his arms, to hold her and Edward both—to hold them all.

"All right!" he shouted, recoiling from that overwhelming surge of male protectiveness. "You can go. I'll find someone to watch the children. But you'd better be ready at six o'clock tomorrow morning, or we leave without you!"

Regina watched the wall tremble as the door slammed behind him. She lay Edward on the bed, put her face in her hands, and sobbed.

That evening she arrived home at dusk to learn that her mother had been asking for her most of the afternoon. She was able to make it to her room without being seen and had Elsie carry a message that she'd had a terrible headache since she'd returned from the dressmaker's and would be down for dinner.

All through their evening meal, her father and mother cast inquisitive looks at her drawn face and suspiciously reddened eyes. Sniffles, she assured them.

"Well, I certainly hope it's nothing that will keep you from helping with preparations for our Christmas Eve gala, Gigi," Alice said sympathetically. "And I simply cannot wait to see what your new gown will be like ... the one you've had Madame de Bouvier slaving over for the last week."

Desperate to explain her supposed preoccupation with fashion and the time she'd been spending away from home, Regina invented not just a dress, but a whole new wardrobe, based on a fictitious new style that the little modiste had predicted would soon be all the rage.

Alice and Charles exchanged glances of concern above their daughter's head and steered the conversation to plans for the upcoming gala. They had apparently invited every eligible son of a noble house for counties around, and Regina knew what that meant. She found the prospect of being scrutinized and assessed as a potential acquisition in a dynastic merger utterly depressing.

Christmas. She wished it would never come.

5

THE next morning, Regina arrived at Nanny Dodd's in
time to make Edward ready to travel, though she had
to sneak out of her bed and her house to do it. The
viscount arrived soon after her with a stout, kindly-
faced woman dressed in nanny gray and a starched
white cap. He introduced her as Mrs. Peabody to the
children, who were just rising from their cots. By the
time he and Regina reached the door, they were being
swarmed by a wailing William and teary-eyed twins.
It took a few minutes to assure them that Gigi and his
lordship would be coming back, even if Edward
wouldn't. Regina watched them say good-bye to the
baby with pats and awkward kisses and felt a tightness
in her throat.

Once they were installed in the carriage and under
way, Max studied Regina from the corner of his eye.
She was wearing a blue, fur-trimmed coat that was
fitted closely over a gown of satin-finished ladine and
a small, saucy hat with a cockade of blue feathers and
a silk net veil. It was most ladylike and feminine attire,
and his eyes fastened warmly on the curves her fitted
coat accentuated. He scowled and released a disgusted
breath as he turned to stare out the carriage window.

Regina shifted the sleeping Edward in her arms and
cast a secretive glance at the viscount. He was the picture of intimidating gray elegance and his expression
was one of tightly reined displeasure. But as she
watched him, her eyes caught on his thick eyebrows
and dark side-whiskers, which hugged the hard, aris-

tocratic angles of his face, as if trying to soften them. He was a very handsome man. And he was utterly furious with her. Pulling her eyes from him, she looked around the carriage, examining it in the daylight and recalling too well how it had looked in darkness. It struck her that on the way back from Kent they would be alone in the darkness again. And she suffered a massive shiver.

It seemed as if half of the populace of Wolesby lined the village's sunlit streets, peering into the viscount's carriage as it passed and whispering amongst themselves. Regina looked past their eager stares and tried not to gawk as she satisfied her own curiosity about the place little Edward would call his home. It was primarily a farming village, with neat stone cottages set on winding lanes and a small stream, spanned by a stone bridge, running through the central greensward.

Daniel and Lydia Craig were waiting for them on the doorstep of a comfortable stone house located on the edge of the village. As Regina alighted from the carriage, she was surprised by the way the villagers pulled their caps, nodded, and tugged self-consciously at their skirts. It took her a minute to realize their respects were aimed at the viscount and that he returned their greetings with terse familiarity. Then her attention was claimed completely by the Craigs, who hurried to meet them and welcomed them into the small well-furnished parlor of their house.

Dr. Daniel Craig was a young man of middling height and sober but kindly features, and Lydia was a petite, gently formed woman with brown hair, expressive eyes, and a slightly wistful smile. Regina greeted them as they were introduced to her, but they scarcely minded it. They had eyes only for the bundle in her arms. Regina watched Lydia's gaze searching the baby and saw her tension melt as she peered past the blankets to Edward's healthy pink cheeks and alert brown eyes. Lydia stepped ever closer, controlling her urge to reach for him by clasping her trembling hands until they paled.

The muffled ticking of the mantel clock and the slow wheeze of the fire in the hearth marked the passage of time. Lydia's eyes glistened as she drank in Edward's presence. She turned to cast a look of longing at her husband, who stood a few steps away, struggling to control his emotions.

"He's beautiful. May I . . . hold him?" Lydia's voice wavered as she met Regina's gaze. In her shimmering eyes were blended all the marvelous and contradictory emotions of motherhood: hope and awe; fear and love. Regina forced a smile and handed the baby into Lydia's shaking hands.

Lydia carried Edward to the settee by the fire, and Daniel hurried to move the crocheted pillows out of the way for her. Carefully, as though the baby was already precious to her, she unwrapped the blankets and removed his cap and sweater. Her hands flowed over his shoulders and fuzzy head and chubby knees, caressing and learning him, even as he studied her. She held up his pudgy little hands one at a time, turning them over, inspecting them with the wonder common to all new mothers.

"Look, Daniel . . ." She raised a teary smile of pure joy to her husband as he leaned over her shoulder. "He has ten little fingers," she announced, as though he were the first baby ever to come so equipped. She kissed Edward's baby palms, then pulled him to her chest and gave him a soft, motherly hug. Both of them were soon engulfed in Daniel's laughter and embrace.

Regina chewed her lip and looked up to find the viscount staring at the new family with an almost stricken expression on his face. When he glanced up and found her watching him, it was he who blushed. A moment later, his consternation deepened as Daniel Craig rushed toward him with an outstretched hand and a smile that brimmed with gratitude. By the time

Lydia finished thanking him as well, he was crimson-faced and squirming visibly under the attention.

Daniel recalled his manners enough to take his guests' coats, and they were soon seated before the fire, while Regina shared what she knew of Edward's history and Nanny Dodd's claiming of him. Daniel had a hundred questions for them, but Lydia seemed content just to hold Edward, who seemed happy to be held. The viscount informed them that he would have his lawyers see to the legal work of the adoption. At length Lydia remembered her duty as hostess and relinquished Edward to her husband's eager hands while she went to prepare a cold luncheon and tea.

Regina joined her in the kitchen and offered to help, insisting that it would do her good to move about after such a long ride. She soon found herself buttering bread and satisfying her own curiosity about the Craigs' connection to the viscount.

"Daniel grew up here, in Wolesby. He's known his lordship all his life," Lydia said, pouring boiling water over tea in a china teapot. "The village needed a physician badly and since the village rests on his lordship's lands, he took it on himself to provide one. Daniel had always been good at his studies and his lordship offered to sponsor Daniel financially if he would take medical training and establish a practice here."

"You mean his lordship paid for Dr. Craig's medical schooling?" Regina paused, mid-stroke, with her knife and looked at Lydia, who nodded with a smile.

"He's always bent over backward to help the village. Whatever's needed, his lordship is there to provide. He even paid out of his own pockets to have a new well dug when the old one proved unfit." Lydia paused in the midst of arranging cups and saucers on a butler's tray. "And he knew that Daniel and I didn't have children . . ."

Her smile brightened and she turned a glowing look on Regina. "Now he's provided for us again, with your help. Thank you, Miss Lofton. Having a little one means so much to Daniel and me. And little Edward, he's so . . ." Her eyes filled with tears.

Regina reached out to pat Lydia's hand while holding back tears of her own. "I'm pleased he'll be with you."

Tea was served amidst small talk and shared news of the village and the viscount's nearby estates. Afterward, they had a peek at the garden and paddock, and watched as Lydia fed Edward his first meal as Edward Craig. Daniel brought their coats and saw them to the viscount's carriage. Regina's last glimpse of Edward was as he lay nestled in Lydia's arms, being lulled by her dulcet tones.

The sight of mother and son lingered in Regina's mind and weighed on her heart as the carriage lurched into motion. She felt emotion welling and turned to look out the window. They were good people, the Craigs. The viscount had been right about them; they were the perfect family for little Edward. The joy in Lydia Craig's face had been almost painful to behold. If only Noni could have seen it . . . Tears splashed down Regina's cheeks; she couldn't seem to stop them.

Her handkerchief was more lace than linen; not much use for tears that came in unladylike quantities. Over her right shoulder came a folded square of white linen and she took it gratefully, dabbing at her eyes and wiping her nose as she struggled for control. It was some minutes before she could take a deep preparatory breath and make herself face him.

"I owe you an apology," she began.

"I believe you do," he said quietly, settling a tight look on her.

He wasn't going to make it easy for her. But then, she hadn't shown him much credence or consideration, either.

"I'm sorry for mistrusting your judgment. The Craigs are wonderful people." She looked down at the handkerchief she'd just dampened; his linen, her tears. It suddenly felt as if there was a hole in her heart and its contents were sliding toward her knees. The viscount had provided for the village, for the children, for the Craigs, for little Edward, and now for her. He was probably the most self-contradictory man she'd ever known, the most generous robber baron in all of England. She couldn't bring herself to look at him directly, and so glanced up to collect his reaction from beneath lowered lashes.

Across the carriage, Max nodded gruffly at her, wishing he could muster something stronger. Why couldn't he stay angry with her? It would make everything so much easier. He pulled his gaze away and her image came with it as he turned to look out the window. Long, wet lashes shading sapphire-blue eyes, lips like swollen cherries, dark hair that somehow managed to steal a bit of fire from the cold winter sun. Lord, it was happening again. He was collapsing internally into a humiliating mass of heaving, inarticulate desires. And the only way he could combat it was to retreat into an absurd and uncompromising bastion of nobility.

If he could only unbend in her presence and talk to her like a normal man instead of either lapsing into verbal impotence or issuing pompous declarations and ultimatums . . .

"Are there other families?" she asked, wishing he would say something, anything. The wary look he turned on her raked her conscience.

"There are two other possibilities," he said in a businesslike tone. "But it will be a few days before I know."

"There isn't much time. Seven days left . . ." She watched the muscle in his jaw flex slowly.

"I am well aware of that."

"I don't mean to . . . It's just that I'm afraid I may not be able to care for the children regularly." She braced, waiting for his reaction. "I have family obligations, and I'm running out of excuses to be gone for hours on end."

"Your family?" He looked as though the mention of them made him slightly ill. "You mean . . . they don't know about the children . . ."

She shook her head. "They didn't like it that I visited Nanny Dodd in the East End. They'd be furious to learn of my promise to her. They'd insist the children be packed off to orphanages straightaway. So I can't let them find out."

He groaned. The full implications arrayed themselves in his mind. If they'd be upset to learn she was *visiting* the East End, imagine their fury upon learning their precious daughter wandered alone through London's roughest boroughs in the dead of night, spent her days in a dingy flat with six orphans and no protection, then went jaunting about the countryside in a randy nobleman's carriage! He closed his eyes. It didn't bear thinking about.

"I'm sorry," she said, feeling guilty for having brought it up when he'd done so much to help already. It was *her* problem, after all, not his. "Do you think Mrs. Peabody would come daily?" She turned her shoulders to face him and he felt as if he'd taken a full naval broadside.

"I think it could be arranged," he declared thickly. Every muscle in his body had tensed in anticipation but he was still unprepared for the way she lifted her gaze directly into his.

"Why are you helping me?" she asked softly.

Panic bloomed briefly in him as he felt a warmth from her that he both craved and feared. "I pay my debts and keep my promises, Miss Lofton."

"Yes, you do," she responded, a wealth of meaning in her tone. "And apparently you pay others' debts as well."

It was a softly spoken charge, aimed at the very middle of him, and it struck, dead on center. His heart began to thud in his chest and his mouth went dry. Her jewel-blue eyes were tugging at him, stirring suppressed desires and mislaid hopes.

"*Noblesse oblige*," he said tautly. "A nobleman has his obligations."

"But they rarely include rash young ladies with re-

former sympathies and a half dozen little 'ragpickers,' "
she said.

Then she smiled. It started small and broadened and
curled delectably, growing slowly into a full, luscious
crescent. It was the first time she'd ever really smiled
at him and his face flamed, even as his expression
froze. Juvenile, red-eared, tongue-tied chagrin seized
him, and he shoved it from him in a full, roiling panic.
He clenched his jaw and propped his long legs up on
the opposing seat. Pushing his shoulders into the padded seat-back, he tipped his elegant hat down to cover
the humiliating hunger in his eyes.

"It's going to be a very long trip, Miss Lofton," he
said, crossing his arms over his chest. "I suggest you
take what rest you can."

His abrupt, emphatic withdrawal stunned her. She
had tried, really tried, to express her gratitude for all
he'd done. She had wanted to speak to him as a person
instead of an opponent, to recognize the generosity of
his efforts. But just as she thought they might be able
to meet and talk as equals, he withdrew into his imperial self, closing her out completely!

When her first flare of anger passed, she glanced at
his insolently sprawled form and chided herself for her
romantic fancies about him. He was arrogant and high-
handed and impervious to the mere mortal experience
of "feeling." If he acted nobly or generously at times,
it was only to serve his own high-flown notions of duty
and to bolster his own sense of superiority! Typical of
a robber baron . . . every bit of it. She jerked a folded
lap robe from the opposite seat, settled it over her
knees, and closed her eyes to blot out the sight of him.

The carriage was dark and a good bit colder when
her eyes opened again. Night had fallen and apparently
she had too; she was sitting at an odd angle, leaning
against something. She felt her arm moving and looked
down to find her gloved hand captive in the viscount's
bare ones. She blinked, trying to make sense of it, then

followed his arm upward to where it ended in a shoulder . . . beneath her cheek.

She raised her head quickly and found herself nearly nose to nose with him. She could see his features in the dim light cast by the carriage lanterns outside and could feel the scented warmth he radiated filling her head and lungs.

"Are you cold?" His voice resonated in her ears at such close range, and the vibrations trickled down the side of her neck to glide seductively through the skin of her breast.

She just managed to shake her head, feeling rattled by his nearness. What was he doing, so close to her?

"You *are* cold," he declared. He nudged her shoulders forward to slide his arm around her and pull her against his side. She stiffened and looked up at him in confusion. But there was no confusion in the glimmer in his eyes, or in the direction his head was bending. Her lips parted, but his lips touched hers before she could speak. It was a warm, lingering caress that deepened slowly and moved in softly undulating patterns over her mouth. When he pulled away, her heart was beating erratically, her lips felt thick and moist, and her face was suffused with warmth.

She couldn't tear her eyes from his when she felt the leather sliding from her hand. He was removing her glove, finger by finger, and she saw in his eyes that he intended to remove even more . . . like her notions of propriety and her girlish reluctance. And as much as she knew she shouldn't, she wanted to surrender them to him.

Max straightened, pulling her eyes into his, offering her heat from the flame she had started inside him. He had watched her fall asleep, had watched the slow, seductive rhythm of her breathing, and had quietly given her his shoulder for support when her head began to droop. Somewhere in the midst of those one-sided intimacies, he gave up all pretense that he'd spent such time and effort on finding the children homes to prove his word and salve his pride. He'd done it—he made himself face it squarely—to be near her.

He had wanted to savor her warm curves and unconsciously sensual movements at close range. He had wanted to feel his blood surge in his veins and his loins quicken when she raised her stubborn chin so that her lips were within inches of his. Then as the forgiving darkness enveloped them, past and future had melted away; barriers of anxiety and doubt had crumbled. Desire had become possibility. In the darkness she was that warm, fragrant presence, that soft, responsive being he had experienced before in that same darkened carriage.

When she shivered, he drew back, unfastening the buttons of his greatcoat. With a twist of his body he opened the heavy overcoat and pulled her into it, wrapping it around her so that she lay pressed against his chest with her forehead grazing his cheek.

"Is that better?" he murmured. She shivered again and he laughed, a low, charming rumble. It wasn't cold she was reacting to now, it was heat. Once more he pulled away, this time to unbutton his inner coat. He seized her bare hand and slid it beneath his waistcoat, trapping her palm against the lean musculature of his ribs.

"Your lordship—"

"Max," he said, placing his hand over hers to hold it against him, while he nuzzled the silky skin of her temple. "My given name is Max, and no one ever uses it. Say it, Gigi."

"Max." She tried it softly, raising her face to him. He covered her mouth with his, coaxing, searching hungrily for her response. Beneath his waistcoat, her fingers splayed and began to move, exploring the tantalizing difference between his shape and hers. He was hard where she was soft, straight where she was curved. Suddenly her curiosity was freed to wander over the rest of him as her hands could not.

She opened to him, accepting, then welcoming the seductive dance of his tongue over hers and the sensual claiming of her it implied. Somehow the buttons of her coat were open and his hands grasped her silk-wrapped waist and slid up her sides, luxuriating in the tightly bound contours of her body and, at the edge of her confinement, the soft flesh mounded above that stern boning. His fingers closed sinuously over her breasts, then discovered buttons and began to work their way inside to touch warm, naked skin.

Something, a sigh of delight, a subtle shift of her body, betrayed her longing and his fingers sank beneath the rim of her corset to find the tingling tips of her breasts. She moaned helplessly as his fingers rubbed that sensitive flesh and her body arched instinctively against his hands, seeking more. And when his mouth left hers to trail down her throat, she somehow knew its destination and wanted to feel his mouth on her there, too.

His tongue traced the heated swell of her breasts as his fingers prised one budded, velvet nipple above her corset. He kissed and tongued, then finally suckled that tender flesh, sending wild shivers of pleasure through her taut, aching body.

She scarcely realized she was pushing against his shoulders until his face came up to hers. "You don't like it?" he whispered, turning his kisses to the borders of her face.

"I do . . . but I . . ."

His eyes opened into hers, glowing, reaching for her. Honest eyes, filled with desire. Honorable eyes, filled with need . . . for her. Her own eyes closed as she reached for his mouth with hers. Then his hand flowed, unhindered, over her breasts and waist and down over her skirts, pausing, caressing, drawing heat into her woman's flesh as his palm lay pressed against her skirts. She felt a thickening, a burning, in her woman's mound. And she began to understand that it was both the locus of her desires and the focus of his. It was a powerful realization that he desired something that lay hidden, deep within her, accessible only through her own giving of herself.

She moved against his hand as it molded over her. Undulating slowly, she sought that promised heat, that elusive, forbidden pleasure of touch. Flashes of hot, quivering vibration radiated upward through her as he pressed harder, reaching for her through layers of worsted and silk and muslin. Then she felt his body arch and flex beside her and he moaned, part in pleasure, part in pain. His hand stilled and then withdrew, and she opened her eyes to his.

"Do you know about men, Gigi?" His voice was deep and thick, full of need. She swallowed with difficulty and shook her head, unsure what he meant. His knowing smile had a twinge of wistfulness to it. And she realized that he was about to teach her.

"We're all made alike..." His gaze flickered over her love-warmed face as he searched for a way to explain. "Like Edward," he whispered into her eyes. "Our bodies are made like Edward's. Only as we grow up... we *grow up*." He slid her hand down his front to the bulge in his trousers. Her hand recoiled when she touched him, but she let him lead it back and press it gently over his hardened flesh, covering it with his own.

After that first shock, curiosity took over and she absorbed and studied the sensations of his columnar hardness with her fingers. Her gentle explorations through his trousers made him draw a hard breath and shudder. She blushed and whispered with girlish candor, "Then you must be quite... *grown up*."

His laugh held that same odd mixture of pleasure and pain as he pulled her into his arms and held her tight against his pounding heart. "I wish I could show you... love you with my body. Oh, God, Gigi—talk to me!"

They did talk, in passionate whispers between soft, opulent kisses that explored both sensual preference and response. And there were caresses, lighter than before, but somehow the more intimate and arousing for all that had passed between them.

Max sat straighter, suddenly, looking around them. The carriage had stopped . . . seemed to have been stopped for some time. He released her to look out the window. "This is my house," he said in some puzzlement. He opened the door to give his driver instructions and when he came back inside, Regina had begun to button her bodice with trembling hands. He watched her fumble for a moment, then gently shoved her hands aside and did up the fastenings for her. A tide of warmth for him flowed through her. When she finally stepped onto the wet pavement of the alley near her home, she was fully, properly covered, yet every inch of her body felt shockingly exposed and excited.

Max watched her go to the side door of her house. As he drove away, past a garish electric street lamp, he caught sight of a small white glove on the floor. He picked it up and fingered its silky leather. A wry smile acknowledged the immediate billow of heat in his loins. He pressed that glove tight against his throbbing flesh and undulated slowly against it. Someday, he thought.

When Regina climbed into the middle of her large tester bed that night, she was still in shock. Her whole body was humming with strange and wonderful excitations. He'd touched and kissed and fondled her, and she couldn't seem to muster a single drop of contrition about her wild and abandoned behavior. She wanted it, wanted Max Strand . . . in the dark . . . again . . . And at the same time she wondered if she'd ever be able to face him in the light again.

The next evening, when Sir Charles arrived home from his office, he found his wife and daughter finishing the hanging of fresh greens and scarlet ribbons throughout the lower floor of the house. He launched into a description of his day, but stopped short, watching Regina's unladylike yawn.

She blushed to find both parents staring at her and blamed her fatigue on a restless night. Alice prescribed a toddy of warm milk and brandy, and packed her off to an early bed. As soon as she was out of hearing, Alice turned to her husband.

"This isn't like her, Charles. She has me a bit concerned . . . this social whirl and not sleeping well at night. I'm going to insist that she stay home a day or two to rest." Her face suddenly lit with remembrance, and she pulled him by the arm to the sofa. "You simply must hear the latest, dear." She paused at his frown, then reminded him, "The viscount!"

"Oh!" Charles lay his newspaper aside and eagerly turned his attention on his wife.

"Sir Lawrence saw him in his carriage last night . . . parked outside the viscount's very own house." Her eyes glowed. "He was with that woman and, Charles, they were . . . well, you know. And right there, on the street!" She pinkened becomingly. "The last word is—and it's all over town—he's moving the hussy straight into his own house!"

6

It was another entire day before Regina was deemed fit to leave the house for a long visit with a friend. Only five days remained until Christmas. She was frantic to reach Nanny Dodd's flat and when she arrived, she found Mrs. Peabody there, packing William's things and preparing him for the trip to his new home. The starch went completely out of her. She pulled William onto her lap and watched desolately as his few clothes were folded and stacked and his favorite wooden blocks and picture books were placed on the pile.

Mrs. Peabody didn't know anything about the people his lordship had mentioned, but she recalled that the place was north of London, in Essex. Shortly, the door opened and Max entered, filling the room, filling Regina's senses. Anxiety washed over her as she looked up at him. How should she act? What must he think of her, after what had passed between them in his darkened carriage?

"You found a home for William. I'm sorry I couldn't come yesterday . . ."

"We got the note," he said evenly, searching the uncertainty in her face. Was it caused by William's leaving or by what had happened between them the other night? He watched the pained look and desperate hug she gave William and determined to steer a neutral course with her until he could decide.

"I have to come with you." Her voice contracted to a whisper as she lifted her face to him. "Please."

He braced as he felt the ignominious slide of his reserve. Neutrality just wasn't possible with her. He retreated miserably from his chaotic feelings into his customary efficiency and drew himself up, nodding. A moment later, he looked down to find Jonathan hanging on his sleeve, calling his name.

"Me, too, your lordship? I'll sit still as a church-mouse," Jonathan begged, slipping his hand into Max's. "I never been in a carriage before."

Max looked down into the raw hope in the boy's big eyes and couldn't deny him. Just now, hope was all he had, too. He nodded, and Jonathan whooped with joy and ran to get his coat.

The trip north seemed endless. William was constantly in motion, climbing over Regina, then Max, then harrying Jonathan, who was trying hard to keep his promise to sit still. Regina tried stories and pointed out sights from the carriage window, all of which Jonathan absorbed and William flagrantly ignored. She found herself praying that the home would be right, simply to escape having to ride all the way back to London with him!

Finally at wit's end, Max hauled the squirmy two-year-old onto his lap, ordered him to sit still, and promised to tell him about his new home and family if he complied. It wasn't quite a magic charm, but it worked almost as well. William sat with his little shoulders rounded and his hands clasped between his knees as Max began to tell of a farm, and a solid stone house with a big friendly stove that produced molasses cookies in quantity.

"Henry and Grace Bower are the mother and father. And there are three older boys . . . you'll have big brothers right away. And since it's an estate farm, there are big barns and lots of animals—"

"Piggies?" William wanted to know.

Max nodded. "And calves and rabbits and lots of kittens. And you'll have to learn to take care of them. You think you can do that?"

William was held in thrall . . . as was Regina.

They soon turned onto a country lane leading toward a cluster of cottages and barns, heading straight for a large house set slightly apart from the rest. Three boys of incremental ages poured out the door to greet the carriage, and just behind them came a genial, barrel-chested man dressed in Sunday clothes, and a plump, bright-eyed woman in her late twenties, also wearing her best.

The couple greeted Max heartily and cast anxious looks into the carriage behind him. Max turned to lift little William down. Everyone became extraordinarily quiet as he clung to Max's hand and eyed his new family. Grace came forward and knelt beside him.

"So you're William." As she studied him, the tension in her face drained. "What big, bright eyes you have," she said, beaming. "Just like our other boys. An' I trow I see a bit of a scamp in there somewhere." She smiled the kind of smile that little boys seem to know means

love. And when she opened her arms, he hesitated
only a second before lunging into them.

There was happy chaos as Regina and Jonathan were
introduced. Then Henry scooped William into his burly
arms and carried him into the house, teasing and
laughing in his booming voice. Grace ushered the rest
of them inside and somehow produced tea and milk
and the fabled molasses cookies while never taking her
eyes from her new son. After a while, she allowed the
older boys to take Jonathan and William outside to see
the animals and barns. As she stood in the doorway,
watching them cross the frozen yard, Henry turned to
Regina with a solemn look.

"Since we lost the baby, near two years back, she's
been grievin'. Quiet-like," he said, watching his wife,
"but grievin' all the same. That little Willie . . . he'll put
the sparkle back in her eye."

Regina nodded, unable to speak. She looked at Max,
stunned by the fact that he'd apparently known about
their loss and meant to help both William and them.
How could he act with such compassion and insight,
while seeming so aloof and imperial?

William was too busy with the wonders of his new
home to give them more than a perfunctory hug when
they left. It was Jonathan's eyes that filled with tears
as they mounted the carriage step and pulled out of
the yard. Regina saw him struggling manfully with his
tears as he watched the farm fade behind them. She
asked if he'd like to come and sit by her, but he shook
his head and wiped his eyes on his coat sleeve. She
bit her lip and looked up at Max, hurting visibly for
the boy.

Their eyes met. Max cleared his throat and asked
Jonathan if he would like to see something wonderful.
He pulled the boy to the window and pointed out a
huge, rambling stone manor house with long windows
that shone in the sun and acres of trimmed and tended
gardens. Jonathan nodded, but with far less than his
usual enthusiasm. Then Max revealed that the great

old house was where he had grown up, and it was still his favorite home. Jonathan's eyes widened.

"Would you like to hear about it?" Max asked.

"Yes . . . please."

Max pulled Jonathan onto his lap and began to tell stories about his home and parents and the pony he had been scared of until he was twelve years old. He spoke of a nanny and a schoolroom and reciting for a tutor . . . and of lumpy porridge and a plump, tart-tongued cook who sneaked big, sugary cookies to him from time to time.

Regina watched Jonathan's glowing eyes grow heavy as Max's voice and the motion of the carriage lulled him. When Max lowered his sleeping form to the seat between them, Regina took the boy's head onto her lap and stroked his unruly brown hair.

"Thank you for that . . . Max." She risked using the name he'd given her in the intimacy of another moment and held her breath as he turned to her. His expression softened as he searched her face, and her heart lurched and began to beat again. She looked down at Jonathan and hid her roused feelings in concern for the boy. "He's so bright and he tries so hard . . . Do you think you'll be able to find a real home for him?"

"It's not so easy to find a place for an older child." Max said quietly. "I still have possibilities, but none of them have . . . books."

Her head came up. She could see him struggling with his emotions and held her breath. His feelings slowly became visible in his eyes. He was hurting a little, clinging stubbornly to hope. She suddenly wanted to know everything about him, to explore and discover the man inside that formidable exterior.

"Will you tell me more about your home?" she asked, her shimmering eyes entreating him.

Her request obviously surprised him, but a moment later, he settled back in the seat and slowly began to tell her. After a while, he realized he'd been talking a great deal and that, as often happened, he'd lapsed into talking about his acquisitions and financial achievements. He caught himself and paused, looking at her. Did she think him an insufferable braggart?

"You see, my family's fortunes, while respectable, have never been particularly lavish . . . until the present generation," he said, reddening a bit. "I seem to have a way with managing financial investments." He drew a deep breath and self-consciously turned his gaze out the window. "Unfortunately, I don't seem to have the same talent for managing other things, including younger brothers."

"What happened with your brother . . . after the other night?" she asked.

"He's been banished to the country," he said a bit defensively, "to spend a quiet Christmas thinking about his life and deciding what to do with himself." When he glanced at her and found her watching him with warmth and interest, he went on. "Perhaps I should have given him more to do, or spent more time with him when he was younger. But I wanted him to have time to grow up and not have responsibility thrust on him at too early an age."

"As it was on you?" She hardly realized she'd spoken it until he turned to her with a shaken look.

"I was fifteen when I inherited, and there were debts. I never had carefree years at Oxford or a grand tour. So I saw to it that he had them. And now it seems he wants nothing else."

Fifteen and a viscount . . . a young boy with a double burden of family pride and inherited debt. She watched the pensive set of his aristocratic features and knew now that he'd had to harden that sensitive face in order to survive. He'd learned to submerge his inner needs and feelings beneath more easily fulfilled hungers for pride and wealth. As the thought struck her, she swayed on the seat.

The man inside that hard shell must be tender, indeed, to need so much protection.

In that moment she knew she was falling in love

with Maximilian Strand . . . the tough and tender Max, the hard-nosed and heroic Max, the grandiose and generous Max. The thought released a hot, painful spiral of pleasure through her. She wanted to reach inside, to touch those vulnerable feelings he couldn't seem to show. And she knew only one way to reach him.

"Max . . ." She gave his name a noticeable caress as she straightened and leaned slightly forward. "Would you . . ."

"Would I what?" He looked at her with a wariness that she knew hid other feelings, feelings that he had allowed to show only in the permissive dark.

"Would you kiss me? Now . . . in daylight."

It took a moment for him to react. Fully five different emotions crossed his face before pleasurable surprise claimed undisputed control. His hands trembled as they closed on her shoulders and he drew her toward him, over Jonathan's sleeping form.

His kiss was rich with nuances of caring and with hungers he couldn't deny. Her fingers came up to cradle his face, then slid down over his wide shoulders. When he would have drawn her closer, Jonathan shifted on the seat, reminding them of his presence between them. Max flushed and looked a bit humiliated by his eagerness. But before he could withdraw yet again, she caught the front of his coat and held him.

"Talk to me, Max. Please," she said, feeling his gaze searching her as he wrestled with something inside him.

"I'd rather kiss you," he said very quietly.

It would be easier for him than talking, she sensed. A persuasive smile curled her mouth. "Who says you can't do both?"

That same evening Sir Charles arrived home late from a meeting at his club to find his wife waiting for him in his study, pacing. "Charles!" She pulled him to a chair before the blazing fire. "You won't believe it . . . it's just too horrible!"

He took her icy hands in his and bade her calm herself and tell him everything. His shock grew with every syllable she uttered.

"The viscount . . . oh, Charles! Sir Lawrence saw him with that woman of his . . . and two older children. He doesn't just have a girl in a family way, Charles, he has a whole family!"

Sir Charles's jaw dropped. "The bounder!" he growled. "A mistress is one thing, but a whole blessed family! To think that all the while he was negotiating a marriage with our Gigi, he was producing bantlings on some poor mill girl!"

Max hurried to Nanny Dodd's the next morning to meet Regina as they had agreed. He had wonderful news: a probable home for the twins. He imagined her delight when he told her and conjured in his mind's eye the seductive softening of her shoulders and the through-the-lashes look that would belie the prim smile she would give him.

But she didn't come. The afternoon dragged by as he waited with Jonathan and the twins, occupying both them and himself. Afternoon slid into evening and still she didn't come. He told himself that she was probably having difficulty finding an excuse to use with her parents and found himself increasingly uncomfortable with the idea. Those long, empty hours reminded him pointedly that he and the children were a secret part of her life, one she couldn't afford to reveal. He was unnerved by the realization of how important the time they spent together was to him. He'd all but set aside his precious businesses to devote his time and energy to her problem . . . and her.

The next morning he made a frantic trip to New Tilbury to finish making arrangements for the twins, then raced back with the good news . . . to find only Mrs. Peabody and the napping children. Regina still hadn't arrived. Some time later a brief note from her was delivered. A party, it said. She was caught up in helping prepare for her parents' Christmas gala.

Max stood in the midst of Nanny Dodd's flat, staring at that note and feeling suddenly alone and vulnerable. She had parties and family and probably suitors . . . and he had no access to that part of her life. He had only the time she stole to be with the children. After the children were placed in homes, what then? Doubt began to contract around his heart like a steel band. When she had what she wanted of him, would she just walk out of his life, having roused and used his most tender feelings? Was he merely a means to an end?

Four days left, Regina thought as she paced the small parlor under her mother's gaze, feeling like a prisoner in her own home. *Three children and only four days.* But it was Max's face she kept seeing in her mind and longed to see in reality. If he somehow managed a miracle and found homes for the children, what then? Would he make an effort to see her again when Christmas was past? Would he dismiss the intimacy he'd allowed her and just walk out of her life, taking her heart with him? Would there be time to make him want more than just the warmth of her kisses?

When Barnes entered, bringing her an envelope on his silver tray, she tore into it with unladylike enthusiasm, hoping it was an invitation that would allow her to escape the house. Instead, she found a note penned in powerful, masculine script, bearing the news that Ruthie and Betty would be traveling to a new home at nine o'clock the next morning. It was signed simply "Max."

Her heart jumped at the signature and she turned to her mother with telltale color in her cheeks. "It's from Victoria Macomber. You know she's leaving for the continent just after the holidays . . . well, she wants me to help her with the final shopping and to have luncheon with her tomorrow. I simply must go!"

Max's carriage was parked in the street outside Nanny Dodd's flat when Regina arrived the next morning. She hurried upstairs, her thoughts a confusing jumble of anticipation and anxiety. When she opened the door, Mrs. Haskins was dressing the twins in their new smocks, shoes, and sweaters, while Max waited stiffly on the edge of the only other chair, wearing his caped greatcoat and turning his hat over and over in his hands. He looked up and his face darkened as his eyes caught in hers for a brief moment before he tore them away.

"You might have sent word you were coming," he said in a growl, pushing to his feet.

"I—I had difficulty finding anyone to bring a message," she said, taken aback by his combative mood. "I was barely able to get away. . . ."

For the last two days, she had imagined how it would be when she saw him again. His eyes would glow and her heart would pound. Her lips would redden in anticipation and he'd watch them with a soft, knowing smile. Instead, he was acting like a perfect stranger. Worse—like the cold, imperial robber baron she'd blackmailed into helping her. A trill of dread ran up her spine and she scrambled to respond.

"You should have known I wouldn't allow the children to go without my . . . coming along." Cold crept up her limbs and seeped inward, toward her heart. What could have happened to him in only two days? "Who are these people that Betty and Ruthie are going to live with? Where do they live?"

He straightened abruptly, his eyes narrowing. Was she questioning his judgment again? He'd thought they were past that. "They're Jennings and Helen Walker of New Tilbury. He has a solid income as the foreman in a mill. They have two older daughters and they want more but can't seem to have them. Anything else you need to know?"

She bristled at his caustic tone. "The other family, what about them?"

"There is no other family," he said sharply. "That's it. They go together or not at all."

Regina pulled her chin back, stunned. "You mean they're both going to the same family . . . they'll be together still?"

"Any objections to that, Miss Lofton?" The muscle in his jaw that served as a gauge of his irritation was pulsing.

Miss Lofton? She tried not to melt too quickly under his stare. "None, your lordship."

When she turned away, her eyes fell on Jonathan, who was putting on his coat as if he expected to go along. She looked around and realized Mrs. Peabody wasn't anywhere in evidence. When she asked about the nanny, Max thrust Ruthie into her arms with the terse comment that she'd found a permanent post and had had to leave them. Then he picked up little Betty and ducked out the door.

She paused for a moment, looking at that open door and feeling utterly bereft. Today, Ruthie and Betty would have a new family. There would be just one little body left to care for, one trusting little heart that needed a home. *No,* she realized, *two.* Jonathan's heart . . . and her own. She willed away her hurt, lifted her chin, and stepped into the dingy hall.

At fifteen months, Ruthie and Betty were each quite a handful. Together they were overwhelming, even for two laps and two pairs of hands. They were constantly in motion in the carriage, standing and climbing and yanking noses and hair. They drooled and stuck fingers and miscellaneous clothing in their mouths, exploring everything in sight. And it was twice as bad in the unbearable silence of the coach. Regina was unspeakably grateful when Jonathan chanted a rhyme about baking cakes and the twins began to pat stiff-fingered hands together, over and over, imitating his motions.

When she looked up at the expression of grim fortitude on Max's face, her heart sank. He was obviously regretting every minute he spent with them, and she couldn't blame him. Was he regretting every minute he'd spent with her as well? Was he regretting the kisses and confidences he'd shared with her? Would he be as eager to be rid of her and the burden of keeping his word to her as he was to be rid of the twins?

New Tilbury was a planned development of mills and small factories built alongside company housing for workers. The Walkers, like other mill employees, lived within sight of the knitting mill where Jennings Walker was foreman of operations. His status as manager entitled him to a stylish house with a small garden, nestled proudly amongst the homes of other mill officers.

The Walkers met them at the door with eager faces and anxious hands. Jennings was a short, rotund man who was balding, and Helen was a thin, meticulously dressed woman who wore spectacles and had a watch pinned to the shoulder of her starched blouse. As Max and Regina peeled the blankets from Ruthie and Betty, Helen's veneer of reserve melted like morning frost under their sunny smiles. She came to take first Betty, then Ruthie into her arms, settling each one on her slender hips and bearing that considerable burden into the parlor with perfect grace.

She sat down on a new-looking fringed parlor settee with them both on her lap, touching them and saying their names so that she was able to learn who answered to which name. Her husband came to squeeze onto the seat beside her, smiling and making rubbery, exaggerated faces that fascinated the toddlers. Helen finally glanced at Jennings and put her arms around the girls with tears in her eyes.

"I want them, Mr. Walker," she declared firmly. His

face beamed with pleasure at that determined pronouncement. From a far doorway came a scuffle and what sounded like a stiffled giggle.

"Perhaps we'd best let them come see their new sisters." Jennings inclined his head toward that door. When Helen nodded, he stood and motioned his older daughters into the room.

They squealed and came rushing and stumbling over each other, then slowed to a more dignified pace under their mother's disapproving eye. The Walker girls were of equal height and their red curls were the very same length and texture. Their noses had the same impertinent tilt and their blue eyes the same eager glint. Regina watched in utter amazement. Twins. The Walker girls were identical twins . . . just like Betty and Ruthie!

Jennings turned to her with a beaming countenance. "We had to have twins, don't you know. So Amelia and Amanda could each have their own baby sister to spoil." His grin broadened. "My missus has a bit of experience with girls that come in twos."

Max read the surprise in Regina's face as she looked at him and a painful chasm opened in his chest. She'd seen firsthand the homes he'd found for the other children. Did she really think he'd do less for the twins? As her disbelief scored itself into his heart, he feared he knew the answer. Her doubts about him had apparently faded only in his mind, not in hers.

Jennings Walker insisted they have a quick look at the mill itself before they traveled back to London, and Max was hard-put to refuse. They walked through the cold sunshine in silence across a paved square to a massive brick building with large, frosted glass windows.

Whatever Regina had expected, it certainly wasn't a large, well-lit facility with clean air and safety railings and numerous young women wearing hair nets and tidy smocks. Mr. Walker showed them around, pointing proudly to the separate rest and hygiene facilities

for the young women and a schoolroom for both training and basic education.

"We run a progressive establishment," Mr. Walker
boasted. "We're the best-equipped knitter in the business. An' with good markets and progressive ideas,
we turn a tidy profit, which we share with the workers
themselves. Incentive, that's what the owner—" Mr.
Walker stopped in mid-sentence, looking at Max, who
was scowling fiercely at him.

Regina saw Mr. Walker's puzzlement and Max's
scowl and felt her heart sink. Mr. Walker had obviously
forgotten Max was a mill owner too. For a while, she'd
forgotten as well. The walk back to the Walker home
was solemn indeed, as was Regina's farewell to Helen
and Ruthie and Betty.

Her eyes filled as the carriage pulled away from the
house and she dabbed quietly at her tears, trying not
to be too conspicuous. But Jonathan climbed off his
seat to come and put his arms around her. She hugged
him tightly and tried desperately to compose herself.
Her tears were for more than the loss of the twins.

They were well down the road before she could make
herself face Max. When she turned to him, he was
staring out the window with the same tense and irritable look he'd worn after Mr. Walker's unfortunate
comments at the mill. He was obviously regretting all
the time and effort he'd spent on her promise while
his precious businesses went begging.

"Max," she said, touching his sleeve to draw his
attention, "it was the perfect home for Betty and
Ruthie. I don't know how you managed to find
them . . ." He glanced at her with a hard look, and she
retreated into silence for a few minutes. The walls between them were rising higher and higher, and she
was desperate to reach out to him. If she could only
make him talk to her, about anything, even his businesses.

"I'd never seen a knitting mill," she began again.
"I'd heard such terrible stories about the conditions.

But with education and safety and incentives...
they're wonderful ideas and Mr. Walker said they
work." She screwed her courage to the limit and
touched his sleeve again to draw his gaze to her. "Perhaps you could use some of those ideas in your
mills..." She was unprepared for the twitch of his
shoulders, which made it seem she'd cut him unexpectedly. Pained anger crept into his face.

"That was one of my mills," he declared.

She felt as if he'd melted every bone in her body
with the controlled heat of that blast. "Y-you m-
mean..."

"Jennings Walker works for me. How do you think
I came to know about him and his family?" He looked
at her as though he were seeing all the way into her
mind... and into her ill-cloaked shock at learning he
was a humane and "progressive" employer. Then he
jerked his gaze away to stare out the carriage window
as though he was unable to stomach her lack of faith
in him for a minute longer.

His mills. It drummed in her mind. *His foreman. His
ideas.* He'd known about the Walkers wanting more
children because Jennings worked for him. The Bow-
ers' farm flashed through her mind, nestled beside
Max's family home—undoubtedly on his family estates. Max had placed each of Noni's children with
people who were a part of his life, people whose hopes
and problems meant something to him. And with each
placement, he'd revealed just how insightful and compassionate a man he truly was. And she had presumed
to suggest he "humanize" his mills!

From the very beginning she had let her notions of
his wealth and power control her perceptions of him.
Her smug, self-righteous prejudices had doomed her
to think the worst of him, even while he was doing
his best for her. He had never been cold or amoral or
greedy... he had never been a *robber baron* at all, except
in her naive and girlish mind. He was a man who'd
overcome his own personal trials to shape the world

around him into a better place. He was a man who'd allowed her privileged glimpses of the tenderness and passion that lay at the core of him. And how poorly she'd guarded that rare and precious trust!

"Max—" She turned to him, desperate to take back those words and those wretched, hurtful doubts about him. "I didn't know. Please . . . I'm so sorry . . ."

When he looked at her, the coldness in his eyes froze the rest of her apology in her throat. She lowered her gaze to the damp handkerchief in her hands. It was too late for words, the imperious look declared. And from his rigid and inaccessible manner and the deep chill in the air between them, she believed it was true. Mere words could never fix broken trust . . . or a broken love.

They rode the rest of the way in a miserable silence interrupted only by Jonathan's hesitant questions and their separate and self-conscious answers. This time, when the carriage stopped in the alley beside her house, Max gave his driver orders to go around to the front. He descended first, then helped her down, feeling a sense of finality between them. It might be the last time he saw her and he intended to escort her properly to her door. When Jonathan scrambled down behind them, Max stopped him and asked him to climb back in the coach and wait. When the five-year-old's shoulders rounded with disappointment, Regina stooped and opened her arms to him.

When she released him and Max lifted him back into the carriage, she could scarcely breathe. It had felt like a good-bye hug to her.

Halfway up the walk she stopped and turned to him. There was still the matter of the fate of one little heart between them. "I've been thinking about Jonathan. Mrs. Haskins would keep an eye on him, I'm sure. And I can pay her until I find someone who wants him . . ."

Max felt as if he'd just been gut-punched, but Regina was looking at his coat buttons and didn't see his blanched look. "I'll see to the boy," he declared gruffly.

"No, really, your lordship, you've done more than enough. It was my promise, after all." And he'd carried that burden in his capable hands and on his broad shoulders . . . "I'm sorry I involved you in it. I was just so desperate . . ." She got up the courage to look at his face. His jaw was stony and his eyes unreadable.

"I'll see he's taken care of, Miss Lofton."

Each word had a "Viscount Lloyd" ring of finality to it and seemed to be pulled from deep within him. She nodded. She trembled with the need to touch him, perhaps for the last time. "Will you send me word?"

This time he nodded. They stood awkwardly, each feeling the inches between them as though they were miles. Then he stepped back, tugged at the brim of his hat, and strode briskly back to the carriage. She watched him drive off and though a haze of tears caught a glimpse of Jonathan at the carriage window, smiling at her, waving. Her heart felt as if it was shattering into a thousand pieces.

Sir Lawrence Trexel stood down the block, getting an eyeful of the stylishly dressed young woman as she turned and entered the front doors of Lofton House. He'd seen the Viscount Lloyd's carriage draw up and had watched as the viscount handed down the young woman. He'd seen the boy and the hug and the intimate conversation afterward. He'd seen them together before, but they'd been too far away and he had never expected to actually *recognize* the viscount's "ladybird."

It took a long moment to sink in, then his face nearly split with a grin. He was suddenly delirious with glee. What a morsel! The viscount's mistress and the mother of his children wasn't some pathetic little mill creature . . . it was none other than Regina Lofton!

7

By the next afternoon, the day before Christmas Eve, Lofton House was polished and glittering, and Regina was burning with frustration at the way her mother had monopolized and frittered away her time. She had managed to pull an under-footman away from silver polishing to send a message to the flat. There was no reply. In desperation, she persuaded Barnes to have a message carried to Max's house. Still no reply.

She lay in bed that night, staring through the dimness at the new gown she'd ordered, sight unseen, to wear to her parents' gala the following night. It was a lovely dress: lush sea-green satin with tiers of white Belgian lace, trimmed with dark silk holly leaves down the elegant bustle and train. And it was a lie. Just like the rest of her life of late. She was forced to pretend that the things and people that mattered most to her didn't exist, while things she found trifling and absurd assumed preeminence in her life.

Her relief when a message finally came the next morning was short-lived. Terse to the point of cutting, it read simply: *The boy is well.* It was signed "V.L." for the Viscount Lloyd. No more "Max." The note fell from her numb fingers into the grate in the small parlor and she felt as if her heart was being singed by the flames that consumed the paper.

Christmas Eve arrived, accompanied by big, soft flakes of snow that accumulated quickly on the cold paving stones and roof tiles and dusted the shoulders of forms huddled around vendors' carts in the markets. Max and Jonathan sat on the edge of a low stone wall in a bustling market square, peeling and eating roasted chestnuts Max had purchased from a street vendor. Their faces were red, their noses cold, and they were laughing at the way they had both burned their fingers in their eagerness.

Max watched Jonathan's eyes sparkle, and his face softened with a full smile. Over the last few days he'd spent considerable time with the boy, talking, reading, playing checkers—something Max hadn't done since he was fifteen. Yesterday he had taken Jonathan out with him for the day in his carriage. They'd seen Big Ben and the queen's palace, attended an exotic animal exhibition, then gone to a restaurant for a huge dinner, which ended in an overindulgence in sweets. Today he'd taken Jonathan to his offices in the City, London's legendary financial district, then explored the sights and sounds of bustling open-air markets and numerous shops. Every time he looked into Jonathan's eyes, which were uncannily close to his own in color, he saw the child in himself that he'd somehow lost. And he prayed it wasn't too late to find it again.

When Max caught Jonathan secreting a few leftover chestnuts into his pocket to carry home to Jennie, he declared they would buy some for Jennie, and some for the rest of the Haskins children as well. As they stood waiting for the vendor to wrap up the chestnuts, Jonathan looked up at Max, beaming.

"I wish Gigi were here."

A sudden, volcanic rush of anguish erupted in Max's chest. Panic seized him as his eyes began to burn and his throat closed. All it took was the mention of that name . . . It was a long, harrowing moment before he could force a pained smile. It didn't do any good to pretend.

"I do, too."

* * *

Guests began to arrive at Lofton House at nine o'clock that night. Regina came downstairs at nine-thirty, wrapped in elegant green satin and a ladylike air of graciousness that cloaked inner misery. She greeted guests with her parents and groaned privately whenever an eligible bachelor was introduced. Then one intrepid young guest had the audacity to introduce a friend he'd "brought along." Regina and her parents were both appalled to find themselves confronting the Viscount Lloyd's brother, Jared Strand, though for very different reasons.

Jared's disturbing resemblance to Max made the party almost unbearable for Regina. She watched the bold and sometimes reckless attentions Jared paid to every girl present. Apparently it was poor mill girls one week, fashionable debutantes the next. Max was right about him, she realized. Max was right about everything . . . except her.

She wandered from room to elegant room, collecting compliments and feeling increasingly detached from the gaiety of the people around her. How could she, how could they, participate in such frivolity when there were needy, homeless children in London who were even now lying down to sleep with empty bellies? And how could she go to bed tonight, knowing that in the morning Jonathan would have nowhere to lay his head?

Bright, irresistible little Jonathan. The image of his brave grin settled into her beleaguered heart. If there wasn't enough room for him at Lofton House, she vowed, then there was no room for love at all . . . or for her!

Just before midnight Max fled the emptiness and silence of his elegant house near Hyde Park. He barely saw the snow falling, scarcely heard the muffled thud of hooves or the creak of carriage and harness as vehicles drew past him. For a long time he stalked the streets, wrestling with the memory of the tremulous smile Jonathan had given him when they parted. Jonathan knew what the coming of Christmas meant for him, and his unspoken fears had made his eyes luminous and his laughter haunting.

As Max strode along, his thoughts focused on that bright mind and pliant nature, on the child who wanted only a few books and someone to belong to in order to be the happiest boy in the world. In Jonathan's presence, seeing the world afresh through his eager eyes, Max felt younger and lighter himself.

Regina Lofton had blown a gaping hole in his heart and Jonathan had crept in through it. Regina . . . Gigi—with her brash spirit and her irresistible sensuality and her tender touch. Would he ever see her again? He found himself on a street corner, holding his chest. When the pain eased, he looked up and found a cab stand nearby, with one lonely cab waiting.

Max charged up the stairs of the tenement on Channel Street and roused the Haskinses with a storm of banging. He wrapped the sleepy Jonathan in a blanket and lifted him into his arms. If he never saw Regina Lofton again, he vowed he would have at least this much love in his life.

Jonathan looked up from the cradle of Max's arms once they were settled in the cab. "W-where are you taking me? To a new home?"

"Yes." Max's chin trembled and his throat was too constricted for him to say more.

"Well . . ." Jonathan was confused and suddenly a little frightened. "Who's my new family?"

Max managed just two words.

"I am."

The Lofton carriage sped through the predawn gloom with Regina huddled inside, still clad in her evening dress and bundled in a heavy cloak. Her mind was fixed on her destination and her face was radiant with the joy she knew would fill Jonathan's face when she told him he was coming to live with her. Through the waning hours of the party she'd tried to imagine giving him up to someone else and couldn't. Jonathan was a special child, filled with a loving and hopeful spirit. He was her last link to Noni . . . and to the precious time she'd had with Max. Bringing him to Lofton House was the only acceptable solution. And if worse came to worst, she would have a modest inheritance from her grandmother at her next birthday and could probably manage to set herself up in a small house of her own.

The door to Nanny Dodd's flat was locked and she panicked briefly before she recalled that Jonathan was probably staying with the Haskinses. She hurried across the hall and pounded on the neighbors' door. Mrs. Haskins answered, looking sleepy and expressing bewilderment at finding Regina on her doorstep when the viscount had already come to get the boy.

"He come in the middle of the night," she volunteered. "Somethin' about a new home . . ."

"In the middle of the night?" Regina choked out, feeling caught between loss and rising anger. "Without telling me? Where?" A cold hand gripped her insides. "Where was he going?"

Mrs. Haskins shook her head; she hadn't the faintest notion. But by the time Regina reached the street, she knew exactly where *she* must go and told her driver, "Hyde Park, Horace—quickly! We have to find the Viscount Lloyd's house!"

Across London, at that very moment, the last stray guests at Lofton House were being located and poured into their respective cabs and carriages by the servants, while Alice Lofton was fainting into her stunned husband's arms.

"Oh, Charles! That man—that wretched little man!" she wailed, pressing a limp wrist against her forehead. "And to think he'd say such horrid things about our daughter . . . when a guest in our own house!"

"What man? What horrid things? Make sense, my dear—"

"S-sir Lawrence, Charles—" Her lashes fluttered swooningly, but Sir Charles's authoritative shake brought her back to her senses. "I overheard him telling Muriel Chamberlain that the Viscount Lloyd's mistress is actually *our Gigi!*"

"But that's absurd!" Sir Charles staggered with the impact of it. "Impossible! Lloyd's mistress has a passel of children, for God's sake!"

"It makes no difference," Alice said with a groan. "Muriel dislikes me so, it will be all over town by Boxing Day . . . and our Gigi will be ruined!"

When Sir Charles finished roaring and stomping, he sent for Regina. Barnes returned shortly, looking ashen, and reported that Miss Lofton had taken their driver and their carriage earlier. She hadn't returned.

"Where would she have gone at this hour, Charles?" Alice wailed. "You don't think she heard Sir Lawrence and . . ." Her eyes widened with horror. "You don't think she would have been so distraught as to try to confront the viscount?"

"Dammit!" Sir Charles let out a rare oath. "There's only one way to find out. Someone ought to have called that bounder Lloyd to account a long time ago!"

Horace had to stop twice to ask directions, but in the rising gray of dawn, he located the viscount's elegant four-story house in London's most fashionable section. Regina snatched up her skirts, bolted from the carriage, and dashed through the front gate and up the stone steps. Her face was hot and her gloveless hands were icy fists of determination.

Every block, every mile from Channel Street had fueled her anger at him. How dare he spirit Jonathan off in the dead of night without a word to her! She pounded savagely with the brass knocker. If he wasn't here, she was going to wait. She wasn't going home until she got Jonathan back and gave the almighty Viscount Lloyd a sizable piece of her mind!

A half-dressed butler sputtered and fell back before her forceful demands to see the viscount. When his eyes flicked nervously toward the great carved staircase, she was quick to perceive his dread and fulfill it, rushing for the stairs. The harried butler trotted ineffectually at her heels as she mounted the steps. She tried first one door, then another, venting fury into each empty room she encountered.

She finally stopped before a pair of lacquered mahogany doors that looked like the entrance to a master suite. The butler's frantic entreaties confirmed that she had found her quarry. She squared her shoulders, narrowed her eyes, and wrenched the brass handle to charge inside.

In the center of the cavernous half-lit room was a massive tester bed in whose opulently draped confines a half-dressed male form sprang up. *Max.* She hurried toward the bed, her eyes fixing on his face to avoid the sight of his unbuttoned shirt. At a glance she realized he'd been lying atop the covers and seemed to be wearing trousers.

"What have you done with him?" she demanded. "Jonathan—where have you taken him?"

"Gi—Miss Lofton?" Max rubbed his face and blinked as though he disbelieved his eyes. "What are you doing here?" He glanced around his bedchamber in befuddlement.

"I demand to know what you've done with Jonathan! I went to Channel Street to take him home with me and Mrs. Haskins said you took him. How dare you just waltz in and drag him off, dispose of him as if he were some—"

"See here, Miss Lofton, I did not *dispose* of him!" Max glared at her, his defenses rising as her heat burned the remaining fog from his senses. But before he could say more, another, smaller figure pushed up from beneath mounded covers.

"Gigi?" Jonathan squinted and rubbed his eyes.

"Jonathan?" Regina started for him then stopped, astonished. She looked between the boy and Max. Her mouth worked before any sound came out. "W-what is he doing here? Mrs. Haskins said you had taken him to a new home."

"I did take him to his new home," Max declared irritably, rolling off the bed and stalking toward her. "*This* is his new home."

The words hit Regina like a runaway carriage, leaving her reeling and grasping for a response. He had brought Jonathan to his home . . . he meant to keep him? Instantly, she knew it was true and she suffered a searing slash of remorse because the possibility hadn't even crossed her mind. It was always her wretched doubt that had erected the barriers between them, and here she was, accusing him again! Had she learned nothing? This was her Max, the one she'd discovered as he measured tummies in a dingy East End flat, the one who had tenderly introduced her to her own body's pleasures in a darkened carriage, the one who had given himself fully to a shameful bargain that she'd had no right to require. This was the Max she'd come to understand, to respect . . . to love.

She stared at his burning eyes and, even as her chest ached with despair, her mind filled with the sight of those eyes as they could be . . . roused and loving. The slice of bare chest that was visible through his half-open shirt, his rumpled clothes and tousled hair produced in her a hot, painful stab of longing for the intimacy his appearance invited. The sound of Jonathan's voice as he scrambled to the end of the bed penetrated her shock.

"It's true, Gigi . . . his lordship's going to adopt me. I get to stay here with him, always, and be his boy." Confusion crept into his face. "It's all right, isn't it . . . if he's my new family?"

Regina searched the strained joy in Jonathan's face and felt something squeezing her throat and scratching at the back of her eyes. Max . . . the tough and tender, the hardheaded and softhearted. He had decided to open his life, his heart, at last.

It was what she wanted . . . a good home for Jonathan with someone who would really care for him. She knew how loving Max could be . . . She made herself nod, then hurried to enfold Jonathan in a desperate hug.

"It's fine, Jonny. You and his lordship . . . you'll make a wonderful family." A terrible ache pounded through her as little arms reached beneath her cloak to squeeze her waist. Her sense of loss deepened with each beat of her heart. Max and Jonathan would belong to each other now. And neither would belong to her.

Max felt the desperation in her hug as though it were his own. She wanted and cared for the boy, he knew, but was there any chance that she could want him too? His eyes ached, his gut tightened, his lungs felt weighted with lead. He stood watching the wetness of her long lashes, the flush of emotion in her skin, the way she bit the inside of her lip. He recalled the feel of those lips, parting beneath his; relived the sweet sympathy of those eyes as they drew him out of himself; remembered the eager responses of her body to his questing fingers. To live without her, without that warmth in his life . . .

For once in your life, Max, take a risk! His heart banged against his ribs, demanding he do something. Forget looking ridiculous and sounding desperate. Forget your suffocating self-control. For once, let your feelings free—let your heart lead. For God's sake, reach out to her—*try*. If she walks out the door, you'll never see her again!

She pulled back and briefly cradled Jonathan's face in her hands, placing a kiss in the region of his forehead . . . she couldn't see exactly where. She turned blindly and was halfway to the door when Max said her name.

It was just "Gigi." But those bare syllables carried a deep vibrato of longing that found perfect resonance in her heart. With a desperate swipe at her wet face, she turned back. He was standing there with his eyes dark and luminous in the cool gray of dawn. He didn't seem to be breathing either.

"It's just like you, Maximilian Strand, to do something perfectly noble and admirable and unselfish." She swallowed and threw her heart at his feet by adding, "*And loving.*"

For a long minute neither moved, neither breathed. Then Max took one step and Regina took one. She took another... and kept walking, straight into him. His arms clamped fiercely around her as she buried her face in his half-open shirt. The desperate force of his embrace sent relief crashing through her.

"Oh, Max, I'm sorry. It seems as if I'm always saying I'm sorry to you," she whispered, crying, "when what I really want to say..."

"Yes?" He loosened his embrace enough to lift her chin and look into her teary blue eyes. "What is it you always want to say, Gigi?"

"I love you, Max." It came out in a whisper, but it seemed to echo like a thunderclap around the room. It was an unthinkably reckless thing to say. A desperate confession. A shameless bid for a gentleman's affections.

And it worked. Max's face nearly split with a wild, delirious grin as he lifted her and whirled her around in his arms, shouting her name like a man joyfully possessed. Then he set her back on her wobbly feet and his head bent, only to come up abruptly as Jonathan threw himself against them, wrapping his arms around them. Regina pushed back in Max's arms, cheeks wet and eyes shining, and Jonathan wriggled into their embrace.

"You're not mad at us?" Jonathan asked, smiling.

"No." She laughed, squeezing him. "I'm not angry. Not at all."

"His Lordship let me sleep in his bed last night so I wouldn't be scared. But I'll have my own room and lots of books. Want to hear?"

"I want to hear every last word," she said, beaming.

Jonathan and Max pulled her to the bed with them. She shed her cloak and hiked her elegant skirts and climbed up between them to lean against the bolsters, to hear all the things they'd done together in the last two days and all the things they planned to do.

In the midst of Jonathan's excited chatter, Regina felt the heat of Max's chest migrating into her shoulder and grew tinglingly aware of his gaze sliding over the liberally bared skin of her breasts. He interrupted Jonathan with a brief comment.

"Lovely dress, Gigi. Quite an effective neckline."

"My parents' gala was tonight. I didn't have time to change." She flushed and lowered her lashes, suddenly aware of the subtle shift of his hip and thigh, tighter against hers. "Go on, Jonny . . . about Big Ben."

Moments later, Max's lean fingers were stroking her bare arm, sending hot shivers through her that made it impossible to concentrate on ponies and roasted chestnuts. She was suddenly measuring the distance to his lips with her eyes.

"Jonathan," Max interrupted again, "turn your head, please."

"Huh?"

"I said, turn your head, please." Max's voice was exceptionally deep as his head bent toward Regina. "I'm about to kiss Gigi, and I don't think you should see it."

Regina's jaw dropped as Jonathan huffed disappointment and turned around. Max seized her jaw and covered her mouth hotly with his. She was stiff with shock at first, but the beguiling circles his velvety tongue made over her lips soon dissolved her ladylike protests of propriety. Her lips parted, remembering, welcoming the wet heat of his mouth. Slowly she turned in his embrace and threaded her arms around his ribs, pressing her half-naked breasts harder against him.

"Can I look now?" Jonathan sounded impatient. Max

raised his head from Regina's mouth just in time to meet Jonathan's curious gaze.

"Ummm . . . do you think you could find Heywood, the fellow who showed Gigi up here? Tell him I said we're all starving and we must have a huge Christmas breakfast soon or we'll all perish. And then tell him I said you deserve a big cup of chocolate, right away."

"Well . . . aren't you coming?" Jonathan watched the way Max cradled Gigi in his arms and frowned, puzzled.

"There are some things I need to speak with Gigi about. Grown-up things. Family things." When Jonathan agreed, Max gave him a huge smile and watched him slide off the bed and walk to the door. During the exchange, Regina's crimson face had been buried against Max's shoulder. Now he lifted it on his fingers and his eyes twinkled wickedly. "Where were we?"

One very long and plundering kiss later, Regina surfaced to remind him, "We were going to talk—"

"Talk . . . yes. Later." He nipped her lips with his, then nibbled her chin and continued down her throat.

"I do have a few things to say to you, Max Strand," she murmured, closing her eyes to savor the fiery thrill of his mouth heating her skin. "All I heard about you before we were introduced was how wealthy you were and how shrewdly you ran your business affairs. Before we even met I was convinced that all you cared about was money."

His head came up and his eyes were dark with emotion. "And money was all I could seem to talk about with you," he replied. "I wasn't used to being around women and you made me feel things . . ." He flushed and looked down at the maddeningly desirable display of her breasts, recalling how speechless it had made him that first night and how desperately he'd tried not to stare at it. Those same powerful longings suddenly surged in him again.

"I do love this dress, Gigi." His hand ran up her

side and flowed possessively over her breasts, perched precariously just inside her corset.

"Oh, Max," she murmured breathily, forgetting the rest of what she meant to say and arching back over his arm in invitation. He accepted, burying his nose in the perfumed crevice.

"And I love your breasts, Gigi. You can't imagine how much sleep they've cost me." He kissed her and pulled her tighter against his entire length, flexing his body so that she could feel just how sincere he was. "And I love you." Deep tenderness mingled with the currents of desire in his expression. "I think I've loved you since the first night I ever set eyes on you, Miss Lofton. And I've had to wait a long time for you to decide to love me. I don't want to waste another moment..."

His lips captured hers while his hands trembled with eagerness at her bodice and she moaned softly, abandoning herself to the steamy pleasures he sent flooding through her senses. Their hands moved as they sank onto the bed. Their bodies pressed together and sought each other, straining to come closer through the barriers of clothing. Minutes later, there was a rattle and a thumping at the door handle, and they managed to pull apart, frantically smoothing clothes and hair and forcing passions into hot retreat.

Jonathan padded in, his whole concentration fixed on the cup of chocolate in his hands. "It's too hot. I have to wait until it cools," he explained.

Max groaned with frustration, then laughed at himself and lunged from the bed to rescue Jonathan and the cup of chocolate that he'd undoubtedly carried all the way from the kitchen. Max set the cup on his nightstand and plunked the boy on the bed. Soon all three of them were laughing and teasing like children. When Max made a tickle bug of his fingers and attacked Jonathan's ribs, the boy retaliated. Regina decided to help even the odds, and together they discovered that Max was squeamish about his upper ribs. He fell back on the bed and rolled, carrying them over with him.

At that very moment Sir Charles and Lady Alice shoved their way past poor Heywood at the top of the stairs and located the double door that was the sign of the master chamber. They exchanged outraged looks at the giggles and protests and wicked laughter that were coming from inside. Heywood tried valiantly to insert himself between them and the door, but Sir Charles brushed him aside and pulled Alice along into the master suite.

They took half a dozen steps and stopped dead at the spectacle that greeted them. Their precious, highly refined young daughter was engaged in a wild tussle with the viscount and a small boy in a nightshirt . . . in the middle of the viscount's rumpled bed! A strangled scream issued from Alice Lofton's delicate throat, and all movement on the bed froze.

Regina looked up to find her parents staring at her in utter horror. She was braced on her hands and knees over Max's prone body, holding him down so that he could be tickle-tortured by five-year-old Jonathan. An erstwhile curl slid down her neck, and she tore her eyes from her parents to look down at herself. Her bosom was all but falling out of her crushed and rumpled dress and her lady-like coif was a shambles. Oh, Lord . . .

"Regina Elizabeth Lofton!" her father bellowed. "What in God's name do you think you're doing?"

"Come away from that wicked, unprincipled wretch this minute!" her mother railed. "Oh, Charles!" Her eyes widened on Jonathan. "Look—he's got one of his . . . one of those *children* with him!"

Sir Charles was, indeed, looking . . . at the shocking bounty about to spill from his daughter's bodice and her obviously kiss-swollen lips. "How dare you, sir!" He tore his gaze from Regina to spear Max. "Trifling with my daughter . . . and in the same bed with one of your . . . with that child. Damn you for the veriest, lowest scoundrel and blackguard in all England!"

"Papa, p-please!" Regina gasped, covering Jonathan's ears with her hands and pulling him against her side to shelter him. "I can explain—honestly I can if you'll just—"

"Sir Charles, I can imagine you've reason to be upset—" Max rose to his knees beside Regina, pulling her against him with the same protective gesture she'd just made toward Jonathan. "But there are explanations to be made, if you'll only give us—"

But Sir Charles was beet-red and hearing virtually nothing but the clamor of evil tongues all over London, ruining his daughter, dragging the name of Lofton through the gutters. "To add to your other vile offenses," he charged blindly, "you've just linked my daughter's spotless reputation to your own foul perfidies. It's all over town—or will be by tomorrow night—that she's your mistress! You've been seen with her and your bantling bastards—the whole brood of them—and they're even saying she's the mother! Good God, Regina, whatever possessed you to be seen with this bounder when you knew what sort of man—"

Gossip, Max realized as Sir Charles ranted on. They'd been seen out and about together and been grossly misunderstood. And unless he acted fast, he might be misunderstood again! In the midst of Sir Charles's tirade, he grabbed Regina by the shoulders and turned her to face him.

"Marry me, Gigi." He ignored the Lofton's sputters of outrage and brought up his hands to cradle her face. Fire flickered in his eyes and there was a pulsing, irresistible urgency in his voice. "Marry me, Regina Lofton, and live with me and Jonathan . . . and be the heart of our family. Marry me and love me." His throat tightened so that the last part came out with a rasp. "And let me love you."

Regina's eyes filled even as joy burst across her face. "Yes—oh, yes!" She pushed onto her knees and threw her arms around Max's neck. His face beamed reckless pleasure as he looked past her shoulder into Jonathan's scowl.

"Is it all right?" Jonathan said anxiously.

"It certainly is." Max laughed, hugging Regina fiercely. "Gigi's going to be your mother!"

"H-his m-mother—*Oh!*" Alice blanched, her pupils shrank to pin-point size and she crumpled at her husband's side.

"Not now, Alice—for God's sake!" Sir Charles declared, catching her halfway to the floor. He strained and heaved and dragged her to a chair by the marble hearth. He was torn between helping his swooning wife and venting his outrage at the sight of his baby daughter accepting a proposal of marriage from a man with a whole flock of illegitimate children . . . whose bare chest was showing, hair and all! Alice moaned limply and he ripped the hat from his head to fan her with it.

Max lurched from the bed and stalked toward the Loftons in his stocking feet, his shirttail flapping. Each step he took straightened his spine, squared his shoulders and hardened his chin. Before Regina's startled eyes he seemed to grow, becoming again the imperial and intimidating Viscount Lloyd . . .

He planted himself three feet from Sir Charles, pointed to the other empty chair by the hearth, and ordered, "Sit!" After a long, volatile stare, he added, "I'm going to explain and you're going to listen!" Sir Charles blinked and pulled back his chin, simmering, then thrust himself down on the edge of the chair.

"Sir Lawrence Trexel himself saw you out with your common 'convenience'—and with your bantlings— more than once," Sir Charles charged. "You can't deny it."

"I'll not deny that your daughter and I were out together, and in the company of children," Max declared in hot, withering blasts that forbade interruption or rebuttal. "It seems Nanny Dodd, Regina's old nurse, took in foundlings on the pension you provided her.

When she died she had six orphans living with her. Regina promised to find them homes and she persuaded me"—he shot a meaningful glance at Regina and tactfully skipped the details of his recruitment—"to help her find those homes. In the last two weeks that is precisely what we've done, found homes for all six children."

Regina and Jonathan now stood three feet away, watching him with big, expectant eyes. Regina listened to his lordly tone and savored his sharp, commanding glare, his chiseled aristocratic features, and his wide, intimidating shoulders. He could be so high-handed, so absolute and authoritarian . . . it was perfectly marvelous. She smiled adoringly at him.

"Jonathan," he said, pointing imperiously to the boy, "is about to become my son by adoption, and he's the reason Gigi came here this morning. She was worried to find him missing from Nanny Dodd's flat and came here to learn what had happened to him. I had just informed her that I intend to adopt Jonathan myself." His explanation was perfectly emphatic and logical until he added, "You had the misfortune to arrive in the middle of our celebratory tickle."

Regina bit her lip to stifle an involuntary giggle and he looked at her. His fierce expression melted slightly, warmed by the flame in his eyes. He turned back to the glowering Sir Charles and the very dazed Lady Alice.

"I have no mistress and no 'bantlings,' as you so delicately put it. I intend to marry your daughter in a vulgarly huge and public wedding and to live openly and honorably with her for the rest of my natural life. We're going to raise Jonathan to be a fine and decent man, and we're going to produce the next Viscount Lloyd together . . . and maybe a raft of other little Strands, as well. And if you don't want your respectable names linked to our infamy, I suggest you set your heads to thinking of some way to counter or squelch the filthy, baseless gossip someone has spread about Regina and me."

He studied their drained faces, drew himself up, and took a deep, satisfied breath. "Now, if you'll excuse us," he said, beginning to button his shirt, "it is Christmas . . . my first with Gigi and my new son Jonathan. And I'm hungry as a bear."

Max put one arm around Regina and the other around Jonathan and led them out the door. At the top of the main stairs he paused and gave Jonathan's hair a tousle. "Why don't you go ahead and warn Heywood we're coming for breakfast?"

Jonathan looked up at him and grinned. "You gonna kiss her again?"

"Very likely. Now go."

Jonathan went thumping down the steps in his bare feet and Max chuckled. "Sharp as a tack, isn't he?"

"He ought to be wearing shoes," she observed with a proud, motherly smile. Max laughed and turned her face up to his. She instantly forgot about shoes and young boys and unhappy parents. Nothing mattered now but Max and the joy of loving him and being loved in return.

"You were wonderful, Max," she said, threading her arms around his neck as he embraced her. "So lordly and arrogant and overwhelming. Are you really going to marry me in a vulgarly huge wedding?"

He blinked at her left-handed compliment, then smiled. "The biggest."

"But people may talk . . ."

"Only about what a beautiful bride you'll make and how lucky I am to have snared you. I'll be so blessedly proper and upstanding in public, they won't be able to think anything else. One thing about being wealthy and arrogant and overwhelming—people tend to think you're a juiceless prig along with it." He laughed wickedly. "Look what a time I had changing your mind about me."

She blinked, then blushed, then laughed. "Merry Christmas, Max."

"Merry Christmas, Gigi," he responded with a rakish, adoring smile. "This is going to be the best Christmas I've ever had."

Then he did kiss her. It was a warm, welcome-home sort of kiss. And somewhere in the midst of it, both realized that in finding homes for Noni's children, they'd each found a home for their own heart.

On the chairs in Max's bedchamber, Sir Charles and Lady Alice sat limp with shock, trying to think how many people they'd told the secrets of the viscount's perfidies.

"I haven't the foggiest idea how one would go about *stopping* gossip." Alice shook her head in disbelief. "I'm not even sure it's possible."

"Certainly a most radical idea..." Sir Charles wagged his head, looking slightly ill. Moments later, Alice straightened and turned to her husband with a blush of excitement blooming in her cheeks.

"The only thing a gossip loves better than a juicy story is a *juicier* story. Charles, we'll simply have to think of something better and get to Sir Lawrence and Muriel before they get to anyone else." Her eyes flitted about as her mind worked feverishly, then she turned to him with the flame of true inspiration burning in her eyes. "I have it, Charles—we'll tell them the *truth!*"

On the day after Christmas, England's traditional Boxing Day, the story of the "six little angels" began to spread. There were six little angels, the story went, six orphaned children who desperately needed homes. And there were two perfectly matched but unthinkably stubborn hearts that desperately needed to fall in love. And when the six little angels touched the two stubborn hearts, a miracle of love was born. The story had a tantalizing ring of truth to it. Details of a bargain and a tryst in a darkened carriage and a tickling match and a bold marriage proposal on a great tester bed usually slipped into the telling, shocking some and titillating others. Thus was a small scandal traded for a grand romance. And the resulting tale set sentimental hearts sighing all over London. Christmas was, after all, the season for angels and miracles . . . and loving.

SEASON'S GREETINGS
from ...
BETINA KRAHN

BETINA KRAHN lives in Eagan, Minnesota, with her physicist husband, Don, her sons, Nathan and Zebulun, and a feisty salt-and-pepper schnauzer. With an undergraduate degree in biology and a graduate degree in counseling, she has worked in the fields of teaching, personnel management, and mental health. She loves butter cookies and quiet snows at Christmas, routinely kills poinsettias, and (much to her sons' horror) leaves Christmas shopping until the last minute. She believes the world needs a bit more truth, a lot more justice, and a whole lot more love and laughter. And she believes deeply in the One Great Love that is the source of all others. She is the author of the historical romance *Caught in the Act*, from Avon Books.

A Match Made in Heaven

Linda Ladd

1

❄❄❄

"Look, Josh, it's startin' to snow. I wanna go build me a snowman!"

"Katelyn, you know you can't go out! It's black as pitch out there!" Joshua Wright jabbed the poker at the logs piled in the hearth, vigorously attempting to rekindle the dwindling fire. His exertions had an immediate effect, generating a burst of licking, red-orange flames. Satisfied, he watched a shower of glowing sparks flee up the chimney like a swarm of fireflies, then returned his full attention to Katelyn.

His baby sister was only four years old and an awful pest to him and his brother, Lucas. But sometimes he had to admit that Katelyn could be real sweet, too, especially when she minded him and told him she liked him better than Lucas. But right now she wasn't minding him at all. Instead, she had climbed up on the window seat and mashed her stuffed-up nose flat against the cold windowpane, trying to peer through the frost that crusted the glass like fine white lace.

"Katelyn, you come down from there right now and get in bed! You still got the sniffles and a runny nose,

191

too, and you ain't even got on your nightcap or nuthin'. You're gonna be sicker than a big dog."

As if attempting to verify his prediction, Katelyn wriggled her nostrils and let loose with a delicate *ker-choo*, a funny, clogged-up sound that made him and Lucas laugh. Then she scampered like a frisky kitten to her frilly, white-linen–swathed cot on her side of the nursery.

His brother Lucas, on the other hand, wasn't nearly as apt to follow Joshua's orders.

"Criminy, they're big old flakes," he said in awe, lingering before the tall casement window. "Look, Josh, they're as big as those shiny silver dollars Uncle Chris always gives us on our birthdays. You think it's gonna get deep enough to go coastin'? One of my sled runners is broke, but we can fix it up so it'll work, I reckon. 'Member how we went sleddin' down the pasture hill last year, Josh? 'Member how scairt you was when you got goin' so fast you crashed into that snow-bank by the creek?"

Like a flash of fire, a painful image flared, burning an indelible imprint into Joshua's mind. He saw his mama again in her pretty red wool cloak, running down the slope, her face all worried when she wrapped her arms around him and asked him if he'd hurt himself. An ache clutched his heart real tight and hurt him something fearful, and he tried not to think about his mother hugging and kissing him. She had gone to heaven almost a year ago. That's when Lucas, Katelyn, and him had left Oak Haven Farm up in Pennsylvania and come to live in Washington with their papa's brother.

Now Uncle Chris was their official guardian. He was real nice and stuff, but Joshua couldn't help missing his mama. When he remembered that she was down in the ground back in the Oak Haven cemetery in the cold and snow, he felt real sad inside. And she was all by herself, too, because his papa, John Wright, had been shot by the Rebs somewheres in Tennessee. He was buried down there with a bunch of his soldiers, but his name was on the big marble monument right beside hers. Joshua was sure glad about that.

Upset by thoughts of his parents, Joshua hid his grief with a harsh bellow aimed at his brother. "Hey, get in bed, Lucas! You know how Miz Abernathy fusses at us when we're up and runnin' around when she comes up to hear our prayers!"

"Just quit tellin' me what to do, Josh! You ain't my boss. You're just my brother, that's all."

Joshua traded an impressive glare with Lucas. "I'm the oldest one, though. Uncle Chris said so. And he says I get to be the man of the house when he ain't around. And you heard him say it, too, 'cause you was hidin' behind the door when he was givin' me that man-to-man talk. I done saw you!"

Lucas didn't bother to deny his transgression. His face settled into sullen, defiant lines, and his answer was impenitent. "I don't give a rat-tailed hang what he says. 'Tain't fair anyways. There's just two little bitty years' difference in us, not even that really. You're nine and I'm seven and a half. Why should you always get to be the man?"

"'Cause I'm taller, that's why, and I can spell better, too. Now go on 'fore we all get in dutch with Miz Abernathy!"

His freckled face wrapped in a massive scowl, Joshua attacked the poor fire with renewed vigor. Brutally, he shoved the fire iron in and out, like the most proficient piratical swordsman. A moment later he abruptly stopped his abuse of the flaming hickory and cocked his head to listen.

"By jings, she's out in the hall now!" he cried, dropping the metal rod. Both boys flew like startled pigeons to the large bed they shared in the corner. When the door opened, they were snuggled deep in the soft feather mattress. But the face that appeared in the doorway was not that of the stout, elderly housekeeper who watched them while their guardian was working. Instead, it was their tall, black-haired uncle himself. All three children popped up in bed, grinning with pleasure.

"Uncle Chris! We didn't know you was comin' home tonight in time to see us! Are you gonna tell us a bedtime story like you used to?"

"Wish I could, Josh, but I just have the time to tuck you kids in, then I've got to meet with President Johnson. It's important, or he wouldn't have called me into work late again."

Joshua frowned, watching his Uncle Chris lean down to give his sister a kiss. Katelyn clutched her little arms in a stranglehold around her uncle's neck, like she always did, and his uncle laughed, like he always did. To Joshua's way of thinking, his uncle looked real grand in his Union uniform with its gold buttons and shiny braid on the shoulders. He was a real important major, and he'd gotten lots and lots of ribbons and medals and stuff, too, for being so brave in the war against the Confederates. Joshua's mama had said that was why Uncle Chris got to work in Washington on the president's staff.

"Can't you even stay long enough to read us a good story or somethin'?" he asked as his uncle came over to his and Lucas's bed.

"Sorry, Josh," Uncle Chris answered as he arranged the red and yellow patchwork quilt over them. "Maybe tomorrow night I'll have more time. Now you two go to sleep like good boys. Mrs. Abernathy'll be downstairs if you need her. I won't be gone too long."

After his uncle had turned down the gaslights flickering in their green glass bowls and taken his leave, Joshua lay very still. His brows furrowed in a disappointed frown, he shifted on his side and ignored Lucas's chatter about sneaking out to the woods behind the house in the morning to shoot at crows with their slingshots.

After a while, Lucas and Katelyn got real quiet, and Joshua figured they were finally asleep. It was about time, too! Real sneaky-like, he slid off the bed, retrieved the stub of candle he always kept hid under his pillow, then tiptoed to the hearth to light the wick. Shielding the flame, he ducked under the heavy brown velvet tablecloth hanging off the round table in the center of the nursery. To his chagrin, he'd barely got himself settled in his most privatest hideout when Lucas lifted the fringed edge and peered askance at him.

"What you think you're doin' under there, Josh?"

"Hey, you're 'posed to be in bed. Go on to sleep, will you? I got some important thinkin' to do."

"What 'bout?" Lucas asked, ignoring Joshua's command and squirming underneath the table.

"'Bout Uncle Chris."

"Why you thinkin' about Uncle Chris?"

"'Cause I want to, that's why, so just clam up and let me be."

Lucas lapsed into silence, but only momentarily. "We don't never see him much anymore, do we? He's always busy workin', and he's always too tired to play games with us like he used to." He expelled a gigantic sigh as he drew his knees up and rested his chin atop them. "'Member when we was home with Mama and Papa, 'fore Papa went off to fight? Uncle Chris was always happy and smilin'. He weren't no fancy major then, and he was always at all Mama's parties. 'Member all the people who came, and all the cakes and puddin's Mama made, and how good her homemade fudge candy was?"

Joshua remembered and wished everything was just like that again. But it wasn't. When the tablecloth stirred again and a tiny heart-shaped face appeared, Joshua frowned. But before he could say boo, Katelyn had wriggled in between him and Lucas.

"Katelyn, we're talkin' about important boy stuff here. Stuff girls can't hear."

"I can too hear it," Katelyn said, looking hurt. When moisture gathered in her cornflower-blue eyes and a big fat tear rolled off her lashes, Joshua felt himself weakening.

"Oh, all right, you can stay, I reckon, but you can't say nuthin' or start whinin' 'bout stuff, you hear? Lucas and me got plans to make."

"We do?" Lucas asked, obviously surprised but intrigued, too. "What sorta plans?"

"What sorta plans?" Katelyn parroted, then stuck her thumb in her mouth as she snuggled close against Joshua, the raggedy baby blanket she still slept with clutched tightly in her fist.

"Don't be suckin' on your thumb, Katelyn," Joshua ordered absently. "You're too old now, and anyways, Uncle Chris says it's sure to make your teeth stick out all crooked and ugly."

"What kind of plans, Josh?" Lucas demanded again, impatient to find out just exactly what was going on.

"Plans to make Uncle Chris act happy like he used to so he'll play games and stuff with us."

"Yea!" Katelyn cried, sitting up and clapping her hands. "Let's make him play hide-and-seek! And I get to be it first!"

"Hush up, Katelyn, or Miz Abernathy'll be up here in a wink to put us to bed," Joshua hissed in his lowest, meanest whisper.

Katelyn took heed of his warning, but Lucas's brown eyes shone with excitement.

"How? How can we get him not to be so busy and quit workin' so hard?"

"Well, first off, we got to get him to stay home with us more."

"But Miz Abernathy tole us that bachelors like him go out all the time and ain't used to watchin' little kids like us."

"What's a batcher?" Katelyn interrupted, her question muffled by her thumb.

"It's a man who ain't got no wife." Lucas's condescending look plainly announced his superiority.

"Who *don't* have no wife," Joshua corrected impatiently, "and you ain't supposed to say ain't."

"You just said it yerself, so there!" Lucas cried, always indignant when Joshua tried to tell him how to talk.

"Maybe I did," Joshua replied, irritated at Lucas's observation, "but I know better, now don't I? So sayin' ain't don't count none against me."

Lucas appeared to contemplate that muddy scrap of logic, but a moment later he let the argument drop, apparently more fascinated by Joshua's profound plan. "You mean if Uncle Chris gets hisself a wife, he's gonna start smilin' and playin' with us again?"

Joshua nodded, draping an arm around Katelyn when she yawned sleepily and began slurping on her thumb.

"So all we got to do is figure out how to get him a wife," Joshua decided. "One we like a lot."

"But where do you go to find ladies who want to be men's wifes?" Lucas wanted to know.

"Well, I don't know everything yet," Joshua snapped, annoyed that he always had to be the one who thought up stuff. "Just hush up, and let me consider on it for a spell."

Lucas held his tongue, and after a long moment of inner study, Joshua decided to solicit suggestions.

"Well, what kind of ladies does Uncle Chris like, Lucas?"

At that question, Katelyn roused herself. "Purty ladies," she mumbled, half-asleep.

"That's right, Josh!" Lucas agreed, impressed by his sister's perceptiveness. "He always takes off his major's hat when purty ladies pass by, even when he's totin' Katelyn on one arm."

"And he always smiles at them, too, real big," Joshua remembered, growing equally excited. "And you know what? Once I heard Daniel talkin' to Lola in the kitchen, real quiet-like, and he said that women chase Uncle Chris all over the place."

"I like to chase Uncle Chris, too," Katelyn admitted

through a wide yawn. "He always lets me be it and I always catches him, too, 'cause I runs so fast."

"Criminy, Katelyn, Josh don't mean that purty ladies play tag with him!" Lucas's tone dripped scorn. "Daniel means they follow him 'round town and try to get to be his wife. Ain't that right, Josh?"

"I guess so, but I wonder why none of them's never caught him yet?" Joshua was stumped for a moment, then he suddenly realized what the answer must be. "I guess he's just been too busy for pickin' a wife. But if that's what's wrong, maybe we can find a purty lady for him, so he won't have to bother with the lookin' part!"

"Yep, that's it!" Lucas seconded.

"Yep, dat's it!" followed Katelyn's drowsy mumble. Silence fell.

"But who?" Joshua asked at length. "We don't know many ladies, 'cept Miz Abernathy and the maids, and they all got good husbands they like fine."

"Well, give me a minute to think. Who's the purtiest lady we know?" Joshua was momentarily stumped, but seconds later, the answer came to him in one of his most brilliant flashes of genius.

"Cousin Abigail is the purtiest one I know of!" he cried, quickly amending that glowing endorsement out of loyalty to his mother. "'Cept for Mama, of course."

"Cousin Abigail?" Lucas sounded dubious. "The one painted inside Mama's big locket?"

"Yep, her. She's real nice, too. She used to come visit Mama and Papa at the farm all the time before the South started fightin' with us. I can remember her. Can't you?"

Lucas shook his head.

"Well, I can. And she's the funnest lady I ever saw. She used to play games with us, but you was real little then. And she likes chickens and pigs, even if she's a grown-up lady." As he listed his cousin's attributes, Joshua became increasingly sure she was the best choice to catch his uncle. "She used to take you down to the pigpen, Lucas, don't you even remember that? Uncle Chris's sure to like 'er!"

Katelyn sat up, rubbing her eyes with her doubled fists. "Who's Cousin Abigail?"

"She's Mama's cousin from Georgia, and she looks like Mama, too. But she's got yellow hair, just like you, Katelyn, and her eyes are funny, kind of silver, you know, like Mama's bestest locket chain."

"Where's George's?" Katelyn wanted to know.

"It's a state way down south somewheres. You got to ride on a train for a long, long time to get there. Mama told me so. That's where she used to live when she was little like you. Then she married Papa and came up to Pennsylvania to live on the farm with him and Uncle Chris."

"Oh," Katelyn muttered, but the conversation had obviously lost its appeal, because she lay down again and snuzzled her face up into her blanket.

Joshua lowered his voice, wishing she'd just hurry it up and go to sleep. She was too little to be trusted with such important talk.

"If Cousin Abigail lives so far off, how can she get married to Uncle Chris?" Lucas asked. "Does she know him?"

"I dunno. He was around sometimes when she visited us, I think, before he went off to fight the Rebs. She's a Reb, too, I guess, but she's a nice one. I reckon she didn't fight us or kill nobody or nuthin'."

Joshua pondered the perplexing questions facing him for several more minutes. "Well, we just got to think up a good plan to get 'm to meet each other."

"But Uncle Chris's too busy to go see her. How's he gonna 'member she's so purty?"

Both boys once more lapsed into serious meditation. When Joshua began to smile, Lucas's face lit up like birthday candles.

"I got it! What if Cousin Abigail comes up here to spend Christmas with us?" Joshua's grin widened. He had liked Cousin Abigail more than any other lady he'd ever met, except his mama, of course. They'd all have a grand time if she came for Christmas!

"Why would she wanna do that?"

"Well, if we tole her Uncle Chris was goin' off somewheres on a business trip and we was gonna hafta spend Christmas all alone, I bet she would. Hey, I could write her a letter! She sent a note to Mama once, last spring after that ole General Lee surrendered. I guess she din't know 'bout Mama bein' in heaven. And I saw Miz Abernathy put it in Mama's blue satin stationery box with all Papa's letters. And Miz Abernathy'll post our letter to her for us, I know she will. We could tell Cousin Abigail that we're all alone and Katelyn cries every night for Mama. That's true, anyways. Cousin Abigail likes us a lot. I 'member that real well. I know she'd come if we can make her feel real sorry for us!"

"We could say Uncle Chris works all the time and never pays us no mind," Lucas added, his voice growing bolder as several other promising possibilities occurred to him. "And we can tell her that we're all sad and lonely and—I know, Josh! We'll tell her we're sick! Real sick, so she'll feel so sorry for us that she can't hardly stand it!"

"That's a real good idea, Lucas, but not us. Katelyn should be the sick one. You know how bad everybody feels when Katelyn's sick with her bein' so little and sweet. And then we really won't be fibbin' to Cousin Abigail 'cause Katelyn's still got a snotty nose, see?"

Lucas peered down at his sister and wrinkled up his own nose. "Ugh, why don't you wipe it off with your handkerchief? It's gettin' down close to her mouth."

Joshua gave him a highly contemptuous look. "Just where am I s'posed to keep my handkerchief in my nightshirt, numbskull? Just go on and use the tablecloth to rub it off with. Nobody's gonna see the underneath side of it, anyways."

The suggestion obviously made sense to Lucas, because he took the gold fringe and poked gingerly at his sister's nose while he posed their next problem.

"When can we write the letter, Josh? We got to do it soon, or she won't make it in time for Christmas."

"Right now. We got our own writin' paper, and don't you worry yourself, neither, 'cause I'm gonna write it real good. I'm gonna make Cousin Abigail feel so sorry for us that she's sure to bawl her eyes out, then she'll write us a letter to tell us when she's a-comin'. Then she'll ride up here on the train just like she did last time. Then Uncle Chris'll see her and like her real good. And they'll get hitched up like Mama and Papa, and adopt us, and all in time for Christmas!"

Lucas slowly shook his head, plumb awestruck at the extent of his brother's brilliance. "By hokey, Josh, I guess you are the smartest. I never could have thunk up such a good plan."

Joshua's chest swelled with pride, but he leaned back on his palms, trying to look as if he received such praise all the time. Actually, it was rare indeed for his brother to compliment him so lavishly. But he *did* deserve it.

"That's why Uncle Chris says I'm the man now. And there ain't no such word as thunk."

"You just said *ain't* again, so there," Lucas accused him, suddenly less inclined to admire Joshua's brain-iness. "And even if you are smarter at stuff like this, you really ain't the man of the house 'cause you're not that much older than me, or Katelyn neither."

"If you're so good, Lucas, then you write the letter to Cousin Abigail."

Lucas frowned, defeated. "Criminy, I guess you get to be the man of the house then. I can't spell nearly as good as you, and you know it, Josh."

"All right, but I guess I can let you help me think up what-all to say," Joshua conceded, mellowed by a sudden feeling of magnanimity. "After all, you were the one who thought up the part 'bout one of us bein' sick."

"Gee, Josh, thanks. Do you really think we're gonna

get Uncle Chris to marry up with Cousin Abigail real quick-like, in time for Christmas?"

"Well, that's pretty serious stuff, I guess, gettin' married and all, so it might take a few days. Maybe even a whole week. But no longer than that, I reckon. It's gonna be fun havin' Cousin Abigail visit us again. But c'mon, let's write the letter now. Go get me some paper and a pencil out of my school box."

Moments later, Lucas had returned with the necessary writing materials, and Joshua squirmed over to lay flat on his stomach, his pencil poised purposefully over the paper.

"What if Uncle Chris likes bein' a bachelor?" Lucas sounded worried.

"He won't, not after he meets up with Cousin Abigail. How many girls do you know who like horses and pigs as much as she does? Grown-up ladies like her is hard to find, and Uncle Chris is real smart. He's gonna probably marry her so fast we won't know what's happenin'."

"'Course, I knew that," Lucas was quick to murmur.

Nurturing dreams of a fun-filled Christmas with Uncle Chris and his pretty new wife, who liked pigs, Joshua clutched his pencil tight and began to write:

Dear Couzin Abigale,
Please come see us. We are all alon and its teribul. Uncle Chris isn't even gonna be home for Christmas cuz he is goin off somewheres else to work. He nevr plays with us and that makes my sistr Katelyn cry. We miss Mama and Papa and we remembr that you like pigs very much (and othr animals). Please come in time for Christmas.

> Yores truly,
> Yore pore orphan couzin,
> Joshua T. Wright

P. S. Katelyn is real sick and there's no medisin. She mite die, but probly not.

2

EVERYWHERE Abigail King looked she saw a sea of dark blue uniforms. Even eight months after the war's end, the major train terminal in Washington, D.C., was overrun with military personnel. Federal troops, mostly soldiers assigned to keep order in the conquered Confederacy, lolled carelessly on the long wooden benches lining the walls of the station house or congregated together in loud, boisterous groups awaiting expresses headed to Southern states ruled by harsh martial law.

How very different was this scene from the dreary one in the city of Savannah, from where she'd just come. There, no gay mood of victory prevailed among the returning Confederate warriors. Ragged, broken, dressed in tattered, dirty gray, they straggled home like living scarecrows, defeated, demoralized, dead of dreams.

And Abigail knew how they felt. She had lost everything, seen her home burned by the Yankees. Determined not to succumb to the melancholy that threatened, she forced herself to concentrate on the reason she had made the long journey into enemy territory. Miriam's orphaned children needed her.

Hot tears burned her eyes, but she quickly suppressed the desolation inside her heart, as she had learned to do throughout the last few years. She had wept too much and too often during the war—enough tears to last her forever. She had to be strong, for Joshua and Lucas and their little sister.

If nothing else, the children's desperate plea for her to come had shown her just how terribly lonely they were. They hadn't seen her since her last visit to Oak Haven Farm nearly five years ago, when the children had been mere babes. Joshua had been four, she recalled, and Lucas a toddler of two. And poor little Katelyn had not yet been born. Abigail was amazed the boys could remember her at all, much less want her with them for Christmas.

Nevertheless, she could understand how forsaken the children must feel with their parents gone. Abigail was alone in the world, too. The fighting between the States had taken the lives of both her father and her brother Ralph. Once more, bitterness sliced through her heart with razor-sharp agony, threatening to engulf her. Mentally, she fought that poisonous emotion, but the bustling atmosphere of postwar prosperity in the capital city made her painfully aware of the Confederacy's ignominious defeat. Worse, most of the fighting, killing, and atrocities had taken place in the South, where the land itself was a scarred and devastated reminder of the terrible destruction.

In Georgia alone, where she had been born and reared, Sherman had led his army in the work of the devil, leaving from Atlanta to the sea a sixty-mile-wide swath of razed fields, burned factories, and demolished railbeds, the metal rails twisted around trees and telegraph poles in "Sherman hairpins." How she despised William T. Sherman and what he'd done to innocent civilians under the guise of war! No soldier with any sense of honor would make war on starving women and children!

Don't think about it, don't, she told herself, trying to relax her rigid jaw. It was over, all of it, after four long, terrible years. Forcibly, she emptied her mind, thinking instead of poor Miriam.

Miriam had been Abigail's first cousin, a lovely woman and a devoted wife and mother. It was hard to think of the tall, energetic brunette no longer working indefatigably in the kitchens or gardens of Oak Haven. But she was gone forever, taken prematurely by a throat infection within months of her husband's death on the battlefield.

They'd been like sisters, she and Miriam. Yet Abigail had not even known about her cousin's death until a few months ago when Abigail had written to Miriam at Oak Haven, just after postal service had been restored between Pennsylvania and Savannah. Miriam's housekeeper, a Mrs. Abernathy, had written back with the sad news.

Tired to the bone and wanting a moment's rest, Abigail sought out an isolated spot near a loaded luggage cart, setting down her single bag and glancing around. How good it felt to breathe fresh air again, after spending several days riding north, surrounded by Union soldiers with their coarse talk and the foul, stale odor of their cigars. And her head was pounding. How lovely it would be to curl up atop a nice soft bed!

A soldier passed by, close enough to brush her full skirt—a tall, broad-shouldered man with captain's bars decorating his epaulets. Against her will, Christopher's face came winging softly across the misty edges of her consciousness, bringing a bittersweet longing. He had worn such a uniform the last time she had seen him, when he had said good-bye to her at the depot near her father's cotton plantation. It had been so warm that March day, the sky as brilliant as a bluebird's feathers. The wind had tousled Christopher's wavy raven hair, feathering it over his forehead as he gazed down at her. He had held her hands very tight, his dark eyes full of love and regret at having to leave.

Oh, Lord, could that day really have been over four years ago? Had they ever really been engaged to marry? It all seemed a dream now, a wonderful, sad courtship she'd read about in some fairy tale. The war had torn them apart, as it had the entire country. She hadn't seen him since that day and had long since resigned herself to the fact that their relationship was over. Too much time had passed, too much hardship and bitter heartache. She was glad he was away for the holidays and she wouldn't have to see him. If he'd been home she probably wouldn't have come to visit at all. No doubt he was equally anxious to avoid her, and that's why he'd allowed the children to invite her while he was gone.

Sighing, she clutched her black silk reticule with a few precious coins tucked inside, all the money she had left. The railway ticket to Washington had been expensive, but the journey was well worth any sacrifice. The children needed her.

Uncertain where to wait, she scanned the crowd, hoping someone had been sent to collect her. But how could they? She hadn't had the money to telegraph that she was coming, so they had no idea which train to meet. Perhaps they had left a message for her with the ticket master, she thought hopefully, picking up her father's old black leather valise. She headed down the platform, jostled first one way then another by the swarming crowd. When she had finally fought her way through the soldiers to a small ticket office situated at the far end of the station platform, she tapped lightly on the open door. An old man looked up from where he sat behind a desk cluttered with all manner of papers, dirty dishes, and train schedules. He scowled at her, his manner harried and disgruntled. He looked to be in his sixties, with long hair the color of dirty cotton and a thin, straggly gray beard stained brown around his mouth from tobacco juice.

"Pardon me, sir, but would you happen to know if anyone has inquired after me? My name is Abigail King. I've just arrived here from Savannah."

Instantly, the man's lips compressed into tight, vicious dislike. "I ain't got no time for any gawdanged, filthy Reb," he growled harshly, "and don't go tellin' me you ain't one, neither. I done heared it in yer voice. You Johnny Rebs kilt my sons at Manassas, both of 'em, and fine men they was, so you just git outta here.

Go on back down south with them other traitors where you belong. We don't got no use for yer kind around here."

Shocked, and more than a little frightened by the cold loathing that burned in the old man's faded blue eyes, Abigail retreated in haste, gathering her silk skirt in one hand and hurrying to the brick steps that descended to the busy street in front of the depot.

By now she ought to be used to Yankee prejudice. Had she not lived in conquered Savannah for the past year? Yankee military rule had taught her plenty about hatred and hostility. For so many people, south and north, the war was not yet over. Abigail wondered if it ever would be.

Outside, the afternoon was quickly fading into dusk, and undecided how to proceed, she looked up and down the wide street. On her right, high atop a hill, she could just make out the alabaster dome of the capitol, shining white against the gray sky, but in the other direction lay a long muddy mall crisscrossed with train tracks and swampy ponds. Finally, she stopped a young boy with an unruly shock of tan hair as he hurried past her with half a dozen floral bandboxes stacked in his arms.

"Pardon me, but could you tell me how I can get to Georgetown?"

"It's thataway, ma'am, near five or six miles, I reckon. If you go up to the end of the Mall there," he pointed toward the capitol building, "you'll find Pennsylvania Avenue, and it'll lead you straight up to the president's house and Treasury Building. You'll have to go around them, but if you find Pennsylvania Avenue again and just keep going on it, it'll take you all the way out to Georgetown. But it's a real long walk, ma'am. You might ought to hire you a hack."

Dismayed at the distance, Abigail thanked him, then gazed longingly at the cabs awaiting fares along the curb. She certainly didn't have any money to squander on such a luxury, so she set her chin at a particularly determined angle and pulled her worn black cape together at the throat. After a band of Sherman's men had torched her house, she had walked all the way from Richmond Hill to Savannah. Thirty miles, in December cold. And she had been exhausted then, too.

Taking a deep breath, she began to head in the direction the lad had indicated. If she ever again did have access to a nice, comfortable carriage, or to plenteous food and warm clothing, she would never, ever take such privileges for granted. She had come close to starving on that trek to Savannah. She had been reduced to begging for food from complete strangers.

From a hidden corner of her mind appeared the image of one man in particular, his face snarling and feral, just before she had pulled the trigger of her father's derringer. Oh, God, would she never be able to erase the horror of that moment? Would the shame and guilt never leave her? Her stomach knotted, and she swallowed down the nausea that crept up her throat each time she let herself remember what she had done that day.

Trudging along with renewed purpose, determined not to think about anything, she kept a wary eye on the dark clouds swarming in over the city in great black mounds, like wrathful warriors preparing to attack. The temperature was falling, the frigid breeze biting into Abigail's cheeks and snapping the hem of her cape.

Afraid she wasn't going to make it to the Georgetown address before the storm swept down on her, she increased her pace, eager now to reach the children. She skirted the big white mansion at the end of the street, looking up at the windows of the house where Abraham Lincoln had lived throughout the war years. He was dead now, too, assassinated: mourned by the North, hated by the South.

She walked past a building fronted by columns which she assumed to be the Treasury, then picked up Pennsylvania Avenue once more. The carriage and pe-

destrian traffic thinned out as she left the confines of
the city, and when she began to despair of ever reaching her destination, she finally reached the quiet village
with its prim streets and brick houses.

It took a while to find Cox's Row, but once there,
she hurried along its wide sidewalk, watching the
house numbers. At length, she found the two-story,
white brick town house with its raised stoop and beautiful stained-glass front door. Christopher's house, she
thought, distressed by the fierce longing that gripped
her. Oh, Christopher, she cried silently with the stabbing regret she thought she'd subjugated, why did
everything have to go so wrong?

Thunder growled threateningly, very close, and as
cold raindrops began to spatter on the pavement
around her, she hurried through the black iron front
gate.

From a spot in the bay window of the parlor, Joshua
kept his eyes on the woman in the black cape. She sure
was awful little for a grown-up lady, he thought as she
clanged the heavy gold knocker. She was soaked, too.
She didn't even have an umbrella or nothing, and it
was raining to beat the band. After another moment
of observation, his jaw went slack.

"Lucas, Lucas!" he cried, jumping down from the
window seat. "It's her! It's Cousin Abigail!"

"She got our letter, din't she?" Lucas yelled with an
ecstatic whoop. He spun around on one foot, knocking
down Katelyn, who'd picked up Jenky in her arms and
come running lickety-split to see the long-awaited lady
who was going to catch her uncle.

"And she's still purty, too!" Joshua cried gleefully,
rubbing out a bigger spot on the foggy windowpane.
"Just look how purty she is, even all soppin' wet with
that funny feather in her hat droopin' down over her
eyes! I tole you she was purty, din't I, Lucas, din't I?"

"Uncle Chris's gonna marry Cousin Abigail! Uncle
Chris's gonna marry Cousin Abigail!" Katelyn shrieked

in a tone so ear-threatening that Joshua cringed until his shoulders nearly touched his ears. Even her kitten was squirming to get away. Sometimes his sister's voice was shriller than the iron-works whistle downtown by the president's house. And she was being a big mouth already!

Sobering instantly, Joshua knelt beside his little sister and narrowed his eyes in his sternest look.

"Now you listen good, Katelyn. You ain't to say nuthin' to nobody 'bout Uncle Chris gettin' married to Cousin Abigail, you hear?"

"Why can't I say it?"

"'Cause neither one of 'm knows nuthin' about it yet, silly goose," he explained impatiently. "Instead, you gotta tell Cousin Abigail how lonely and sad you are. And cry sometimes, too, so she's sure to feel real sorry for us. Hey, maybe you oughta start bawlin' right off, the minute we open up the door for her." His face totally serious, he turned to Lucas. "What do you say 'bout that, Lucas?"

"Yep," Lucas agreed. "Cryin's good. But we got to hurry 'fore the maids comes in to answer the door! Cry, Katelyn! Hurry, so Cousin Abigail will get all choked up and be extra glad she came!"

"Uh uh." Katelyn crossed her arms and jutted out her dainty jaw. "I don't wanna cry. I is glad Cousin Abigail's here, so Uncle Chris won't be a batcher no more."

"But you *have* to!" Lucas hissed, his voice threaded with a hint of hysteria. "She's here! Din't you hear the door knocker clangin'?"

"No. I don't wanna cry," Katelyn repeated stubbornly.

"Aw, criminy, Katelyn, pleeese. I'll snitch some more cookies for you. A whole batch, and you can hide 'm and eat 'm in bed."

Katelyn considered the bribe, found it wanting, and shook her head, her long, blonde banana curls bobbing.

"Now what are we gonna do?" Lucas cried, wild-eyed with panic. "Cousin Abigail ain't gonna feel bad a'tall if none of us are sick or cryin' or nuthin' good like that!"

"I know what! You can do the cryin', Lucas!"

Lucas appeared mightily offended by Joshua's insulting suggestion. "Boys don't cry, not even when they're sick as sin."

Joshua frowned. He certainly didn't want to be a big crybaby in front of Cousin Abigail. "Well, I guess we could slap Katelyn." Dubiously, he eyed his little sister. "That oughta make her cry real quick."

"Or we could pinch her!" Lucas added.

Katelyn's little face screwed up and turned beet-red at the mere idea of such abuse. When she began a sloppy sob, Joshua and Lucas grinned in triumph, then raced each other to the front door.

Standing on the porch, wet and shivering with cold, Abigail was beginning to think no one was home. She was about ready to make her way around to the servants' entrance, when the big oak door was suddenly flung wide. Two fiery-haired little boys stood on the threshold, beaming huge welcoming smiles. She gasped in surprise as they catapulted against her, making her stumble backward.

"Cousin Abigail, we're so glad you're here!" cried one.

"We been waitin' for you ever' day!" cried the other.

Abigail laughed, delighted by her warm reception and truly happy to see the children again. She held the boys at arm's-length so she could look at them.

"Joshua, can that really be you? My gracious, you've grown so much. Why, you're almost as tall as I am. And you're so handsome with those big brown eyes of yours."

Abigail smiled at the way the nine-year-old's face darkened, making his abundant freckles blend into his embarrassed flush, but then he smiled the seraphic smile she remembered so well. Miriam's sons had always reminded her of tiny cherubs, with their coppery curls and big eyes. Lucas still held back, however, watching her shyly. Smiling, she took his hands and drew him closer.

"And you're Lucas, aren't you? I remember that the last time I visited you had a whole family of pigs in the barn. Do you still have them?"

"Yes, ma'am, we sure do," he answered, gazing up at her out of brown eyes lighter than those of his brother. "I reckon the ones you saw are all grown up to be big pigs now, but there's a new litter of piglets back at the farm for us to play with. Josh, he tole me you ain't afraid of pigs." His wide smile revealed a gap where two front teeth were missing.

Abigail hugged him tight, then looked around for the only one of Miriam's children she'd never met. "Now, where's little Katelyn? I've been anxious to meet her."

"She's in the parlor with her cat, Jenky," Joshua said, taking her hand. "C'mon, I'll show you."

In the next room behind a rose-sprigged sofa they found their sister, a forlorn little figure clutching her kitten and peeking at them over the curved back.

Abigail slipped out of her wet cape as she moved toward her. "Katelyn?" she said, kneeling beside the child.

"She's been cryin'," Lucas informed Abigail at once, coming up close beside them. "See, her cheeks are real wet. Just lookee at all these here tears she's been cryin'! Ain't it sad?" He wiped a finger down his sister's damp cheek and proudly held the wetness out for Abigail to examine. He grunted as Joshua's elbow landed ungently in his ribs.

"Ouch! What'd ya do that for, Josh?" Lucas scowled.

"What's the matter, my little precious?" Abigail was crooning, tenderly drying Katelyn's face with her handkerchief. "You can tell Cousin Abigail. Are you still feeling bad?"

"She's been real, real, real sick, and I mean real sick, too," Joshua answered in a hurry for fear his sister would spill the beans with that flappy mouth of hers.

Katelyn's huge blue eyes considered Abigail for a moment, than an expression of pure misery crumpled her face.

"You looks just likes my mama," she cried, her voice breaking into harsh sobs that quickly gained momentum and became full-fledged bawling. "I wants my mama to come back home! I don't wants her to be an angel and live up in heaven!"

Abigail's heart twisted, and she enfolded the child in a tender embrace, closing her eyes as Katelyn's thin arms squeezed tightly around her neck. Oh, thank God, she had come. They did need her, desperately.

"Hush, darling," she whispered through her own rush of tears. "I'm going to take care of you, I promise. Just like your mama would have wanted me to. We were very good friends, you know." She turned slightly to gather the two little boys in the circle of her arms. "Don't you worry, my little angels. Now that I'm here, you aren't alone anymore."

As she hugged them close, over her head Miriam's two freckle-faced sons exchanged smug grins. But their hard-earned triumph was short-lived, for only moments later a door slammed outside in the foyer, followed by a man's deep voice calling to the children.

"It's Uncle Chris!" Lucas shouted, pulling away from Abigail. "He's come home early, Josh! He's here!"

3

ABIGAIL'S entire body tensed. Her heart stopped for a fraction of a beat, then resumed with such a wild thudding that she was sure she'd collapse. She found she couldn't move a muscle, even as Joshua and Katelyn took off toward the foyer after Lucas at a full run. They met their uncle at the front door, screaming their welcome, and when she heard the familiar rumble of Christopher's laugh, involuntary shivers erupted, sending gooseflesh down her arms. Oh, Lord, it *was* him! After so long, what would he think when he saw her? What would he say? What would *she* say?

The children's joyous shouts continued, and Abigail took a deep breath to fortify herself. She *had* to compose herself. She had to face him. But his appearance was so unexpected. Why, she had barely set foot inside the door. Somehow she managed to force one foot in front of the other and approach the doorway, deliberately staying out of his line of vision.

She had often fantasized about such a meeting, trying to imagine how she might feel to see him again— the man she had once loved.

He was as lean and tall as she remembered, dressed now as a Union officer in a well-fitting, dark blue uniform, each broad shoulder decorated with fancy gold braid signifying his rank of major. While she watched, he swept off his plumed hat and performed an exaggerated bow for the children, then tossed the hat carelessly onto a chair beside the door.

His hair was longer than it had been the day they

214

had parted, curling almost to his collar. He seemed a lot taller than the six feet three inches she knew him to be. And he wore a beard now, as black as his hair and close-cropped around his chiseled chin and jaw in a style that accentuated his fine, aristocratic features. The children were still jumping up and down, and he grinned, stooping forward to hoist Katelyn into one arm.

"Don't get too excited, kids. I'm only here to collect a report I forgot this morning, but I am on leave all day tomorrow, so I thought we'd go cut a Christmas tree."

The second part of his announcement was met with a burst of wild approval, and Abigail wet her dry lips with the tip of her tongue, more drawn to the sight of him than she could ever have imagined. Her strong attraction after so long both startled and dismayed her.

Across the room, Joshua was frantically tugging on his uncle's coat sleeve. "Uncle Chris! We're so glad you came back early, 'cause we got a real big surprise for you! Just wait 'til you see what it is!"

"Well now, I just happen to like big surprises. Don't you, Katie-girl?" Christopher winked at Katelyn.

"Just lookee over there and see what you see!" Joshua grinned smugly and pointed at Abigail.

Abigail's breath caught as Christopher, smiling widely, Katelyn still in his arms, swung around to her. He froze, and Abigail watched his glad expression dissolve. Pure astonishment replaced it as all color drained from his handsome face. For what seemed an eternity, their eyes locked.

"See! It's Cousin Abigail, Uncle Chris!" Joshua cried, dancing around his uncle's long legs. "She's come for Christmas! Ain't it grand? And ain't she purty?"

Christopher still stared wordlessly at Abigail, and when she saw the children exchange worried glances, she forced herself to speak.

"Hello, Christopher," she said quietly, and was immediately appalled at how weak her voice sounded.

"Good God! Gail?" Christopher managed finally, not taking his eyes off Abigail as he put Katelyn down. He frowned slightly, and Abigail began to feel that something was wrong. Why did he look so shocked? Surely when he'd allowed the children to invite her he'd been prepared for the possibility that she would accept.

"I can't believe it's really you standing there," he said, then shook his head as if confused. "But I don't understand. What are you doing here?"

His question was the last one Abigail had expected. Surprised, she glanced at the children.

"Why, because Joshua invited me," she explained, then was mortified as the truth hit her like a mallet blow. "You did know I was invited, didn't you?"

"No, I did not," he answered, his brows drawing together as he turned to Joshua. "What's the meaning of this, Josh? Surely you didn't invite Cousin Abigail without telling me."

Joshua looked scared. "We sent her a letter and tole her to come for Christmas." The admission came reluctantly, and his next words were full of dismay. "Don't you like her at all?"

"He don't like Cousin Abigail?" Katelyn shrilled out in absolute horror. "Now what is we gonna do, Josh?"

Feeling like a complete fool, Abigail wished she could disappear. All three children looked frightened, and for good reason. A stern, displeased scowl had settled over Christopher's face. Silence reigned for a moment or two, until Abigail endeavored to speak.

"I'm sorry if I've inconvenienced you," she said to Christopher. "I understood the children were going to be here alone for the holidays. That's the reason I came so quickly. I realize now, of course, that I should have contacted you first."

"It's hardly your fault, Gail," Christopher said, her words obviously doing little to assuage his anger as he turned back to Joshua. "But you, young man, have a great deal of explaining to do. I cannot believe you'd do this without asking my permission." He paused, his fists on his hips. "Gail and I will have to decide what's to be done. Go on now, Josh, take your brother and sister up to the nursery. I'll speak to you in the morning."

Abigail watched Joshua hang his head, shamefaced, then take Katelyn by the hand. Sympathy coursed through her. Despite Christopher's calm rebuke, she was well aware that he was furious about her unexpected arrival, and judging from the looks on the children's faces, they all knew it. As they moved up the steps under a cloud of guilty gloom, she herself was not anxious to face Christopher alone.

"I feel very foolish and presumptuous," she began quietly. "I can't imagine why the children deceived us, but I'm sure they meant well."

Christopher shook his head. "Forgive me, my manners leave a lot to be desired. I didn't mean to sound as if you weren't welcome. I was just so startled to see you."

"That's understandable under the circumstances. I wouldn't have come, but I got the impression from Joshua's letter that they've been very lonely since their mother died."

"Yes, they have been. And I've been so busy with work that I'm sure they've felt neglected."

Their eyes met, and Abigail felt as if he'd reached out and touched her. Alarm bells pealed in her head as his black eyes delved into hers, so deeply that she feared he was reading her soul. She lowered her lashes, shocked at herself. She was glad when Christopher spoke because she found herself at a complete loss for words.

"Let's go into the parlor where we can sit down and talk. Would you like some tea?"

Abigail nodded, and when he moved toward the back of the house to summon a servant, she walked into the parlor, wishing she had not come. What had possessed her not to write back and verify the invitation? It just hadn't occurred to her that the children would act on their own behalf. She couldn't stay, of course. Not now.

She glanced out the windows. It was dark outside with cold rain pattering loudly against the windowpanes. Where on earth would she go so late? She had no money for a hotel or a room in a boardinghouse. She seated herself on a small silk settee near the crackling fire, feeling chilled both inside and out.

A moment later Christopher rejoined her, seating himself in a green brocade wing chair opposite her. For several long, uncomfortable minutes they each groped for something to say.

"You're looking well," he remarked at length.

Abigail knew he couldn't possibly mean that. She had caught sight of her damp, bedraggled appearance in the gold hall mirror.

"Thank you. I'm afraid I'm still a bit wet."

"I would have sent someone to meet you if I'd known you were coming. I'm sorry you had to wait for a hack in this weather. Usually the drivers at the depot hover like vultures around the new arrivals."

Abigail was reluctant to admit that she'd been forced to walk until a surge of pride stiffened her spine. "Actually, I walked here."

Christopher's concerned expression became one of incredulity. "You can't mean you walked here from downtown? By yourself?"

To her surprise, his astonishment amused Abigail. The Abigail he had known wouldn't have dreamed of walking anywhere, except perhaps to take a leisurely stroll through a garden. She wondered what he'd think if he knew all she had done to survive during the last four years. For the second time that day she was haunted by the face of that vile Yankee . . . She spoke hastily, wanting to banish the ghostly visage.

"I've grown accustomed to walking." She lifted one shoulder in a slight shrug. "Few of us in Georgia have carriages anymore, or anything else of value." Although she hadn't meant to sound bitter, she did.

Abruptly, Christopher rose and moved to the hearth. She watched him bend to stoke the fire. When the flames were jumping and darting, he turned back to face her.

"I heard about Richmond Hill, Gail. I'm very sorry it was destroyed. I know how much you loved it."

Abigail looked down at her lap, endeavoring to hide her pain. "How did you know?"

"After the war ended I made inquiries through army channels. I was concerned about you and your family." He hesitated before his gaze captured hers. "All I could learn was that the plantation had been burned to the ground. No one knew what had become of you, your father, or your brother."

"Papa and Ralph are both dead," she murmured, fighting to control the emotion that threatened her voice. "They were both killed in the fighting."

"Gail, I'm so sorry—"

Unable to bear speaking of her grief—she hadn't since her father had died during the siege of Atlanta—Abigail rose, suddenly afraid. She felt so sad, so vulnerable. Uncomfortable now that the conversation had turned personal, she changed the subject. "I really shouldn't intrude on you any longer," she began hastily, anxious to get away. "You weren't expecting me, and I know my presence here is a terrible inconvenience—"

"Nonsense. It's late and pouring rain outside. You'll stay here tonight. I insist. The children are obviously eager to have you, and there's more than enough room."

Abigail hesitated, harboring distinct reservations about remaining in Christopher's house where she would be in such close proximity to him.

"I'm not sure that would be entirely proper, my staying in your house and—"

"Please don't concern yourself about that. I'll stay elsewhere tonight."

"But that would be putting you out."

"It won't be any trouble. I often stay at my officers' club if I have a late night." He paused. "But I'm afraid I have to leave now. I have an important conference with the president, and I'm already late."

"I understand."

Their gazes held briefly, then separated when a heavy-set, older woman hurried into the room carrying a tray laden with tea and biscuits.

Christopher rose. "Mrs. Abernathy, allow me to present Miss Abigail King. She'll be staying the night. You will make her comfortable, won't you?"

"Yes, sir, I surely will. The children are just thrilled she's come to visit."

"Yes, I know," Christopher answered, looking apologetic as he glanced back at Abigail. "I really have to go, but I'll be back tomorrow. We can discuss your visit further then. Is that agreeable?"

"Yes, thank you."

"Good night, then." He turned to his housekeeper. "Mrs. Abernathy, would you see that some of my clothes and necessary toilet articles are packed and sent over to my officers' club? I'll be staying there tonight. Now, I imagine Gail would like to rest. She's come a long way."

Abigail watched him leave the room. When the front door closed behind him, her shoulders relaxed for the first time since he had entered the house. Seeing him again had been much more of an ordeal than she'd expected, but at the moment she was so exhausted that she was more than willing to follow Christopher's friendly housekeeper up the steps to a nice soft bed, where she could forget all her troubles in welcome sleep.

4

AT half past eight o'clock the following morning, Christopher Wright let himself into the front foyer of his town house. Glancing toward the parlor, he mentally reviewed his uncomfortable interview with Abigail the night before. The whole situation still seemed unreal. Never in his life had he expected to find her in his house again. He was still partially in shock, but immeasurably relieved to find her alive and well. He had feared the worst when his inquiries into her whereabouts had led nowhere.

All through the night at his officers' club, he'd lain awake staring at the ceiling and thinking how Joshua had unwittingly brought Abigail back into his life. Now he was trying hard to decide just how he did feel at seeing her again, having her near.

Four years ago he had loved her to distraction. He had wanted to marry her more than anything he had ever wanted in his life. But the war had ended their betrothal, abruptly and without warning.

Christopher's mouth thinned into an ironic twist. If Beauregard had fired upon Fort Sumter one month later, in May instead of April, his wedding to Abigail would have already taken place. She would have spent the war safely in his house in Pennsylvania with Miriam and the children. One month more, thirty damn days, and she would have been his wife for the last four years. More than anything else, that thought twisted through him, as corrosive as acid.

At first, in the days right after her father had called

off the engagement, he had been so furious he had refused to accept that their relationship was over. He had thought about her constantly, worried about her, wondered where she was and who she was with. But when long years had dragged by with no word from her or about her, his own weariness and disillusionment with the war had worn down the edge of his anger into a sad, wistful longing for what could have been, what should have been.

"Good morning, Major. You're back early this morning."

As Mrs. Abernathy came forward from the back hallway, Christopher shrugged out of his heavy wool military greatcoat.

"Yes. Did everything go well? I mean, did Miss King get settled in comfortably?"

"Oh, yes, sir. That poor little wisp of a thing was thoroughly exhausted. Did you know she actually walked all the way here? Lawsy me, I was just shocked to hear that."

"So was I. Is she up yet?"

"Oh, yes. She's been in the nursery nearly all morning long. I declare, it's been many a day since I've seen those children so happy."

"Is that where they are now?"

"Yes, sir."

"Thank you, Mrs. Abernathy."

Mocking his own rush of eagerness, Christopher took the stairs three at a time and paused at the newel post on the second-floor landing. A burst of children's laughter floated down the quiet hall, and he went quickly to the open nursery door.

Abigail sat cross-legged before the warm hearth, the children gathered around her. She was telling them a story, using her hands and voice to enliven the tale, her animation far different from the quiet, wary demeanor she'd exhibited the previous evening. This was the real Abigail, he thought, the woman he remembered so well.

Grateful for an opportunity to look at her without her being aware, he stood unmoving, examining her face. She looked better this morning, rested and refreshed. Last night he'd been concerned at her weary, travel-worn appearance. Now, as his gaze slid down over her black silk dress, he realized she had lost a lot of weight. Her thinness made her petite build seem even more fragile. But her beauty remained undiminished—her small, exquisitely sculptured face was lovely, her fair skin still smooth and flawless. Her thick golden hair was caught up in a black velvet snood in a style she had often worn before the war.

A treasured memory crept like a phantom mist across his mind, and he held her hand again in the privacy of a white latticed gazebo hidden among the tall, fragrant pines of Richmond Hill. She had been seventeen, he twenty-six, when they'd sat there together, the sweet scent of trailing honeysuckle perfuming the warm June evening. She had permitted him to tug a similar hair net free and gather her soft, shiny hair into his hands. How he had savored the texture, so like the finest Chinese silk. He had kissed her for the first time that summer evening, and from the moment his lips had touched hers and he'd felt them tremble, his desire had been confirmed.

How many times during the long dark days of fighting and killing had he lain on the cold hard ground, wrapped in his bedroll, hungering to touch her, to stroke her satiny skin and twine his fingers through her finespun golden hair? Although he had hidden the pain of their separation deep in his heart, his mind had rebelled, plaguing his sleep with sweet, honeysuckle-fragrant dreams of their time together.

"And then the handsome prince married the beautiful princess," Abigail was finishing with a smile, "and as they rode away on his big white horse to start a wonderful life in their new kingdom, all the townsfolk cheered and showered them with wildflowers because they were very, very happy that the evil king was no more."

As Joshua and Katelyn continued to gaze wide-eyed at Abigail, still caught in the story's spell, Lucas spoke, his face serious. "How many days did it take the beautiful princess to catch that handsome prince? Did it take more than a week and five days, do you reckon?"

Christopher smiled, but Abigail answered with utmost solemnity.

"Well, Lucas, I'm not sure how many days it took, but it doesn't really matter because true love always wins out in the end."

"Maybe that prince and princess will ride that big white horse to our house and adopt us, so we can have a mama and papa again," Katelyn whispered hopefully. Abigail drew Katelyn close and kissed the soft blonde curls atop her head.

Joshua, however, was quick to scoff at his sister's remark. "Don't be a numskull, Katelyn. That's just a made-up story, like the ones Mama used to tell us. There ain't no real prince or princess. It's all just a bunch of pretend. Ain't that so, Cousin Abigail?"

"I'm afraid so, darling." Abigail's voice softened as Katelyn's face fell. "But you mustn't feel as if you haven't got any family. I'm here, aren't I? And I love all of you very much."

"And so do I." Christopher spoke up, making his presence known.

As Abigail swung around to face him, Christopher stared like a man mesmerized into her wide, limpid eyes as deep and silver as summer moonlight. Desire, swift and powerful, threatened to overwhelm him as she rose quickly to her feet.

"We didn't hear you come in," she murmured, patting her full silk skirt into more ladylike folds. Christopher's gaze lingered on her slender hands. Her nails were short, as if she was used to hard work, and he realized once again that the war years had not been easy for her. The thought of her suffering, perhaps alone and afraid, pierced him with a new kind of pain, and he fought the desire to ask her where she had been all this time, what hardships she had endured.

"That's because I just got here," he answered instead. When he glanced at the children, they had hopped up as well and were staring at him with obvious wariness—except for Katelyn, who was skipping happily over to him, her arms outstretched. "Are you still mad at us, Uncle Chris?" she asked.

The devil himself could not have refused her, and Christopher smiled, swinging her up into his arms. "No, I'm not angry. But"—he captured Joshua's gaze—"you're never to invite anyone here again without asking me first. Understood?"

"Yes, sir." Joshua's long-drawn-out sigh plainly indicated that he'd expected a much sterner dressing-down for his crime.

"Then can Cousin Abigail stay for Christmas? Pease, can she? Pease, Uncle Chris?" Katelyn begged, placing her palms on either side of his bearded jaw and forcing it around so she could peer into his face. "She tells us the bestest stories, and she's gonna be the princess! Josh says so! So does Lucas!"

When Christopher raised his gaze to Abigail, a heated blush had already climbed halfway up her cheeks. He laughed.

"I suppose that whether Gail stays with us or not is up to her. She's certainly more than welcome to spend the holidays here."

His two nephews immediately clutched Abigail's hands and began such an enthusiastic petition that she finally nodded her head.

"All right, I guess so," she said. "If you're sure you don't mind," she said to Uncle Chris.

"I'm pleased to have you," he answered with great understatement. To hide the storm of relief hurtling through him, he turned to the children. "Didn't I mention something about fetching a Christmas tree today? Run, get your coats and mittens, and we'll find a big one. And don't forget your caps! The rain turned into snow during the night."

Squealing with delight, the three little ones flew from the room, leaving Abigail and Christopher to share a smile. Again, Christopher was struck by an uncharacteristic and very disconcerting shyness now that he was alone with her.

"You're coming, too, aren't you?" he asked. "The children will be disappointed if you don't."

"I'd like to," she answered simply, and further conversation between them was effectively curtailed as the children burst back into the room, eager to get started.

After spending several minutes buttoning wool jackets, wrapping knitted mufflers around pulled-up collars, and securing furry hats beneath chins, Abigail followed Christopher and her three young cousins across the long, narrow, snow-crusted lawn stretching behind the house. A thick wooded tract lay on the other side of the wood-slatted back fence, barely visible through the softly falling snow. The morning air seemed hushed and muffled by low-hanging gray clouds, and Abigail breathed deeply, invigorated by the crisp, cold air.

A few yards in front of her, Christopher turned and waited for her while the kids scampered ahead, the boys bending to scoop up snow, then tossing snowballs at each other.

"Are you warm enough?" Chris asked when she caught up to him.

Hot color warmed Abigail's cold cheeks as he eyed her thin wrap, the black fabric shiny with age, but she gathered her pride and smiled. "I'm just not used to such chilly weather. Why, I guess I haven't played in the snow since I spent Christmas with you at Oak Haven—"

Abruptly, she cut off the words, her teeth catching on her lower lip. Their eyes held for a brief moment as they silently shared a fond memory. On that Christmas Eve, kneeling before her at the base of a twenty-foot, candle-lit Christmas tree, Christopher had asked her to marry him. Not a single Christmas had passed since then but what Abigail hadn't remembered his loving proposal and yearned for the contentment she'd felt that night enfolded in his strong embrace.

"That was a long time ago," Christopher said quietly, his face somber. "How could we have known then how quickly things would change?"

His ebony eyes bore into hers, and Abigail fought her desire to lay her head against the solid wall of his chest the way she used to do. She wanted to be comforted, to share the regret that suddenly overwhelmed her. Her pulse lurched into a powerful cadence as he raised his hand and gently brushed snow from her cheek, his warm fingertips lingering against her cold skin.

Oh, Lord, I still care about him, she thought, terrified by the realization and the way her heart was slamming against her rib cage. Always, from the first day they had met, his mere touch had left her giddy. She felt breathless, her emotions roaring like a runaway train, and she realized she wanted him to kiss her. The spell snapped like a dry twig as Lucas's shout rang out from somewhere ahead of them.

"We're coming!" Christopher called back, withdrawing his hand and taking Abigail's elbow.

She tried to get a grip on herself, horrified by her weakness. She had thought her attraction to him would have faded by now, just as some of her memories of their courtship had begun to dim. But now, being with him, talking with him, their engagement seemed like yesterday. It wasn't yesterday, she told herself firmly. It was a very long time ago, and Christopher was now a different man. She had noticed that at once.

His demeanor was more serious and dignified than it had been before. Occasionally she caught glimpses of a deeper sadness in his eyes. There was a faint vertical indentation between his brows, as if he frowned often. What had etched that line there? Had he, too, suffered during the war?

Swallowing convulsively, she cursed the stupid war and all the grief it had caused. She was glad when Katelyn came running back to tell her about the beautiful spruce tree they'd chosen. Abigail took the child's hand, glad to be able to concentrate on less painful thoughts.

Later that evening the family gathered in the front parlor to decorate the tree. Surreptitiously, as he had all day long, Christopher watched Abigail's every movement. He wasn't certain he still loved her, but he sure as hell wasn't indifferent to her. Good God, he thought with self-disgust, he had trouble keeping his eyes off her for even five minutes at a time.

Despite his inner chagrin, he hazarded yet another glance across the room to where Abigail sat on the rose-covered, camel-backed sofa, helping Katelyn string fluffy white popcorn. Annoyed with himself, he steadfastly forced his concentration back to the task of setting in a large wooden bucket the full, heavy-branched ten-foot spruce with its heavy ball of roots and dirt. Not far from him, Joshua and Lucas were whispering together like a pair of conspirators. They'd been peering periodically across the room at Abigail, too, and suddenly they sidled up to where Christopher continued to wrestle with the uncooperative evergreen.

"You know what I think, Uncle Chris?" Joshua ventured, lowering his voice. He glanced toward the sofa. "I think Cousin Abigail's 'bout the nicest, kindest, sweetest lady I ever did see in my entire, whole, live-long life."

Christopher stopped manhandling the waving branches and fixed questioning eyes on Joshua. "Am I to take it that you like Gail, Josh?"

"Yessiree, we sure do," Lucas chimed in with whole-hearted agreement. "She's surely the most beautifulest and wonderfulest lady, and she's smart, too. And she likes animals, just like you do, Uncle Chris. Do you like her yet, Uncle Chris? Christmas is gettin' real close."

Christopher frowned, at a loss to figure out what Christmas had to do with him and Abigail, but his nephews were right to think that Abigail liked animals. Her affinity for horses was one of the first things he had noticed about her. He had first seen Abigail when he and his brother, John, had gone to Richmond Hill plantation to escort Miriam back to Oak Haven after an extended visit with her Southern kin. Miriam had met her husband at the front portico, but Christopher had taken their mounts around back to the stables.

He had barely dismounted there when Abigail had come rushing out of the stalls, frantically grabbing his arm and pulling him after her. Inside, a mare was laboring to give birth, and together with a groom they had worked to deliver the colt. It had been an exciting, moving experience. Even at sixteen, she had been the prettiest, the most intriguing girl he'd ever met, and within a month, he had asked her father for permission to court her.

The boys were still watching him expectantly, and he grinned to think of how eager they were for him to like Abigail. If they only knew. "Well, I suppose I like her as much as you do."

"Oh, boy, oh, boy, things are cookin' now!" Lucas cried, clapping his hands until Joshua gave him a shove.

"Don't fight, boys. You'll knock over the tree, and I'm having enough trouble getting it to stand up straight." Christopher told them. "There, I guess it'll stay put now." He let go to make sure, and when the spruce quivered then held, he nodded, satisfied. "All right, that's done. Why don't we go help Gail and Katelyn make the ornaments?"

The boys had no objection to the idea and ran ahead, kneeling around the low table where Abigail had begun to cut out paper angels. Sitting on the sofa across from

her, Christopher watched her carefully turn a stiff sheet
of white paper in her slender hands as she snipped out
the intricate pattern. Her delicate blonde brows were
drawn together in concentration, but Christopher's
eyes were dragged inexorably to her full pink lips,
pursed slightly as she labored. His gaze riveted there
as if fused, and he remembered how soft her lips had
felt beneath his, how sweet they'd tasted, and, even
more distressing, how she had moaned in soft surrender each time he had stolen a kiss.

When Abigail suddenly looked up and caught him
in his keen-eyed scrutiny, Christopher jerked his gaze
away as guiltily as if he'd been caught leering through
her bedchamber window. He was inordinately pleased
when Mrs. Abernathy called the children to help her
decorate the sugar cookies she had just taken from the
oven. They obliged with all due haste, accompanying
her to the long table in the adjoining dining room,
giving Christopher a chance to be alone with Abigail
for the first time all day. He had never seen anything
like it; the children had clung to her from morning to
night, as if sewn to her skirts.

"The angels look very nice," he commented, striving
for some neutral topic with which to open the conversation. He picked up the one she had just finished and
pretended to examine it.

"Thank you. Mama taught me how to draw them
when I was little. Ralph and I used to make them every
Christmas . . ."

Her voice trailed away, and Christopher immediately
regretted initiating a subject that reminded her of her
brother.

"I'll cut one out for you if you like."

His offer earned him a surprised look, followed by
a grateful smile.

Inordinately glad to have pleased her, he accepted
the shears she held out. "The children are thrilled to
have you here. They haven't been so happy in ages."

"Perhaps that's because you're with them, too."

"I know. I regret having had to leave them alone so much lately, but I can't neglect my work. It's too important. We're trying our best to get Lincoln's plan for reconstruction of the Union through Congress before Thaddeus Stevens and his Radical Republicans totally alienate the South with their harshness."

Abigail stared down at the angel in her hand, but her scissors remained idle. "I think it will be difficult to reestablish the Union. People are still very bitter, especially in Georgia." Her fragile jaw went hard. "What Sherman did to us was too cruel to forget or forgive."

All at once the bottom seemed to drop out of Christopher's stomach. Oh, God, she'd hate him when she learned of his own association with William Sherman. And he couldn't blame her. Sometimes he hated himself for the things he'd been forced to do.

For an instant he faced the phantoms he'd tried hard to forget—southern civilians, watching, weeping, as he ordered their homes set afire. Had Abigail stood and watched Richmond Hill blacken and crumble under the flames? He had no idea where she'd been or what she'd been doing. Suddenly, he felt he had to know.

"It's been nearly a year since Richmond Hill was burned, Gail," he said gently. "Where have you been? What have you been doing?"

She was silent at first, her long dark lashes shielding her eyes. "I've been living in Savannah."

She didn't want to discuss it, Christopher perceived at once. She was hiding something painful.

"Alone?"

"No, I've been living there with a friend of the family. You wouldn't know him."

"A man?" he asked quickly, appalled at his intense, irrational jealousy.

"Yes. Robert's an old friend of my father's from the legislature down in Milledgeville. He gave me a room in the back of his newspaper office and let me work as a typesetter. I don't know what I would have done without his help. I had nowhere else to go."

"You could have come to me."

"Could I have?" Slowly, she raised her face, her silver eyes shadowed with sadness. "I didn't think you'd want to hear from me again after I broke off our engagement. I wasn't sure how you'd feel."

"I imagine I felt the same way you did."

Eyes averted, she was quiet for a moment, then she spoke, her voice barely audible. "Then you must have felt like dying."

The sorrow in her voice was like living pain, and Christopher reached out to her, placing his hand over hers.

"Yes, that's exactly how I felt."

A glimmer of tears shone in her eyes, then she withdrew her hand and stood, impatiently wiping away the wetness with the back of her wrist. Christopher remained where he was as she moved toward the children.

Abigail had been in his house for only one day, and already he knew that he still cared for her very deeply. But how did she feel about him? And even if they could bridge the long years of separation, would Abigail want to reconcile when she learned he'd served under Sherman in Georgia? He ought to tell her the truth, he knew that full well. Now, without a moment's delay.

But God help him, he couldn't bear the thought of her looking at him with hatred in her eyes. Not yet, not before they had at least a chance to get to know each other again. Later, when the time was right, he would find the best way to make her understand. Sighing, he stood and went to join the others in the dining room.

5

"Look, Cousin Abigail, right there in the window by the red and blue spinning top—see, that's the baby doll I want! See her yellow hair and fancy dress? Ain't she the bestest thing you ever did see?"

"Yes, she is perfectly lovely," Abigail agreed, dutifully admiring the ruffled pink and white creation in the display case of Theodore Berry's mercantile establishment. "I can certainly see why you want her."

"And I been so good. I know St. Nick'll bring her to me!"

Abigail laughed at the way Katelyn was jumping up and down in anticipation. She was glad that Christopher had insisted that she join him and the children in a Christmas shopping excursion. She exchanged a significant look with Christopher, who had already brought home the identical doll the day before. As the little girl pressed her nose against the glass and peered enraptured at the delicate porcelain toy, Abigail smiled inwardly, relishing the idea of Katelyn's delight come Christmas morning.

Gazing through the shop window again, she realized how happy and light-hearted she had felt since she had arrived in Washington several days ago. The children had been adorable, so openly joyous to have her with them that they glowed with excitement.

Even she and Christopher were beginning to relax in each other's company. At first, they had been so stiff and self-conscious, so afraid they'd say or do the wrong thing, that it seemed they were tiptoeing around each other on eggshells.

Abigail wondered if he was grappling with emotions similar to hers. Most of the time, she wasn't sure how she felt, and she was increasingly afraid to find out. Often, she caught him watching her, his eyes filled with the same look of longing as when they were engaged. But if he still had such feelings for her, he didn't show them overtly. Instead, he always glanced away, as if mentally distancing himself from her.

Perhaps his caution was for the best. Both of them were very different people now. Certainly they were no longer a young, innocent couple, head over heels in love. They had chosen opposite sides in the war, believed in different principles. He had won; she had lost. In truth, everyone had lost.

"Shall we browse for a while?" Christopher asked, leaning close, his proximity arousing in her a heightened awareness that made her shiver. She almost trembled as he took her hand and tucked it securely in the crook of his arm.

The snow was like soft white down, sifting lightly all around them as they followed the children down the crowded sidewalk, while dray horses struggled to pull freight wagons and carriages through the thick mud and dirty slush of Pennsylvania Avenue. Abigail gazed down the street at the three- and four-story buildings fronting the wide avenue, thinking again that Washington seemed brash and upstart after the ancient, tree-lined streets and old iron-galleried houses of Savannah. And the snow! Abigail had never experienced so much cold weather! But she loved the wintry landscape, the tree branches bending low under loads of snow and huge windblown drifts lying up against the windows and porches. White rooftops with black smoke curling from their tall chimneys reminded her of pictures in her childhood storybooks.

They window-shopped for a time, strolling along past the storefronts with their green awnings and gold-lettered signs, all festively bedecked for the holiday season with swags of thick, fragrant pine boughs. Sprays of evergreen draped doors and lined windows, and showy red and green bows were tied around the lampposts. Tiny silver bells tinkled each time customers entered the shops, and many establishments prominently displayed a scene of the nativity. One, in a tobacconist store, particularly intrigued Abigail, enough to cause her to linger for a while so that she could admire the miniature figures of Mary and Joseph kneeling reverently before a manger.

As the December twilight thickened over the narrow brick sidewalk still bustling with holiday shoppers, they paused before a dressmaker's shop where Abigail gazed with wistful yearning at a lovely midnight-blue evening gown displayed on a dressmaker's form. Lush velvet fell in graceful folds with black lace inserts caught up in draped scallops and tied over the small bustle by a stylish black satin bow with trailing streamers.

Abigail tried in vain to remember the last time she had even seen such a beautiful ball gown. Certainly not since the Confederates had fired on Fort Sumter and Federal gunboats had begun the blockade of the Confederate coastline that had continued throughout the war. Foodstuffs and other necessities were still hard to come by in the South, lavish velvet and satin ball gowns impossible to obtain.

"You're drooling over the dress just like Katelyn did over the doll."

Abigail had to laugh at Christopher's observation. "It is splendid, isn't it? The dress shops were empty during the war. Not even day dresses were available—"

Her words faltered, and as it did each time the subject of the war came up, a vague sense of unease settled like an imaginary wall between them.

"Chris! Wait!"

The feminine voice brought them both swinging

around. A pretty young woman was rushing headlong toward them, hurrying around treacherous patches of ice on the sidewalk. Somehow, she made it safely to them, and laughed up into Christopher's eyes, her youthful face flushed with becoming color. She was a good bit taller than Abigail and was elegantly attired in a fashionable mauve velvet cloak, the hood and cuffs lined with soft ermine. The curly dark brown hair on her forehead was artfully frizzled, and a matching pink velvet bonnet set at a jaunty angle flattered her fair skin and hazel eyes. She couldn't be more than sixteen or seventeen, Abigail decided.

"Christopher Wright, where have you been keeping yourself? You haven't come to visit all week! Papa's quite annoyed with you, you know, and so am I!"

Abigail looked elsewhere as Christopher's friend clung to his arm. To her chagrin, she was both irritated and hurt by his familiarity with the woman, and she wondered if they were courting. It's none of your business, she told herself firmly, then made as if to move toward the children, who were clustered around a baker's establishment, eyeing the confectionary delights. Christopher, however, effectively prevented her escape by firmly catching hold of her elbow.

"Wait, Gail, I want to introduce you to a friend of mine. This is Miss Katherine Ladyman. Her father is a colleague on the president's staff. Katherine, allow me to present Miss Abigail King."

"How do you do, Miss Ladyman," Abigail murmured politely, and watched surprise fill Katherine's greenish-brown eyes.

"Why, you're a Southerner! I can tell from your accent!" she exclaimed as if truly horrified by the realization.

Christopher didn't hide his displeasure over Katherine's comment, but his tone was politely civil. "That's right, Katherine. Abigail's from Georgia. She's my guest and will be visiting us through the holidays."

Katherine's face quite clearly revealed her dismay at

the news. She surveyed Abigail with new interest, then returned all her attention to Christopher.

"I see. Well, I just wanted to make sure you still plan to attend our holiday ball on Christmas Eve. Everyone will be there. Even the president himself is expected. It's sure to be a wonderful evening!"

Breathlessly, she waited for his reply, and Abigail remembered a time when she had hung on Christopher's every word in a similar fashion. Katherine Ladyman was in love with him; Abigail knew it at once.

"Actually, I doubt I'll be able to attend now that Gail's here, but I do appreciate the invitation," Christopher was saying.

Katherine's alarm registered first, followed swiftly by disappointment, all of which Abigail could read on her face as easily as newsprint. Then the girl turned to her. "Then you must bring Miss King with you. By all means, we'd love to have her, of course."

Although the words were uttered with a good deal of feeling, Abigail wondered how much sincerity lay behind the invitation.

"That's very kind," Abigail murmured courteously, not eager to attend any such party.

But before she could formulate a gracious decline, Christopher said, "Thank you, Katherine, we'll be delighted to come. Please give my regards to your father."

"Oh, I will. Now don't change your mind, you hear? We're all expecting you. Papa's waiting for me now in the carriage, so I really do have to run. I'll see you next Sunday night at ten, don't forget!"

Then she was gone, leaving Christopher and Abigail to watch her scurry toward a fine, black-lacquered carriage waiting at the next intersection.

Christopher shook his head. "I do believe Katherine is the most scatterbrained young woman I've ever met."

"She seemed pleasant enough," Abigail lied, not at all sure Katherine Ladyman was nice.

"She's all right, I suppose." He smiled down at her.

"You don't mind going to the ball with me, do you? It's an important social event here in Washington, and I really should make an appearance. But if you think you'd feel uncomfortable, I'll send my regrets."

Abigail imagined herself in a glittering ballroom waltzing in Christopher's arms, laughing and having a good time. She loved parties and dancing, but here in the North she was an outsider, still the enemy. And Katherine had recognized her origins from the first word she had uttered.

"Come with me, Gail, please," he implored. "I really think you'll enjoy yourself."

Abigail found it hard to resist him when he smiled warmly at her, his dark eyes earnest. She wavered, unsure how she would fare among his Yankee friends. "I don't know if I should. Do you think the children would mind?"

"I think the children will have only one thing on their minds on Christmas Eve—Saint Nicholas."

His grin was the slow, infectious one she had always loved so much, and Abigail couldn't help but smile back. "All right, if you're sure you want me to."

"I want you to, believe me, but you'll have to have something formal to wear. We'll go back and get the blue dress you liked so much."

"Oh, no! I couldn't let you do that!"

"Why not?"

"Well, because it's not a proper gift."

"It's more than proper since you're only going to the ball as a favor to me. The least I can do is supply a suitable gown for you to wear. We'll call it a Christmas present from the children, if that will make you feel better."

Without waiting for her answer, he called to the children, then Abigail felt herself being pulled along beside him. She knew full well she shouldn't accept such a personal present from a gentleman, but as they approached the display window, and she saw how beautiful the gown was, her good intentions took an abrupt backward slide. Just this once, she thought, perhaps it wouldn't hurt to accept Christopher's generosity, especially since he was so insistent. After all, it was Christmas. She smiled ruefully at her own illogic and let herself be drawn into the dressmaker's shop.

"Where we gonna find that mistletoe stuff anyways, Josh?" Lucas asked, scooping up a handful of snow. He slapped it between his palms, shaping it into a good-sized ball which he sent in a long, spiralling arc toward the stable doors. He watched it splat, then hurried to catch up with his brother at the edge of the woods behind the house.

"It grows way up there." Joshua said, pointing at the tree branches high above their heads. "Papa used to shoot it down for Mama when he went huntin' back home. And he tole me hisself that it's magic or somethin' 'cause when a man gets some and hangs it over a lady's head, they always wanna kiss and stuff. I seen it done a bunch of times, and it works real good, too."

"Sure sounds awful dumb to me, Josh."

"Me, too, but it does work. Guess it's kinda like catnip is to cats, and you know how crazy Jenky acts when we pick a bunch of that and let her roll around on it. I guess grown-ups act like that with that mistletoe stuff."

"Do they roll around on it, too?"

Joshua looked disgusted. "'Course not. They just kiss and giggle and act real silly."

"Oh."

"Anyways," Joshua went on, "it's the only thing I can think up to make Uncle Chris kiss Cousin Abigail. And he's sure to like it lots 'cause you know how good she always smells when she kisses us good night. And her face's real soft and smooth, too, just like Katelyn's. Uncle Chris ain't one not to notice stuff like that."

"What do this kissin' weed look like?"

"I forget exactly. Just look up in the branches for something green. There oughta be some hangin' around somewheres. But we got to hurry 'fore Uncle Chris takes Cousin Abigail off to that big fancy party tonight.''

Just after nine on Christmas Eve, Christopher pulled his heavy gold pocket watch from the inside breast pocket of his black evening jacket, clicked it open, and checked the hands, then glanced yet again up the curving staircase. Abigail wasn't late, but he was afraid she might change her mind at the last minute. She was obviously reluctant to accompany him to the Ladymans', and he had barely been able to persuade her to accept his gift of the blue velvet gown.

During his visits to Richmond Hill during their betrothal she had worn a beautiful gown of a different vibrant hue every night, each one in the height of fashion. Now she owned only a handful of dresses, all the same mourning black worn for her father and brother, and all old and threadbare. She had lost everything—her family, her home, her whole way of life—and with each passing day, Christopher was more eager to provide her with all that and more, beginning with the blue dress she had wanted so much.

Dread assailed him, curling over him like a huge, sluicing wave. Would she ever accept even one gift from him once she learned of his part in Sherman's Atlanta campaign? He had to tell her, the sooner the better, but how could he? They were still too tentative in dealing with each other. He didn't want to risk pushing her away, not until they had time to decide how they felt about each other. Inwardly, he mocked himself for being a fool. He already knew damn well how he felt.

"Uncle Chris! Come see Cousin Abigail!".

Katelyn's excited shriek brought Christopher's head around. Abigail stood on the stairs above him, the three children behind her. He stared at her, his timepiece held forgotten in his hand.

The dress could have been created exclusively for

her, the lustrous blue a perfect complement to her blonde beauty. Her hair was caught up in an elegant French twist, the silky strands interwoven with the white rosebuds he had sent up earlier with the children. Long white gloves encased her bare arms, and her shoulders gleamed like fine alabaster in the lamplight. Never had he seen her look so lovely, not even on the night of their engagement party when she had worn pale yellow lace and he had sworn she was beautiful beyond compare.

"Don't she look plum grand?" Joshua cried. He wore an exceedingly smug look on his face, as if he was single-handedly responsible for Abigail's ravishing appearance.

"She certainly does," Christopher agreed, slipping his watch back into his pocket and moving to the bottom of the stairs.

As Abigail descended, he realized he was smiling up at her like a besotted fool. Despite his unwavering fascination with her, his attention was momentarily distracted by his nephews. They stood behind Abigail, presenting Christopher with the most ridiculous display of exaggerated winks and silly grins that he'd ever witnessed. Then, to his utter amazement, Joshua dug something wilted and green from his pocket and waved it back and forth over Abigail's head, as if he were conjuring up some magical spell, while Lucas pointed at her and urgently beckoned Christopher forward. Nonplussed by their actions, Christopher shook his head.

"I give up, boys. Why are you swinging that dead ivy around?"

"Uncle Chris!" Lucas accused sternly. "You just ruined everything!"

"That ain't no dead ivy!" Katelyn cried, her yellow curls bouncing as she leaned over the banister. "It's missy toes!"

"We got it so you can kiss Cousin Abigail anytime you want to, and she'll like it." Joshua explained in slow, succinct syllables, as if his uncle were very, very dense.

Grinning, Christopher looked up at Abigail as a crimson flush colored her high, delicate cheekbones.

"Joshua!" she murmured, mortification hoarsening her voice. "What in heaven's name are you thinking of?"

"Kiss her, kiss her!" Joshua shrieked.

"Go ahead, you'll like it!" Lucas predicted just as loudly.

Despite the small, enthusiastic audience eagerly clustering around to watch, Christopher wasn't the least bit averse to the idea. He mounted one step so that their faces were level. Though Abigail smiled, she looked afraid. His gaze lowered to her mouth, found the full softness of her lower lip trembling, and felt his blood heat and surge in a racing, rushing flood through his veins. Swallowing around a hard lump in his throat, he realized how long it had been, how many times he had dreamed of such a moment. As he brought his face closer to hers, her long lashes drifted down. When he finally felt the sweetness of her lips, his heart lurched as if jerked on a string, and though he knew he should not, he tasted them again, gently, his own self-control slipping as he became aware of the faint scent of honeysuckle in her hair.

The sound of the children laughing finally filtered through his clouded mind, and with extreme effort he drew back. Abigail opened her dreamy eyes, and he knew in the breath of a pulsebeat that he loved her, had always loved her.

Shocked by the force of his own realization, he turned and faced the children, trying hard to hide his inner turmoil.

"Better get to bed, kids. Christmas is tomorrow, remember?"

"Oh, we remember!" Katelyn cried, "and I'm gonna go right off to sleep, so it'll come sooner!"

With that, she raised the front of her long white

nightdress and tripped up the steps. The boys hesitated only long enough to yell good night to Abigail before they raced up the stairs after their sister.

"Shall we?" Christopher said, offering Abigail his arm. She had been as affected as he by their kiss, he could see it in her gray eyes. Suddenly, he felt exhilarated and optimistic, certain that they would have a second chance at love. When he led her outside to the carriage, she looked so warm and happy that he was even more confident that things were going to work out between them.

The elegant Ladyman mansion was located only a short carriage ride from Christopher's house, and was set amidst lush lawns along the banks of the Potomac. As they left the winding drive and the huge house appeared, the windows glowing with welcoming candlelight, Abigail was filled with trepidation. She shouldn't have come. She didn't know anyone, and all the guests would be Yankees.

Stiff with dread, she sat very still as they reached the massive front portico. Christopher stepped from the coach, then held out his hand to her. His strong fingers settled around hers, and she fought for control of her emotions, which had been spinning since he had kissed her. His lips had been gentle, undemanding, yet totally devastating. And what had he felt? He had turned away so quickly, while she had been breathless for long moments afterward.

"Are you all right, Gail?" he asked as they passed the columns and paused before the impressive double doors. "You're awfully quiet."

"I suppose I'm just a little nervous." She glanced back to where a long line of carriages stretched down the snowy drive. "There are so many people here."

"This is the event of the season. Just relax, Gail, and enjoy yourself. I'll introduce you to everyone."

Despite his reassurances, as they entered a wide central foyer extending toward the rear of the house Abigail wished she were back home with the children. A tall, handsome Negro servant dressed in spotless white livery took her silk cape and Christopher's top hat and gloves, and almost at once, Katherine Ladyman materialized from the crowd and looped her arm through Christopher's.

"Chris, you're late!" she scolded coquettishly. "Everybody's been asking about you."

Christopher smiled. "Sorry, Katherine, but I don't see anyone who seems unduly concerned about my late arrival."

Except for Katherine Ladyman, Abigail thought, immeasurably gratified when Christopher put his hand around her own waist and drew her close. Katherine didn't look nearly as pleased.

"Good evening, Miss King," was her courteous greeting, but her regard lingered on Abigail for only seconds. "I've saved you a waltz, Chris," She waved her lace-covered dance card with a smile of invitation.

"Perhaps later, Katherine. At the moment, I would be remiss to leave Gail on her own since she isn't yet acquainted with any of my friends. I'm sure you understand. Now, if you'll excuse us, I'll see if I can remedy that lack."

Katherine's mouth formed a pout, but Christopher didn't seem to notice. Purposefully, he guided Abigail toward the ballroom at the rear of the house, pausing often to introduce her to female acquaintances and fellow officers. Abigail made a resolute effort to be gracious, but more often than not, she detected a faint disapproval in people's eyes when they realized she was from the South, usually followed by an effort to hide their feelings out of respect for Christopher.

"Would you care to dance?" Christopher was asking.

Abigail nodded. She did love to dance, and as he smiled and took her in his arms, she was transported back in time to another night, another ball. He had been dressed in West Point gray, she in pale yellow lace with white daisies woven through her hair. She had gazed up at him and realized she was hopelessly in love . . . just as she was doing right now.

Christopher was glad to see Abigail looking so happy. More than anything, he wanted her to have a good time tonight. He longed to hear her laugh, easily and often, the way she used to. Since she had come back to him, a specter of sorrow had haunted her gray eyes, and he wanted to banish that look forever.

Even now, as he held her lightly in his arms and whirled her around in time to the lilting strains of the stringed orchestra, he detected a hint of melancholy shadowing her beautiful face. He hungered to draw her aside and kiss her until she forgot the past.

Gradually, as the evening progressed, Christopher noted with relief that Abigail seemed to relax and begin to enjoy herself. They danced nearly every dance and chatted with his friends between the sets. As he led her off the floor after one such waltz, Ben Carpenter, a young officer from his own staff, stopped him and requested the next dance with Abigail. Though Christopher was childishly reluctant to hand her over to the young adjutant, he stood back and watched as Ben twirled her gracefully around the polished parquet floor, Abigail's dress a blur of blue among the revolving dancers. He leaned back against a marble pillar, his gaze riveted on Abigail until Katherine Ladyman's voice intruded upon his thoughts.

"Do you really think it's a good idea to bring Miss King here tonight, Chris? There's a lot of talk about her being a Reb and all," she continued blithely. "Papa said such gossip will hurt you politically if you flaunt your association with her so soon after the war."

Coldly, Christopher disentangled his sleeve from her clutching fingers. "Abigail's my guest, Katherine. I won't stand here and let you insult her. Now, if you'll excuse me, Gail has promised me the next dance."

Katherine's face darkened with anger, but Christopher left her without another word, wending a path to where Abigail was chatting with Ben near the terrace doors. Katherine had infuriated him, but her remarks had also made him realize a few things. One, that he didn't give a damn what anybody thought of his relationship with Abigail, and two, that it was high time he told her how he felt. After enduring a moment's conversation with the younger man, Christopher finally clasped Abigail by the arm and drew her aside.

"Gail, I've got to talk to you."

"Why? Is something wrong? Is it the children?"

"No," he answered, leading her through knots of milling guests, his destination the glass-walled conservatory adjoining the ballroom.

A man and woman stood together in the doorway, and he nodded to them, then led Abigail deeper into the vaulted greenhouse filled with towering potted palms and long tables of Boston ferns, their lacy fronds swaying. In the shadows of a recessed alcove, before a tall, frost-crusted window overlooking the vast snow-glazed garden, he stopped and turned a bewildered Abigail to face him.

"What are we doing in here—" she began breathlessly.

"This," Christopher muttered, sliding his arm around her waist and finally giving in to what he'd been desperate to do ever since he had seen her again. He sought her lips, urgently, hungrily, passionately, pressing her back against the wall, no longer caring if she was offended or not, only craving the feel of her, the sweetness of her smooth, fragrant flesh beneath his mouth.

It felt so good to hold her at last, and a muffled groan escaped him when she slid her palms up his chest and around to the back of his neck. His passion intensified, his blood roaring out of control. He kissed her until she moaned helplessly and clung to him, her body trembling.

"Oh, God, Gail, I've wanted to do this for so long," he muttered hoarsely, his mouth moving against her temple. "I couldn't wait any longer—"

"I wasn't sure you cared anymore," she whispered, and then his lips sought hers again, ending any other admissions, their mouths mingling fiercely and hungrily. A few moments later, Christopher pulled back, but still he held her tight, his fingertips sliding down the satiny skin of her cheek and caressing her soft lower lip.

"God knows I still care about you, Gail. I thought it was over between us, I really did, but after I saw you again, spent time with you, I knew better. I was afraid to hope you'd feel the same way. So damned much has happened to keep us apart, but now, here, it doesn't matter anymore. We're together, and that's all I care about."

"I feel that way, too," she murmured, the words muffled against his cheek.

He crushed her to him again, kissing her over and over, unable to stop. He did not release her until another couple wandered too close to their leafy hiding place. Abigail stepped away from him, but he pulled her back into his embrace as soon as he could, feeling empty without her in his arms.

"Let's go home," he whispered. "I want to be alone with you."

Abigail's legs were so wobbly from his draining kisses that she could barely walk as Christopher escorted her swiftly from the dark, intimate confines of the garden room into the bright candlelit world of music and merry laughter. But her heart was singing with happiness. He still loved her. He had said the words. He had held her and kissed her as if he couldn't bear to let her go.

"Wait for me here," he whispered when they reached the front foyer. "I'll order the coach around, then fetch our wraps."

Abigail nodded wordlessly, watching him take long strides across the floor. An erotic shiver fanned ripples of pleasure over her flesh. His lips had seemed on fire when he had pressed them to her mouth and throat.

And he would kiss her again as soon as they were alone in the coach. She wanted him to. She couldn't wait for him to press his body close against her own.

"Are you and Chris leaving, Miss King?"

Abigail winced inwardly. Katherine Ladyman was the last person she wanted to see, but she faced the other woman with a polite smile. "Christopher's tired tonight, but we've had a lovely time. Thank you for inviting me."

"He certainly didn't appear tired earlier. He danced nearly every dance with you, didn't he? I usually have to drag him out on the floor."

Abigail looked away, not ready to reply to such a barbed question, then stiffened at Katherine's next remark.

"Rumor has it that Chris was engaged to a Southern girl before the war. They say she jilted him, and he never quite got over it."

Abigail's gaze didn't waver. "Oh?"

"Yes, and he's still in love with her, which is why he has never married."

Abigail searched the perimeter of the assemblage and picked out Christopher's tall form just starting back toward her. She wished he would hurry.

"But if that's true," Katherine continued, her eyes watching Abigail closely, "he wouldn't be paying me court, would he? He's escorted me regularly during the past few months, you know." Abigail said nothing, and her silence seemed to annoy Katherine. "Even if he does still love some girl from down south, I'm sure there could be no future for them, considering what he did. I bet it's hard for you to forgive him, even though you're practically part of the family."

"A lot of families were divided by conflicting loyalties during the war, Miss Ladyman. Now it's time to forget all our differences and start anew. The war is over." Abigail meant it with all her heart. She and Christopher would begin again, tonight.

"I must say that's very generous on your part, Miss

King. I'm not sure I could be so forgiving. I spent most of the war up north where there wasn't much fighting, but if a relative of mine had helped to burn Boston, or had spread such devastation as Sherman did in Georgia, I'm just not sure I could forget it."

Abigail frowned, confused. "I don't understand. What do you mean?"

"Why, I'm talking about Chris serving under General Sherman. Surely you knew that he participated in the burning of Atlanta."

In the first moment, all Abigail could do was stare at her. Then, a terrible heaviness settled over her chest, squeezing her heart until she felt she could not draw a single breath. Christopher, one of Sherman's officers? No, it couldn't be true!

"Oh, dear me, you didn't know, did you? I can see it in your face." Katherine's eyes were filled with grim satisfaction. "I'm so sorry. I just assumed you knew. I hope I haven't upset you. Please don't tell Chris I told you, or he'll be furious with me. I'm sorry, but I really must go now. But I'm so pleased you were able to come tonight."

Still shocked to the core, Abigail struggled with the raw, ragged emotions raging inside her as Katherine Ladyman glided away. She tensed when Christopher came up to her, their cloaks in his hands.

"Sorry I took so long," he said, then hesitated, examining her pale face. "What's wrong?"

She didn't trust herself to speak as he placed her cape around her, his hands lingering on her shoulders.

"I saw Katherine talking with you. Did she say something to upset you?"

"Please, I'd like to leave."

Trembling now with shock and anger, Abigail walked stiffly at his side into the cold air. She remained silent as he assisted her into the coach. Christopher watched her intently as the driver slapped the reins and the wheels began to roll, but Abigail kept her gaze fastened on the darkness outside the window, trying not to cry. She felt as if he had thrust a sword keep into her soul.

"Katherine told you, didn't she? Damn her!"

"Is it true?" Abigail turned to look at him, her face a tight mask. "Were you one of Sherman's devils?"

She could see his face clearly, bathed in the dim light filtering inside from the coach lamp, and there was no need for him to admit his guilt. It was written plainly on his face.

"Let me explain, please."

"Did you burn down houses, Christopher? Did you turn out women and children and leave them to starve?"

When he remained silent, Abigail's mouth clamped into a thin, tight line. A moment later, the carriage stopped, and she put her hand on the door handle, her eyes glittering in the lamplight when she looked back at him.

"I could forgive you for a lot of things, Christopher, but not this. Not any more than I could forgive Sherman himself."

6

HIGH on the second floor of Christopher's town house, Joshua leapt up from the nursery window seat where he had been keeping a diligent vigil for Saint Nicholas.

"C'mon, they're home early!" he cried, his freckled face alight. "Let's go see what they're gonna do now. They might even kiss each other some more, and we can watch 'm!"

Intrigued with that idea, Lucas and Katelyn tossed

back their blankets and scurried barefoot after their big brother. Just outside their room, all three drew up in the shelter of a recessed doorway, then peeked around the corner just as Abigail rushed up the steps in an angry rustle of velvet skirts and satin petticoats. She ran to her bedchamber, and the door slammed resoundingly behind her.

"Whatsa matter with her?" Lucas demanded in a hissing whisper.

Joshua placed a forefinger to his lips to hush up his brother as his uncle's broad back loomed up the curving stairs. Peering cautiously around the wall, they watched him head straight to Abigail's room.

"For God's sake, Gail, let me in," he said in a low voice, tapping a knuckle softly on her door. "You know we have to talk this out. Refusing to discuss it won't solve anything."

Joshua leaned forward, straining to hear her reply, but as far as he could tell, his Cousin Abigail didn't say anything back.

"Good gravy, Josh," Lucas whispered, leaning behind the wall as his uncle knocked a second time. "Don't they know it's Christmas Eve and everybody's supposed to be nice to each other and think 'bout baby Jesus bein' born?"

"Shhh, he'll hear you and make us go back to bed!" Joshua peered down the dim hall again, watching his uncle take a few agitated strides back and forth in front of Abigail's bedchamber, muttering a whole bunch of real bad words under his breath. Some of them Joshua had never even heard before. Joshua ducked back out of sight and expelled a heavy sigh. "Well, I sure did think Uncle Chris would be better at catchin' ladies than this. Now he can't even get Cousin Abigail to talk to him, and I thought that mistletoe stuff was gonna help him bag her for sure."

"I wanna see, too!"

To stop Katelyn's whining, Joshua pulled her around where she could take a quick gander at their angry uncle. Joshua watched, too, as Christopher knocked a few more times, received no answer, then entered his own bedchamber, banging the door behind him almost as loud as their Cousin Abigail had hers.

"Now what are we gonna do? This sure ain't a very good Christmas, after all, is it?" Lucas said, his face glum.

"It ain't Christmas yet, Lucas. And I guess if Uncle Chris can't even get her to talk to him by hisself, then we're gonna have to do that for him, too."

"How we gonna do that, Josh?" Lucas asked, looking worried.

"We just got to fix it so she got to open her door up and listen to him, like he wants her to."

Joshua herded Katelyn back into the nursery, and the three children settled around the fire to think. Lucas and Katelyn waited and watched while Joshua stared morosely into the flames. His brow wrinkled into a disturbed frown, his chin was propped on his fist as he mulled over different plots and plans to get Cousin Abigail to see what a good husband his uncle would make. Suddenly, like a hammer coming down on the top of his head, he knew what had to be done.

"I got it!" he cried, jumping to his feet. "C'mon, we got work to do! And we don't have no time to lose!"

Abigail paced back and forth at the foot of her mahogany four-poster, wrestling with her shattered emotions. She was being childish by refusing to talk with Christopher, but she just couldn't bear to quarrel with him, not yet. She was too upset and stunned that he could have had any part in such despicable acts.

Horror swept her again, and her fingers tightened around the smooth bedpost. She rested her forehead against the carved wood, and a vivid scene revisited her mind, the day she had hidden among the pines and watched the long column of blue-coated soldiers march up the winding, sun-dappled drive of Richmond Hill. In her ears, she heard again the muffled crunch of hooves upon the white shells paving the road and the jingling of hundreds of harnesses.

A cold shudder skittered up her spine as she remembered the sounds they had made entering her house, boots clomping hollowly on the veranda, the front door crashing down. Then the destruction had begun in earnest as the soldier shattered mirrors and china and smashed precious possessions that had been treasured by her family for generations. After they had gotten their fill of ransacking and looting, they had set the house and barns aflame, lingering to make sure they burned all the way to the ground.

Christopher had not been with those men, she knew that, but her heart cried out to think he was capable of such crimes against other people. Had he done the very same things? Had he ruined other lives the way hers had been destroyed? The hurt that thought brought to her was like a razor embedded in her heart.

Nestling her face into her palms, she sank down on the bed and tried to think. She went over all that Katherine Ladyman had said, the same numbing heartbreak gripping her. Oh, God, she just couldn't believe it was true, but it was. Christopher hadn't even denied it. What was she going to do? She loved him. Less than an hour ago, she had been so happy and hopeful that they could be together again.

A loud yell from down the hall brought her out of her miserable thoughts. She jerked up her head and came to her feet as Joshua's shouts came again, closer this time. Then he was pounding on her door. Alarmed, she ran and fumbled with the key until she finally got it to turn. Joshua rushed in, his wild-eyed panic terrifying her.

"Come quick, Cousin Abigail! It's Katelyn! Jenky climbed out on the window ledge to catch some pigeons and before we could stop her, she done crawled out after him! Now she's all scairt to come back in! It's all snowy and slick out there, and she's gonna fall! I know she is!"

"Oh, my God, no!" Abigail cried with mind-churning horror, rushing past him and out into the hall. "Hurry, Josh! Get Christopher! Quick!"

But as she raced toward the nursery, she saw that Christopher was running down the hall ahead of her.

"Hurry, Christopher!" she cried as he disappeared into the children's room. She ran after him, stark fear riveting her when her eyes settled on the wide-open window, the white organdy curtains blowing in the cold December wind.

Christopher was already at the casement, leaning over the sill, and Abigail came up behind him, putting her hand over her mouth to fight her rising hysteria.

"Katelyn! Where are you?" Christopher cried frantically, peering along the ledge in both directions before he ducked back inside. "I don't see her! Josh! Where is she? What window did she go out?"

Across the room, the nursery door slammed shut, followed by the distinct sound of a key scraping in the lock.

"What the hell?" Christopher muttered furiously, stalking back to the door and angrily rattling the door-knob. "Joshua! Lucas! Dammit, what do you think you're doing?"

"Sorry, Uncle Chris." Joshua's voice sounded very small and apologetic. "We just want you two to quit fussin' with each other and get married, is all. It's Christmas Eve, 'member?"

"What?" Abigail cried, pushing Christopher aside and pounding on the door with the flat of her hand. "Joshua Wright! You and Lucas better open this door right now, do you hear me? Don't you know how badly you scared us, telling us Katelyn was in danger! Is she all right? Where is she?"

"I'm fine, Cousin Abigail, and so is Jenky. I gots him right here," came Katelyn's babyish voice from the other side of the door. "Listen, he's purrin' real purty, 'cause I'm scratchin' the back of his ears."

Abigail's lips parted in a gasp, then snapped shut.

She frowned. "Joshua, let us out! Right this minute, if you know what's good for you!"

Her threat prompted a good bit of low, muffled discussion outside in the corridor.

"Can't. I'm real sorry 'bout it, though."

"Joshua! What are you thinking of to do something like this?" Abigail turned to Christopher, who had the audacity to grin at her. She glared back, then furiously shook the doorknob again.

"Please, Joshua," she begged, her voice taking on a wheedling note. "I know you mean well, darling, but you really must let us out. Katelyn? Dear? You'll open the door for me, won't you, sweetheart? Please."

"Josh says I can't 'til you marry Uncle Chris," replied the girl equably. "Are you gonna do it?"

"Children, please! You really don't know what you're doing!"

"Don't worry 'bout us, Cousin Abigail, we're gonna take good care of Katelyn for you while you're locked up in there. We're gonna go on off to bed now, down in your room."

Then to Abigail's dismay, there were sounds of the children talking together as they moved off down the hall.

"Children! Come back here!" she cried, looking desperately at Christopher, who was leaning calmly against the wall behind her, his arms folded over his chest.

"This is *not* funny, Christopher."

"I'm not laughing."

"I bet you'd like to, though."

He lifted his shoulder in a small, noncommittal shrug.

"Did you put Joshua and Lucas up to this?" she demanded, planting her hands on her hips.

"No, but I might have if I'd thought of it. They did get you to open your door, didn't they?"

Furious, Abigail looked toward the window. "Why don't you climb down and get help?"

Christopher arched a raven brow. "If you'll remember, Gail, we're on the second floor. I'm no acrobat."

Abigail swiftly retraced her steps to the windowsill, her gown fluttering around her legs. She leaned out and looked down the thirty-foot vertical drop to the backyard, then righted herself. She frowned, considering the feasibility of shouting to the next-door neighbors for help.

"Before you go yelling out the window, I'd consider what people are going to say when they find us locked in here together at this time of night."

Stricken with a new kind of dismay, Abigail gasped. "My reputation will be ruined."

"Not to mention what'll happen to mine. I can only imagine what my men will say if they find out I was locked up all night in a nursery with my beautiful cousin-in-law, held captive by nephews demanding marriage."

Abigail frowned at him, not amused. "Christopher, don't be ridiculous! How are we going to get out of here?"

"We could get married, I suppose." Jet-black eyes delved into hers, intense and completely serious.

His cavalier attitude angered her, and she turned away, not able to look at him. "Do you really think I could ever marry you after what you did? Sherman and his men were nothing but animals, cruel, despicable animals, and that makes you one, too—"

He reached her so quickly, a gasp was wrenched from her as he jerked her roughly around to face him. She quailed at the dark fury flushing his face.

"Do you really think we were the only ones who did cruel things during that goddamn war?" he ground out through clenched teeth. "Do you?" He gave her a violent shake, and Abigail tried to pull away, but his fingers bit deeper into her arms, holding her in place.

"Don't call what you did war!" she cried, her voice shrill with fury. "The only war Sherman made was on women and children! Is that what you Yankees call courage, Christopher? Attacking people who can't fight back? Are you proud of winning the war that way? Father was right about you all along, wasn't he? He kept telling me you weren't the man I thought you were! He said you were the enemy and would do whatever it took to crush us! Now I'm glad he broke it off! It sickens me now to think I was going to marry a man like you, a man without any honor—"

"Honor!" Christopher exploded, the single word heavy with derision. "Is that what you call sending me that goddamn note telling me that loving me was a mistake, that I could never be anything but your enemy?" His teeth clamped, a muscle in his cheek working furiously. "And you want to know when I got it, Gail? The day I left to join my regiment. Do you have any idea what that did to me?"

Abigail trembled under his hoarse, brutal words, but caustic resentment ruled her, and after months of suppression, she let the strident, biting words pour out of her.

"Do you think I didn't suffer, too? Do you think I just forgot all about you and had a wonderful time while the war went on and on and on until I thought it would never end? Do you think I enjoyed Ralph getting killed at Shiloh and Papa dying at the siege of Atlanta? Do you think I liked watching Sherman and his terrible army march through Georgia, burning and looting and destroying Richmond Hill and everything else I ever loved!" Pain swelled up into her throat, making it hard to speak, but she bit it back under the onslaught of the suffering that had lain in a hard, suffocating knot inside her breast. Her despair came flooding out, harsh and grating. "It wasn't easy for me, either, Christopher! How many times do you think I wished I was at Oak Haven with you and Miriam, where it was safe, where there was plenty of food to eat, where I wouldn't have to be alone, and scared, and hungry—"

Abruptly, he released his tight hold on her, and she

stumbled a few steps away, leaning unsteadily against the bedpost. They stared at each other, both shaken by the accusations they had hurled at each other. The pain and remorse on Christopher's white, stricken face hit Abigail like a fist. Tears sprang up with such force that she couldn't stop them, and she dropped to her knees, breaking down in a way that, on the night she had watched her home burn to the ground she had vowed never to do again.

When she felt Christopher's hands on her shoulders, she couldn't find the strength to resist and she let him turn her and clamp her close against his body. She didn't struggle, couldn't, just weakly laid her cheek against his shirtfront, clutching the silk lapels of his evening coat and weeping as if she would never stop.

"Oh, God, Gail, don't cry," Christopher whispered into her hair, but it was as if a great floodgate had burst apart and released a rain-swollen river of grief. Wracking sobs shook her as Christopher lifted her and drew her onto the bed with him. She clung to him, afraid to let go. She never wanted him to take his arms from around her again. She was so weary of being alone, tired of fending for herself and being brave in the face of hardships. She felt so weak, her heart all broken up into little pieces.

At first, Christopher said little, stroking her back and soothing her with indistinct words, but in time, as Abigail's grief began to diminish, he spoke softly, his words muffled against her hair.

"I'm sorry about your father and Ralph, Gail. I know how close your family was."

She sat back, wiping away her tears with her fingers. "I didn't think I could stand it when I found Ralph's name on the dead list." Her voice quivered, and she took a steadying breath. "He was so anxious to join his regiment and so proud of his new uniform. He left at once, right after war was declared, because he was so eager to fight. He'd been gone only a month, Christopher, and I'd already lost you and regretted breaking our engagement, because I loved you and missed you so desperately."

"Then why didn't you come to me? I sent a telegraph message begging you to come to Oak Haven while you still could. Why didn't you answer?"

Heartsick, Abigail shook her head. "Papa wouldn't let me. When I told him I wanted to go to you, he called me a traitor." She looked down, twisting her fingers together. "He said he'd disown me if I left Richmond Hill. He said I'd be dishonoring Ralph's memory if I married a Yankee, and he'd never speak to me again. I just couldn't go against him then, Christopher. He was all alone, and grieving terribly for Ralph. I couldn't add to his hurt. Then after he left to join the fight to save Atlanta, I knew it was too late for us."

Christopher leaned back against the headboard and pulled her across his chest, burying his face in her pale gold hair. "Dammit, Gail, I missed you so much. All those months I was fighting, I told myself over and over that I didn't care, but I was so worried about you I couldn't think straight. That's why I requested an assignment in Georgia. Because you were there. I didn't know then the awful things we were going to have to do in Atlanta. God help me, I did things that went against every principle I held dear."

"How could you have done them then?"

Christopher rose abruptly, paced a few agitated steps away from the bed, then stopped, raking his fingers through the thick black waves at his temples.

"For God's sake, Gail, what do you want me to say? I did what I had to do to survive. When the war started, I was just like everyone else. We all went into battle carrying our high ideals like banners and spouting patriotic speeches, but it didn't take a hell of a long time to find out what war really was. It's not some grand holy mission. It's just blood and gore, misery and suffering." Tense, tight lines remolded his face. His voice came lower, gruffer. "And you know the worst part? Fighting against other Americans, hearing them scream with pain, watching them suffer and die, knowing they weren't foreign invaders with alien languages and customs, but only people like you and Ralph and Miriam, who just happened to live a few hundred miles south of us."

He paused as if to get a grip on himself, then began again. "I'm sorry the war happened, Gail. I'm sorry the South seceded and caused the bloodshed, but I have no excuses for my part in it. I'm a soldier. I fought, and I killed. But that doesn't mean I liked it. I hated what we did in Georgia. I tried to be humane, to keep my men under control, but I did lead a unit like the one who took Richmond Hill. I ordered houses burned and food confiscated, and I left people like you homeless and hungry. And I can't forget it, either, Gail, not any more than you can. I've been living in my own hell, I can promise you that."

Abigail's teeth caught at her lower lip as he stopped in front of the window and stared into the night. When he continued, he did not look at her.

"By the time we took Atlanta, we'd been fighting for three years, and still there was no end in sight. We knew we had to finish it, stop the stupid, bloody battles where thousands of men died horrible, agonizing deaths. I know that what Sherman did was cruel and callous. I cringed at being a part of such senseless destruction. But I knew it had to be done. We had to bankrupt the Confederacy. We had to disrupt your supply routes and communication lines or we'd still be fighting. If we hadn't done those things, all the men who are home right now with their loved ones would be spending this Christmas Eve in some godforsaken battlefield. We wanted the war to end for good, for everyone."

He turned, imploring her to understand. "And after you came here, and I saw you again, I was afraid to tell you what I'd done. I couldn't bear to see the pain in your eyes. Can't you understand that the thought of you despising me tore me apart? Haven't you ever done anything you were ashamed of? That you just wanted to forget, but couldn't, no matter how hard you tried?"

Abigail felt bitter bile rise in the back of her throat. She did know how that felt, and she hated it.

Christopher watched her blanch and his heart was wrenched at the terrible look of hopelessness that overtook her face. He went to her, taking her hands in his.

"I love you, Gail. I can't help it. Even when I thought I'd lost you forever, you were always with me. A single day didn't go by but what I didn't think of you, wonder where you were, if you were all right. We've gotten another chance now, don't you see? We've got to forget what happened to hurt us and go on. Don't let what I did in the war rob us of this chance. Don't hate me for something I had to do."

"I did something, too," she whispered brokenly, averting her face. "Something so awful I feel sick every time I think about it. I've never told anyone. I was too ashamed."

Christopher frowned, then put his arm around her shoulders. "Do you want to tell me?"

She laid her head against his shoulder and was quiet for so long that Christopher thought she wasn't going to answer. Her muscles were tense, and he stroked her hair gently, waiting.

"I killed a man," she mumbled, her face hidden against him.

Christopher's heart ached for her as she went on, her words low and thick with emotion. "He was a Yankee soldier. I was alone, trying to get to Savannah. He came down the road on a horse, and I was so hungry, I hadn't had anything to eat in three days, and I asked him if he had any food to spare, but he said no. Then he got down and he grabbed me, and was going to'—her words faltered as a sob escaped her—''hurt me. He was holding me down and tearing at my dress, and I knew I had to stop him. I had Papa's gun with me, in my skirt pocket, and when I finally got it out, I put it against him and pulled the trigger.''

She squeezed her eyes shut, as if to black out the memory. She began to speak faster, her words becoming desperate. ''He fell on top of me, groaning and clutching his stomach, and there was blood all over my clothes and on my hands, and all I could think about was getting away so he couldn't hurt me anymore. And I ran and ran until I couldn't breathe, until I couldn't go any farther—''

''Hush, Gail, don't tell me any more,'' Christopher whispered, aware she had probably already relived it every day since it had happened, as he did the worst of his own deeds. He suddenly hated himself for not being there to protect her. ''You only did what you had to do, just like I did. The man was probably a deserter. We called them bummers because they stole away at night or in the heat of battle so they could rob and terrorize the civilians. He was evil. I know it's hard, but you have to make yourself forget what happened.''

''But I can't. I keep remembering how he looked, even how he smelled, like stale coffee and whiskey, and the way he was touching me—''

Something twisted deep in Christopher's gut. ''Then don't forget, sweetheart. Maybe if we all remember how horrible the war was, we won't ever let it happen again. That's what I've been working for here in Washington, Gail. President Johnson wants to bring the South back into the Union with some kind of dignity intact so this bitterness and hatred will end.''

''Oh, Christopher, why did the war have to happen? Why did there have to be so much suffering and killing? Why did Papa have to die? And Ralph and John?''

Christopher shook his head. ''I don't know, but if nothing else, the war made us appreciate how precious life is and how important love is, if you're lucky enough to find the kind we had.''

He leaned back and held her by the shoulders. ''Marry me, Gail. We need each other, don't you see that?''

Abigail couldn't answer, could only nod, tears rolling down her cheeks, and Christopher smiled, tenderly wiping the wetness away. Then his lips found hers, and he slowly pressed her backward on the bed. She closed her eyes and moaned when his fingers combed loose the intricate coils of her hair, then tangled tightly in the silky tresses. His lips forged a warm path down her arched throat, so hot and eager that her heart thundered with desire.

"I love you," she managed, wanting him to know how she felt, needing to say the words.

Christopher held her tighter, his groan tortured. "God, I need you so bad it hurts inside. But I won't do anything you don't want. I love you, but I can wait for you. Forever, if I have to."

Abigail cradled his lean cheek. His eyes were warm with love as he gazed down at her. "I don't want to wait," she whispered, pulling his head down until their lips met, tenderly at first. But as he molded his mouth to hers, she was lost to her own raging desire, her flesh trembling wherever he touched her. She closed her eyes in total surrender as his fingers worked to loosen the buttons of her bodice, allowing her breasts to swell free, then she closed her eyes and held him tightly to her, wanting the closeness, the intimacy, willing his strength to merge into her body.

Fate had cheated them for far too long. This night of pure, tender love was meant to be. They were meant to be, as surely as if their union had been made in heaven, their names written side by side in some celestial book, long before either of them were born. She smiled, her heart full, and gave herself to the man she loved, had always loved, without guilt or fear or regret.

7

Misty rays of early dawn light slanted through the drapes like bars of smoke as Joshua and Lucas tiptoed down the shadowy second-floor hallway, leading Katelyn by the hand. When they stopped in front of the nursery, no sound could be heard from behind the locked door. Nervously, Joshua laid one ear against the wood panels and listened intently.

"Do you hear somethin'?" Lucas whispered anxiously. "Tell us, quick!"

"I don't hear nuthin'. They're real quiet in there."

"Is Cousin Abigail and Uncle Chris gonna get out in time for Christmas?" Katelyn cried, tugging on Joshua's pants leg.

"Shhh, Katelyn. We just don't know yet. If they're ready to get married, then we're gonna open up the door."

"But I wanna be with Cousin Abigail. There weren't nobody to rock me last night."

"Hush, I say! Lucas tried, din't he? You just didn't like the way he did it."

"'Cause he kept wrigglin' around and jigglin' me up and down. And he can't sing good, neither."

"Hush! Or I'm gonna put you back to bed and you can just forget seein' what Saint Nick brought you!"

His appalling threat effectively subdued his little sister, and Joshua listened again for telltale movement from inside the nursery.

"I don't hear nuthin' neither," Lucas hissed from

where he was kneeling and trying to peer one-eyed through the keyhole.

"Told ya."

"You don't think they got in a fistfight or nuthin' like that, do you?" Lucas asked, his brow furrowing with sudden worry as he belatedly doubted the wisdom of locking them up together. "Cousin Abigail was mad as a riled-up hornet when we din't let her come out."

"Naw, Uncle Chris'd never hit no lady. And he likes her, anyways. He's probably glad we locked him in there with 'r."

When a few more minutes of eavesdropping brought no inkling as to what was transpiring inside the room, Joshua withdrew the weighty iron skeleton key he had taken from the kitchen the night before. Carefully, he inserted it into the lock, turned the key, and eased open the door.

"What're they doin', Josh?" Lucas asked in too loud a voice, trying to push past him.

"Shhh. They're sleepin'."

"Do they look like they're gonna get married?"

"How can they look like that?" Joshua answered, disgusted with his brother's dumb-cluck question. "They just look like they're sleepin'!"

To Joshua's dismay, Katelyn squeezed between him and Lucas and skipped across the room. Both boys followed at a more sedate pace, until all three children stood looking down at Katelyn's cot. Their Uncle Chris and Cousin Abigail lay closely entwined in each other's arms, still all dressed up in their bestest party clothes, but sound asleep.

"Lookee there, Josh, she's got her head on his shoulder!" Lucas pointed a finger at his discovery. "She wouldn't be doin' something like that, would she, Josh, if they weren't gonna get married?"

"I dunno," Joshua whispered back. "Maybe we oughta wake 'm up and see what they have to say for theirselves."

"You do it!"

"No, you!"

"You're the man of the house!"

"Oh, criminy, Lucas, I always got to do everything—"

Their argument ended abruptly as Katelyn suddenly
jumped up on the bed and yelled as loud as she could.
"Wake up, Cousin Abigail! It's time for Christmas!"

Abigail and Christopher lurched upright with a start,
and Joshua watched Abigail cautiously, thinking she
looked might messed up with her long yellow hair all
down around her shoulders and sticking out all over.
She sure had been real mad the night before, beating
on the door and yelling at him, he remembered warily.
He never saw her get riled up enough to raise her voice
before.

"Good morning, children," she murmured, her face
turning real red and embarrassed as she straightened
her blue velvet gown, which was all rumpled and stiff,
and patted her wild-looking hair. Then she glanced
over at their equally disheveled uncle. His shirt was
unbuttoned down the front and all wrinkled from
sleeping on it, but to Joshua's heartfelt relief, he gave
them a great big grin.

"Thank you, boys. Your trick worked like magic.
Cousin Abigail likes me now. A lot."

The children swung their attention back to Cousin
Abigail, just to make sure he was telling the truth, and
she laughed and pulled them down on the bed with
her and Christopher.

"You *should* look guilty, you little imps, locking us
up in here like you did. But I guess I'll have to forgive
you since it's Christmas."

Joshua blew out a long, vastly relieved sigh. He
hugged her, then backed away, wishing someone
would tell him what he really wanted to know.

"Is you gonna marry Uncle Chris now or not?"
Katelyn demanded, turning Abigail's face around with

her hands. "Josh ain't gonna let you outta here 'til you does, you know."

Christopher smiled at Abigail. "Well, my love, answer the children. Are you going to marry me? Or do we have to spend another night in here, all alone together with the door locked? It's up to you. Joshua there still has the key clutched in his hot little hand. One wrong word from you, and we'll have to suffer through another night like last night."

Abigail gave him a look of mock concern. "Well, if you're sure it's the only way to attain our freedom, I guess I'll just have to marry you and be done with it."

A trio of glad cheers and gleeful hoots drowned out any more conversation, and to Katelyn's delight, Christopher pulled Abigail to her feet, then swooped her up into his arms and swung her around.

"Merry Christmas, my love!" he shouted, loud enough for the whole neighborhood to hear. "You've made me the happiest man alive."

"Christopher! Stop!" Abigail protested, but she laughed as he put her down, then stood still for the long, thorough kiss he gave her as the children ran around, shouting with as much excitement as if a circus parade was passing.

"Now who would like to open their presents?" Christopher asked, causing even more of an uproar, followed by the children's screaming race downstairs to the Christmas tree in the parlor. The tree had been off-limits since yesterday evening when Christopher and Abigail had put out the gifts.

Christopher and Abigail followed more slowly, pausing in the parlor doorway to watch.

"Lookee at all them boxes of stuff!" Lucas was yelling at the top of his lungs.

Joshua, however, had wasted no time on idle conversation, and had begun searching through the boxes for gifts affixed with a tag bearing his own name.

"Here, Katelyn, here's one for you," he was saying, "and here's another one. And this here one's mine, just look how big it is! I bet anything it's gonna be a brand-new sled, Lucas! Look how long the box is!"

They were so engrossed in their long-awaited Christmas that the children hardly noticed that Christopher had stoked up the fire and drawn Abigail down beside him on the sofa near the warm hearth.

"When?"

"When what?"

"When can we get married?"

A sensual shiver raced up her arm as he picked up her hand and pressed his heated lips to her slender fingers. It had been so beautiful between them, she thought, so wonderful and right. She would never forget how tender and loving he had been. "Whenever you say."

"Then I say now." His lips curved roguishly. "I can make you happy, you know."

"I'm already happy."

"Tomorrow then?"

"Tomorrow's not soon enough."

They shared a slow smile.

"Then tomorrow it is."

Christopher glanced at the children, his voice lowering to a whisper. "And we're going to spend our wedding night in a hotel where we don't have to worry about the kids bursting in on us."

Abigail slanted him a wicked look. "Why, I got the impression you rather enjoyed helping me put my clothes back on."

"Not nearly as much as I liked taking them off."

Abigail smiled. Their lips brushed gently, but they broke apart guiltily when across the room Katelyn screamed in absolute ecstasy.

"My yellow-haired doll from Mr. Berry's window! You got her, you got her! Oh, at last, at last, she's my very own!"

"I know exactly how she feels," Christopher whispered, quirking a dark brow at Abigail. Then they laughed together and went, hand in hand, to join the three devilish little angels who'd worked so very hard to give them their wonderful new future.

HAPPY HOLIDAYS
from ...
LINDA LADD

LINDA LADD lives in Poplar Bluff, Missouri, with her husband, Bill, and their two children, Laurie and Billy. She is the author of five historical romances, including the Avon Romances *Dreamsong*, *Fireglow*, *Moon Spell*, *Silverswept*, and *Wildstar*, as well as *Frostfire*, the first book of her "Fire" Trilogy. Book Two, *Midnight Fire*, will be available from Avon Books in February 1991. She has just finished the concluding book in the trilogy.

Christmas is Linda's favorite time of year—a season to celebrate love and caring with her family, surrounded by warm candleglow, fragrant pine boughs, and laughter. Linda sends all her readers her very best wishes for holidays that are warm and happy and as full of love as Christopher's and Abigail's.

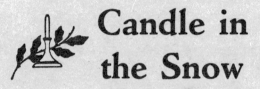

Candle in the Snow

Barbara Dawson Smith

1

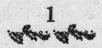

Wiltshire, England
December 1855

"CHELSEA!"

The distant voice echoed from her past. Heart leaping, Chelsea Devlin clutched the brown paper parcel tight against her gray wool mantle. Bracing a hand on the stone market cross, she swung sharply and scanned the street. Sunshine glistened on the shop windows. The frosty Saturday in early December rang with the jangle of harness and the clopping of hooves as the townfolk of Rossbury bustled past, tradesmen with mufflers framing their reddened cheeks and housewives hastening about their daily errands. Across the green a trio of boys teased a girl walking her dog.

The scene looked commonplace, nothing out of the ordinary.

The tension prickling her skin eased. It couldn't have been him, Chelsea reasoned. She'd imagined that deep, resonant tone. The snug velvet bonnet must have addled her hearing. Taking a deep breath to compose herself, she resumed her progress toward Miss Maxwell's Academy for Young Ladies, beyond the outskirts of the village.

"Chelsea, wait!" the voice called again, closer this time.

She froze for a single protracted moment; then with the sluggishness of shock, she pivoted. The midday brightness dazzled her eyes and lit the cramped, honey-hued buildings of High Street. Only half-heeding the inquisitive glances aimed her way, she squinted frantically at the passersby.

Then she saw him.

Tall, lean, and self-assured, he elbowed through the throng of shoppers. Sunlight kissed his broad shoulders, the thatch of coal-black hair, the rakish angles of his face, and the bluest eyes she'd ever seen. Familiar eyes that had once sparkled with laughter and darkened with passion.

He stopped in front of her. The parcel slipped from Chelsea's nerveless fingers and tumbled to a grassy patch beside the road. The world tilted giddily; her gloved hands whisked to her mouth.

"Sean?" she said in a strangled whisper. "Oh, dear God, Sean!"

He smiled, his teeth a white flash against healthy bronzed skin. His hands were perched at the waist of a fine navy overcoat which gaped open as if welcoming the wintry weather. "Aye, love," he murmured, " 'tis your Sean."

She struggled to grasp the inconceivable. Her husband, alive and well, standing before her! A tumult of emotion burst from her stunned heart: disbelief and joy and panic. He couldn't be here, he couldn't be! Not when she'd finally reconciled herself to his death and made plans for the future...

His smile wavered. Stepping closer, Sean grasped her shoulders. "Faith, Chelsea," he said, the words raspy with emotion. "Is this how you welcome your prodigal husband home?"

Her tongue felt tied in knots. Fleetingly she noticed that the lilting caress of his voice had acquired an intriguing hint of an American accent. She could only shake her head and gaze at him in wonder.

With abrupt impatience, he snatched up her parcel. Then he tugged at her arm. Feeling as wooden as a Punch-and-Judy puppet, she let him lead her into the shadows of an alley between two shops.

"Let me show you the homecoming I've long fancied," he said.

Setting down the parcel and pressing her against the rough stone wall, Sean lowered his mouth to hers.

No, her mind cried out, even as her body softened against his hard chest and her eyes drifted shut. He pushed off her bonnet, so that it dangled by its velvet strings, and worked his supple fingers into her prim blonde bun. Her reason scattered before a torrid wind of rapture. Long lonely years flashed away as she drank in his astonishing presence, breathed the outdoors scent of his skin, absorbed the firm familiarity of his embrace. Sean . . . her first love. Sean . . . the man who had introduced her to the mysteries of passion and the bliss of love. Tears pricked her eyelids. How many desolate nights had she dreamed of such a moment, to lose herself in his arms again, to relive the precious brevity of their youthful marriage?

At last he lifted his head. "Wood sprite," he said, his voice breaking, his hand stroking her cheek. "Forgive me for staying away so long. Forgive me for ever leaving you."

Her mind danced from the long-ago memory of their final, bitter argument. In a daze, she noted the subtle tracery of lines around his eyes and mouth, lines that had deepened during six years of separation. He was still the handsomest man she'd ever seen. No longer a youth, he looked hardened by adventure and more roguish than ever.

She couldn't keep from laying a gloved finger against the cleft in his chin, as she'd done a hundred times before. "Sean . . . Sean. I thought you were dead."

His arms bracketed her; his black brows clashed into a frown. "Didn't your agent report back to you?"

Your agent. Like a blast of winter air, alarm iced her giddy joy. She swallowed. "Yes. He said you'd perished in a landslide in California."

Chuckling, Sean shook his head. "I wasn't even working my claim at the time. You must have hired a bletherin opportunist who'd lie to gain his fee."

"I didn't . . ." Chelsea gulped back a hazardous explanation.

He brushed his lips over her temple, his breath warming her cold skin. "Pleased I was to hear you tried to find me, love. For so long I feared you were ashamed of me, that you never wanted to see me again. But, bless Saint Brenden, you really did care whether I lived or died."

His husky words cut deeply into Chelsea's soul. She opened her mouth, then closed it. Dear Lord, she thought. Oh, dear Lord, what can I say to *that?*

"We'll start anew," he went on, anointing her forehead with kisses. " 'Twill be better this time. We've both had a chance to grow up, to realize how much we need each other. I can provide for you at last, Chelsea. I can give you everything you've ever fancied. I love you—"

"No!" Wrenching away, she sucked air into her paralyzed lungs. Once she had dreamed of hearing his tender declaration again, but no more. Reality smacked her like a frozen fist, and she shivered. What had she been thinking, to kiss him like that?

"You're assuming too much, Sean. You can't simply appear after so many years without a word, and expect me to welcome you with open arms."

He propped a hand on his hip, drawing back his natty braided coat. "Seems you did just that. And 'twas a fine welcome, indeed, m' love."

His knowing expression infuriated her. The pain she'd suffered over his callous desertion struck with staggering force. She raised her chin. "You haven't changed at all, Sean Devlin. You still think you can sail through life, relying on charm and wit. Unfortunately for you, I've learned that a woman requires much more from a husband."

He leaned closer until their eyes were level. "Such as?"

"A steady provider. A respectable man who won't run away on a whim. Not a laggard who squanders his life chasing rainbows."

"And just supposing there's a pot of gold sitting at the end of that rainbow?"

"A pot of gold more important than me?" She scoured her hair into a proper twist at the back of her head. "You and your ridiculous Irish folklore. Imagine, a grown man believing in leprechauns and banshees."

He cocked a black brow. "You can't take pleasure in fanciful tales anymore, can you, love? Old Lady Quincy trained you well . . . too well."

"My guardian preferred me to read the classics, and rightly so. Perhaps that's something a man of your background can never understand."

The cruel insult hung like a stormcloud between them. Suddenly remorseful, Chelsea yearned to call it back.

A faint bitterness shadowed the blue brilliance of his eyes. "I couldn't help my lack of schooling," he murmured. "We were both orphans, but I never had the advantages you did."

"I'm sorry. I didn't mean . . ." What *did* she mean? Her head ached; all level thinking seemed to have flown away. One painful truth remained: as always, she and Sean were arguing. They couldn't hold a sensible conversation without hurting each other. They'd known only one way to settle their strife: in bed. She was far better suited to a man like—

Panic punctured her anew. With shaky hands, she rammed the bonnet atop her head. "It's six years too late for amends and sweet talk from you, Sean. I've made a life of my own—I'm an English instructress at Miss Maxwell's Academy for Young Ladies."

He frowned. "A schoolmarm?"

"And a happy one," she stated. "So you see, you can cease worrying about my welfare and go back to America. No one need ever know you came here."

Sean's features went dark. "So you're saying you *didn't* want me to come back? Then why did you send your agent asking after m' whereabouts?"

"I . . ." Her insides clenched into a wretched ball. "I wanted only to learn what had happened to you," she hedged. "To find out if I was a wife . . . or a widow."

A muscle jumped in his jaw; his gaze swept her sedate gown of claret wool, the mantle of gray merino. "So you learned of my supposed death. Yet you aren't in mourning."

"When I moved here from London, people assumed I was a widow. I knew you'd never come back, so I let them go on thinking so. I had to get on with my life, you see." Knowing she was babbling, she picked up her parcel and edged toward the roadway.

Sean followed. "And why," he asked in a razor-edged tone, "did you feel the sudden need to prove your marital status?"

She wasn't about to answer *that* question so near a busy street. Her hotheaded husband might very well make a scene.

"What are you hiding, Chelsea, m' love?"

Her boots slipped on the cobbles and she clutched at the limestone wall. Too late she saw the trap she'd set for herself. Concentration furrowed his brow and his breath fogged the frosty air. His eyes had held such resolution once before, when he'd declared his intent to seek his fortune in the goldfields of America . . . alone if necessary.

"Tell me, Chelsea," he commanded again.

He gripped her arm none too gently; an unreasoning excitement quivered over her skin. She clasped the parcel like a shield against her breasts, yet her husband's crisp scent embraced her like a beloved friend. A pang of longing squeezed her abdomen as tightly as the fingers holding her arm. *Her husband.* Yet she scarcely recognized this hard-eyed stranger, who seemed bent on plunging her plans into disaster.

Sudden anger heated the cold ashes of her heart. Why *should* she guard the truth? Unveiling the facts might drive him away forever.

"I'll tell you, then, since you're so keen on knowing. I'm affianced to a gentleman. We're to marry come summer."

Sean stood perfectly still. Blankness descended over his handsome features, and apart from the faint tensing of his fingers, she might have thought he hadn't heard her. Odd, he didn't look at all surprised . . .

"What gentleman?" he demanded.

She hesitated. How could she lay her fiancé open to Sean's wrath? Yet, dear God, her husband must exit her life before anyone discovered his existence.

"Tell me," he warned, "else I'll ask around the village."

She forced out the name. "Sir Basil Spottsworth."

" 'Tis a shame for Sir Basil," he said flatly. "And for you. 'Tis sorry I am to smash your dream of marrying into the gentry, m' love, but bigamy is against the law."

"I'll seek a divorce."

"You'll have to prove adultery. And are you fancying his lordship would stand by you through a sordid trial?"

Brutal reality crushed Chelsea. Tears of fury and frustration stung her eyes. Blindly she struck at his chest with the hard edge of her parcel. The jarring contact with solid flesh shot frissons of pain up her arms and into her heart.

"Why did you have to come back, Sean?" she said, sobbing. "Didn't you do enough damage to me six years ago?"

"Chelsea . . ."

His voice was tender, contrite, ripe with yearning and the remembrances of days gone by. Through the blur of moisture she saw his dark head loom closer. She knew he meant to kiss away her resistance, just as he'd always done. And with fatal alarm she feared she might succumb.

"Stay away from me!" she snapped. "I despise you, Sean Devlin. I don't ever want to see you again."

Yanking free, she dashed into the cold sunshine and hastened along the street, driven by the agonizing need for escape. She saw the village as if through a rain-washed window. Her legs felt numb; her insides ached. Frosty air seared her lungs. She was vaguely aware of startled looks from the passersby, but she didn't care. A single thought pounded through her head: Sean Devlin had hurt her once already. She wouldn't let him do so again.

At the outskirts of the village, someone caught her arm. Blinking, Chelsea looked down at the white-gloved hand detaining her, then followed the black sleeve up to a narrow face with pinched lips and a perpetual grimace. A plain bonnet framed the stark features.

Chelsea's heart plunged to the paving stones. "Miss Maxwell!"

"Mrs. Devlin." The headmistress peered closely at Chelsea. "You look a fright. Is something wrong?"

Only then did Chelsea realize what a sight she must have made, barreling along like a madwoman, with tears streaking her face. Mortified, she groped inside her pocket for a handkerchief and dried her eyes. "No. No, I'm perfectly fine now."

Miss Maxwell leaned on the handle of her rolled umbrella. "I got quite a different impression, as did half the town. You were making a spectacle of yourself. What is the cause for such unseemly behavior?"

"I . . . I left a basket of damson jam with Mrs. Dickerson. She's so frail and ill . . . I suppose I was overwrought by her suffering."

The clumsy explanation wasn't entirely a lie. Chelsea *had* visited the elderly woman before embarking upon her shopping. And before Sean had embarked upon *her*.

"An admirable sentiment," said Miss Maxwell, her thin eyebrows still arched. "But next time, kindly limit such a display to the privacy of your chambers. We must at all times embody the dignity of the academy."

"Yes, ma'am."

"I trust the state of your emotions shan't interfere with the pantomime rehearsal." Giving a curt nod of farewell, the headmistress marched toward the shops, her back as stiff as the spine of a King James Bible, the tip of her ebony umbrella tapping the pavement.

Chelsea took a shaky breath. Praise heavens, the lame excuse had extricated her from a sticky explanation. Miss Maxwell employed only spinsters and widows of impeccable character. How was Chelsea to justify the miraculous resurrection of her brash Irish husband?

Clutching the parcel, she trudged out of the village. Along a winding lane, the steeple of a Norman church poked above the barren tops of hawthorn and oak. An occasional thatched-roof cottage, smoke drifting from the chimney, hunched alongside the stream. Icicles dripped from the rain gutters, and the black beds of flower gardens lay in winter silence.

Chelsea looked away from the dismal scene. In her mind, she traveled back to the fragrant springtime of her girlhood when she had first met Sean Devlin.

She'd been hiding in the darkened morning room of the London town house, and peeping through an opened window at the formal garden, where couples strolled in the cool evening. The strains of a waltz drifted from the ballroom. Leaning on the casement, breathing in the scent of climbing roses, she sighed dreamily and tapped her slippered foot in time to the music. Tonight marked the come-out ball of Daphne, Lady Quincy's youngest daughter. Barely seventeen, Chelsea had to wait until the next season for her own debut.

She ached with all her young heart to be courted by

a dashing nobleman. He would be handsome and rich, of course, and kind enough to overlook her humble birth. Dipping into the curtsy she had practiced with the three Quincy girls, she pretended to accept his invitation to dance. Then she twirled around and around, imagining herself not in drab schoolgirl navy, but fine gold taffeta over a score of flounced petticoats. In her mind, the shadowed chamber faded into the candlelit brilliance of the ballroom.

"As lovely a dancer a man could ever hope to see."

The faintly foreign lilt of a male voice banished her fantasy. Gasping, Chelsea whirled to an ungraceful halt. In the doorway, the low light from the hall defined the broad-shouldered frame of a stranger.

"And as nimble as a wee fairy beneath the moon of May," he went on, walking toward her. "Might I have this dance, miss?"

Without awaiting a reply, he spun her around in time to the faraway music. Astonishment tied Chelsea's tongue. Though his steps didn't precisely follow the waltz she'd learned, he moved with the confidence of a gentleman. The gloom hid his features, and intensified her awareness of his hand at her waist. Never before had she been held so intimately by a man. She felt breathless and giddy as he swung her around. A queer fluttering warmed her insides, and suddenly the night vibrated with promise, like a wish about to come true.

The dance carried them around wing chairs and tables, then past the long row of windows. Here, the faint starlight touched strong and handsome features, framed by thick black hair. He gazed down at her with an intensity that lifted her girlish hopes to the stars. Afraid she was dreaming, Chelsea lowered her eyes to his maroon coat. The shiny gold buttons bore the Quincy crest, and a telltale knot of braided cord draped his right shoulder.

Scandalized, she jerked free. "Why . . . you're a footman!"

"You wound me, m' lady. I fancied me a man admiring a pretty colleen."

He took a step closer. She retreated until her back met the drapery. "Come near me again and I'll scream the house down."

He stopped, palms upheld. "Faith, now don't be getting your dander up. I'm only a poor Irish lad who's lonesome for a bit of gaiety. I thought we were kindred spirits in that."

Chelsea felt mortified that she'd mistaken him for a gentleman. Kindred spirits, indeed. It was a bold presumption coming from a servant, yet somehow his endearing grin inspired trust.

"I've not seen you before," she said slowly, studying him in the shadowy light. "You must be the new man I heard the maidservants whispering about."

"Sean Devlin, at your service." He swept into an exaggerated bow. "Her ladyship, bless her kind soul, took me from the workhouse and saved me from an early grave."

He didn't appear as if he needed saving from anything, though now she noted a leanness about him, the hungry look of a hard life. And despite his air of confidence, Sean Devlin couldn't be much older than herself.

"Lady Quincy *is* wonderful. Why, she took me in, too..." Chelsea stopped. Why was she confiding in him?

"So I heard," he said. "She found you, a wee babe, on the doorstep of her charity hospital in Chelsea."

"You've been gossiping about me?"

"Now, don't go high and mighty again. I saw you strolling in the garden yesterday, and I only asked who you were." Lowering himself onto the casement, he patted the cushion beside him.

She loathed the thought of returning to her empty bedroom. Yet it was highly improper for her to visit with a man unchaperoned, let alone a man who was her social inferior. "I can't—"

"You can. Faith, I want to hear more about the fairest colleen in Londontown."

His smile radiated a charm that made her legs wilt. She sank onto the window seat. "I'd rather hear about you," she ventured.

Sean spoke freely about moving from Ireland to London as a lad of eight, his parents' quest for a better life and their untimely death, and his subsequent harsh life on the streets. Fascinated and appalled, she knew that but for Lady Quincy's intervention, she might have shared such hardship. Despite his coarse background he displayed an innate courtesy. His easy manner soon had Chelsea pouring out thoughts she had shared with no one else, the painful awareness of being a part of the Quincy family, yet not a part, the veiled antipathy shown her by the three Quincy daughters, and the diligence with which Chelsea had worked at her studies as a way of securing Lady Quincy's esteem.

All the while she was intensely aware of him. She sat straight so that not even her skirts brushed him, yet she felt his warmth mingling with the cool breeze from the opened window. In the starlight, his eyes gleamed a dark and unsettling blue. The night air grew thick with tension. She gripped the folds of her gown and glanced down at her lap, looking anywhere but at him.

"I must go," she said, stiff with confusion. "I shouldn't be here and neither should you."

"You fret too much about shoulds and shouldn'ts."

Sean leaned over and brushed his lips against hers. The sensation evoked a strange breathless excitement in her. While she sat trembling, unable to speak, he sauntered from the room.

Chelsea tried to summon outrage that a footman had taken such liberties. But her conscience whispered that she bore the blame as much as he. A true lady would never have put herself in such a compromising position. By being alone with him, she had displayed a loose moral character. Henceforth, she would treat him with chilly disdain.

Yet through the long summer months, each time she heard an orchestra play, she remembered her time with him. While the family ate dinner, Sean waited on the table and flashed her that heart-stopping grin. When she went calling with her ladyship, he opened the carriage door and surreptitiously brushed her hand. Once, when she sat sewing in the library, he entered and closed the door. She straightened, her heart pounding. Did he mean to kiss her again? But he only asked her to read him a letter from a cousin in Ireland.

A pang of surprised concern stabbed her. "You must learn to read," she urged. "You'll never rise above your station without schooling."

He frowned. "Faith, Chelsea, is that how you measure a man? By how much book-learning he's had?"

The rare glimpse of his defensive side, his vulnerability, reached deep inside her. She tried to deny the way he made her heart pound, the unseemly impulse she felt to touch him and to relive the magic of his kiss. She cared for him, Chelsea assured herself, only out of a natural sympathy for the less fortunate.

As summer waned, Daphne became betrothed to the Earl of Huntsborough, a match as brilliant as the ones her sisters had made. Feeling lonely amidst the whirl of wedding preparations, Chelsea dreamed of the day she would have her turn.

One autumn afternoon, Lady Quincy called Chelsea into the drawing room. Lucille, the eldest daughter, sat beside her mother. Lucille had always given herself airs over the lowborn Chelsea. It had been a relief four years ago when Lucille had married and moved away.

"It's time to settle your future," Lady Quincy said, her smile as kindly as ever.

Excitement tingled inside Chelsea. "Yes?"

"I believe we've found the perfect situation. Lucille has been so generous as to offer you the post of governess to her dear little Edward."

The bottom dropped out of Chelsea's stomach. Lucille had often taunted her about being denied a come-out, but Chelsea had kept blind faith in Lady Quincy's generosity. "Governess? But . . . what about my debut . . . my chance to marry . . . ?"

Consternation on her elegantly wrinkled face, her ladyship stared. "Oh, my dear. I never imagined . . . Surely you can't have believed you could assume a place in polite society?"

Her compassionate expression only heightened Chelsea's shock. Their class difference opened like an unbridgeable chasm. She glanced at Lucille's smirking face. No! Chelsea thought in wild denial. She could never work for such a haughty employer, could never resign herself to the empty life of a spinster.

Devastated by betrayal, blinded by tears, she ran from the room, straight into Sean's arms. He drew her into the butler's pantry and held her close until her sobbing subsided. When she explained what had happened, fury tightened his handsome face, a fury that turned quickly to resolution.

"You'll not wither away in bondage to that harridan," he declared. "Better you should marry me."

Stunned, she huddled in the strong circle of his arms. Crazy feelings tumbled inside her: longing and hope and need. She shook her head in bewilderment. "We'd never make do."

" 'Tis a poor man I am," he acknowledged, his mouth twisting in bitterness. "I can't give you fancy trappings, but I can keep a roof over your head and food in your belly."

The pain dwindled to a warm fathomless ache. "But . . . you don't love me."

His harsh expression softened and he stroked her cheek. "Ah, but you're wrong, Chelsea, m' love. I've loved you from the moment I saw you, a wood sprite dancing by herself in the starlight."

The declaration left her reeling. Suddenly with all her heart she wanted to belong to him, wanted to shed the past and meld their futures. With all the pent-up passion inside her, she'd kissed Sean and let him talk her into eloping to Gretna Green.

Now, as Chelsea walked alongside the rural road, her shoes crunching the frozen grass, bittersweet remembrance constricted her throat. She had never been able to forget how it felt to make love with him, the fierce rapture of linking their bodies and the mellow sweetness of lying in each other's arms. Even now, her loins throbbed with a ghostly hunger for the past.

Praise God he was alive. *Alive!*

She squelched an errant surge of joy. Of course she wouldn't wish him dead. Nostalgia for the brief happiness they'd once shared accounted for her wild pleasure at seeing him today.

She took a deep breath of cold air and slowly released it. Their marital bliss had endured scarcely more than a fortnight. They'd lived off his meager savings while Sean searched for employment. Loath to work again in the demeaning role of servant, he came home one day and proclaimed his intent to seek his fortune in the goldfields of America, where a man's achievements were limited only by his character, not by the circumstances of his birth.

Chelsea had been aghast at the notion of gallivanting thousands of miles to a foreign country rife with outlaws and savages. She wanted to stay in England and become a lady, to rise above her orphan roots. She offered to educate Sean, to help him find a respectable post. He rejected her plan and insisted that a wife should obey her husband. Furious, she said she wouldn't waste her life in a shantytown. He threatened to leave without her. Torn between hurt and anger, she retorted that she'd made a terrible mistake; she ought to have taken the governess post and lived with the gentry. She threw her wedding ring at him and declared the marriage was over.

He'd stormed out of their humble lodgings in London. At first she didn't believe he was serious, and she left a candle burning beside their bed so that when he returned, he wouldn't stumble in the darkness. She'd say *I'm sorry.* He'd say the same. Then he'd do all those delicious things to her body and her heart.

But he never came back. Until today.

Fresh tears welled in her eyes, but she dashed the moisture away. With each step down the country lane, she felt her scattered emotions solidifying into a tight knot of anger. The devil take Sean Devlin! How dare he saunter back into her life and try to pick up where he'd left off! As if she were still an impressionable girl, craving love and a dashing adventurer to soothe her hurts.

I despise you . . . I don't ever want to see you again.

The memory of her outburst whispered through the bleak sunshine. Now that he knew the depths of her antipathy, surely he would go back to his beloved America. She would likely never see him again. Why did the thought carve a hollow place inside her?

Because he'd destroyed her future, she told herself bitterly. The law permitted divorce only for adultery, not desertion. To prove his culpability, she would have to track down some nameless hussy Sean had slept with. No doubt the rascal had seduced many.

The very notion turned Chelsea's stomach. Sir Basil would never marry a divorced woman, anyway. Like it or not, she was well and truly wed to a reckless man who made his home thousands of miles away.

A low stone fence marked the grounds of the academy. In the distance the tidy complex perched like a brooding hen atop a low hillock. A few girls in their regulation gray coats and bonnets strolled the barren lawns.

Chelsea hesitated, one hand clenching her parcel, the other resting on the wrought-iron gate. The pantomime rehearsal would begin in an hour. But she shouldn't put off what must be done.

She turned abruptly and set out across a pasture,

the stubble from last July's haying crackling beneath her feet. Normally she would take the longer route back toward the church and around the lane. But today impatience dogged her. She must face this unhappy task. Now that the shock had worn off, she knew better than to hide the past.

A short time later, she walked up the drive leading to Sir Basil's manor. The stately stone dwelling had an ancient ambience, the aura that came from housing gentlefolk for centuries. This could have been hers, Chelsea reflected, as she mounted the steps to the front door. Her children might have played on these lawns. Her children might have known a time-honored heritage. The sour taste of loss burned in her throat.

Winchester answered her knock. Uttering his customary grunt of greeting, the old retainer took her wrap and parcel, then led her down the dim and musty hall. Stuffed birds perched inside the tall glass cases lining the walls. Poor things, she thought involuntarily. Trapped, just like me.

The library doors stood ajar. A man lounged in a blue wing chair near the window. His sharply handsome profile and broad shoulders made her heart shudder with shock.

Sean!

2

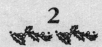

RISING, he inclined his dark head to her. Even if his eyes weren't steady and probing, she would have guessed his determined mood from the way his jaw tightened. So he hadn't stormed out of her life again. A confusing meld of consternation and pleasure thickened her throat.

"A timely entrance, m' love," he said. "I've just finished introducing m'self to your . . . former fiancé."

His audacity drove the paralysis from her limbs. "Dear God, surely you haven't come to blows—"

Chelsea hastened into the library. To her relief Sir Basil stood, hale and blustery, by the fireplace. He must have recently come in from shooting, for he wore a checked cap, tweed hunting garb, and Wellington boots. His ruddy face with the tidy gray mustache bore an expression that was more disgruntled than heartbroken.

"Terrible turn of events," he grumbled. "Terrible." He turned to Sean. "Not that I'd wish you dead, old chap."

Sean gave a grave bow. " 'Tis sorry I am to be the bearer of such tidings."

"Humph." Sir Basil began to pace. "Who will keep up my lists of birds, I ask? Who will catalogue my specimens? Who will copy my articles for *The British Ornithologist*?"

"Ah," Sean said, "so Chelsea worked for you."

She met his speculative stare. *He* wouldn't understand that marriage was a bargain; for the sake of children and an impeccable background, she'd gladly play the secretary. So why did she feel suddenly discomfited?

"The change in circumstances needn't interfere with your work, Sir Basil," she said. "I can continue to transcribe for you."

"I think not." Sean took a firm step forward. "M' wife will be a trifle busy from now on." He looked at her, his lashes lowering slightly in smoldering promise.

Unbidden heat flashed through Chelsea, a sensation she attributed to anger. Busy, indeed! She clamped her lips and silently counted to ten. It wouldn't do to make a scene . . . not here, at least.

"I say, Mrs. Devlin," Sir Basil said musingly, "perhaps you could recommend someone else."

"To marry you or secretary you?"

He looked taken aback by her vehemence. "Why, a secretary, of course."

Chelsea drew a calming breath. This wasn't *his* fault. "My husband's resurrection must be as much a shock to you as it was to me. Your London agent swore—"

"Incompetence!" Sir Basil shook a liver-spotted fist. "Incompetence is the bane of this world. Why, the housemaids cannot even dust my cases properly. Nor can the under-footman keep the fires burning at the temperature necessary to preserve my specimens." He aimed a glare at the low blaze in the hearth.

Hands in his trouser pockets, Sean wandered to one of the glass cases stacked nearly to the cornices. "A grand collection, to be sure. Did you shoot all these birds yourself?"

"A fair number of them." Sir Basil clumped to the display. "The others I procured from dealers and correspondents all over the globe."

Sean studied a small dark bird, its wings spread in perpetual flight. "Faith, this one looks like a shag. I recollect seeing them when I was a lad in County Wicklow."

"Ah. *Phalacrocorax aristotelis*. A marine bird, nesting on the rocky coasts of Ireland."

Fuming, Chelsea listened to them discuss the migratory patterns of various seabirds. Neither man seemed to care that they'd rudely excluded her. Sir Basil's middle-aged features lit with zeal as he gestured at the stuffed birds. Odd, she thought, in the year she'd worked with him, she'd never noticed him ever regarding *her* with such unabashed devotion. Odder still, the realization aroused only a vague pang inside her, more of hurt pride than the agony she'd once suffered over losing Sean. She didn't understand the dizzying sense of liberty that suddenly lifted her spirits, as if she'd sprouted wings and could soar out of this decaying manor . . .

Sean swung toward her. "You look positively shaken, m' love. Might you need a breath of fresh air?" Before she could reply, he addressed their host. "Thank you for being such a sport."

"Come back anytime, old chap," said Sir Basil, offering a hearty handshake. "Be delighted to take you shooting on the estate. Delighted, indeed."

Winchester glided in, carrying their wraps; Sean put his coat on, then silently held her parcel while she donned her mantle. His features remained sober, though laughter lurked in his eyes. His deft management of Sir Basil made her steam with resentment. She ought to insist on staying, yet the awkwardness of remaining daunted her.

"I'll clap that cheating vulture in gaol," Sir Basil groused, as he saw them to the door. "Never you fear, Mrs. Devlin, I shall recover my ill-spent money."

The instant they walked outside and the door clicked shut, Sean said, "Oh-ho, so *he* paid the agent who prematurely reported my demise."

"It was a token of his regard for me," she said, stiffly descending the stairs. "He was most anxious to marry me."

"So was I, once upon a time."

"*He* would have supported me properly."

"He would have acquired an unpaid assistant."

The perception stung. "Our betrothal was a mutually satisfactory arrangement," she snapped. "And speaking of his work, I can't recall you ever showing such an interest in birds before. Must you practice your charm on every person you meet?"

"An Irishman always knows which side of the bread to butter." He made a grand gesture with her parcel, and went on softly, "Were I the bashful sort, wood sprite, I'd never have danced with you the night we met. And I'd never have asked you to marry me."

Swallowing a knot of nostalgia, she yanked on her gloves. "I shouldn't have been so naive as to believe you could actually see your commitment through. This is one person who's had enough of your blarney to last a lifetime. Now give me my package."

She tried to grab it from him. The vivid blue of his eyes snared her as he clasped the parcel against his coat. "I'll carry it for you, m' love. I won't have you thinking me any less than one of your fancy gentlemen."

"On the contrary, I don't think of you at all."

His sigh condensed on the frosty air. "Faith, Chelsea, 'tis sorry I am that today has been such a trial for you. I know how you must have relished the prospect of spending your life dusting feathers and polishing glass eyeballs."

A twinkle lurked in his gaze. She'd never admit that all those dead creatures gave her the shivers. "I wasn't going to be a maid. I was going to be a titled lady. Much more than you ever offered me."

"Ah, but I have something greater than riches. Love."

She repressed the leap of joy in her chest. Skirts swishing, she stomped down the graveled drive. "You've a peculiar way of showing *that*."

With easy strides, he kept pace with her. "I'm the first to admit I made a mistake in leaving you."

"You made another mistake in going to see Sir Basil. Six years ago you forfeited all right to meddle in my life."

"Ah, but I feared the devil might tempt you not to tell his lordship about me. 'Twould be simple indeed to let the unwanted husband slip quietly back to America. No one need ever learn he's still alive and hale."

Her cheeks burned. "Of course I meant to break the truth—more gently than you did, I might add. I'm a woman of honor. Why else do you suppose I came straight here?"

She tossed Sean a challenging glare. All mockery vanished from his face; he gazed at her with an expression as bleak as the December scenery. "Ah, Chelsea," he murmured. "Can you truly love him, then?"

The agonized undertone caught at her heart. The most ridiculous urge to caress the cleft in his chin swept over her. Clenching her fingers into fists at her sides, she concentrated on walking through the shorn hayfield.

"Tell me, Chelsea. I'll have no secrets between us."

She stumbled over a root and he reached out to steady her, his grip firm on her arm. Again she found her attention trapped by his sober sapphire eyes. When he looked at her like that, somehow she could not bring herself to lie.

"I was . . . *am* fond of Sir Basil."

"Fond of him or his pedigree?"

"Him, of course." The words sounded hollow, weaker than she'd intended.

"And did your fondness make you burn to share his bed? To let him kiss that glorious beauty mark on your hip? Did you fancy he could carry you up to the stars?"

"Stop it!" She pulled her arm free and stalked onward. "There's more to marriage than pretty words and a romp in bed."

"Aye," he conceded, falling in beside her. "There's devotion. A wife willing to follow her husband to the ends of the earth."

"And dependability. A husband who'd never abandon his wife."

He scowled. "Faith, woman, we've strayed from the subject. You know how much pleasure a wife can reap from making love with her husband. Would you deny yourself such happiness?"

She *did* remember. Too well, too poignantly. Even now, in the brisk icy air, she felt flushed with the memory of Sean caressing her beneath the quilts, his warm mouth suckling her bare breasts, his clever fingers stroking the moist heat between her legs until she writhed with unrestrained bliss . . .

"I don't deny that one can enjoy the marital embrace. But not with a husband who'd desert me."

"We were both young and prideful. Give me half a chance, love. Half a chance to show you I've changed."

Chelsea couldn't resist slanting a look at him from beneath her bonnet brim. Sunshine cast his rakish features into sharp relief. Panic surged in her as the low stone wall surrounding the school property loomed in the distance. The desperate need to escape him beat against her ribs.

"You gave up your right to second chances a long time ago," she said. "Why are you following me, anyway? I told you I don't ever want to see you again."

"Aye, but we need to talk."

"I've nothing more to say to you."

"Then 'tis I who'll do the speaking and you the listening."

She blew out a breath. "What will it take to convince you, Sean? Our marriage is over, in my heart if not by law. Now give me my package and go away."

She tried to snatch it from him. He held the square of brown paper out of her reach. "Faith, you're more protective of this parcel than a mother cat of her kittens. What might be in here?"

"Nothing of interest to *you*."

"More secrets, Chelsea love?"

His chiding tone grated on her nerves, like chalk

dragged across a slate. "All right," she said. "I'll show you, since you're so keen on knowing."

Black brows quirked, he handed her the parcel. The paper crackled as she tore it off to reveal an Audubon watercolor of a kingfisher. Mournfully she regarded the crack in the glass and the gilt frame that hung askew.

"I must have broken it when I hit you," she said. "But it's the least of the damage you've done, I suppose. It was to be my Christmas gift to Sir Basil."

Sean's face softened. Before she could draw back, his hand brushed her cheek in a quicksilver stroke that threatened her precarious equilibrium. " 'Tis grieved I am to have caused you distress. But our marriage *is* true in the eyes of Our Lord. I'll not give up until I've had m' say."

"I'll meet you tomorrow, then. On the old stone bridge at Bradford-on-Avon."

"Oh, nay, I'm not fool enough to travel five miles away, just so you can keep me your own dark secret. We'll meet now, right there."

He nodded toward the gray stone bulk of the academy. By his steadfast expression, she knew with sickening frustration that he would follow her inside if necessary.

The cupola clock crowning the front entrance chimed the hour of four. No one strolled the side garden; the girls must already be gathering for pantomime practice. Gritting her teeth, Chelsea decided it might be safe to sneak him into her private apartment, let him say his piece of blarney, then spirit him out again while everyone assembled for dinner.

"All right, then," she said. "But you must promise to stay out of sight. The girls aren't used to men wandering the halls."

"I'll be as good as California gold." With a flourish, he pushed open the gate. "After you, love."

She rewrapped the parcel and started up the carriage drive. How casually he spoke of love, she reflected bitterly. He had abandoned her once; now he seemed intent on wreaking havoc with her life again. If anyone saw them . . .

Nervousness quickened her steps as she led him behind the main classroom building. Here, several smaller structures formed a quadrangle: refectory, dormitory, library, and chapel. In the central square, chestnut trees spread barren limbs over the empty flower beds. A squirrel scampered along the brown grass. The wrought-iron benches, which provided a fine place to sit in balmy weather, now looked cold and forlorn.

" 'Tis most impressive," Sean said, slowing to study the stately Georgian architecture. "Imagine, m' wife a respected teacher. How many colleens study here?"

The pride on his face oddly gratified her. "Seventy-six in all. Come this way." She started toward the dormitory.

Yet he lingered, hands in his pockets, as he continued his leisurely survey of the school. "And how old might they be?"

"Between the ages of twelve and seventeen." Prickles crept down her spine. Did anyone peep at them from the mullioned windows? "Do come along."

Grinning, he saluted her. "Aye, Mrs. Devlin."

With relief, she entered a doorway at the end of the dormitory and mounted a steep flight of stairs. At the top, she turned left and opened a plain wooden door.

"Please, come in," she said, politely standing back.

Her formal manner made Sean feel a twist of dismay. Faith, but his wife had honed the noble talent of gazing straight through a man. He prayed her touch-me-not air was but a shield to guard against further hurt. He ached to turn back time, to kiss her again, to unpin the prim blonde coil of her hair, to see her gray eyes go misty with love.

Drawn by the vision, he leaned toward her, his hand brushing her elegant face. "Chelsea," he murmured.

She flinched, then marched inside. Quelling his frustration, he shut the door and looked around. The bed-sitting-room was small but cozy. In the corner, behind a chintz-covered screen, he glimpsed a narrow bed covered by a painstakingly tidy blue counterpane. The lack of luxury struck straight into his heart. Had her lot been hard? Or had she changed? Did she no longer need expensive trappings to make her happy?

Yet she'd wanted to marry a titled man. Jealousy still burned in Sean's heart, along with an alien uncertainty. He and Chelsea had both changed in subtle ways. He glanced at the multi-paned window. No longer did she keep a candle on the sill, lighted in hope for an errant husband's return . . .

Her movements bore a familiar grace as she set down the parcel, hung the bonnet and mantle on a hook, then wrapped herself in a gray woolen shawl. Shrugging off his overcoat, he wandered around, running a hand over the striped armchair, then the matching chaise longue. Several books lay on a side table. Was she content to curl up by the fire on a cold night, with only a book for company? Yearning pressed at his throat, the need to absorb every detail of her life, to unravel the mystery of the woman his wife had become.

At the modest dressing table, he fingered the set of silver hairbrushes, the only extravagance in the room. The brushes had been a wedding gift from Lady Quincy. He winced to remember himself insisting Chelsea return the costly present. Back then, he'd had too bloody much pride and was too ignorant to know the difference between a gift and charity. Their heated argument had ignited a blaze of passion that dissolved into a night of lusty love . . .

Chelsea cleared her throat. "At least we have a private place to meet. I spent my first five years here chaperoning the girls downstairs in the dormitory. Only last autumn did I gain my own apartment."

She stood near the door, hands clutching the fringe of her shawl. She looked poised yet uneasy, a wood sprite on the verge of flight. Softly he asked, "Are you truly happy here, love?"

"Yes. I have everything I could ever want."

Her certainty blasted more doubts into the bedrock of his confidence. Picking up the poker, Sean stirred the glowing embers in the fireplace. Sparks danced like a shower of tiny stars. Needing time to think, he added coals, the shovel scraping the grate. He'd understood Chelsea as a wistful girl. But her leap into womanhood left him baffled. Only the memory of her initial reaction to seeing him again, the naked joy that shone in her eyes and the unguarded eagerness of her kiss, could rekindle his spirits.

"All these years," he said, "I fancied you living in a noble house, tutoring little Lord Edward. What happened, Chelsea? Did Lady Lucille refuse to hire you?"

"I never even went to see her. I . . . decided to make a clean break from the past."

"Aye, I'd wondered. When I arrived in England a fortnight ago, I thought to find you through Lady Quincy. I had the very devil of a time getting in to see her." He paused, remembering her chilly reception. " 'Twas she who gave me your address. Yet she said she scarce knew what had become of you, that you rarely bothered to write, let alone pay an old woman a visit."

Sadness tugged at Chelsea's lovely mouth; then the brief gentling firmed into a bitter line. "Speaking of not writing, Sean, surely *you* could have found someone to pen a letter to me, if only to let me know you were still alive."

"Have you forgotten our last quarrel? 'Twas you who said you never wished to see me again."

"We'd had arguments before, but you never stormed out." Her expression wavered again, softening with grief, as if she could no longer restrain her emotions. "Why, Sean? Why did you stay away so long? Why didn't you come back until it was too late?"

He stared, riveted by the misery on her face. Had

their separation been no more than a colossal blunder? Had his hotheaded pride cost them years of happiness?

He took a halting step toward her. "Faith, you told me you regretted marrying me," he said, his voice hoarse. "I thought if I went away and never returned, you needn't be held back by a low-class husband. You could become a governess. You could live in one of the fine houses of the gentry. 'Tis what you wanted, isn't it?"

Her gaze fell. "Yes, but I like what I'm doing now. So you needn't trouble yourself."

The sadness about her gnawed at Sean. He walked nearer, until he stood close enough to catch her elusive violet scent. "I meant only to do right by you, love. I swear by all the saints, I never meant to hurt you."

Her eyes remained stubbornly downcast. He wished he dared tell her the truth about California, but he couldn't now, not until he was sure of her unconditional love.

"Come back to America with me," he cajoled. " 'Tis a grand country, a place we can be free. We'll take walks in the redwood forests, where the air is as hushed as a cathedral. We'll see the deep gorges and turquoise rivers of the Sierras. We'll watch the fog rolling in from the Pacific—"

"No!" Her head shot up, her features set with anger. "Sean, how could you even imagine—" A distant clock tolled the quarter hour, and she gasped. "Oh, sweet heavens. I'm late for practice."

She reached for the door; he ensnared her hand on the brass knob. Her fingers felt impossibly dainty, and a river of heat drenched him with the memory of how she had once touched him in love, aroused him with tender devotion. Resolution firmed inside him. He'd accept the fact that she'd never leave here. He'd make a more determined effort to win her back. He'd show her the loving respect she deserved.

"I'm going with you," he said.

She swung around, gray eyes wide with alarm. "You

can't. You must wait here until I return."

The old misgivings rose within him to sour his mouth. "Still ashamed of me, Chelsea love?"

"No! I only . . ."

She bit her lip. Saint Brenden save him, he wanted to kiss her until the sorrows of the past melted into the pleasures of an unreasoning present. Instead, he twisted the knob and yanked open the door.

He stopped in surprise.

A tall woman stood in the hall. A black net imprisoned her graying hair and her sharp features looked as grim as a banshee's visage. One thin hand was poised as if to knock.

Chelsea's arm brushed him as she took a step backward. "Miss Maxwell!"

3

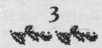

CHELSEA wished the floor would open and swallow her. She'd be dismissed for entertaining a man in her room! She'd have to start all over again at another school. Like a wren caught between a hunter and a cat, she stood trapped between Sean's damning presence and Miss Maxwell's chilling gaze.

"What is the meaning of this?" the headmistress demanded, folding her arms across the black bombazine of her bodice, in a gesture reserved for recalcitrant pupils.

Chelsea swallowed. "I . . ." Sean would probably blurt out the truth; far better that it should come from her. Shoulders squared, she looked at her employer. "I would like you to meet my husband, Sean Devlin.

Sean, this is Miss Maxwell, headmistress of our academy."

Miss Maxwell's taut lips parted. Her gaze darted from Sean to Chelsea. "Husband? What is this nonsense? When I hired you, you presented yourself as a widow."

"At the time, Sean had been gone for months. I . . . I thought—"

"She thought me dead." He lay a firm hand on Chelsea's shoulder, radiating heat over her cold skin. "Through a tragic mistake, she'd heard false word from America, where I'd gone to seek our fortune in the goldfields. Years it's been that I've worked my claim, hoping to strike it rich, so I could give her all the comforts a man dreams of giving his wife. But I realized I'd left my greatest treasure behind."

His tender words might melt other feminine hearts, but Chelsea knew him better. Thank heavens, Miss Maxwell wouldn't fall for such blarney, either.

"Indeed," said the headmistress, skepticism arching her brows. "Did it never occur to you to write?"

He cocked his head in boyish chagrin. "Faith, 'tis ashamed I am to admit the truth to such a fine, clever lady as yourself."

"Admit what truth?"

"As a wee lad growing up on the streets, I never had the chance to learn m' letters. I dearly hope you can forgive such a miserable failing. I wouldn't wish you to think poorly of me—or of m' own Chelsea."

To Chelsea's dismay, Miss Maxwell's stern expression eased as she was sucked in by his charm. "Of course not, Mr. Devlin. One cannot help the circumstances of one's birth." She wagged a knobby finger. "Yet one *can* strive to improve oneself."

"Oh, aye, ma'am."

"You've no reason to wither in the darkness of illiteracy when your wife is such a gifted teacher."

"A grand notion, to be sure." His darkly handsome features remained solemn, though his eyes sparkled at

Chelsea. "Now that we've been reunited, 'twould be a pleasure indeed to take tutoring from m' own beloved wife."

She stiffened. Spend more time with Sean? The very thought shot hot and cold flashes through her. "I have a full schedule of classwork. I wouldn't wish to shirk my duties."

"Nonsense," said Miss Maxwell. "You've unrestricted time in the evenings. And the Christmas holiday will soon be upon us." She peered closely at Chelsea. "Unless you've an objection to helping your own husband."

Beneath Miss Maxwell's gruff exterior lay a heart unselfishly devoted to charity. Her generosity of spirit had drawn Chelsea to the academy years ago, when she'd been a grieving, abandoned wife searching for a secure home.

Pinned by that glare, she had no choice but to murmur, "Of course not."

"Excellent. It is our sworn duty as teachers to open the world of the printed word to people everywhere."

" 'Tis an admirable goal, to be sure." Sean cleared his throat. "Might I impose further on your benevolence, ma'am?"

A faint, encouraging smile touched the headmistress's lips. "What is it?"

"M' own foolish search for treasure has cost Chelsea and me many years of happiness." He feathered his fingers over the sensitive skin of her neck. " 'Tis m' fondest hope that we might live together and rekindle the love that lighted our youth. Yet I mislike the notion of stealing her away from you . . ."

Chelsea's jaw dropped. The nerve of him, acting so affectionate, assuming she'd go off with him! "Don't give a thought to my leaving, Miss Maxwell," she said. "If you'll have me, I'd like to remain right here."

"Indeed. I shouldn't wish to see you depart in the midst of the school year. Perhaps I shall make an exception to my rule about married teachers." A strange wistfulness lit the headmistress's brown eyes. "And you've a point, young man. A married couple belongs together. For the time being, you may reside in the gardener's old quarters over the stables, until I can arrange permanent quarters for the both of you."

"What?" Chelsea gasped.

"May Saint Brenden bless you." Stepping forward, Sean kissed Miss Maxwell's hand. "A more kind-hearted lady I've never before had the honor of meeting."

Her cheeks pinkened. She drew her hand back and lifted her sharp chin to a dignified level. "I must request, Mr. Devlin, that you never venture into the dormitory at night. Our young ladies must be sheltered from the . . . ahem . . . practices of man and wife."

Sean graced her with his devastating smile. " 'Tis grateful I am just to be near m' wife. I'll be the very soul of discretion."

She gave him a quelling look. "I trust you will. Now, Mrs. Devlin, I came to see what was keeping you. Given the circumstances, I'll overlook your being late for rehearsal, so long as you go straight to the refectory."

The pantomime. Head spinning, heart aching, Chelsea struggled to clear the panic fogging her senses. Sean couldn't stay so close by! Yet how could she object without revealing the hurtful details of their estrangement? "But . . . but Miss Maxwell—"

"We were just on our way there, ma'am," he said, clasping Chelsea's icy hand. "I couldn't bear to let m' darling wife out of m' sight. Given me up for dead, she had. 'Tis Our Lord's own miracle that I returned before she remarried."

"Dear me!" Miss Maxwell frowned. "Sir Basil! Someone must inform him . . ."

"Bless you for considering the kind gent," Sean said. "May the Lord forgive me for breaking another human being's heart, but at least he took the news with a stiff upper lip."

"Oh, the poor man! Alone at a time like this. Perhaps I should take him a jar of Cook's orange marmalade, and help him with his specimens. Yes, yes, I must do so straightaway." Turning in uncustomary agitation, she hastened down the stairs.

"Faith, the woman's in a crashing rush. Might I behold a hidden fondness in her starched heart for the bird-loving gent?"

At any other time, Chelsea would have been startled by the headmistress's behavior. But fury had a stranglehold on her emotions.

Gripping the edges of her shawl, she rounded on Sean. "How dare you invite yourself to stay here! What do you want from me? A warm body in your bed each night? Let me make this clear, Sean Devlin, it shan't be mine!"

His eyes darkened. "I want only a chance—"

"There'll be no more chances. How many times must I say that? Yet you persist in using your brash Irish charm, as if by winning over every person in my life, you fancy you can win *me* as well."

"Time was, you liked m' Irish charm."

"That time ended forever when you deserted me. You cared more for your reckless adventuring than for your own wife—"

Tears closed her throat. Whirling away, she headed toward the stairs. He caught her arm and spun her back around, his lean body pressing her to the carved oak paneling. Her senses swam with the outdoors fragrance of him, with the heat and tension emanating from him. Raw emotion made his features stark.

"I tried to forget you, Chelsea, because I knew you wouldn't have me back. As the saints can stand witness, I tried. A man can't hold his head high knowing he arouses naught but shame in his own wife." Bitterness chased across his features, and he moved back a fraction, his arms still bracketing her.

"I never said I was ashamed of you!"

"Oh? All you could talk of was educating me." In a

blend of American brashness and Irish lilt, he went on, "When I heard of that agent nosing around, 'twas impossible to bury m' feelings any longer. I hoped at first you'd changed your mind and wanted me back. But a wee devil whispered the unhappy tale that you'd found someone else, that you wished to remarry. So you see, 'twas the blackest jealousy that sent me rushing back here. I had to know the truth."

"You never cared enough to be jealous," Chelsea countered.

"I did care. I cared so much I was willing to give you what you wanted most—me, out of your life." He paused, his eyes probing hers. "You asked what I want. I want you back in m' life and in m' bed, wood sprite. Most of all, I want you to love me as much I still love you."

Flabbergasted, she gazed numbly at him, from the strand of black hair lying rakishly across his forehead to the candid blue of his eyes, from the firm set of his mouth to the bold cleft in his chin. The sudden certainty of his love robbed her of anger and left a shaky confusion. Heaven help her, she wanted to touch her lips to his, to reawaken the fairy-tale happiness of girlish dreams. But she couldn't bear the heartache again.

"I'm *not* ashamed of you," she asserted again, in a softer voice. "I never have been. If I didn't want anyone to find out about you today, it was only because I feared losing my teaching post."

His face gentled. "'Tis pleased I am to hear you say so. A few weeks is all I'm asking you. A few weeks to see if we can find the gold that pride made us toss away."

She moved her head from side to side. "We've already tried living together for a few weeks, and you left me."

"'Twas youthful pride that drove me away." He stroked her cheek. "You needn't fear I'll be forcing m'self into your bed, Chelsea. I'll play fair. You have m' word on that."

His nearness made her tremble. Was it Sean she mistrusted . . . or herself? She thrust her chin up. "If you expect me to toss away my life here and move to America, you're wasting your time."

"I expect . . ." His face hardened; he slammed a fist against the wall with such force the paneling rattled against her spine. "All I expect, Chelsea, is a wife who'll meet me halfway."

His vehemence disconcerted her. How much of what he said could she believe, and how much was the eloquence of a smooth-talking Irishman? She lowered her eyes. "I must go to rehearsal."

This time, when she moved toward the stairs, he let her go. The tread of his feet behind her lent a comforting sense of companionship. His determination to fit into her life, at least for the time being, aroused a swirl of bewildering emotions inside her—dismay and delight, pain and pleasure. Could the seeds of love still lie buried deep inside her?

They walked across the chilly quadrangle and toward the refectory. Swallowing hard, she stole a glance at him. He stared at the ground, his brow creased in thought. The flawless male beauty of his profile wrenched her heart. *Had* she driven him away by expecting him to fulfill her dream of becoming a fine lady? Had she stolen his pride by not loving him for the man he was, by refusing to open herself to *his* dream?

The troubling questions chilled her more than the icy wind.

Inside the refectory, the last rays of sunlight streamed through the windows and illuminated the far end, where the long dining tables had been pushed against the walls to clear an open space. A cheery blaze crackled in the hearth. On chairs nearby sat the girls, clad in white pinafores over gray frocks, their ringlets neatly held back with white bows. Giggles and chatter brightened the air. The sight of her precious charges brought a measure of contentment to Chelsea's soul.

She clapped her hands. "Young ladies! May I have your attention?"

The noise dropped to a murmur. Eyes agog, a sea of girlish faces swung toward her. The sudden hiss of whispers betrayed a keen interest in Sean.

With an inexplicable lightness of heart, she gestured at him. "We have a visitor today. I should like all of you to meet my husband, Mr. Devlin."

A willowy girl with reddish hair leapt to her feet. "Aren't you supposed to be dead?" blurted Georgina Ives.

"Only in a bumbling agent's casebook," he said, grinning. "I've been away in America."

"America, sir?" piped little Martha Griggson from the back of the group. "Oh, do tell us about the blood-thirsty Indians."

"Did they shoot arrows at you?" asked Jane Yardley, bouncing up and down in her chair, blue eyes big in her china-doll face. "Did they try to scalp you?"

Laughing, Sean ruffled a hand through his hair and perched on the edge of a table. "Nay, I survived un-scathed, though I could tell more than one grisly tale of men who crossed the Great Plains."

"Oh, do entertain us with some stories, sir," begged Martha.

"Yes, please," chorused several others.

His eyes twinkled. "Faith, I'd hoped you'd be more inclined to hearing about m' own adventures. I've been mining gold in California." He looked at Chelsea. "To make m' wife's dreams come true."

"Gold!"

"Are you rich as Croesus?"

"Did you bring lots of fancy gifts for Mrs. Devlin?"

"One special present," he said. "But she cannot find out what it is 'til Christmastide."

He gave Chelsea a mysterious half-smile that started her wondering in spite of herself. What could he have brought her? It didn't matter, she thought, lacing her fingers in the shawl fringe. Undoubtedly he'd be off again before the holiday.

"How very romantic," murmured Alice Archer, hands clasped to her flat bosom. "You're ever so much more dashing than . . ." She glanced at Chelsea and fell silent, blushing.

"Aye," Sean said under his breath, "at least m' wife won't waste her life dusting dead birds."

Chelsea shot him a warning glare, which he met with a grin.

"Oh, dear!" exclaimed Jane in dismay. "You aren't going to leave us straightaway, are you, Mrs. Devlin? You promised to stay through the end of spring."

Distraught exclamations swept the gathering. Tenderness glowed inside Chelsea, for these girls had long eased the aching emptiness inside her. "I shan't be going anywhere," she said. "Now, take your places, everyone. I thought to find all of you practicing already."

Groans and grumbles filled the chamber, along with the scrapings of chair legs and the swish of starched petticoats.

Mincing to the front of the group, one of the older girls, Eliza Phipps, turned up her elegant nose. "I don't see why this is necessary. We needn't rehearse *that* old story."

"Eliza's right," said Laura Hargreave, a typical disgruntled look on her elfin face. "We've done Saint George and the dragon for each of the three years *I've* been here."

"Saint George?" said Sean, casting an inquiring look at Chelsea. " 'Tis a curious choice for a Christmas play."

"It's a school tradition," she explained. "We perform it for the villagers each December."

" 'Tis a queer tradition, to be sure. Were the choice mine, I'd put on a show more in the spirit of the holidays."

"What might that be, sir?" ventured Martha.

"Perhaps *A Christmas Carol* by Mr. Dickens."

Excited chatter burst from the girls.

"A jolly idea," said Jane, blue eyes gleaming. "I could be one of the ghosts. Imagine, all those clanking chains and such."

"*I* must play Belle," said Alice, twirling in romantic grace. "Mr. Scrooge's tragic lost love."

"Oh, what great fun!" exclaimed Dora Lang, clasping her chubby hands. "Cook might even give us real food to use for the Christmas feast."

Smiling indulgently, Sean said, "Bless Saint Brenden, 'tis a grand notion. We might even share the feast with the villagers afterwards." He aimed a devilish look at Chelsea. "Providing the plan meets the approval of Mrs. Devlin, of course."

"Oh, yes!" cried the girls, their eyes shining. "Please, Mrs. Devlin." Everyone started talking at once, the din echoing in the cavernous room.

Annoyance burned inside Chelsea. She might have known Sean Devlin would manage to turn a simple rehearsal into an uproar.

She clapped her hands again. "Enough, girls! We're performing Saint George. We haven't the time to put together a new production."

"We've several weeks yet," said Laura, pouting. "Oh, don't make us do that dull old fairy tale again."

"If you please, Mrs. Devlin," spoke a plain girl from the back. As everyone turned to stare, Prudence Henning adjusted her horn-rimmed spectacles and shrank against the stone chimneypiece. "I . . . I own a copy of the work in question, and . . . and should like to volunteer to transcribe the speaking parts."

Though gratified to see the shy girl offer to participate, Chelsea said gently, "Thank you, but I'm afraid it's out of the question. *A Christmas Carol* is far too long a piece. It would take weeks to write out enough copies for everyone."

"Not if we all pitch in," said Jane, jumping from one foot to the other in an effort to see past the taller girls.

"Prudence is so awfully quick. I'll wager we could have the pantomime script finished within a few days."

"Yes, yes," came several eager voices. "We'll all help."

"Why do you need a script?" asked Sean, frowning. "Isn't a pantomime where you caper about without speaking?"

Georgina's willowy frame convulsed in a giggle. "Oh, heavens, no. It's the English rendition, with lots of singing and dancing and tale-telling."

"That's why Mr. Dickens's story is perfect for Christmas," said Dora. "Don't forget the feasting on cakes and pies and puddings, too."

Chelsea shook her head in exasperation. She ached to see her girls happy, but they weren't viewing the situation sensibly. "I'm afraid I must disagree. There are rehearsals to consider, and props—"

"Leave the props to me," said Sean. " 'Tis many a hurdy-gurdy show I've seen in America."

"Hurdy-gurdy?"

Under her cool stare, he grinned sheepishly. "Musicians, in a manner of speaking. Traveling troupes who perform for the miners."

"Saint George is the patron saint of England. His is a time-honored story, a classic. Hardly mere popular fiction."

He cocked a black eyebrow. "Aye, but even a classic must have had a start somewhere. Who knows, in fifty years perhaps you'll be teaching the Dickens tale, right along with Shakespeare."

Teasing tilted the corners of his mouth. He enjoyed stirring this hornet's nest! Despite her irritation, she had to squelch this most absurd urge to return his smile.

"Miss Maxwell will never agree to a change at so late a date," she pointed out.

"You leave her to me."

His confidence irked Chelsea. "It would take a miracle to be ready on time."

"Have faith, woman," Sean murmured, blue eyes intense in the fading rays of sunlight. "Have you so quickly forgotten about the candle in the snow?"

Her heart went liquid. For a long moment the fire crackled into the silence. She could only stare at him, for she knew he was remembering when he'd first told her the tale, to buoy her flagging spirits on the wearisome ride to Gretna Green.

The girls crowded closer. "What candle in the snow?" asked Jane, eyes round with curiosity.

"Please do tell us, sir," begged Martha.

"With Mrs. Devlin's permission."

He looked at Chelsea and she nodded numbly.

Relaxing against the stone wall, he said, " 'Tis an ancient Irish legend, about a gentleman who lived alone for many years. Though lord of a grand castle, he would not marry, for he'd never met a girl he liked enough. Well, one day a great thunderstorm blew up while he was out hunting, and he took shelter in a deserted hut alongside a lake. The rain ceased as night fell, and the sad sound of singing drew him outside.

"There, to his surprise, sat a woman on a rock, a colleen as pretty as a wood sprite." Sean cast a meaningful look at Chelsea. "She said she'd lived in the hut as a girl, but her parents had sold her to evil fairies in exchange for worldly riches. Until she could win the true love of a human, she was doomed to remain a prisoner of the dark netherworld."

A collective "Oooh" issued from the girls.

"To be sure, the gentleman vowed to love her. He would have kissed her then, but she warned him against touching her, for fear the wee folk might claim him as well. And so they sat and talked until dawn lit the sky. To set her free, she said, he must first prove his faith, and she lit a candle. He must keep it burning in the window of the hut, else she would die. Then she vanished into the morning mist."

Gasps rippled from the girls, and their rapt faces were tilted toward Sean. The web of enchantment snared Chelsea as well, and she sank onto a chair.

Clasping his hands around his bent knee, Sean continued, "For nigh on six years the gentleman kept his lonely vigil, guarding the magic candle. Many a time he was cold and miserable, but he would not give up, for his life was nothing without her. Then one winter there came the most terrible blizzard Ireland has ever seen. Cows froze in the fields and many people died. A fever overtook the gentleman and he awakened much later to find the hut dark and the flame gone out."

Several girls sniffled; fabric rustled as they groped for handkerchiefs.

" 'Twas with great sorrow in his heart that he struck a flint and relit the candle. Then he carried it out into the wild wind and driving snow, sheltering the flame within his coat, for he wanted to die in the place where he'd first seen his true love. He feared the lass would think he'd lost faith, though love still blazed in his heart. In a daze, he fell onto the rock and prayed, 'Dear Lord, You must save her, for I can no longer go on.'

"Suddenly the snow vanished and springtime blossomed all 'round him. He came to his senses with the beautiful colleen embracing him, for the evil spell was broken forever. Tears streaming down her cheeks, she said his faith had wrought a miracle."

Sighs swept like a wave through the audience. A few girls dabbed at their eyes, and even Chelsea had to blink to clear her misty vision, for he'd tailored the story to fit their own estrangement.

"And did they live happily ever after?" asked Alice dreamily.

"Why, bless Saint Brenden, of course they did. I heard they even had a dozen children." Sean paused to aim a soft yet probing look at Chelsea. "You see, even though they'd been separated for many years, the gentleman never stopped loving his lady."

Her throat ached. If only reality could match such

fantasy. If only magic could restore lost love and shattered faith . . .

"We can make a miracle, too, with the pantomime," Jane declared.

"We'll give up our free time to learn our lines," said Laura, her usual sullenness banished by enthusiasm.

"We'll plan extra rehearsals," promised Georgina.

"Yes," Dora added stoutly, "we'll even work through teatime if we must."

Martha wriggled past the older girls and tugged on Chelsea's skirt. "Even I could have a part, couldn't I? I could play Tiny Tim Cratchit. Please, might I?"

An endearing glow lit her dainty, heart-shaped features. Gazing around at the other expectant faces, Chelsea felt the bleakness of practicality dissolve into the warmth of hope. Perhaps this was one miracle even she could believe in . . .

"All right, then," she said. "We'll do *A Christmas Carol*. But you must begin your copying immediately."

Amid cheers and chatter and a mad scramble for the dormitory, she looked at Sean. The tenderness in his eyes made her heart tremble. Quickly she turned and walked out, before she succumbed to the dangerous softening inside her.

Sean vanished after practice and stayed away from dinner, as well. Alone in her room later, Chelsea spied a faint glow in the window of the gardener's old quarters. The knowledge that her husband was alive and near still shook her. Huddled beneath the counterpane that night, she couldn't sleep. The floodtide of memories, the impossible yearnings she'd so carefully tucked away, kept her as wakeful as a candle that blazed without cease.

Not that she intended to revive their marriage. Sean Devlin was still a devil-may-care rogue who might depart at any moment on another wild adventure. Yet she couldn't stop wondering if she'd been too hard on him long ago, if their love might have endured had she been mature enough to bend. Heart pounding, she wondered if she could resist if he tried to kiss her again . . .

But he didn't.

Over the next few days, to her wary surprise, he kept his distance. Yet he was ever-present, a tall and cheerful charmer who chatted with Miss Maxwell after Sunday church service and entertained the girls with tales of the wild West. He sat apart from Chelsea at meals, though his hearty laughter drifted down the long table. Even the snobbish Mademoiselle Daumier, the French teacher, and gloomy Miss Mainwaring, the history teacher, fell victim to his spell.

Chelsea was guiltily aware that Miss Maxwell expected her to teach Sean to read. But he never broached the matter, and she found it easier to procrastinate. In her heart, she ached to help him. Yet she couldn't bear to closet herself alone with him, to sit close to him, to risk awakening emotions best left forgotten . . .

Instead, she kept busy with schoolwork. But it proved hard to forget Sean when the girls bubbled over with jests he'd told them and offered snippets of his conversation. Jane even began to mimic his Irish lilt.

As the week progressed, Chelsea wondered how he occupied himself during the long hours of class time. Each morning, gazing out the window of her schoolroom, she saw him stride purposefully toward the village. Her throat went dry. Was he already so bored he couldn't bear to stay in one place?

At least his return had reaped one reward: excitement centered on the pantomime. She'd never seen the girls work with such inspiration on their copywork. Ink-stained fingers abounded, and many an eye looked bleary during her literature lectures. By Friday, the scripts were prepared, the roles assigned, and rehearsal began in earnest.

At the appointed hour of four, Chelsea entered the refectory. Her steps faltered when she spied Sean hanging his overcoat on a hook near the door. He looked up, grinned, and sauntered over to help her remove her cloak.

"Afternoon, love." His admiring gaze swept the gown of sapphire silk with its modest lace flounces on the skirt. " 'Tis fetching as a wood sprite you are today."

"Thank you," she murmured, secretly glad she'd given in to impulse and worn her best frock. Before she could stay her tongue, she said, "Where have you been today?"

A momentary shadow came over his face. "Oh, wandering the countryside. 'Tis restless I am without you."

In a fleeting caress, his cool hand stroked her flushed cheek. Disobeying the dictates of reason, her heart stumbled over a beat. She ached to rub against his fingers; it had been so long since he'd touched her.

The overcast sky rendered his eyes an opaque blue and the wind had tousled his black hair into a rakish tumble. A snow-white cravat and gray morning coat gave him the jaunty air of a gentleman. She frowned. Now where had her ne'er-do-well Irishman gotten the funds to purchase such stylish clothing?

It was on the tip of her tongue to ask when a querulous voice called out, "Oh, Mrs. Devlin!" Script in hand, Laura waved from the gathering near the hearth. Her temper had improved since she'd been awarded the starring role of Scrooge, but now a frown soured her pretty face. "Do you know where Eliza is? We can't begin without our narrator."

"I haven't seen her since class," said Chelsea, walking closer, Sean beside her.

"I saw Eliza speaking to Miss Witherspoon about her costume," offered Dora, naming the sewing instructress.

"Bless Saint Brenden!" exclaimed Jane. "I'll see what's keeping her." She bounded out the door.

"We mustn't waste a moment," grumbled Laura. She turned to Sean and held out the script. "Mr. Devlin, perhaps you wouldn't mind filling in for Eliza so we can get started?''

Chelsea's throat went dry. Dear heavens, the girls didn't know of Sean's illiteracy. She couldn't stand by and let him suffer the humiliation of being found out.

Her lips forming a hasty excuse, she started to step in front of him. But he shot her a cocky glance, then strode forward and seized the sheaf of papers.

"I'd be honored," he said, and began to read.

4

" 'MARLEY was dead: to begin with,' " Sean recited in a clear, measured voice.

Thunderstruck, Chelsea stared. Despite an occasional slight faltering, he read with a melodious lilt that sent prickles over her skin. Her throat constricted from an upsurge of pride. Why had he hidden his new skill until now?

Concentration creased his brow. He inched a finger along the page to keep pace with the words. When he hesitated over a phrase, she ached to prompt him. She wanted to laugh and cry, to rebuke him and embrace him. Dear heavens, why hadn't he told her?

And what else had he concealed?

The girls sat listening, engrossed. Chelsea snapped out of her own reverie in time to nod at Dora, who played Scrooge's nephew.

On cue, the pudgy girl stepped forward. "A merry Christmas to you, uncle! God save you!"

"Bah! Humbug!" answered Laura, screwing her features into a parody of her usual peevish expression.

The refectory door slammed. Everyone turned. Trailed by Jane, Eliza minced inside and draped her shawl over a chair. "So sorry I'm late, Mrs. Devlin. We can commence rehearsal now."

Chelsea arched an eyebrow. "We already have. Mr. Devlin has been reading your part."

The girl halted. Blushing crimson, she turned doe-brown eyes on Sean. "Oh!"

He handed the script to her. "We left off right here," he said, pointing.

"Oh . . . I do thank you, sir." She dipped a flustered curtsy.

He smiled, then perched on a table near the back wall. As practice resumed, Chelsea had a difficult time concentrating on her role as director. A blend of vexation and bafflement plagued her. *She* was no hero-worshipping girl, so why did she feel this new welling of tenderness? Why should she be so absurdly pleased to learn he'd deceived her?

The play marched on. Impatient to confront Sean, for once she couldn't share in the girls' enthusiasm. At the end of Stave Two, she clapped her hands. "That's enough for now. We'll break for tea."

Shedding the sober countenance of the Spirit of Christmas Past, Jane bounced forward. "Faith, shouldn't we press on? How shall we be ready by December twenty-third?"

Sean frowned. " 'Tis rather late to be going home for the holidays, isn't it?"

"Oh, nay, sir," said Martha, her tiny face cheerful. "Miss Maxwell's Academy is our home. We're orphans, each and every one of us."

He straightened. "A charity school?"

Even from across the room, Chelsea felt the intensity of his gaze. She held herself upright and stared back.

Eliza gave an elegant sniff. "Miss Maxwell's Academy is for girls of genteel birth. She is renowned for educating superior governesses and companions."

"And wives." Sighing dreamily, Alice clasped her

hands over her flat bosom. "Some of our graduates go on to marry fine gentlemen."

" 'Tis lucky we all are to be here," asserted Jane. She wrinkled her china-doll nose. "After I lost my parents to a cholera epidemic in India, *I* very nearly had to live with my nasty Great-aunt Augustine."

"Who supports your education?" Sean asked.

"Friends of our departed parents, sir," Martha said. "And Miss Maxwell goes to London twice a year to solicit subscriptions from other kind ladies and gentlemen."

"I see. 'Tis a benevolent undertaking, to be sure."

He aimed another pensive look at Chelsea. She resisted the urge to squirm.

"Might I go see if Cook has our tea ready?" asked Dora. An expression approaching ecstasy lit her plump face. "She promised currant buns today."

Chelsea nodded distractedly, and the girl waddled off. The other pupils gathered around the fireplace and began chatting amongst themselves. Sean threaded through the throng, his dark head and broad shoulders visible above the sea of white bows and neat ringlets.

Chelsea's heart thumped. She couldn't get used to his presence here. Without fully understanding why, she turned and hastened toward the door. He caught up with her there, his fingers snaring her upper arm.

" 'Twill be a chill walk without this." He held forth her mantle.

His mocking eyes belied the pleasant set of his features. She let him drape the cloak around her and tried to ignore the tingly sensations caused by his hand brushing her high-throated gown.

"How thoughtful you've become," she couldn't resist taunting.

" 'Tis a pleasure to help m' lovely wife."

Slinging his coat over one shoulder, he grasped her hand and drew her into the dreary winter dusk. A glow on the horizon lit the sullen clouds. The wind swirled clumps of dead leaves across the path, and she huddled deeper into the gray merino mantle. Her entire being focused on the man who walked at her side, on the solid warmth of the hand clasping hers. Without speaking, they headed for the dormitory and up the dim flight of stairs.

They entered her room. Her blood surged with a curious blend of excitement and alarm; she hadn't been alone with him in nearly a week. With the impersonal finesse of a gentleman, he removed her wrap and hung it up.

"Now," he said, turning toward her, " 'tis time for you to explain why you haven't been honest with me."

He stood with his feet planted apart, his hands on his hips. Sudden ire flushed her cheeks. "Me?" she said. "How can you accuse *me* of dishonesty when *you* lied—to both me and to Miss Maxwell?"

"I spoke no untruth. Faith, you knew I couldn't read or write when I left for America. You never troubled to ask whether I could *now*."

"When did you learn?"

"A few years ago, from a clergyman's wife. 'Twas many a lonely night I spent practicing m' letters."

"Letters you never wrote *me*."

"Letters I didn't think you wanted."

Pain pierced her anger; she swallowed hard. "Why didn't you tell me right away that you could read, Sean?"

"I wanted to." Bitterness laced his voice. "But maybe I had to see if m' wife could love me for more than mere book-learning."

Chelsea took a step toward him. "Sean, is that what you really thought?" Words seemed inadequate to express the pride and regret and confusion gnawing at her. "I wanted you to educate yourself only so that you could become the finest man possible. I'm pleased to know you have."

One dark eyebrow lifted. "Pleased enough to accept me again as your husband?"

The challenge vibrated in the chilly air. He stood tall

and imperious, waiting for her to close the gap between them.

Beset by a swell of panic, she went to the hearth and used the poker to stir the glowing embers. A gust of wind down the chimney made the fire flare. She had driven Sean away once by expecting him to sacrifice his dreams to satisfy her own. Yet could she give up her beloved pupils, her friendships here, and move to America? Must she suffer the agony of losing him again?

Propping the poker against the fireplace, she ventured a look at him. "Sean, don't press me. I can't just leap back into our marriage. We've both changed."

"Aye. You never let on that you taught in a charity school."

"Does it matter so much?"

Impatience shadowed his face. "By Saint Brenden, you know it does. Six years ago, you led me to think you could be happy only as a lady living with the gentry. Now I learn you took a post teaching orphans. I want to know why."

How could she explain the yawning ache inside her when he'd left? The desire for a place to belong, for people who needed her? "I was a foundling myself. I . . . wanted to give love to others who had no one else to love them."

He paced restlessly around the small bedroom, touching a book here, a china pitcher there. "And yet you were planning to abandon the colleens come summer. If you loved them so dearly, why were you set on remarrying?"

"That's just like you to leap to conclusions," she flared. "I wasn't going to abandon them. With Sir Basil's approval, I'd intended to spend a few hours a week tutoring some of the girls."

"Why marry at all, then? Unless you couldn't be content without being called 'Lady Chelsea.'"

His contempt left her stricken. Unable to deny a familiar emptiness inside her, she walked to the window and gazed into the gray twilight. "It wasn't that at all," she murmured. "The girls never stay here longer than a few years, and I wanted children who would always belong to me. I wanted to feel my own babe kicking within me. I wanted to watch my own children thrive and grow." Leaning her forehead against the icy glass, she went on in a whisper, "I wanted someone who would never leave me. Someone I could love forever."

Silence hung thick in the room. From without came the muffled rattling of chestnut branches and the lonely keening of the wind. Sean's footsteps sounded on the floorboards; then she sensed his warm presence directly behind her.

She squeezed her eyes shut, but before she could master her turbulent emotions, he gently turned her toward him. Through blurry eyes, she gazed at the ivory buttons on his white shirt. Her hands rose to his chest in an instinctive effort to keep him at a safe distance.

His thumb slipped along her cheek and caught a stray tear. "Have you never chanced to consider, little wood sprite, that I could give you children?"

Her gaze leapt to his. The tender intensity of his expression made her sway. Sean's child . . . Long-ago dreams rushed over her, dreams of a boy with his devilish grin and blue eyes, of a girl with his gentle humor and coal-black hair. And memories of how barren she'd felt when, after he'd gone, the onset of her monthly courses had left her with no part of him to treasure.

Beneath her palm, his heart thumped in pace with the sudden wild tempo of her own blood. Without allowing herself to think, she lay her head in the hollow of his shoulder and pressed her lips to his throat. His scent reminded her of the outdoors, clean and earthy and achingly familiar.

A groan rumbled from his chest. "Chelsea, love . . ."

Tilting her chin up, he drenched her mouth in a deep and drowning kiss. She opened her lips and met the delicious stroking of his tongue. Reason burned away in a firestorm of yearning, a yearning too long denied. Hot and hungry, she melted against him and felt the hard strain of his arousal. His hand cupped her breast, the heat penetrating the stiff-boned corset and nourishing the ache between her thighs. She let her hands relearn the contours of hard chest and lean waist. Sean . . . this was her Sean, the only man who could make her feel such wonderful sensations. She wanted him . . . oh, sweet heavens, how she wanted him to fill the void of loneliness within her.

Abruptly his lips left hers. Clasping her shoulders, he thrust her to arm's length. Bereft and bewildered, she opened her eyes to see his chest heaving and his expression turn grim with longing.

"I want to make love to you, Chelsea."

"Then do . . . please do."

He shook his head, his eyes dark and moody. "I'll not risk planting m' seed until you vow to live with me as m' wife."

The chill wind of reality blew away the fever of desire. Struggling to collect her scattered wits, she bit her lip. "I . . . how can I, Sean?"

His fingers clenched her shoulders. "Do you love me?"

The hoarse question hovered between them. Searching herself, Chelsea found an agonizing joy and an icy fear. She bowed her head, unable to speak the words that might seal her fate. "Don't ask me that," she whispered.

"I must. Look at me. Look at me and say you'll be m' true wife now and forever."

She slowly raised her eyes to meet his. "I can't, Sean. How would we live? Where would we live?"

"I'll provide for you."

"But I want my children warm and fed and safe from harm. Do you have the means to support a family?"

Sean stiffened, as if she'd slapped him. "You've so little trust in me. We cannot make our marriage real until you learn to have more faith." He paused, searching her face. "If I said I meant to return to America, would you go with me?"

Confusion cut into her. Could she trail after him on his quest for adventure, could she cart a baby on her hip through a foreign land, could she raise their children without a permanent home? Could she endure the uncertainty that another quarrel might trigger him to storm out on her again?

She'd been abandoned so many times . . . by unknown parents, by Lady Quincy, by Sean himself. Could she throw away her safe niche here at the academy only to risk the pain of being deserted again?

"I . . . don't know," she murmured.

The intensity left his eyes. His hands dropped. " 'Tis best you think on it, then. Time is one of the quantities I'm rich enough in."

Pivoting, he grabbed his coat and strode out. The door clicked shut, then came the quiet rhythm of his footsteps descending the stairs.

Hands shaking, she gripped the sill. His tall figure emerged into view. Instead of heading across the quadrangle and back to the refectory, he walked slowly toward the shadowy woods beyond the school. His hands were plunged into his coat pockets, his shoulders hunched against the cold.

With a pang, Chelsea recalled his swaggering step as a young footman, his cocky grin, his bold kisses. Now she saw him as a man, a man who possessed hidden depths, a man who'd been hardened by experience. For too many years she'd envisioned him as a happy-go-lucky rogue who'd blithely forgotten his wife. But his character had been defined by their painful separation every bit as much as hers had been.

Would they ever reach accord?

The gloom of the forest swallowed him. She ached to call him back, but knew it was too soon. She ached to ease his bitterness, but knew she couldn't yet give him the trust he needed.

Most of all, she ached to become a girl again, to let dreams sustain their love, to believe in that candle in the snow.

Humbug, thought Sean, hauling on the ropes to open the crimson draperies. He paused in the gloom backstage as Laura, a pinch-faced Scrooge, strode out in nightcap and gown to begin Stave Four of the pantomime.

The eerie glow of lamps illuminated the background scenery of painted shop fronts. In the shadowy rows of chairs beyond the footlights, the villagers sat transfixed by the melodrama. Determined to give Chelsea her miracle, Sean had spent the past fortnight transforming the refectory into a makeshift theater, constructing the sturdy wooden platform, painting canvas backdrops, and stringing curtains on ropes worked by pulleys.

Yet sometimes he felt as jaded as Scrooge.

He stared at the opposite end of the stage, where Chelsea stood half-hidden by the curtains. The sapphire gown hugged her slender form to perfection. She looked fragile; he fancied he could smell her faint violet scent. He wanted her weak with need and begging for his love. But with the pencil stuck behind her ear and her blonde hair scraped into a bun, she was unmistakably in charge here. Where was the passionate girl he'd deflowered so tenderly?

He smiled in spite of his black mood. If he'd known as a lad that teachers could look so primly provocative, he might have learned to read earlier.

She bent her head to consult a notebook, then motioned Prudence and Alice offstage, where as laundress and charwoman, the two girls had been haggling over Scrooge's last effects.

Half-sick with longing, he studied his wife. For all his newfound book-learning, he was a bletherin idiot. He knew Chelsea had a dread of abandonment. By pandering to his own foolish pride six years ago, he'd deepened that fear.

So why, after that steamy kiss, had he demanded absolute trust from her? Why hadn't he been content to accept what she offered? Why hadn't he assuaged the plaguing pain in his loins by taking her to bed? He might have gotten her with child, bound her to him in the most elemental way possible, and then worked at winning her faith later.

But Saint Brenden help him, he couldn't. That wee devil of doubt still rode his shoulders. He needed to know she loved him for himself, not for education or riches or background. He needed to assure himself that his wife wasn't ashamed of him.

"No, Spirit!" cried a voice from on stage. "Oh, no, no!"

With a theatrical flourish, Laura fell to her knees before the Spirit of Christmas Yet to Come. Georgina, her willowy form and red hair shrouded by a black hooded cloak, pointed a spectral hand at a gravestone bearing the name *Ebeneezer Scrooge*.

"Spirit!" cried Laura, clutching at the cloak. "Hear me! I am not the man I was. Assure me I yet may change these shadows you have shown me, by an altered life!" Sobbing, she collapsed to the floor.

Sean heaved a sigh. Would that he could change the shadows around him, prove to Chelsea that he, too, could lead an altered life. After what had happened in California, maybe he'd be more acceptable to her now. He might be wrong to deceive her again, but if worse came to worst, maybe his Christmas gift would finally convince her that he was steadier now, more dependable. That he would never again leave her.

Someone tugged at his sleeve. He looked down at Martha's dainty, glowing features. She wore a boy's pants and shirts, and clutched a crude wooden crutch.

"Is it time for me yet, sir?" she whispered.

Aware of a fierce longing for a child belonging to him and Chelsea, he tenderly patted the cap crowning her auburn hair. "Patience, wee colleen."

At Chelsea's signal, he pulled on the ropes; the pulleys squealed as the curtains swung closed. Amid giggles and whispering and much bumping about in the gloom, the girls rushed to prepare for the final act.

He opened the curtains again. Laura cavorted onstage as the transformed Scrooge, carrying a prize turkey from the poulterer's shop to Bob Cratchit's house. Dora, a plump Mrs. Cratchit, rolled in a tea tray laden with mince pie and roast goose, plum pudding and pork sausages. Jane followed, staggering beneath the weight of a great bowl of oranges and pears.

The Cratchit children oohed and aahed. Leaning on the cane, Martha limped to the footlights and said in her sweet voice, "God Bless Us, Every One!"

The audience burst into hearty cheers and deafening applause. The curtains closed, then opened again to the entire cast crowding onto the stage. A grin tickled Sean's lips as he leaned against the ropes. How proud Chelsea must be of her colleens! As proud as he was of her.

He spied her still standing in the wings, her face wreathed in a smile. She looked happy, content, the way he remembered her from the early days of their marriage. A pang struck his heart. Would she ever smile at him that way again?

He ducked behind the stage, where the back curtain muffled the applause. Dodging props and costumes, he made his way to her side. This time, the delicate aroma of violets was real. He couldn't resist touching her shoulder. Her warmth radiated through the fine silk of her gown.

She turned, smiling. Her cheeks were flushed with pleasure and her gray eyes glowed. "Wasn't our pantomime splendid? The villagers loved it!"

Pleased that she'd included him, he said, "Your colleens brought down the house."

"Don't be modest. You've worked as hard as the girls." Her face sobered. "I haven't yet thanked you for suggesting we abandon Saint George. *A Christmas Carol* gave the perfect aura of sentiment to the season."

He shrugged. " 'Twas your fine directing that wrought the miracle. Go on out there now and take a bow."

"I couldn't."

"Now who's being modest?" Pressing a hand to the small of her back, he gave her a slight push. "Go on with you, wood sprite."

She laced her fingers with his. "Only if you'll come with me."

Her hand felt like a small warm bird nesting in his palm. Any protest he might have uttered drowned in a wave of longing. He wanted to say he'd go to the ends of the world for her.

She drew him onto the stage and into the throng of girls. After a renewed bout of clapping, the applause began to diminish. At the edge of the audience, Miss Maxwell directed several teachers to light the oil lamps.

"Isn't this great fun, sir?" said Martha, bouncing up and down, Tiny Tim's crutch thumping.

" 'Twas a grand entrance I made as Marley's ghost," said Jane. "But I confess those clanking chains almost toppled me off the stage."

"*I* very nearly sneezed from this white face powder," Georgina added, still clad in spectral robes. "Now *that* would have been a disaster."

"You were all grand," said Chelsea, "and Scrooge in particular."

Nightcap askew, Eliza dipped into a much-practiced bow. "Perhaps I shall pursue a career on the stage."

"But for the moment," Dora said, "we can all pursue our Christmas feast." She gazed hungrily toward the tempting array of meats and pastries contributed by the villagers.

"Not yet." Alice pulled Chelsea and Sean to center stage, where she pointed demurely to the ceiling. "You should know, Mr. and Mrs. Devlin, that you're standing beneath the mistletoe."

Sean looked up. Some imp had indeed hung a sprig from the rafter. A smattering of giggles erupted from the culprits.

He couldn't help but grin. "Faith, we mustn't ignore an old English Christmas custom, must we, Mrs. Devlin?"

"Sean . . ." Chelsea warned, casting a glance at the girls.

She looked charmingly flustered, her cheeks pink as peonies, her eyes soft as smoke. It seemed the most natural move in the world to slide an arm around her slim waist. "You fret too much about shoulds and shouldn'ts," he murmured, echoing the words he'd uttered before their very first kiss.

The memory left him aching. For one breathless moment he wished they weren't standing in a sea of avid observers. He wished he could kiss his wife with all the passion burning inside him, passion that had survived the years of loneliness, passion that blossomed brighter with each season. But determined to act the gentleman and prove himself worthy of her trust, he merely brushed a chaste peck across her smooth brow.

When he drew back, she was staring solemnly at him. Did she resent him for taking even such a small liberty?

Hiding his uncertainty behind a jovial smile, he winked at the girls. " 'Tis a custom I'll carry along wherever m' path leads. If you grande dames of the theatre will excuse me now, a man can't let grass grow under his feet."

Chelsea watched him stride away to help the village men move the chairs. The phantom touch of his lips lingered, as did the ache haunting her loins. How could she feel such a turmoil of yearning for the man who'd deserted her?

Still, he *had* worked hard on the pantomime, and she owed him a debt of gratitude for that. But now, with the show over, she couldn't help wondering how much longer he'd stay before wanderlust seized him again.

A lump lodged in her throat. Had that been a kiss of farewell?

Someone tugged on her hand. "Come join the party, Mrs. Devlin," said Martha.

Chelsea made an effort to fill her heart with the bright joy of the festivities. Talk and laughter echoed off the stone walls of the refectory. On a platform in the corner perched a Christmas tree, the tradition Prince Albert had brought from Germany. The branches wore red ribbons and gingerbread and the fairy-tale glow of a hundred flickering candles. The fir scent mingled with the heavenly aromas emanating from tables piled high with ham and beef, roast chestnuts and French plums. A great steaming bowl of wassail sat in a place of honor, presided over by Miss Maxwell.

The headmistress's cheeks bore a faint flush. Sir Basil hovered nearby, looking stiffly proper in a checked suit and high boiled collar.

Out of obligation, Chelsea walked to him. "I'm pleased you were able to attend tonight."

"A jolly good show," he said. "Seems you're as skilled at directing plays as you are at cataloguing specimens."

"How *is* the bird collection?"

His ruddy face took on the fever of animation. "You'll be interested to hear, Mrs. Devlin, that I've finally acquired that rare great auk egg. My foreign agent delivered it last week, all the way from Iceland."

As he rambled on about his new treasure, she found herself stifling a yawn. How could she have ever thought to spend the rest of her life listening to a middle-aged man's dull prattle? Great auk egg, indeed!

Yet Miss Maxwell looked fascinated, and posed an occasional scholarly question which sparked a youthful smile on Sir Basil's lips.

Chelsea's restless gaze halted on the broad-shouldered form of her husband. The tedium whirled away before a gale of yearning. Sitting with his back to the wall, his hands casually bracing one knee, Sean spoke to a cluster of girls. By their starry-eyed faces she knew he must be spinning more yarns of gold miners and claim jumpers, bold pioneers and wild Indians. Chelsea ached to join the girls and listen to his vivid tales. How different would her life have been had she gone with him? Would they have a bevy of darling children? Regret sliced through her. She felt a sudden yearning to see this untamed land for herself, with Sean to guide her.

Pride and self-preservation held her back. She mustn't open her heart until she was certain his stated desire to resume their marriage was more than mere blarney, that his roaming days were over.

Sir Basil and Miss Maxwell were discussing the mating habits of the woodcock. Unnoticed by them, Chelsea slipped away and threaded through the crowd. Forcing herself to nibble on a slice of ginger cake, she paused to speak to some of the townfolk, complimenting Mr. Honeycutte, the grocer, on his contribution of figs and raisins, then asking after old Mrs. Dickerson's health.

"Bless you, girl." Eyes like black currants in a wrinkled face, the tiny woman peered up at Chelsea. "We'll miss you, child, when you leave for America with your handsome husband."

"I. . . shall be staying out the school year at the very least."

"A joy to hear so. You must come visit again soon. Your youthful cheer always brings me a ray of sunshine."

As Mrs. Dickerson hobbled away, Chelsea wondered why she hadn't denied that she would be moving to the States. It was an awkward topic, she decided. Best to let people think what they would for now.

The evening dragged on. Across the crowded room, Sean spoke to the solicitor and acted as much at ease with that proper gentleman as he'd been with the girls. He seemed to be avoiding her as much as she avoided him. Doubts weighed on her spirits. If he truly wished to make amends, why didn't he speak to her? Had she turned him away at last? Was that why he hadn't seized the chance to kiss her properly under the mistletoe?

Her fingers tightened on her plate. By his own admission, restlessness made him rove the countryside. Perhaps he already chafed within the confines of a quiet village life. Perhaps he longed for the excitement of a newly settled land. Perhaps his love for America exceeded his love for her.

Then why had he come all the way here? Because he needed financial support? Not for the first time, she cast a jaundiced glance at his fine clothing, the white cravat that set off his tanned features, the navy frock coat and trousers that fit him to perfection. Had he squandered what little coin he'd earned on expensive trappings?

No, Sean had always been fiercely independent, a hard worker below the veneer of a carefree manner. He hadn't changed in that. He'd balk at living off his wife.

I want you to love me as much as I love you, he whispered inside her heart.

She set down her plate and stared at the crumbs. God help her, she did love him. But she was afraid to trust him, afraid that his promises to love her forever might be no more substantial than a candle in the snow, its flame snuffed by a breath of wind.

"Are you ill, Mrs. Devlin?"

She whirled to see Miss Maxwell's plain features. "No . . . I'm fine. Perhaps a bit tired, that's all."

"I see." The headmistress's gaze strayed to Sean, who was now charming the blacksmith's stout wife. "Pardon me for prying, but you and your husband don't seem to have much to say to one another. People are wondering . . ."

Chelsea's throat went dry. "What do you mean?"

"Over the past weeks, I've noticed signs of trouble between you two. It disturbs me to see one of my teachers so unhappy."

"Un . . . unhappy?"

"Come, sit down, Mrs. Devlin. It's a schoolmistress's duty to counsel her staff."

She marched to a pair of empty chairs in a secluded corner. Uneasy, yet loath to disobey her employer, Chelsea followed, gingerly perching on the edge of the hard seat.

"Now," said Miss Maxwell crisply, "to set your mind at ease, perhaps we may begin with my telling you a story." She paused, then continued in a subdued tone, "There once lived a young girl, an orphan who lived with a distant cousin, a country vicar. She wanted for none of the essentials in life, food and clothing and a good home. Yet her cousin was too involved with church work to pay her much heed. And so she frittered away the hours reading tales of Ali Baba and genii, and dreaming of far-off lands."

"I beg your pardon," said Chelsea, "but I fail to see . . ."

"Patience, my dear." The headmistress stared down at her clasped hands. "One day, a group of missionaries came to visit the vicar, and she listened raptly to their tales of China. Afire with zeal, she declared her desire to join them in that foreign land. But she'd forgotten the young curate, with whom she'd spent many a contented hour discussing books. On hearing of her plan, he asked her to marry him instead. Although very fond of him, the girl was appalled. Squander her life in a dreary English village? Never! And so she struck off on her Chinese adventure, but instead of a rich exotic land, she found poverty and loneliness, and a people who stubbornly clung to their Buddhist gods. Disillusioned, she returned to England four years later, only to find her curate had married another." Sadness haunted Miss Maxwell's dark eyes. "Too late she realized she'd given up something precious. She'd given up her best friend . . . and she'd given up her chance at love."

Chelsea's heart went liquid. She touched the headmistress's hand, the skin dry and fragile as parchment. Odd, she'd never before thought of Miss Maxwell as fragile. "That girl was you, wasn't she?"

Miss Maxwell nodded. "Perhaps, Mrs. Devlin, your troubles with Mr. Devlin bear no relation to my own bitter regrets. Yet I dislike imagining that you may be denying yourself happiness out of misbegotten pride. Or because you value the safety of the schoolroom more than taking a chance on the man you love."

Chelsea looked away. Near the stage, Martha yawned and several of the other girls slumped tiredly in chairs. Sean helped the blacksmith and the tailor restore the tables to their customary position. Half-ill with longing, she watched him work, remembering his easy laughter in their marriage bed, how he'd made her comfortable with her own nakedness . . .

She glanced at the starched woman beside her. Would she end up as unfulfilled as Miss Maxwell? Was she clinging to the familiarity of England, the security of the academy, only because she feared being abandoned again? Could she risk committing her life to the man she loved?

"What are you thinking?" prompted Miss Maxwell.

"I hardly know what to think anymore," Chelsea murmured. "But thank you for being honest, for caring about me. You've certainly given me much to ponder."

"It is my vocation to make people think. And it is never too late to learn from one's errors." Miss Maxwell glanced toward the door, where Sir Basil stood expounding to Mrs. Scarbrough, the parson's meek wife.

"No, I don't suppose it is." A sudden wild hope took root in Chelsea's heart. Before rationality could wither the seedling, she said, "Might I beg leave to go to Bristol tomorrow?"

Miss Maxwell's brows arched. "Of course—you've more than earned a holiday. But tomorrow is Christmas Eve. The young ladies will be disappointed if you fail to return in time to celebrate Christmas Day with them."

"I'll be back by late afternoon. I need only to purchase a gift." Chelsea glanced back at Sean, and a smile trembled on her lips. "A very special Christmas gift."

5

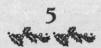

THE heavy oak door boomed shut behind Chelsea. By the uncertain light of the December dusk, the interior of the chapel loomed dim and chill, the pews empty, the pulpit deep in shadow near the altar. The smell of musty stone underlay the aroma of fresh greenery. Strings of holly looped the communion rail in preparation for tomorrow morning's Christmas service.

Her footsteps echoing, she walked down the side aisle to a stained-glass window near the front. There, she rummaged in her reticule and drew forth a beeswax candle, carefully setting it on the ledge.

With cold-numbed fingers, she struck a match on a bit of sandpaper. The tiny flame flared as she carried it to the wick. The window glass took on the rich glow of rubies and emeralds. She blew out the match, then sank to her knees, bowed her head, and began to pray.

That was how Sean found her.

A few minutes earlier, he'd been taking tea in the refectory with the colleens when he'd spied Chelsea crossing the quadrangle, the brisk wind tugging at her gray mantle. She'd been out on an obscure errand since early that morning; he'd spent the day concluding the final details of his plan and then prowling in impatience for her return.

Now, his hair tousled from his dash through the icy twilight, he paused in the shadows of the nave. An angelic vision, his wife knelt with her fingers laced, her eyes closed. A lone candle gleamed golden light over her profile and gilded the blonde hair peeking from her bonnet brim.

His heart squeezed in painful longing. What prayer held her so absorbed? Did she beg the Lord to make her unwanted husband cease plaguing her?

The old shame washed over him; he struggled to master his emotions. Quickly he composed his own fervent petition: *Heavenly Father, please grant Chelsea and me a second chance. Please open her heart to me.*

He paused a moment to memorize the image of her, to guard it forever in case she spurned his gamble to win her trust. As the saints could stand witness, he'd tried his best these past weeks to prove himself a worthy husband. He'd charmed her friends. He'd treated her with loving respect. He'd curbed his hot urges when he wanted nothing more than to rediscover the joy that brash youthful pride had made him run from six years ago.

His efforts thus far had earned him only a greater wrench of longing, for now that he knew the admirable woman she'd become, he loved her all the more.

Fighting despair, he reminded himself that regaining Chelsea's love was like panning for gold: a man could labor for weeks, uncovering only pebbles and sand. Then one day there it would lie, a treasure glinting in the sunshine.

He exhaled a ragged breath. God, grant such a miracle tonight.

She turned and squinted into the gloom. "Who's there?"

He hesitated, torn between sustaining fantasy and facing reality. Then he walked slowly down the aisle. Her expression changed, but he couldn't read the emotion on her fine features. Surprise? Gladness? Uncertainty?

When he reached her side, he said, "I've been waiting to speak to you. But don't let me disturb your devotions."

Chelsea gazed up at the towering figure of her husband. Her heart thumped. Had he come to tell her he was leaving, that he would no longer bother with a wife who refused to trust him?

If only he knew *he* was the answer to her prayers.

"Don't go," she said quickly. "I'm finished."

She started to rise. He gently grasped her hand and helped her up, but made no move to release her. A shimmering circle of candlelight guarded them from the darkness of the chapel. Her legs felt suddenly frail. She thought he must surely hear her pulse throbbing in the quiet air.

Yet his handsome face remained grave, as if he pondered a weighty problem. "For what were you praying so fervently?"

Taking a moment to shore her courage, she moistened her lips. "I was following a custom."

"Custom?"

The words sat on the tip of her tongue. Overcoming her fear, she forced out the confession. "Every Christmas Eve since you left, I've lit a candle here, before the image of Our Lord."

His fingers tensed around hers, and his gaze flicked to the window and back. "Why?"

She held a breath, then murmured, "In the past, I've asked God to protect you in the coming year, wherever you might be. This time, I said a prayer of thanksgiving for your safe return."

He stared. Fever as bright as sapphires burned in his eyes. "You lit candles for me, even though I'd left you?"

"Every blessed year, Sean. I drove you away by refusing to share your dreams. But I've never stopped loving you."

The strain sharpening his features dissolved into tenderness. Uttering her name in a hoarse cry, he gathered her close and buried his face against her throat. His heart beat in quick strokes against her breasts. Brimming with love, she rubbed her cheek against his hair and breathed in the wonderful masculine scent of him. It was heaven to feel his arms enclosing her, cherishing her again, the answer to her prayers.

He lifted his head and kissed her. "Chelsea, love, I need you. Saint Brenden help me, I need you so."

Joy bubbled inside her. The worries and fears of the past weeks melted like snowflakes in the sun. "I need you, too, Sean. I don't want us to ever be apart again. I want you to know I'm willing to go anywhere with you—"

"Hush." He planted another warm, stirring kiss on her lips. " 'Tis Christmas Eve, and there'll be no talk of anyone going away. Now, before you say another word, I've a surprise for you."

Grasping her hand, he pulled her down the aisle. She felt cold without his loving embrace, and his swift gait forced her to run, her skirts swishing, threatening to entangle her legs.

"Sean, slow down," she said, laughing as they emerged into the wintry dusk. She reached for the reticule that dangled from her wrist. "Can't we stop a moment so I can give you my Christmas gift?"

"No," he said, his arm at her waist as he urged her across the quadrangle. "Weeks it's been that I've wanted to give you m' own gift. A little token of regard for m' darling wife. We'll be going to the stables first."

"The stables?"

"Aye. To borrow a carriage."

"Why?"

His grin gleamed through the deepening darkness. "You'll see soon enough."

His mysteriousness kept her wondering. What trinket could her husband afford? She fretted briefly that the expense of her own present might wound his pride. No, she decided, he'd realize that her gift was enough for the both of them.

The smell of hay and droppings pervaded the stable. By the light of a single lantern, he harnessed the horse to an ancient curricle. Watching his deft movements, she asked, "Does Miss Maxwell know you're using her carriage?"

He winked. "Show some faith, wood sprite. She said I could borrow it anytime I liked."

Chelsea smiled wryly. "I should have guessed. You could charm money out of Ebeneezer Scrooge."

A few minutes later, she sat beside him as the horse trotted down the pebbly drive. The twin lamps shed barely enough light to see the road and the leather top provided scant protection from the frigid wind. As the glowing windows of the academy vanished into the night, she huddled deeper into her cloak.

One pinprick of ice, then another, struck her cheek. She peered at the black, moonless sky. "It's beginning to snow," she said, marveling. "Perhaps we'll have a white Christmas."

He transferred the reins to one hand so he could hug her. "We'll have a grand Christmas, no matter what the weather. Just you wait and see."

She wondered again why he was being so secretive about his gift, and ached to give him her own, the gift that would prove her commitment to their marriage. But for the moment she contented herself with cuddling against him for warmth.

The carriage rolled up and down hills, and the wind rushed through the barren treetops. Sean guided the horse away from the village, to a part of the Wiltshire countryside unfamiliar to her. At last the curricle rumbled up a darkened drive and halted before the inky silhouette of a manor house. Stately rows of mullioned windows held the welcoming gleam of candlelight.

"Why are we stopping here?" she asked.

The horse blew robustly. The seat springs creaking, Sean turned and took her gloved hands in his. "Because, love, 'tis my Christmas gift to you. The first of many."

"What is?"

"Why, this grand manor, of course. Isn't it what you've always dreamed of?"

Her mouth dropped open. She stared at the imposing mansion. "I don't understand."

" 'Tis simple enough." He made a sweep of his arm. "All this is yours, from the polished brass doorknobs to the antique stones, from the rocking horse in the nursery to the crystal chandeliers in the ballroom. And a thousand acres of wooded parkland besides."

"But . . . the money . . ."

In the pale lampglow, he shifted uncomfortably. "Aye, the money. Now, there's something I have yet to tell you, Chelsea. M' first year in California, I must have had the luck o' the Irish, for I happened into a bit of gold."

"How much gold?" she said faintly.

He eased a finger under his collar. " 'Twas what the forty-niners call a bonanza. Then I invested in a string of mercantiles and reaped another fortune selling supplies to the miners. I did it all for you, love. You see, you're wed to a wealthy man."

Shock rushed over Chelsea. So that explained his expensive garb and his lack of concern over his ability to support her. Half of her heart swelled with pride; the other half squeezed tight from an acute sense of betrayal.

Bitter hurt inundated all reason. "I'm wed to a man who couldn't be honest if his life depended upon it."

Reeling from the pain, she scrambled down from the curricle.

He leapt out after her. "Where are you going?"

"Anywhere!" she shot over her shoulder. "Anywhere that's away from *you*, Sean Devlin."

She stalked down the drive, her shoes scuffing through the thin layer of snow. His footsteps crunched from behind; he grabbed her arm and spun her around.

"Faith, woman! Aren't you pleased?" The night shrouded his features, but his anger rang clear. "You always wanted to marry a rich man."

Did she anymore? He'd given her the house, but not her heart's desire. "I was young and foolish when I wanted wealth. All I want now is a man whose love I can count on. A man who won't try to buy my love. But you deceived me again, Sean. You deliberately made a fool of me . . ." The lump in her throat thickened. She turned her head away.

" 'Tisn't entirely true." His cold fingers forced her chin back toward him. Snowflakes jeweled his midnight hair. "I wanted you to choose *me*, not m' bank account. And as the saints can stand witness, I've never made a fool of you, Chelsea. Never."

"But you did," she whispered, and fumbled inside her reticule. "I have the proof of that right here." She slapped two bits of paper at his chest.

"What's this?"

"Read it." Her anger surged. "You misled me about *that*, too."

Sean stood still, the paper pale against his dark coat. Then he took her arm and said in a more cautious tone, "Come inside. 'Tis cold out here."

Furiously blinking back tears, she marched beside him, up the wide stone steps of the manor house. An elegant Georgian pediment crowned the entryway. With the ease of ownership, he opened the door and ushered her into the warmth and light of a lofty foyer.

Despite her battered emotions, Chelsea couldn't help but admire the pastel-striped wallpaper and polished marble floor. The fresh scents of beeswax and Christmas greenery perfumed the air. Curving staircases swept upward from either side, joining in a majestic balcony at the second floor.

Yet she felt like a stranger in a strange house. The shallow girl she'd been, craving baubles and ballrooms, had fled. In her place was a woman who finally understood that the essence of love had nothing to do with money, and everything to do with the agonizing doubts in her heart.

A white-haired butler, as dignified as the house, emerged from the hall straight ahead. "Good evening, sir, madam. May I take your wraps?"

Still clenching the papers, Sean helped her remove mantle and bonnet, then handed his own coat to the servant. "Thank you, Hamilton. I should like you to meet Mrs. Devlin."

Hamilton bowed. "A Merry Christmas to you, madam. May I say, I look forward to serving you for many years to come."

She forced a smile. "A Merry Christmas to you, too."

"See to our carriage, please," Sean told the butler.

"Of course, sir." Hamilton paused. "I have prepared everything according to your directives."

"Thank you," Sean said, lifting a hand in a dismissing wave. "That'll be all for tonight."

He acted as if he'd been born to privilege and fortune. Renewed dismay quivered through Chelsea. How well did she really know her husband? Was he gentleman or rogue? Saint or sinner?

He led her into a sumptuous drawing room, where several candelabra lent a golden sheen to the rosewood furnishings. The quiet ticking of a tall case clock mixed with the crackling of a Yule log in the black marble hearth. Trapped in a bubble of unreality, she walked to a window and touched the tasseled gold cord securing the crimson drapery.

"These are the curtains we used in the pantomime last night!"

"Aye. I had the housemaids rehang them today."

"You must've bought this place weeks ago."

"Aye, 'twas a lucky chance Lord Fitzwayne was keen on selling, furniture and all, to settle a gambling debt. Don't you like the house?" Sean's anxious voice came from behind her. "I thought you'd prefer to be close enough to teach at Miss Maxwell's."

Arms folded across her breasts, she rounded on him.

"When I've a liar for a husband, it might as well be a hovel."

His eyes narrowed. "If my humble choosings don't suit your tastes, then change whatever you like. Faith, you can refurbish the whole bloody house if you so fancy."

Unreasoning pain choked her. Tonight should have been a dream come true. Instead it was a rude awakening. "You haven't yet bothered to examine my gift to you."

"Your gift? Oh." Looking down, he unfolded the papers in his hand. His handsome features sharpened with amazed disbelief. "Two tickets. You've bought passage to San Francisco."

"In steerage. It was the best I could afford."

"Chelsea, love." He touched her cheek. "You must have spent your life savings."

She steeled herself against the tenderness shining in his eyes. "I took the early coach to Bristol because I wanted to give you something special for Christmas. I wanted to prove my commitment to our marriage. I wanted to give you what I believed you wanted with all your heart. Now I learn you could have bought the whole bloody steamship . . ." Tears burned in her eyes again, and she whirled away, biting down hard on her lip.

His arms embraced her from behind, drawing her against his solid length, holding her as if she were fragile porcelain. "Chelsea, darling. Don't weep, please don't. 'Tis a wonderful gift . . . the most wonderful gift of m' sorry life."

"I'm *not* weeping," she insisted, sniffling. "I wanted you to know I'd renounce my post, my friends, everything, and go off to America with you. I was willing to live in a shack so we could be together. Now I find out my gift means nothing."

"Faith, it means everything. To think I agonized over you loving me for m'self. I bought this grand house to show you I was willing to live in England, to please m' wife."

He nuzzled her hair, but she denied any softening and held herself stiffly upright. "Kindly release me."

His arms tightened. "Chelsea, look at me."

"No."

"Aye." Without giving her a choice, he twisted her around. To her angry astonishment, he was smiling. "We're doing it again."

"Doing what?" she snapped.

"Forgetting how we really feel. Letting the pride in our hot heads come before the love in our hearts."

The absurdity of the circumstance struck a chord deep inside her. He was right; the impetuous couple from the past had matured. Gloom and doubt dwindled, banished by a bright ray of hope. A breath of wry laughter pushed past her lips.

"Oh, Sean. What a fix we've put ourselves in. I've finally decided to go to America and you're determined to stay here."

"Perhaps we should pray to Saint Brenden for guidance."

His lopsided grin washed her in giddy longing. She smiled at Sean, her beloved Irish rogue, the dashing youth she'd married in haste and the steady man he'd become through years of hard work. The man she loved beyond reason.

Cuddling her head against his shoulder, she murmured, "I've already said my prayers this evening. They've been answered . . . or will be soon, my darling." She slipped a finger inside his shirt.

His dark brows arched. "Why, Mrs. Devlin. 'Tis shocked I am at your boldness." He made a show of tucking the steamship tickets into his shirt pocket. "I shall keep these close to my heart forever, so I'll always remember this moment."

His eyes burned into hers. Then he lowered his head. Their mouths met in a kiss of fire and fantasy, of madness and miracles. She wrapped her arms around him, her hands luxuriating in the thickness of his hair, then trailing downward over the crisp starched shirt and the rippling muscles of his shoulders. The hard heat of his chest and thighs pressed into her, yet still she strained against him, unable to get close enough. The slide of his tongue promised the ultimate joining, the joy of becoming one with him and the anticipation of sating the hunger that licked like wildfire through her veins.

His lips moved over her face. Against her ear came the warm whisper of his breath. "Ah, wood sprite. Where we live can't matter so long as we're together."

"Sean, I want to see all the places you love in America. I meant what I—"

He silenced her with a swift exciting kiss. "Hush, now. We can go to Timbuktu if you like. But before we go making any rash decisions, let me show you the rest of the house."

Impatience coursed through her. "Can't it wait until later?"

He chuckled. "If you wish, love. Though I did have a mind to show you the upstairs . . . unless you've no interest in viewing the master bedroom."

"Oh!"

She straightened so quickly, he laughed again. "You look as keen as a forty-niner hankering after his first nugget of gold."

"I've something more precious than gold," she said softly, caressing the cleft in his chin, then the faint stubble of his cheek. "I fancy myself more like a bride, eager to know all of her husband."

His eyes darkened to sapphire smoke. "More talk like that, wife, and you'll get a fine long look at the ceiling."

He scooped her into his arms and strode out the double doors. The foyer tilted; the lovely walls and high cornices rushed past in a dizzying blur. As he mounted the grand staircase, she clung to his neck and savored his masculine scent. Against her breast, his heart beat in wild rhythm with hers.

He carried her down a vast shadowed hall and shouldered open a gilt-framed door. She caught a glimpse of an intimate bower, aglow with candles, the four-poster bed swathed in midnight-blue brocade and yards of ivory lace. On a table before the hearth, a Christmas feast of cheeses and sweets and a bottle of wine awaited. But she had no interest in food or drink; neither did Sean. Even as he let her feet slide to the Persian carpet, he was kissing her again, his hands skimming her curves, stealing awareness of all but the magic of his touch.

"Years it's been that I've dreamed of making love to you again," he murmured, his lips gliding over her face and throat. "Many's the night I've tossed and turned, tormented by memories of you . . . and feeling so lonely for m' wife that I wanted to die."

As he spoke, he unfastened the buttons down her back, and the bodice dropped to her waist. Her corset melted away as well; then he buried his face in the valley between her breasts. Wondrous sensations shivered through her, and she gasped, her knees weak.

Need flared into a reckless fever that swept through the both of them. Hands trembling, Chelsea unbuttoned his shirt and threaded her fingers through the wiry mat of chest hair, over the sleek warm curve of muscle. He left her clothing in a tangle on the floor and stripped off his trousers. Magnificently naked, he caught her up into his arms again and carried her to the bed. Laying her on the cool silken sheets, he braced his hands on either side of her, holding himself back.

"Chelsea, love," he gasped, his features taut with restrained passion. "Help me . . . else I'll lose control. I want to show you all the love I've carried in m' heart."

"My dearest Sean." She moved her hips against his. "It's been too long since I felt the miracle of my husband inside me. Don't make me wait any longer."

A shuddering groan tore from his throat. He melted atop her, his hand sliding toward the places that ached for him. Memory merged into the agonizing bliss of reality, and she cried out his name. He'd always known just how to touch her, how to stroke her until she knew naught but the drowning desire for a rapture only Sean could grant her.

"Please," she moaned, reaching down to caress him.

He entered her in one powerful surge. "Sweet," he muttered, his voice low with wonder. "You feel like a virgin again. Am I hurting you?"

"You're pleasuring me." Awed by the fullness of him, she feathered a kiss over his jaw. "I've loved only you, Sean."

"And I intend to keep it that way, Chelsea, m' darling."

His fierce words accompanied the sudden forceful rhythm of his body. They shared another open-mouthed kiss, and more whispered words of a love that had withstood time and trials. She wrapped her legs around him until the muscles in her thighs tensed with urgency and the fire in her loins blazed out of control. The splendor broke over her in brilliant tremors. Holding her close, Sean stiffened, her name pouring from him in a husky groan.

For long moments, she savored the pleasurable weight of his body. Then he carefully rolled her over with him, so they lay facing each other. Still embedded within her, he pushed onto an elbow and gazed unabashedly at her breasts and thighs.

"Fancy," he said, grinning. "No one would believe a wanton's passion from a woman who once declared she hated me."

Reaching up, she ruffled his already tousled black hair. "Nor would anyone believe the penniless youth who walked away from me would come back a successful and admirable man."

"All I have belongs to you, m' lady wife." He paused, sobering. "Wouldn't Lady Quincy be proud to see you mistress of a home that makes her London manor look like a carriage house?"

The bittersweet tug of nostalgia stayed Chelsea's

hand. "Perhaps we could visit her ladyship. I'd love to share our happiness with her."

His eyes softened. Bending, he kissed her gently. "A grand notion, m' love. We've the leisure to go anywhere, do anything you like. 'Tis the season to lay old hurts to rest."

" 'Tis the season for miracles," she averred, embracing him. "Praise God you came back to me, Sean."

" 'Twas the magic of the candle. You'll call me superstitious, but for the past fortnight, I've kept one burning for us." He nodded beyond her.

"Have you?" She wriggled up against the masses of pillows and followed his gaze to one of the windows. The blue draperies were drawn back with silver cords, and a gust of wind struck the night-darkened glass with a flurry of snowflakes. On the windowsill rested a tall white taper, the tiny yellow flame dancing in the draught.

Misty-eyed, Chelsea wrapped her arms around her husband. "Oh, Sean. Sean, we mustn't ever let our flame go out again."

"Aye, Mrs. Devlin," he said, answering her impassioned hug. "I want naught else but to devote m' life to tending the warmth and love between us."

She drew back slightly. "Perhaps at tomorrow's Christmas service, we could renew our wedding vows."

He smiled in approval. " 'Twill be a fine lesson for the colleens to witness the undying love between a husband and his wife. But what I've in mind for tonight," he added, cocking a wicked brow, "is not for the eyes of children . . . 'tis more for the making of our own children."

He drew her down on the bed and their lips melded in a kiss of passion, a kiss of promise. This time, without the frantic urgency of six lost years, they came together in a slow, sweet outpouring of love.

And through the long winter night, the candle in the window burned steadily against the snowy sky.

MERRY CHRISTMAS
from . . .
BARBARA DAWSON SMITH

BARBARA DAWSON SMITH has experienced two different kinds of Christmases: the traditional white holiday of her native Michigan and the balmy Decembers of her present home in Houston, Texas, where she lives with her husband and two children.

Besides collecting antiques, she enjoys researching Victorian England, a period which gave us many of our favorite Yuletide customs. *Candle in the Snow* takes place soon after the introduction of the Christmas tree in 1840 and Dickens's *A Christmas Carol* in 1843.

A winner of the Golden Heart Award, Barbara Dawson Smith is the author of six novels, including the Avon Romances *Stolen Heart, Silver Splendor,* and *Dreamspinner.*

Silent Night, Starry Night

Katherine Sutcliffe

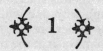

1

Arizona
December 1882

Anna Wilder stood in the doorway of the *Delgadito* outpost, situated halfway between Nogales and Tombstone. It had belonged to her father until six months ago, when he got himself scalped by an Apache out near Skeleton Canyon near the New Mexico border. Anna wouldn't admit it outright, but she was secretly relieved that the old coot had died at the hands of Geronimo. Few people had been born as cantankerous or as mean as her pa. No doubt he'd given the Injuns hell before he gave up the ghost.

She dried her hands on her apron and watched the passengers reboard the coach bound for Nogales, another twenty miles southwest of the *Delgadito*. Not one of them had offered so much as a thank you for the food that she'd slaved the last hour to prepare for them, but that was nothing new. Why she was continually surprised and disappointed by people's lack of manners and respect she couldn't figure. The last four years, since her marriage to Billy Joe Wilder, she'd learned to deal with prejudice; most everyone in the territory held her accountable for her dead husband's hell-raising, even though she'd been ignorant of his crimes when she'd married him. Still, with Christmas only days away, the passengers might have shown a little consideration for her efforts.

Anna wrist-wiped a smudge of grease from her wind-blistered cheek as she watched Dewayne Crabtree, driver of the stagecoach, walk her way, his breath flowing through his lips in a white stream. Dewayne was one of the few friends she could count on if there was trouble, though with one whiff of him it was all she could do to keep her breakfast down. More than once she'd made him wash in the trough before sitting down to her table. One look at his apparel and it was easy to understand why. His buckskin shirt, leggings, and moccasins were stiff with bear grease and dirt, as was his chest-length beard and his bushy red hair that spilled over his shoulders. Anna was certain that neither soap nor water had touched his grimy hide since the last time she'd ordered him to bathe.

He stepped inside, out of the bitter cold, and placed his Golcher plains rifle against the wall as he dug inside his coat pocket, withdrawing a wad of money which he proceeded to count into Anna's hand. "Them was mighty fine vittles, Anna."

She smiled.

"You got any plans for Christmas?" Dewayne asked.

"I suppose I'll be spendin' it alone this year."

He shook his head. "Christmas ain't a time to be alone for anyone, least of all a sweet little woman like you. You ought to set yer sights on some bowlegged, rangy cowboy and git married agin, have you a buncha young'uns."

"Show me some bowlegged cowboy who's willin' to overlook that I'm the widow of the most notorious bank-robber who ever lived and I'll marry him, Dewayne, just on principle." She smiled again, and Dewayne winked.

"Darlin'," he said, "I 'spect there's one out there somewheres who's jist as lonely as you. You'll find 'im one of these days."

"Maybe." She rubbed her arms against the cold and cast a last lingering look toward the stage. "I reckon I'm gonna have to take a ride back to civilization on that conveyance first, Dewayne. Nobody but losers and loners would ever find me way out here."

"You never know, Anna." He smiled kindly at her, and his eyes twinkled merrily; his cheeks glowed warmly as coals as he teased, "Come Christmas mornin' yer liable to find yerself a husband all wrapped up in ribbon under yore tree. I happen to know that Santy looks right favorably on sweet little gals like you."

Anna felt herself blush. Another time she might have argued with him, pointed out that such grand dreams and aspirations for a branded woman like herself were silly and childish; such fantasies had grown as dusty in her mind and heart as all the Christmas decorations she had put away years ago, telling herself each Yuletide that she couldn't remember where she'd stored them.

Dewayne buttoned his coat and tugged on his gloves, his round eyes sweeping the mountainous landscape before coming back to Anna. "It don't seem wise, a woman livin' out here alone. 'Specially in light of the recent trouble."

"I'm used to dealin' with trouble, Dewayne, but I sincerely appreciate your concern."

He tugged his hat down on his brow and turned up his coat collar. "Soon as I git to Nogales I'll report the stage holdup to the sheriff. I 'spect he'll be ridin' out here with a posse, try to pick up the trail of the two varmints who robbed me. 'Course, with any luck them shots I took at 'em found their mark in their no-account hides. If I didn't kill 'em outright, they's liable to crawl off in the mountains and die. Still, to be on the safe side, you'd best keep yer doors locked proper."

Anna folded the money and tucked it into the pocket of her skirt. "I'll do that," she said, stepping aside as Dewayne left the house. Pushing the door partially closed against the frigid wind, she watched as he boarded the stage, plunked himself on the driver's seat, and took up the lines. "Heeyaw!" he yelled to the horses, and the stage lumbered off into the shadows of the Chiricahua Mountains.

Alone again, Anna moved to the table and, with her hands in her pockets, gazed at the picked-over food and dirty dishes, hearing the wind howl and her spotted hound thump his tail against the floor. She cursed herself for firing Hoss Lovejoy the day before yesterday. Drunken scoundrel he might've been, but he did get the cow milked and mule fed, though it took her prodding him every step of the way. And even if he wasn't worth the fifty cents a week he demanded in salary, he'd been company on occasion, even if his conversations had dwelled too much on his lumbago and the closing down of the bordello up near Fort Huachuca.

She hadn't minded his reminiscing about the finer days when he'd visited the whorehouse once a week, but she hadn't appreciated his suggestion that she might go into the business herself. "A man might pay plenty to take a poke at Billy Wilder's widder," he'd declared, then she'd fired him, tossed his long underwear and spare shirt into the dirt, along with his Sunday-go-to-meetin' boots, and told him if he ever showed his weasel face at the *Delgadito* again she'd shoot him between the eyes. She meant it. She'd had a stomach full of every man in two territories thinking that just because she was once married to a no-account, good for nothin' outlaw she was promiscuous.

She'd been a sixteen-year-old virgin when the handsome Billy Joe had ridden up to the post to get his horse shod. How was she to know he was really wanted by the law for bank robbery and murder? He'd told her he was a rancher up near San Carlos, and that he was on his way home from Texas where he'd done some deals with cows.

Well, he'd done deals all right. Everything from rus-

tling to killing to holdups. She'd known him less than
a week when they married, and she'd paid for her
foolishness for the next three awful years as she was
dragged from one hideout to the next, threatened with
death any time she so much as mentioned that she
wanted a divorce, and beaten each time she defied Billy
Joe's authority. Thank God he was finally caught, tried,
then hanged at Fort Bowie. Of course, by the time she
arrived back at the *Delgadito* her reputation had been
ruined. Her father, though claiming to disown her,
allowed her to move back in with him because he
wanted someone to wait on him, which she did to keep
peace between them . . . and besides, she had no place
else to go.

Dog chewed at a tick on his rump, and Anna went
about clearing the table, spooning the scraps into a
bowl, ladling pork grease over it all, and plunking it
on the floor where the hound rolled his eyes up at her
and thumped his tail in gratitude. "You're welcome,"
she said.

She'd earlier put water on to boil, and now she
poured it into the dishpan in the dry sink, dumped the
greasy plates into it while blinking the steam from her
eyes and shouldering away the moisture that collected
on her brow and made the pale hair at her temples
droop around her ears. Dog whined, making Anna
look around, surprised to find him at the side door,
hackles raised and ears perked.

Bang . . . bang, bang!

Grabbing up a dish towel, Anna moved to the door
and gazed out the frosty window at the barn. "Door's
come open," she said aloud, frowning and flinging the
cloth aside. She reached for the Sharp buffalo rifle she
kept by the door and threw open the door. She paused
as the icy wind hit her full force, snatching away her
breath. Every time she made the trip to the barn she
cursed her father's stupidity in constructing the building so far from the house. More than once Apaches
had sneaked into the barn and stolen a cow, and once,

they'd taken a hog her pa had been on the verge of butchering for winter. Anna had always argued that if the barn had been built nearer the house the Indians wouldn't have been so likely to rob them. Her pa had reasoned that if a savage wanted a shoat, he would take it come hell or high water, no matter where it was housed. Better the heathen go slinking into the barn than their bedroom. Maybe he was right.

She hadn't taken the time to put on her coat. The wind seemed to drive right through her as she hurried down the path to the dilapidated structure, her eyes watering and nose turning numb. She peeked inside the building to make certain her mule and cow were still there. The chickens had roosted on the rafters and in the hay spread over the barn floor. Her eye caught on a particularly fat hen she'd named Pugnacious because of its penchant for pecking anyone careless enough to wander too close. Pugnacious squatted on the plow for which her father had once traded their best horse; a sad circumstance, since without a good horse to pull the plow they were flat out of luck when it came to earth-turning. But then, her pa had never been known for his forethought.

Scrutinizing the hen, Anna caught herself speculating that the bird would make a fine Christmas meal, if she could get close enough to wring its ornery neck; then she reminded herself there would be no point in going to so much trouble for only herself and Dog, who would be just as satisfied with a bowl of beans and an old ham hock. She secured the barn doors and turned back to the house, too cold even to breathe before stepping into the cozy shelter, slamming the door and leaning against it until she stopped shivering. Dog had moved to the front entrance and was sitting on his haunches, tongue lolling out one side of his mouth as he gazed back at Anna with a *You'd better let me out quick* look that sent her hurrying for the door and throwing it open without her usual precaution.

The man came at her from nowhere, falling against

her so forcefully that the impact sent her stumbling back, his weight driving her down with a horrified scream before she hit the floor. Dog let out a ferocious racket as Anna beat at the man's wide shoulders and dark-haired head, which was lying suspiciously still between her breasts. Then the realization hit her that he wasn't fighting back. A warm wetness was seeping into her skin through her dress. Warily, she slid her hand between their bodies and froze as her fingertips drew back to expose blood.

Nausea reeled through her, then confusion, and finally fear. Shoving the stranger away, she crawled from beneath him and rolled away as soon as it was feasible, scrambling to her feet while grabbing up the rifle she had dropped, aiming it at him and backing away. The man lay sprawled, face-down. Anna couldn't tell whether he was alive or dead.

Dog, having dashed outside for a hike against the hitching post, returned to the door and proceeded to bark. The man still didn't move, forcing Anna to ease toward him and nudge him with the rifle barrel, then her toe. A dozen reasons for his being shot flashed through her mind, but only one made sense. This was one of Dewayne's stage bandits. No doubt about it. Spying the saddlebags beneath him, she cautiously tugged them away, and with her rifle still aimed at his back, bent to one knee, flipped open the satchel, and looked inside. Money, and lots of it, just as she'd expected. What now?

The stranger groaned and stirred, causing Anna to step away. Raising the rifle, she stared hard down the barrel at the back of his shaggy head, her heart thumping as he struggled to lift his shoulders from the floor, his bloody hands clawing at the rag rug beneath her feet as he dragged himself up, then over, spilling onto his back with a cry of pain.

A silent moment passed as Anna stared at his face. Pain had a way of distorting a person's features; she'd seen enough gun-shot men during the years she'd lived with Billy to know agony when she saw it. But this one . . . Despite his suffering he was incredibly handsome . . . in a rough sort of way. Not pretty by any means. His skin was too dark and weathered, his cheeks too sunken and in need of a shave to make a proper lady take notice. He was young, no more than twenty-five or -six, she estimated. His dark brown hair swept down to his broad shoulders. He wore a longtailed coat, and beneath it, a blood-soaked black shirt. His pants were tucked into boots that were worn nearly through in the sole. And he was dying from the gunshot wound in his shoulder.

What to do?

She briefly considered saddling her mule and taking off after Dewayne, then thought better of it. It was too blasted cold, and besides, there was no way that old bag of bones could catch up with Dewayne Crabtree, who drove his stage as if the devil himself was hot on his heels. Besides, why bother? The no-account outlaw deserved to die for what he'd done. She had a good mind to drag him out of the house and let him bleed or freeze to death out by the water trough.

Reluctantly, she put her rifle aside, stooped, and took hold of the man's shoulders, then dragged him out of the doorway and further into the house so she could close the door against the cold. But first she stared long and hard into the frigid night. Somewhere out there was the other outlaw. Where was he? Had he taken a deadlier bullet than his companion, or was he watching and waiting to jump her when she least expected it?

Anna stepped into the house, slammed the door, and drove the bolt into place. Shaking her head at Dog, she took a deep breath, then said, "I got a feelin' I'm gonna regret this."

By midnight his fever was soaring. Anna had managed to remove the bullet from his shoulder—she'd had plenty of experience doing that while married to

Billy—but the bleeding hadn't stopped. She changed the bandages for the third time, wondering aloud how a man could lose so much blood and still live.

Since she had put him in her bed, Anna sat in a chair, dozing on and off, waking with a start each time he groaned, rushing to the bed to mop his brow and check his wound for infection. So far so good. She'd done a pretty fair job of cleaning it up and stitching it closed, though why she had gone to the trouble, she couldn't figure. Soon as the sheriff and his posse showed up, the outlaw would be transported to town to stand trial. If robbing stagecoaches was his only offense, he'd be hauled off to prison. If he was guilty of murder . . .

She found herself studying his features; they didn't look like a killer's. She'd learned that a man capable of cold-blooded murder had a certain look about him, then she reminded herself that she'd been duped easily enough by Billy Joe's handsome appeal. Then again, at sixteen, she'd been young and naive, and so desperate to get away from the *Delgadito* and her father that she probably would have ignored the signs even if Billy Joe had rattled at her like a snake. Still, she knew now what to look for, the signs of ruthlessness and cruelty that turned a man into a monster.

Her patient moaned, and as she pressed a cloth to his brow, he opened his eyes. Anna's breath caught, but as she attempted to move away, he grabbed her wrist faster than she would have imagined possible considering his weakened state. His fingers bit into her flesh, and as his blue eyes burned up at her, he rasped, "Who the hell are you?"

She refused to wince, though she thought her bones would snap at any moment. Men like Billy Joe—and this man—thrived on bullying people. To show weakness of any kind was to set yourself up for more abuse.

"Who are you?" he repeated.

"Anna Wilder."

"Where am I?"

"Barrancas Pass."

Confusion flickered over his features, then alarm. As he focused harder on Anna's face, his grip relaxed, allowing her to free her wrist and step away, wringing the rag in her hands as she deliberated over whether she should grab her rifle for safety's sake. Then his eyes drifted closed, flying open again as she stepped toward the door, where Dog lay sprawled on the floor.

"Please," came his whisper-thin voice. "Don't go. I . . . need help. Gotta get out of here before . . ."

"Before the posse comes?" she asked sharply. "Sorry, mister, but you're goin' nowhere. Not with that shoulder. You've lost too much blood."

His heavy black eyebrows drew together, and he rolled his head as if confused, spilling his long, dark brown hair over the white casing beneath his head. Then he tried to sit up, forcing Anna to leap to his aid without thinking that he might use the opportunity to overcome her. She forced him down on the bed, her hands pressed to the fever-slick flesh of his hard chest, her shockingly sensitive fingertips registering the feel of the coarse hair there. In a moment, his breathing eased; his eyes closed. He lapsed again into a state of semiconsciousness, rousing occasionally to ramble incoherently.

"No. No!" he shouted. "Don't shoot, Pa! Damn. Damn! Ah, God, you killed him. Why did you have to kill him, you stupid old fool? They'll hang us now for sure. Hang us!"

He groaned and thrashed while Anna did her best to subdue him, trying to soothe him with words. "Hush. No one's goin' to hang you—"

"I told him . . . no more. Please, no more. I'm tired of runnin'. It ain't right what we're doing. This is the last job, I swear it. After this you'll do your thievin' by yourself. We've had enough, me and Paul and Clint. We've had a gut-full of hurtin' folks and runnin' . . . No more . . ."

She smoothed his heavy hair back from his brow,

sponged the sweat from his cheeks, wiped away the single tear that crept from the corner of his eye. She spooned water past his dry lips, coaxing him with gentle persuasion to drink, all the while his haunting pleas reverberating in her mind.

"Prison," he whispered. "Serves me right. They ought to lock us all up and throw away the key. Hang him. They're gonna hang Pa tomorrow . . ." His eyes flew open and he fixed Anna with a piercing blue stare that froze her blood. "They're gonna hang me too," he told her. "That jury's done changed their minds and decided to hang me too. I can hear them building the scaffold. I can see it out my jail cell window—"

"No," she told him. "No one's hangin' you tomorrow."

His head fell back; his eyes rolled closed. He groaned and said so softly she was forced to bend nearer, "Oh, Lord, they're gonna make me watch Pa hang. He's scared. He can't stand up and they're holdin' him up so they can get the rope around his neck." He twisted his head into his pillow; his body bowed; his hands clenched around the blankets. Blinking the sweat from her eyes, Anna did her best to hold him down, although her own body and mind were in an upheaval. She understood the stranger's suffering—understood too well that he was experiencing again the instant that floor dropped from under a man's feet, the dull thud of the rope snapping taut with a human weight, the helpless kicking of the hanged man's legs, and the final twitching of the lifeless body before it stilled. One year, almost to the day, she'd stood at the back of a mob of people, watching as her husband and three of his partners in crime were hanged. It was a sight no human with any conscience would soon forget.

At last, the man fell into a deep sleep, allowing Anna to leave the room. She ran from the house and into the December night where she stood shivering with cold and memories . . . and something else. Surely it wasn't pity she'd experienced while holding the outlaw. She'd learned long ago that men such as he were born bad; they were evil through and through, and believing that there might be a spark of good inside their cold hearts led to hurt and disappointment. She'd been down that road before.

Never again.

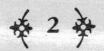

HE thought he smelled biscuits cooking, and ham. But that wasn't possible. People didn't eat biscuits and ham in hell. Something warm and wet touched his cheek, and slowly rolling his head, Steve Burke stared at the hound whose muzzle rested on the pillow near his face. Its lips curled up to expose long white teeth, and its tail began to thump against the floor. Steve decided he was either dreaming or hallucinating; the damned dog was grinning at him.

There came the unmistakable *click-click* of a gun hammer; swallowing, Steve looked toward the end of the bed where a short, skinny woman with wild yellow hair was staring at him through the sights of a Sharp rifle.

"Don't move," came her tense voice.

"Do I look that stupid?" he replied.

"Any man who goes about robbin' stagecoaches is pretty dumb, mister, or just mean to the bone. By lookin' at you, I imagine it's more mean than dumb." Stomping her foot, she said, "Here, Dog."

Steve watched the hound saunter over to the woman, plop down on the floor, and heave a sigh of contentment.

"Who are you?" the woman asked.

"Steve Burke." He moved and pain sluiced through him. He closed his eyes and waited for the discomfort to ease, wondering what the blazes had happened to him. Little by little memory returned: the image of him and his brother Clint riding out of the trees to stop the stage, their guns aimed at the burly driver as they demanded the money. He vaguely recalled the thoughts that had scattered through his head in that frantic instant—the terrible realization that all his good intentions of going straight after leaving prison had been as thin as the morning air; the sudden and shocking awareness that his older brother, who had once stood face to face with their pa and cursed him for involving his sons in his crimes, had adopted his father's life of lawlessness after all. Not only that but he had chosen to involve Steve, whom he had once tried to protect. Staring up into that stage driver's furious eyes, Steve had been swallowed by doom and defeat and the acknowledgment that the last five years of prison had rectified nothing. Calmly, he had holstered his gun after demanding that the driver throw down his weapon—the worst mistake a bandit could make when holding up a stage. Any outlaw with his wits about him knows that a gun is always hidden in the floorboard beneath the driver's feet, and at the first opportunity the driver is going to grab it. The last thing Steve recalled was catching the satchel of money and slinging it across the pommel of his saddle. No . . . that wasn't the last thing. There was the instant when he raised his gaze to the driver, watching as the red-haired Goliath lifted the barrel of the rifle and aimed it at him and Clint . . . recalled the look of confusion and surprise on the driver's face as Clint whirled his horse about and disappeared into the trees, while Steve made no attempt to draw his gun in defense, or attempt to flee. There was nothing left of memory after that . . .

He took a breath and slowly released it, relaxing as the hot, constant pain in his shoulder settled into a pulsating heat. At last he was able to ask, "Who are you?"

"Anna Wilder."

"Wilder." The name sounded familiar, then he remembered. "I knew a man named Wilder. Met him in prison some years back."

"You talk too much," she stated, cutting him off.

He focused on her features. Her face was stark white and her eyes were two glassy green orbs of agitation. "I wish you'd put that gun down," he told her. "I've already been shot once today—"

"You were shot three days ago," she corrected sharply.

"Three . . ." He shook his head and glanced toward the dog. "That explains why I'm so hungry. Is that ham and biscuits I smell?"

Her eyes grew rounder, and, spinning on her heels, calico skirt swirling, she dashed from the room. There came the sound of an oven door squeaking open, then slamming shut. Suddenly she was peering at him around the door frame and asking, "You up to eatin'?"

He nodded.

"You want an egg with your breakfast?"

"I'd be much obliged."

She frowned, then disappeared. Her footsteps thumped hurriedly over the wood floor as she mumbled to herself. A door opened and closed. Struggling to sit up, clenching his teeth against the pain, Steve gazed out the window near the foot of his bed and watched Anna Wilder, rifle in hand, walk with fast, determined strides toward the distant ramshackle barn. He listened hard, trying to determine if anyone else was in the house, perhaps her husband or a child or her parents. There was only silence, and the soft snores of the dog stretched out on the floor. Taking a quick perusal of his surroundings, which was not much bigger than a good-sized larder, he noted a barrel of cornmeal, another of flour, an assortment of dry goods and harness equipment, and small tins of tobacco and snuff stacked untidily in the corner. He was obviously in an outpost, which meant they were secluded—until the next stage or some traveler needing supplies happened by.

His gaze swung back to the window in time to see the Wilder woman run from the barn, a furious flapping hen fluttering at her heels. Anna hurried up the path, head bent against the wind, eggs cradled carefully in her apron. Steve relaxed back on the bed as she entered the house, slamming the door shut. There came the clattering of pots and pans, and soon the smell of heated ham grease wafted to him, making his mouth water. He tried to remember the last time he'd tasted fresh ham and eggs and biscuits. The swill he'd been fed the last five years in prison hadn't come close to resembling edible food.

He must have dozed. The next thing he knew he was opening his eyes to find the woman standing next to his bed, a plate in one hand, a cup of steaming coffee in the other.

"I said to sit up," she repeated. "And don't try anything funny unless you want this scaldin' coffee thrown in your face."

He tried to sit up, but had trouble using his wounded arm. At last Anna was forced to put the food aside in exasperation and stuff pillows behind his back. Suddenly Steve found himself face to face with a woman for the first time in five years, and despite his pain, he couldn't help but acknowledge the effect she had on him. There was something about the smell of a female in the morning that had a way of stirring a man's baser instincts. As ornery as this one appeared to be, and despite her dishevelment and aggravation, she was fair enough to turn a man's head. Her hair, tied at her nape, was butter-yellow and baby-fine. Her face was heart-shaped, her mouth small and petulant; there was a sprinkling of freckles across her nose; and when she bent over him the way she was now, her blouse, unbuttoned at the throat, fell open and he could see all the way to her breasts, visible beneath a thin chemise: they were small and round, with upthrust pink nipples.

She tucked the blanket as best she could around his chest, being especially gentle near his shoulder, and the feel of her fingers against his skin made him catch his breath. Her head came up with a snap, her green eyes meeting his, locking for a shocking instant before she moved swiftly away to grab up his plate of food and plunk it on his lap. Then she hurried from the room without looking back.

"Thank you," he yelled as sarcastically as possible.

The only response came in the scraping of a chair on the floor, the tinkling of silverware. Obviously she had chosen to eat her meal in the other room, as far from him as possible. He stabbed at his egg with his fork before looking back at the doorway. "Hey!" he called. "How the hell am I supposed to cut this slab of meat with one hand?"

Scrape went the chair again, and here she came, fluttering the curtain door as she entered the room, her thin face dotted with color, her green eyes fixed on the plate in his lap and not on his face. She gripped a yolk-caked knife in her small fist and wasted little time in sawing the meat into bite-sized pieces before hurrying from the room exactly as she had entered it.

"Thank you," he called out.

A moment passed before she replied, "You're welcome."

There were chores to do. She couldn't lollygag around the house all day, hopping at the outlaw's every beck and call. Besides, she needed to spend time in the cold fresh air, to clear her mind. There were problems to consider. Burke was too weak now to move about, but what was going to happen when he was strong enough to get out of bed? He could easily overpower her and demand that she divulge where she had hidden his gun and the stolen money. If he was anything like Billy Joe, he would kill her. But first he would rape her and torture her and . . . what about his cohort? What had Burke called him in his delirium? Lord, she was in big trouble if the man showed up. Families that thieved in packs were no better than a lot of coyotes and wolves. They took care of their own and the rest of the world be damned. She'd learned that quick enough the first time Billy Joe had flogged her for taking a bowie knife to his brother Fred. Never mind that the stinking, filthy bastard had been trying to have his way with her; Anna was at fault for leading him astray . . . as if she would want the lice-infested, offal-smelling piece of garbage.

She shuddered with the memory as she left the milking stool, swinging the pail of frothy milk at her side as she grabbed up her rifle and left the barn, then taking a precautionary look up the path and around the yard. Her gaze landed on Pugnacious, who was chasing several hens away from a particularly generous pile of corn feed. Above, clouds were moving in, obscuring the mountain peaks. There could be snow in the next day or two. No doubt there had already been some snow fall between here and Nogales, or the sheriff and his posse would have already been by in their search for the outlaw. The idea that they could ride up anytime made her jittery, though she couldn't imagine why. She supposed it was because she knew there would be trouble. Burke wasn't likely to go peaceably to prison. And Anna, knowing Sheriff Landry would just as soon as shoot a criminal between the eyes as go to the trouble of hauling him into jail, had no doubts that the outcome of Burke's and Landry's confrontation would be deadly.

She kicked open the door, stopping short as she discovered Burke standing buck-naked in the doorway of the bedroom, clutching his bloodied, bandaged shoulder, his face as white as a sheet. She dropped the pail of milk and swung up the Sharp in the same motion, aimed, and cocked the hammer.

His thick brown hair spilled over his shoulders as he leaned with obvious weakness and pain against the door frame. He looked at Anna with glazed eyes. "My gun," he slurred. "Wh-where is it?"

"Gone."

He frowned and shook his head, as if uncertain he understood.

"I flung it down the well," she lied.

His mouth twisted in something short of a smile, and with great effort he glanced around the room. "You live here alone." It wasn't a question, so she didn't reply, just kicked the door shut and stepped over the puddle of milk at her feet, keeping as much distance between them as possible, trying equally hard not to allow her eyes to roam down his tall, lean, sinewy body. He gave a dry laugh. "Go ahead and shoot me, lady. I dare you. You might even get yourself a reward. I'm prob'ly worth a hundred dollars easy. You could buy yourself somethin' pretty for Christmas."

"I ain't interested in no blood money," she snapped.

"No? Then why all this effort to keep me alive?"

"It's not for me to pass sentence. That'll be up to a judge and jury."

"Well, you might as well pull that trigger because I'm not goin' back to prison. I'd rather die."

"You shoulda thought about that before you held up Dewayne's stagecoach."

"Had Dewayne's aim been better, I wouldn't have had to worry about it."

Strange comment. A flicker of unease passed through her as she stared into the outlaw's eyes. They were a penetrating blue, intense and disturbed. A riot of emotions swam behind those eyes, which had nothing in common with Billy Joe's, whose cold perusal had been like death itself. If she allowed herself, she might even imagine there was a conscience lurking inside Steve Burke.

Gripping the rifle tighter, she motioned toward the bedroom. "Git back to bed before you bleed all over my floor. I ain't up to draggin' you in there agin, and I sure ain't up to buryin' you. Now!" She punctuated the *Now* with a poke of her rifle at his midsection.

He backed unsteadily into the room, his eyes fixed on hers. He dropped onto the bed with a groan of relief and eased down on the pillows as she hurried to fling the sheet over his hips. By now blood had soaked his bandages; they obviously needed changing. She went about the chore with gritty determination, all the while refusing to meet his eyes, which were regarding her with curiosity.

At last he asked, "What's a woman as pretty as you doin' livin' out here all alone?"

She dropped her cloth, then snatched it up again, refusing to acknowledge that his words had both stunned and thrilled her. No one had ever called her pretty before—not her ma or pa or even Billy Joe. Plunging the rag into the pan of warm water, she swished it around, then wrung it out before placing it gently over his wound.

"Anna," he said, "I asked you a question. A woman who can cook as good as you should be married."

"I was, but I ain't no more. My husband's dead."

"How long?"

"A year."

"What happened?"

"That's none of your business."

"Any children?"

"No."

"That's too bad. You look like a woman who'd like children."

She flung the cloth into the water and left the room with the pan, slamming it down on the table so hard that water sloshed to the floor.

"Anna," he called.

"You hush now and git some rest."

"I'm tired of restin'. I've been restin' for the last three days. I could use a little company."

She stared at the Grand and Crown cast-iron cookstove, its heat rising in a wave to make the room stifling. Her heart was beating double time with the realization that she would like nothing more than to share time with the outlaw. Lord, but the many days that dragged by without another soul to talk to seemed to her like an eternity. But no good could come of acquainting herself with such a ne'er-do-well. He was trouble. He was doomed. As soon as Sheriff Landry showed up with his posse, Steve Burke was a dead man.

For supper there was pinto beans and hot-water corn bread swimming in butter. The outlaw lay propped up in bed, the bowl of beans nestled in his lap, while Anna sat in a chair in the doorway, balancing her enamel dish on her knees, the Sharp within easy reach. She was going no closer to him. Taking him his food and checking his bandages were disquieting enough. "I haven't had hot-water corn bread in fifteen years," he told her, licking the butter from his fingers. "Not since my ma died."

Anna broke off a piece of the crisp, steamy bread and lobbed it to Dog lying near the foot of the bed.

" 'Course my ma didn't cook much. Didn't have time. We were too busy movin' from one territory to the next."

She took a bite of fresh onion and followed that with a spoonful of beans.

"By the looks of this place, you've been here a while," he said.

Anna nodded.

Steve frowned. "This your husband's place?"

"My pa's."

"I suspect you get kinda lonely bein' way out here by yourself."

"Sometimes."

"Any brothers or sisters?"

"Nope."

"I had two brothers. One's dead now. The other

makes his home in the Chiricahua Mountains." A shadow passed over his face, and he closed his eyes. He looked angry suddenly, confused and dangerous. He raked one hand through his shaggy hair as he took a deep breath and said, "I've been away for five years."

"That how long you were in prison?" Anna didn't look up as she sopped up bean juice with her corn bread. There had been a biting edge to her tone, but she couldn't help it. She was becoming greatly exasperated with the outlaw. No matter how she tried to ignore him, the feat was becoming increasingly difficult. One look from those intense blue eyes and she felt as if she were drowning.

Realizing he hadn't responded, she looked at him again. The silence rang as loudly as bells as she watched Steve poke at his food, apparently no longer hungry. He looked weary—so weary from pain and . . . what else? Guilt? Despair? Regret?

His eyes came back to hers, and she was caught. She was loath to admit to herself that she found him even more handsome than Billy Joe, and that she experienced a tingly excitement each time she sensed his gaze on her. During the long afternoon, she'd caught herself peeking in on him as he slept, finding too many flimsy excuses to enter the room, to dust here, sweep there, tuck the blankets more closely around his hard chest. Even now, with the width of the room separating them, she felt as if every last bit of air had been sucked out; she could hardly breathe.

"Well?" She swallowed the corn bread and sat back in the chair, tried to ignore the reckless tilt of his shoulders and the angry way his fingers plucked at the frayed patchwork quilt covering him. It was downright dumb proddin' at the wound of an injured animal; she knew that, but she couldn't help herself. "You didn't answer my question."

He nodded, spilling dark hair over his brow. His mouth turned down in a thin line of irritation.

"What were you incarcerated for?" she pressed on.

"Bank robbery."

"And murder."

His eyes blazed as he leaned toward her, clasping the covers in his fists. "I didn't kill that teller. Me and my brothers were never murderers—we never lifted a finger to hurt nobody. My old man shot that teller. I tried to stop him; there were witnesses to testify, which is why I got five years instead of hanged."

Anna shook her head. "Still, you ought to know no good can come from such meanness. Somebody is bound to git killed sooner or later."

"I tried to tell Pa. I didn't want no part of the job; I never did, but you had to know my pa. He could be mighty persuasive when he set his mind to something. Just before each job, he swore it would be the last. He swore no one would get hurt. I don't think he would have killed that teller, if the man hadn't shot and killed my brother Paul."

"It's a little late for hindsight."

Angry, Burke shoved the bowl away. "I don't need preachin' to. I got enough of that in prison."

"Obviously it didn't sink in. They no sooner turned you loose than you were at it agin, holdin' folk up at gunpoint."

"What the hell else was I supposed to do for money?"

"You might try workin' for it."

"Who'd hire a man fresh out of prison? Besides, what could I do? I ain't ever accomplished anything except stealin' and outrunnin' the law—and I didn't even do that too good." He closed his eyes in frustration, giving Anna a moment to study him closely, undeterred by his disturbing eyes. She felt sorry now that she'd upset him. The urge to rush to him and soothe the distress from his features was strong. Too strong. After her experiences with Billy Joe, she should know better. Outlaws could lie their way out of most any kind of trouble, but there was something about this one that made her think that perhaps, if he had the chance, he might go straight.

"You shouldn't have tried to rob that stage," she told him more quietly. "Now they'll put you back in prison for certain."

A moment passed before he replied. "If that damned driver had a better aim I wouldn't have had to worry about it."

Again that odd statement. Anna set her empty bowl aside and moved to the bed. She plucked his dish and spoon off his lap and held them gripped against her stomach as she waited for his eyes to open, which they did. He stared up at her without blinking. She lifted her chin and glared back at him, refusing to be intimidated by the nearness. She'd faced far more dangerous men than him during those years she'd been bullied into following Billy Joe around the country. Men who thought little to nothing of killing a human being in cold blood. Narrowing her eyes, she said, "You talk like a man who intended to git himself killed."

"Why not?"

The abruptness of the response startled her.

Steve shook his head and averted his eyes, his countenance softening as he held out his hand to Dog, who nuzzled his palm. "Funny. The first thought that popped into my mind when the warden told me of my release was that I was gonna be free for Christmas. I rested in my bunk throughout the day, stared at my cramped four walls, and imagined that this year would be different from the others. I'd spend it at some pleasant place, maybe in a house with a warm, cozy fire instead of in some hideout with a lot of cussin', stinkin', no-good losers who think belchin' and passin' gas is a way of spreadin' good cheer." His blue eyes came back to hers, and she started. She'd been staring in fascination and appreciation at his young, miserable face without realizing it. "I guess you wouldn't know about that sort of life, seein' how you had such a nice home and all," he said.

She sniffed and reached for his coffee, gone cold in the cup. She thought of telling him of those nightmarish holidays she'd spent with Billy, then reconsidered. The idea of him judging her on Billy's merits, or lack thereof, shook her to her shoes. Why, she couldn't figure. She really shouldn't give a fig what Steve Burke thought of her. But she did care, Lord help her.

"A lot you know," she replied, moving away from the bed. "Christmas with my pa wasn't no holiday, and that's a fact. My ma, God rest her soul, finally gave up doin' anything special. For years we would decorate the place with candles and fir wreaths and big red velvet ribbons. We'd spend days fixin' whiskey cakes and sugar cookies, and on Christmas Eve we'd search out the fattest hen in the flock for Christmas dinner and prepare her for bakin' the next day. Then we'd go huntin' for a tree and spend the evenin' decoratin' it with glass ornaments she bought once in Chicago."

Anna gathered up her own dishes and piled them atop the outlaw's, cursing the rise of emotion she could feel in her throat. Her voice was thick as she finished. "We'd exchange presents on Christmas mornin'. There weren't much. Maybe a doll Ma had made all by herself, or a pair of new stockin's she'd picked up in Nogales. Maybe an apple, or an orange, and if I was real lucky a handful of pecans. Then Pa would decide to stir up a batch of whiskey punch and the day went downhill from there. By meal time he was roarin' drunk, sloppin' the food Ma had worked so long to cook, and smashin' the tree."

She left the room, dumped the dishes in a pan of hot water, and stared out the kitchen window, doing her best to calm the riot of emotions inside her. She hadn't opened up like that to another person since her ma died; in truth, she had buried the disappointments years ago, refusing to acknowledge them even to herself. Pretending indifference dulled the pain, and besides, she'd never known another person who might understand her feelings, had never even considered that there were other people whose holidays might have been worse than hers. An image of Steve Burke as a little boy with wide blue eyes, spending Christmas with a lot of cut-throats, brought a lump to her throat. Why, Lord, were some innocent folk destined for a life of disappointment and misery?

Condensation trickled down the glass panes, and the wind howled around the weather vane atop the barn, whipping it round and round until it became a blur from this distance. Then a movement caught her eye, and suddenly there was a group of men riding out of the trees toward the house. She easily recognized Sheriff Landry; he sat astride his short piebald ramrod straight, his hat pulled low over his stern brow, the badge pinned to his coat reflecting a melon-colored sunset.

Spinning away from the window, Anna fixed her eyes on the bedroom doorway as her heart pounded as fiercely as the approaching horses hooves upon the frozen ground. She forced herself to move, blindly knocking against the table in her haste, bumping a ladder-back chair askew as she moved to the bedroom door. Steve's dark head lay relaxed on the pillow, but at the first sound of the drumming hoofbeats, his eyes opened.

"It's the sheriff," she managed in a dry voice.

"Where's my gun?" came his steady reply. "I don't intend to go without a fight."

Anna called Dog, looked hard at the man for another instant, then snatched the curtain closed over the door.

"Anna," Steve called. "Anna, girl, don't do this to me."

She covered her ears with her hands and closed her eyes. What was wrong with her? She should be glad the sheriff had finally shown up. He could haul Steve Burke's handsome hide off to jail where he belonged.

"Anna!"

There came a knocking on the door, and Dog

growled, which was nothing new. Besides Billy Joe, Dog hated Sheriff Landry more than any man she'd ever known. Frank Landry was infamous for his reputation of shooting first and asking questions later, and if one could believe rumors, he'd been known for his lawless ways long before taking the job of sheriff in Nogales. Many people attributed his ability to second-guess the criminal mind to his own past, which made him doubly dangerous.

Taking a deep breath, her hands twisting then smoothing the front of her skirt, Anna moved to the door, paused long enough to steady her trembling hands, and took a breath. She yanked open the door to stare into the sheriff's eyes.

He never bothered to remove his hat for Anna, not as he did for the ladies in Nogales. But then, he'd never considered her a lady—not since she'd married Billy Joe. With the wind whipping the hem of his coat, the sheriff took a long perusal up and down her person before stepping into the house, nudging Anna so that she was forced to move aside. He was a tall man, standing well over six feet, with gaunt, pointed features and yellow-brown eyes that reminded her of a Gila lizard's.

"Mrs. Wilder," he greeted her, emphasizing *Wilder* because he knew how it rankled. "I reckon you already know why I'm here."

She glanced toward the gun on his hip, a Colt Frontier .44-caliber six-shooter; she knew her guns, for certain, and this one was primed and ready to go. What, exactly, did he mean?

He looked over at the coffee on the stove, swept up a cup from the dry sink, and poured himself a good portion of the steaming black brew. His sharp eyes took in every detail, from the pot of beans on the stove to the last corn bread patty in the frying pan.

"Well, now, it's a dad-blamed shame that I didn't happen by sooner, ain't it? I might've got myself an invite to dinner."

"Since when did you ever wait for an invitation, Frank?" She always called him Frank because she knew it annoyed him to be spoken to so familiarly by Billy Joe's widow. He'd hated Billy Joe with a passion because Billy had once shot and killed his deputy. He figured anyone who would spread her legs for such a man was as filthy as the outlaw himself.

Frank Landry took up the corn bread patty, paying no mind to the cold grease coagulating between his fingers. He took a big bite and said between chews, "I'm looking for the men who robbed Dewayne's stage."

"Somehow I figured that was the case."

"You seen them?"

"No." She swallowed and the realization of what she had just done rocked her. Merciful heavens, she must be out of her mind to think she could protect Steve Burke! Furthermore, why would she want to?

Frank turned toward the curtain covering the bedroom doorway, making her heart slam in her chest and her skin break out in a thousand pinpoints of sweat. Dog, lying stretched across the doorway, raised his yellow head and growled as the sheriff eased his gun from the holster and thumbed back the hammer. Anna's gaze swept the kitchen, noting the iron frying pan, bringing to mind the memory of once slamming it against Billy Joe's head when he'd become particularly disagreeable. She wondered how much prison time she'd get for assaulting an officer of the law. Then she decided it didn't matter; as soon as he pulled back that curtain she was going to jail anyway for harboring and protecting a criminal.

As he moved aside the curtain, she grabbed hold of a chair, closed her eyes, and prepared herself for the slaughter. A thousand images flashed through her mind in that infinitesimal moment: pictures of Steve fighting for his life, weeping over his past and hurting over his future . . . his haunted and haunting eyes, the scent of his feverish skin. Oh, Lord . . .

It was going to be a long, cold, lonely Christmas in Barrancas Pass.

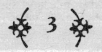

SHERIFF Landry slid his gun back in the holster, took another bite of corn bread, and turned to face Anna. "Sumpthin' wrong, Mrs. Wilder?"

She stared at the curtain, her mind a whirl of fear and confusion.

"You look like you just seen Billy Joe's ghost rise from the grave." He grinned. "But then, I reckon that would give ya a real thrill, not scare ya to death. I suspect a woman like you gets a mite lonely out here by herself."

Her gaze slid back to his, noting the curl of his thin lips, the narrowing of his yellow eyes. "Not likely," she said.

Landry wiped the grease and crumbs from his mouth as he walked toward the door. "You sure you ain't seen or heard nothing of them desperados, Mrs. Wilder?"

"What makes you think I have?"

"Their tracks split up at the scene of the robbery. One set headed for the mountains, the other in this direction. We followed 'em as far as Barrancas ridge a half mile or so down the path. Then we come across his horse where it had broken a leg. He's out there on foot somewhere, and I aim to find him."

Anna glanced toward the pan of soaking dishes—two spoons, two bowls, two cups—

Landry leaned over the dry sink and peered out the window toward the barn, then he tapped on the glass, catching the attention of his posse, and pointed toward the structure. A pair of men broke away from the group and trotted their horses toward it. Turning back to Anna, he said, "You don't mind if we check out the barn, do you, Mrs. Wilder?"

"I suspect you're gonna check it with or without my approval, Frank."

"Well now, you're right about that. I've found that ya can't be too careful when dealing with no-accounts. They're liable to plug a man in the back just for the heck of it . . . like your husband did my deputy."

"I reckon that was a mistake, Frank." She reached for the cold frying pan atop the stove, stopped, and looked at him again. "Billy Joe thought he was pluggin' you."

The smug smile on his face turned hard, but Anna ignored it. As casually as possible she poured the grease from the skillet into a can and carefully placed the iron pan over the top of the wash pot, effectively hiding the other dishes. Try as she might, she could not keep her eyes from straying toward the barn, or her ears from straining for any sound that might hint of the outlaw's whereabouts. Had he slid out the window at the first sign of trouble? Perhaps run to the barn, thinking he would be safer there?

Not possible. He was too weak. Even if he had managed to open the window with his one good arm, he couldn't have walked, much less run, the distance to the barn.

Lord o' mercy, what was she doin' protectin' the man?

Dog ambled to the side door and sat down. Anna hurried to let him out, watching through the window as he loped toward the barn. Then she walked to the bedroom door, drying her hands with a tea towel before reaching up to shut the curtain the sheriff had yanked open during his search for the outlaw. Her eyes swept the room; her mind scrambled for a hint of how Burke had simply disappeared, and—

There was blood running in a stream from under the bed.

Anna slowly drew the curtain shut and turned back to the kitchen. She walked as calmly as possible to the stove and began feeding the fire with sticks of wood. All the while Landry regarded her while sipping his coffee, his yellow eyes rarely blinking, bright with malice and meanness. Of course she wouldn't turn Steve Burke over to the lawman. Frank Landry was as cold-blooded as Billy Joe Wilder. He murdered in the name of justice, but it was murder all the same.

At last a man pounded on the door and announced they'd found no sign of the culprit in the barn. Landry put his coffee cup down and turned for the door. "It's been a real pleasure, Mrs. Wilder. You have a real merry Christmas, ya hear?"

She slammed the door behind him, watched him ride off through the dusk with his posse, then spun and ran to the bedroom. She fell on her knees and peered under the bed. "Oh, God," she whispered, then grabbed Steve by the shoulder and did her best to drag him out from under the bed.

He was unconscious, his weight like a dead man's. Obviously he'd torn his wound open; the loss of blood was staggering. Anna managed to get him back on the bed after long minutes of stumbling and straining, then she hurried for a needle and thread and hot water. Half an hour later she had stopped the bleeding, but his skin was cold and tinged with blue. Even his lips were colorless. She found herself staring at them, touching his sunken cheeks that were badly in need of a shave. Each time she thought of him returning to prison, his words came to mind: *If that damned driver had a better aim I wouldn't have had to worry about it.*

She'd known men who had given up the will to live;

she had met a few while residing with Billy. They intentionally thumbed their noses at the law, waiting for a bullet to take them down because they couldn't work up the courage to put a gun to their head themselves. Those weren't the men who had decided to walk on the wrong side of the law just for the excitement of it, like Billy Joe. They were the lost souls, born into a life of injustice, who'd never stood a chance at a decent existence. Men, and occasionally women, who'd lost all hope of ever knowing anything better . . .

She remained with him throughout the night, quietly carrying on a one-sided conversation as she studied him for any sign of improvement. She held his hand, so large and brown, the back lightly sprinkled with black hair. She wondered if he would be harsh or gentle in his lovemaking, then, realizing where her thoughts had strayed, she shook her head and left the chair, rubbed her arms and hurried to the stove to stoke the fire. Finding she was out of wood, she dashed outside for more and discovered a light snow had begun to fall. She turned her face up, allowing the powdery flakes to dance on her closed eyelids, her nose, her tongue. Then she hurried back indoors, tossed the firewood into the stove, and returned to Steve.

His condition improved very little throughout the following day. Once, he opened his eyes, and her heart skipped with hope.

"Anna," he whispered.

"I'm here."

His large hand closed gently around her own, and his lips curved in a sleepy smile. "Is it Christmas yet?"

"Not yet. I reckon you'll have to hold on a while longer."

"Not sure . . . if I can. I'm real tired, Anna."

"But I insist, else I'll be stuck here all alone on Christmas, starin' at Dog and wishin' for company." She swallowed and briefly closed her burning eyes. "It gets mighty lonely out here by myself, especially at Christmas."

"A lady like you ought not be alone on Christmas. That just don't seem right somehow."

A lady? He'd called her a . . . lady. She looked toward the window and watched the snow fall softly, silently against the panes while inside her breast her heart was thumping like a bird's. "I've been thinkin'," she said. "I hadn't planned too much for Christmas, seeing how there was no point since there's just me and Dog. But if you were here . . ." She looked and found he was asleep again.

"It's not safe, I tell you. With Geronimo raisin' Cain out yonder in them hills, a man ought to keep a good grip on his hair. Pass me them clod potatoes, Jethro."

"Geronimo, my boot. Ain't the savages we got to worry over. It's the shootists. Ain't a stage twixt Fort Worth and San Francisco safe anymore. Blamed outlaws are thicker'n fleas on a coon dog. I'll take another plug of that corn bread, Mrs. Wilder. Much obliged. If'n you want my opinion, prison's too good for 'em. I say strang 'em up by the neck, just as you would a no-account horse thief."

Steve pulled the blanket closer around him. The tiny room was frigid, being cut off from the heat. He shook so hard he could hardly understand the conversation flowing between the stagecoach drivers and passengers. He kept waiting for Anna to speak up, confess that one of the no-account outlaws the travelers were ruminating about was now lying half bled to death in her bed, but so far nothing, not even a word as she rushed to feed the hungry patrons. Why?

He'd understood her earlier refusal to turn him over to Sheriff Landry two days ago. Landry's reputation was well-known throughout the territory. Anna, being the kindhearted soul that she was, knew Steve would never have survived the grueling journey to Nogales; if his injury hadn't killed him, Landry would have. But he was stronger now, had even managed to sit up a time or two during the last days. Another couple of days and he might even manage to straddle a horse, at least long enough to make the journey into the Chiricahua Mountains to find his brother Clint . . . or cross the Mexican border. If he was lucky, he could make Cananea by Christmas.

Steve tossed back the blanket and struggled to sit up. He thought about the money he and Clint had stolen, wondered where Anna had hid it. With his gun, no doubt. If he could get his hands on them—

The curtain door was snatched open, and Steve's head jerked around, expecting to see the burly stage driver named Judd Endsley who'd been shoveling clod potatoes down his throat for the last half hour. It was only Anna, drawing the cloth closed behind her as her green eyes met his in silent communication. She seemed surprised, and somewhat disconcerted, to find him sitting up, his elbows on his knees. At least he'd managed to pull on his breeches the day before, declaring he had no intention of meeting his maker bucknaked, should Sheriff Landry show up unexpectedly again. So at least he wasn't forced to grab a blanket to cover his privates now.

She moved across the room and retrieved a tin of leaf tobacco, holding it against her breast as she turned back for the door. What made Steve reach out and take her arm, he couldn't figure, but he did it before he realized, stopping her abruptly. She gazed down at him, her green eyes bright with fear and . . . what? What, exactly, was she afraid of? Surely by now she realized that he would never hurt her . . .

His eyes went to her mouth, moist and red and slightly parted; he could just see the tip of her pink tongue as it danced nervously across the edge of her white teeth. A sheen of perspiration dewed her face, and a flush of color brightened her cheeks, put there during the last hour of scurrying to feed the hungry travelers who were eager to set off before more snow fell in the pass.

"Mrs. Wilder, can I help with that tobacky?" Judd Endsley called.

"No," she replied, her eyes never leaving Steve's. "I won't be but a minute." At last, she tugged her arm from his hand and swept from the room, leaving him to stare toward the door, his mind in a sudden flux of confusion. His thoughts throughout the morning had been on his brother's reasons for choosing their father's way of life instead of law and order. He'd convinced himself that to dwell on the hopelessness of the situation would drive him insane, so he'd purposefully imagined escaping to Mexico. With the money he'd stolen he could start a new life. Now, however, there was another notion tapping him on the shoulder, absurd though it seemed. Cananea, Mexico, wouldn't seem so bad if Anna was with him.

Christ, what a crazy idea!

Or was it? He'd caught bits and pieces of her conversation with the sheriff those days before, and it hadn't taken long for him to realize just who Anna Wilder was—Billy Joe's widow.

He'd met Billy briefly, soon after he arrived at prison, just before Billy and two of his cohorts had escaped. What he couldn't figure was how a woman like Anna could get involved with a man like Wilder. Then, recalling his own frail mother, he understood. She had loathed everything Jim Burke stood for, but had finally given up all hope of leaving him and simply accepted her sorry circumstances. Eventually she'd died from the grief and humiliation.

He wouldn't put a woman through that sort of hell. If he settled down, he would do his best to build his wife and children a stable home—oh, yes, there would be children. A half dozen, at least, all bright-eyed and happy . . . and proud of their father.

Anna thought Judd and his passengers would never leave. Judd was especially partial to her clod potatoes and had been known to dally an extra hour at her table just so he could finish off the entire pot of spuds. At last, he was ushering everyone to the stage, conjecturing about the snow-laden clouds and whether or not they would make Nogales before the bad weather hit.

"Merry Christmas, Anna!" he called as he climbed aboard the stage and took up the lines.

Anna waved in response, pulled her shawl tighter around her shoulders, and stared at the swaying coach as it rounded the bend. "And by the way," she said aloud, "one of them outlaws you folks are huntin' is laid up in my bed."

The wind kicked up a dust devil and sent it dancing about her feet as Anna turned back to the house. For the second time now she had declined turning Steve Burke over to the authorities. The very idea made her question her own lucidity.

She slammed the door against the wind, leaned against it, and closed her eyes.

"They're gone?"

Startled, Anna looked up to find Steve at the door, shirtless, his breeches slung low on his narrow hips, the bandages white against his dark chest. Her heart gave a sudden leap at the sight; her breath caught, and she couldn't move. His eyes were penetrating, questioning. She knew what he was going to ask even before he asked it.

"Why didn't you turn me in?"

She forced herself to look away, toward the table, then she hurried to collect the dishes, stacking plate upon plate—

"Don't make me walk over there and shake the truth out of you. I don't have the strength."

She slid the dishes into the wash pot, glanced at the frosty window, then plunged her hands into the hot water. He moved up behind her, and she closed her eyes, tried to force her heart to stop racing, mentally chastising herself for experiencing these disturbing emotions over some no-account outlaw. He was too close; she couldn't think. The nearer he stood the more confused she became. All reason told her that she should have turned him in, yet twice now she hadn't. Why? He was strong enough to survive the ride to Nogales. Yet . . .

"Look at me." His tone was deep, drawn-out, dark.

The cup she was washing slipped from her hand, into the water, splashing a wet spot onto the front of her dress. She didn't turn; she wouldn't.

"Why didn't you turn me in?"

"You shouldn't be up."

"Look at me."

"You'll open that wound again, and—"

He touched her hair. She closed her eyes, realizing she was perilously close to allowing herself to lean back against him. How odd it seemed, this sudden need for closeness. For years, while married to Billy, she had spurned his companionship. But then, Billy's sort of closeness brought little pleasure. Oh . . . how long she had yearned . . .

Steve's hands closed on her shoulders and he turned her around so that her back was pressed against the edge of the sink and her breasts were flattened against his chest; her knees were shaking. Steve's eyes searched her face while his fingers brushed the fine wisps of hair from her moist brow, traced the arch of her pale eyebrows, followed the curve of her cheek to the corner of her mouth.

"I'm gonna kiss you," he told her, the words a whisper that was soft and warm against her cheek. "I have to, Anna. You're so damn pretty and it's been so long . . ."

She shook her head. "I—I don't want you to."

"No?"

She sank against the dry sink, elbows holding her up when her knees gave out completely. The steam from the wash pot rose up behind her, making her scalp tickle and her dress grow damp between her shoulder blades. "No," she finally managed. "No."

"Just a kiss." His big hand slid around her jaw, cupping her chin, his long fingers lightly brushing her earlobe and the rapid pulse in her throat. Then his dark head was bending over her and his eyes were closing; she could do nothing more than stand there, breathless, while his gentle mouth brushed hers, once then twice, the contact of his lips on hers a flash as fierce as heat lightning streaking through her. Then she was sinking against him while his arms held her, and she moaned, quivered, lost of all thought but for the delicious feel of his body against hers, hard where hers was soft, hot while hers was shivering with heightened anticipation. What was happening to her that she would ignore the fact that he was an outlaw, wanted by the law, destined for prison or to hang? Had she become so lonely and desperate for the touch of a human hand that she would forget her own sense of decency?

She put up her hands to break his grip, yet he held her, his blue eyes intense, his lips curving in a sensual smile. "Steve, please!" she moaned. "I can't." She pushed at him again, and he turned her loose. An eternal second passed before she found the strength to slide away and run for the door without looking back. Just outside it, she stopped, gripping the door while carefully closing it behind her, knowing her escape had come too late. With one kiss he had thrown open the dam of long-pent emotions—loneliness and grief, hope and desire—that she had tried so hard to bury during the last years. Leaning back against the door, she trembled, stared helplessly down the desolate path to the barn, and wept.

She fed the chickens, doing her best to avoid Pugnacious who watched her with a cocked head and beady black eyes while she strew feed over the ground and cursed herself for being softhearted enough to take in a felon like Steve Burke. There was only one solution. He would have to go. If he was strong enough to seduce lonesome women, he was capable of mounting a horse and hightailing it out of Barrancas Pass.

So . . .

She would tell him to leave. The sooner the better. Next time she would turn him in, and . . .

The darn cow was dry as a bone, not a spit's worth of milk in her teat. Then Anna remembered she'd already milked the animal that morning. She kicked aside the pail, forked hay into the cramped stall, paced about the barn, and scolded herself for being too skittish to face Steve again.

The air was becoming colder; already the sun had set behind the Chiricahua Mountains, casting a pink glow over the western slopes of the snow-tipped peaks. She rubbed her arms briskly, scolding herself for leaving the house without her coat. By the time she made her way up the long path she would be half-frozen. If she wasn't careful she'd make herself ill, and then what? Who would be here to hold her hand? Make her beef-stock stew? Soothe her fevered brow with cool damp cloths?

She shook her head, set her shoulders against the cold, and trudged out of the barn into the twilight, breathing in the pungent scent of piñon pines and the pigsty, thinking her life was no more fulfilling than the hog's that was buried up to his hairy snout in mud and swill and staring at her with tiny round eyes.

Reaching the door, she hesitated, hand on the knob, nose turning numb, and fingers beginning to tremble. Then she shoved the door open and entered the house, hesitating as she was swallowed by darkness and . . . emptiness.

She knew empty when she heard it, felt it. It rang as familiarly as the wind rattling the spiny-leaf barberry shrub growing beneath the kitchen window. Steve was gone.

She moved from the entry to the bedroom where the curtain door had been tossed aside and lay half on and off the top of a spindle-backed chair. The bed was deserted.

The glowing coals in the potbellied stove provided the only illumination in the silent main room. Anna walked to the dry sink and stared down at the water grown cold in the washtub and felt her eyes fill with tears. Silly goose. Imagine her growing fond of a no-account like Steve Burke. He was a stage robber, for heaven's sake; had spent the last five years in prison for stealing money from a bank. She should be glad he was gone. Her life could return to normal. Perhaps she would finally get a decent night's sleep.

The least he could have done was say good-bye.

The front door opened in that moment and Anna spun, staring hard through the shadows as Dog poked his head in and peered at her with his tongue hanging out one side of his mouth. Then the door was nudged again and Steve was there, filling the threshold, grunting and pulling something behind him.

"Well," he managed, breathless, groaning, leaning against the frame and clutching his shoulder, "are you gonna stand there and gape, or are you gonna help me?"

Anna briefly closed her eyes while pressing her palm against her heart, doing her best to calm its irrational thump of relief and . . . happiness she felt over seeing Steve again. "What are you doin'?" she finally asked.

He looked out the door, into the pitch-black night, before allowing her a chagrined, weary smile. "Why don't you give me a hand and I'll show you."

Chewing her lower lip in contemplation, Anna moved cautiously toward the door that Steve pushed further open, enabling her to clearly see the gnarled trunk of a piñon pine. The splintered bark where he had chopped it down was the color of an old mule's tooth and stuck up here and there like barbed wire. She stared at it, oblivious to the cold wind scuttling across the floor and making her skirt billow.

"What is it?" she asked.

"What does it look like?"

"A tree."

"Not just any tree."

Her gaze returned to his; the dim light from the stove painted his features black and gold.

"A Christmas tree," he explained softly. "I figured if I was gonna be stuck here for the holiday I might as well make the most of it."

A heartbeat passed before she managed, "I thought you had gone."

"I considered it."

"Why didn't you?"

He shrugged and massaged his shoulder, his features suddenly weary and etched with pain.

Rubbing her hands up and down her skirt front, clenching them to her roiling stomach, Anna considered the scrawny, bristly bush and what it represented. Then Steve dragged it further into the house and closed the door against the cold night. He struggled to move the pine to the corner of the room; propped it against the wall where its sprawling branches painted swaying shadows on the fire-orange wall. He turned back to face her, and she realized with sudden embarrassment that her throat felt as if it were burning up inside and that tears filled her eyes.

"Oh, Christ," came his words, a whisper of distress in the semidarkness. "What's wrong, Anna?"

Angrily, she swiped at the tears and continued to stare at the tree, visualizing, despite her fury, her mother's precious baubles bobbing from the fragrant needles. "Damn you," she finally choked. "Just who do you think you are, Steve Burke, to come sashayin' into my house with that—that *thing?*"

"It's a Christmas tree," came his even reply.

"I know what it's supposed to be, but I don't recall givin' you permission to come waggin' it in here. Besides, it ain't even a decent tree. It's about the ugliest Christmas tree I've ever seen!"

"Oh, I don't know."

Her gaze went to his. She stared at his face, full of dancing firelight and shadows as he looked at the scraggly shrub, its rounded gray-green crown of stiff, sharp needles dotted with egg-shaped, yellow-brown cones. A smile crept over his mouth, and a bare hint of the desperate young boy he used to be showed in the softening of his features, the eyes that shone briefly with a child's vulnerability. "Never having had anything to compare it to," he stated quietly, "I think it looks pretty good."

What made her move to him in that moment, she would never know. Standing before him, her head barely reaching his shoulder, she gazed up at him until he forced his eyes from the tree to her. "I'm sorry," she confessed. "Sometimes folk have a way of gittin' so caught up in their own sorrows they forget that others' lives might be even worse."

Her hair fell loose over her narrow shoulders. He suddenly imagined what she would look like without the drab, worn dress. No doubt her shoulders were pale as cream and her stomach smooth and sleek and—

"Steve," she whispered, drawing his eyes back to hers. "Don't."

"Don't what?"

"Don't look at me that way."

"How was I lookin', Anna girl?"

"As if . . ."

"How?"

"You know."

"Like I wanted to take you to bed and—"

"Hush!"

He reached and buried one hand in her hair, gave the shimmering strands a tug, just teasingly but enough to make her hands flutter in the folds of her skirt.

"Imagine you out choppin' trees," she scolded nervously. "You should be horsewhipped. I swear, but you lean toward dumb, Steve Burke, and you don't look like a dumb man."

"I must be or I wouldn't be standin' here with a hole in my shoulder," he told her.

"We all make mistakes, and if we're smart we learn from them."

"I guess I didn't or I wouldn't have held up that stage."

"True." She nodded her head, seriously, soberly. "But sometimes desperation makes us blind to common sense and we don't always understand our own motives. The trick is to search deep within ourselves for the reasons—grasp the meanin' and try to do the right thing."

He caught the tip of her chin with his finger, angling her face up to his. "And tell me, Anna girl, what motive did you have in savin' my worthless life?"

She lowered her eyes and he noted the fan of wheat-colored lashes against her wind-brightened cheek, watched her childlike fingers toy with the folds in her skirt before she shrugged, just a simple shift of her overly slender shoulders within the high-collared blouse. "Aw, Steve," she whispered, almost tonelessly. "You ain't worthless. Not at all."

Briefly, he closed his eyes and swallowed back his emotion. "It's been five years since I last took pleasure in a woman's body and here you stand lookin' like some angel from heaven, lurin' me with promises of paradise."

She turned her head and stared off into the cold, black house.

"Come to bed with me, Anna, and let me hold you for a while."

She shook her head, refusing to look at him.

"Please."

"It ain't right."

"I won't do anything you don't want me to."

"No point in startin' something we can't stop."

"I'm thinkin' you're just as hungry as I am to be held."

She concentrated on her hands, her fingertips lightly tracing the feminine patterns on her calico skirt. Long strands of hair spilled like sunlight over her shoulders.

"Anna—"

"My husband used to hurt me," she began.

"Billy Joe?" Her head came up. "I heard you talkin' to the sheriff—"

She spun and fled toward the door. "Anna!" he called, stopping her so she stood still and ghostly in the dark. "I don't give a damn who your husband was and neither should you. You have to stop condemnin' yourself for past mistakes—"

"Look who's talkin'," she interrupted angrily, turning back to face him. "I'm lookin' at a man who tried to git himself killed because he held no hope for the future. Who's so ashamed of his past he can't sleep at night. Don't tell me how to run my life, Steve Burke, until you git your own under control!"

Steve smiled. "Why don't you come on over here and help me do that?"

She shook her head, yet her feet moved forward, just inches at a time, while her hands clenched and unclenched on her skirt. At last she stood close, so close he could easily reach out and take her nervous fingers in his own and draw her near. Lord, she smelled good. Like a woman, all clean and fragrant, a little like soap, too, and the musty redolence of sweet wet hay that clung to her shoes. He closed his arms around her, and though at first she stood stiff as a fence post against him, she relaxed little by little, until her arms inched around him and hugged him tightly, like a child's.

They stood in the shadow of the ugly Christmas tree, exalting in the wonder of each other's touch, until the magic drove the chill away and the bliss of communion filled up their hearts with warm, glowing hope.

At last Steve backed away to the bedroom door, his

eyes beckoning, his smile persuading. And she followed.

In the cold and dark, he shed his clothes, heart pounding with an eagerness that made him breathless and feeling as if he were a virgin again, experiencing his first woman, wanting so badly to do all the right things, but knowing he was too damned anxious to know the womanly wonder of her to take the time to make it good—truly good, the way Anna deserved it. He eased down on the bed, his gaze locked on her dim form as she appeared to float toward him. Her hands tugged at her clothes, clumsily, uncertain. The garments slid to the floor with barely a whisper, and still she hung back, her fingertips pressed to her lips and her hair spilling like moonbeams all the way to her hips.

He reached for her and tugged her down until he was sliding his hand behind her knees and drawing her legs beneath the covers to that she lay nestled and tense beside him. Her head rested on his good shoulder; her hands were bunched between their chests; her knee pressed against his thigh.

He sighed and said, "Lord, you feel good."

Minutes ticked by as, gradually, Anna relaxed, warming with the pleasant closeness of Steve's body. This was nice. So very nice. How long had it been since anyone had actually held her, touched her with tenderness and consideration? Surely this was wrong, but what harm could come from it? Who would know except them, and who would care?

The cold and dark encompassed them as they lay cocooned in the warmth of the heavy blankets, their arms and legs entwining as the heat of their bodies soothed them into a state of sleepy contentment. How right it felt. How wonderful to share a sense of companionship and closeness with one whom she had come to care for.

She did care; she couldn't deny it. She could tell herself a thousand times that her concern stemmed from nothing more than a desire to help another human being, and perhaps that was how it had started. But she'd learned enough about Steve Burke during the last days to realize that, like her, he'd dealt with life's injustices as best he could. They'd both made mistakes. How many times since returning to Barrancas Pass had she cried alone in the night because the world had chosen to condemn her for her past? Oh, yes, she understood the desperation that had driven Steve to want to end his pain and suffering, yet what a loss to her world it would have been if he had succeeded. At last she was ready to admit to herself that his presence had filled up her life, had given her a reason to wake up in the morning, had occupied her long hours of sleeplessness late in the night with a sweet anticipation of the morrow.

And he felt so damned good. So big and hard and lean. A thrill ran through her as her leg pressed against his, warm where his was warm, smooth where his was rough. She felt liquid inside, shamefully aroused as she had during those first innocent days with Billy, when she'd imagined his lovemaking would be like heaven. Only it had turned out to be a living hell.

Somehow she knew Steve would be different. She felt it in the gentle touch of his callused fingertips as he stroked her hair, turning her mind into a riot of emotions, her body into a flame of heat and urgency. She couldn't deny it. The need had been growing since the first time he'd called her "Anna girl," since he'd turned those cerulean eyes on her and smiled.

"Anna," came his voice in the quiet.

She raised her head and looked in his eyes, touched her finger to his lips that were slightly parted and moist. The memory of his kisses brought a stirring of warmth inside her, deep down in the private part of her that had known only one man but now ached for another.

"I must be truly wicked to be here," she told him,

"but I don't care. People think me a loose-moraled woman anyway."

"I'll shoot the first person, man or woman, who suggests such a thing."

She smiled, and he smiled back, then brushed aside the hair that spilled around her face and over his chest.

"I want you," he admitted matter-of-factly, his voice husky and deep. "But I won't take you unless you're willin'. Are you willin'?"

Slowly, she lowered her head and kissed his mouth, softly, sweetly, their breaths mingling while their hearts beat as one. His hand skimmed her hair lightly at first, then slid against her scalp, cradling her head while he kissed her deeply.

"Say you're willin', Anna girl," he breathed against her mouth.

She closed her eyes, allowing the pressure of her body against his to say what she couldn't. Then his hand was wandering over her skin, exploring, worshiping, finding her secret places that quivered at his touch, discovering what made her gasp and groan and throw back her head in mindless pleasure. It *was* pleasure, indeed it was, such as she'd always imagined it could be. Because he was not able to mount her, she slid her leg over him as he drove his body home, into the hot tunnel of her that was eager to receive him.

It was glorious, this glide to ecstasy, this coming home of lost souls. He introduced her to tenderness; she offered him hope. Together they found the transcendent recompense for all life's injustices.

Later that night Anna sat on the floor before the tree, a blanket wrapped around her as she gazed up at the pine's lofty branches. It was as if the years of disillusionment had never existed; it was as if she was young again, peering at the sparkling, fascinating symbol of goodness and faith, believing with all her heart that this Christmas would be different. She'd been a good girl all year, had obediently darned her stockings and churned the butter when her mother told her, never sneaking away even for a moment to stare at the sky and imagine the clouds were her guardian angels.

Oh, yes, this Christmas would be different. She was certain of it! Already the stockings had been hung with great care near the stove. Perhaps this holiday her two greatest prayers would be answered: her mother would be cured of the disease that had been eroding her health the last years, and her father wouldn't get drunk on whiskey punch and smash the tree.

Now, sighing a little at the memory, Anna looked up to find Steve beside her, his own face a little dreamy as he studied the tree. Smiling, she opened the blanket and invited him in, nestled her head on his shoulder, and closed her eyes.

Perhaps the tree wasn't as bad as she had first thought. And even if it was, somehow that didn't matter. For she realized suddenly with a fluttering of her insides, that she wouldn't be spending the holiday alone after all.

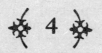

By dawn she had whipped up a whiskey cake and turned out two dozen sugar cookies shaped like Christmas trees—one of which she had labored over for half an hour before baking, carefully shaping it to match the real one residing in the corner. Again and again she caught herself gazing at the pine in silly fascination, enjoying the pungent scent of its greenery and the sharper aroma of its freshly cut trunk. That, and the smell of baking cookies, made her giddy with excitement. She was giggling with a child's enthusiasm, her imagination running rampant as she daydreamed of Christmas morning, of awakening in Steve's arms, of preparing the holiday meal that would be the grandest and most memorable of any she had ever prepared!

She dropped to her knees before the oak sideboard and hunted for the pewter platter on which she would serve the holiday bird. Thinking of Pugnacious reclining plump and succulent on the platter brought a smile to her lips. Ah, the mouth-watering taste of revenge . . .

Spying the Dutch oven in which she intended to bake and baste the foul-tempered hen, she grabbed it and gave it a yank. What fell into her lap, however, brought her to her senses with an impact that made her reel: Steve's gun and the satchel of stolen money.

Angrily, she shoved the abhorrent weapon and the blood-stained saddlebags into the sideboard and slammed the rickety door, only to have it swing open again, as if reminding her that no matter how badly she ached to put Steve's crime from her mind, it would not magically go away. He and his brother had robbed a stagecoach. That brother was still out there somewhere, and so was Sheriff Landry. At any time either of them could ride up to her door. Clint would lead Steve back to a life of crime, or Landry would haul him directly to a hangman's noose.

She wouldn't think about it. Building a future on mistakes from the past led only to failure.

Slamming the door closed again, she struggled to her feet and discovered Steve leaning against the door frame, running one hand through his tousled hair and grinning. He had donned his breeches and one of her father's old shirts.

"Mornin'," he said.

"Good mornin'."

"Somethin' smells awful good."

She beamed at him and looked toward the table where the sheets of golden-brown cookies were steaming. Hands in his pockets, Steve sauntered over and stood by the table with his head bent and his dark hair spilling to his eyes as he regarded the array of sugar-coated confections.

"There's fresh coffee in the pot," she told him.

He touched the tip of one finger to a crystallized currant sparkling at the crown of the largest tree-shaped flat-cake.

"I thought you might like some breakfast. There's buttered grits and a ration of bacon. If you want eggs..." Her voice dropped off in the silence as she clutched the cumbersome Dutch oven to her midriff.

He looked around the room, noting the slightly crumpled red velvet bows she had placed here and there. Then his gaze went to the tree, where a porcelain angel with one wing peered down at him from the crest.

"My pa broke it," Anna explained.

"Stupid bastard."

"That's nicer than what my ma called him."

Steve's laughter sounded warm and easy in the quiet room. The music of it made her blush and grow dizzy. She hugged the blue speckled pot hard against her and prayed to whatever god watched over lonely, desperate widows that Steve Burke wasn't another one of her fanciful daydreams—the ones she conjured up when she lay alone in her bed at night and tried to imagine that the rest of her life would not be as empty as the last year had been.

Finally his gaze swept back to hers. "I'm glad I didn't die," he told her. "I have you to thank for that."

Anna smiled and looked at her feet.

"So this is what Christmas is like. It's just as I imagined it would be." Steve slid his hands back in his pockets. Nothing more was said about his brush with death. There was really no point in dwelling on the issue. That was the past, after all, and had nothing to do with the future.

Turning back to the dry sink, Anna placed the oven to one side and grabbed up a pair of tea towels stained by a generation of meals, then made herself busy removing the whiskey cake from the stove. She plunked the pan on the table. "If you'd like to wash up before your breakfast, feel free."

Steve took a last glance around the room before rubbing one hand over his jaw.

"There's a straight-edge razor in the bedroom if you want it. And a mug and brush. If you'd like, I can heat you some water—"

"No thanks. I'm used to doin' without."

She dried her hands on her apron and watched as he moved for the door, stopped, and turned back. A grin began tugging at one corner of his mouth, then he opened his arms and Anna flew into them, laughing for no particular reason other than that it felt damn good and seemed right.

He closed his arms as tightly as he could and tried to twirl her around. "Stop!" she squealed, stepping on his toes and dancing as quickly off of them. "You're gonna pop your stitches agin!"

"Anybody ever tell you that you're the bossiest woman in this territory?" He goosed her in the ribs and she howled with laughter and wiggled as his hands ran up and down her body.

"Stop. Oh, oh, *stop!*"

"That's not what you said last night, darlin', or this mornin', or—"

Wrenching herself free, Anna stumbled backward, laughing and gasping for breath while Steve cocked his weight on one hip and watched her, that lopsided grin creasing one gaunt, beard-shadowed cheek. His face was flushed from their frolicking, his blue eyes bright. It was odd how happiness could transform a man, she thought. A woman too, for that matter. Anna felt like a girl again.

He crooked his finger at her. "C'mere."

She shook her head and backed away, a bubble of laughter inching up her throat, though she tried—oh, how she tried—to swallow it back.

He moved so swiftly that she had little time for anything except a squeal of surprise as his arm wrapped around her, lifting her off her feet and up against him. Then he was kissing her in that gentle, warm, arousing way that made her toes curl in her shoes. She forgot about her baking cookies. Forgot even that the coffee was boiling and in another five minutes would be as thick as pitch.

Lord, oh, Lord, he could kiss. She loved the circular motions he made with his head when he did it. She liked the feel of his head in her hands and the way his hair slid through her fingers when she stroked it. She relished the smell of him—warm skin lightly tangy with sweat. Her eyelids opened halfway, and even while he continued to kiss her she admired him, the deep creases between his well-shaped brows and his straight nose. Then she suddenly realized he was watching her, too, and smiling against her mouth.

"Know what I'm gonna do now?" he whispered.

She couldn't speak.

He lifted her to her toes and headed for the bedroom. Her feet flapped uselessly at the air. "Not the bed," she gasped. "I'll never git up agin."

"Nobody said anything about a bed." Her eyes flew open as he perched her on the old pine lowboy next to the bed, the one laden with stacks of cans. Then he pried apart her legs and moved between them, inching up her skirt with his fingertips, skimming along her underwear until he found the slit in her drawers. She gasped.

He managed the buttons on his breeches with little effort. Anna watched in fascination and hunger, and when he slid inside her she locked her legs around him and threw back her head in ecstasy, allowing her body to fly and her heart and mind and soul to soar.

The lowboy creaked and groaned, and the clutter Anna had shoved aside to make room rattled and clanked together, faster and faster, until the cans toppled over and rolled under the bed, and the window fogged up so heavily that condensation poured down the panes like rain. Then it was over. Anna, fallen back on her elbows and her hair spilling over the table edge, took a long, shuddering breath before opening her eyes. Steve leaned over her, arms outstretched and palms planted firmly to the lowboy on each side of her. Smiling, she watched his shoulders gradually relax, his head slowly come up, his eyes drowsily open.

"Ho, ho, ho," she drawled, and Steve burst out laughing.

She eyed Pugnacious from behind the barn door. Very soon now the damned chicken would be shut up inside Anna's oven. Each time she shoved another spoonful of corn bread dressing into the hen's gutted carcass she would remember a time when Pugnacious had flown at her from behind some haystack, scaring another ten years off her life.

Anna crept from behind the door and, with a half dozen eggs sheltered in her apron pouch, tiptoed from the barn. She took to the path with wings on her feet. By now Steve would have finished shaving; the fresh coffee would have perked. Another five minutes and the next batch of cookies would be ready to come out of the oven to cool. At the rate Steve was eating them, she'd be forced to whip up an entire new batch by tomorrow morning . . . *Christmas* morning.

She threw open the door and started to yell, "Breakfast in five . . ." but stopped, her voice falling as silent as death as her eyes locked on Steve. He sat at the table, the satchel of money placed before him, the gun drawn from the holster and held in his hand that fingered the hammer back and forth as if checking its readiness to fire. How many times had she watched Billy Joe do the same?

He laid the weapon down gently yet did not take his hand from it. At last he looked up at her while she stood there with her heart in her throat. Her previous joy dissolved like snowflakes against a warm windowpane, and even as she stood rooted to the floor, her eyes on that weapon, the frigid wind beat at her back and sent the first hint of snow scattering around her feet. Silence filled up the space between them; only the pop and hiss of tinder burning in the stove broke the spell.

"I've been thinkin'," Steve said, followed by another silence that seemed interminable and impenetrable. He swallowed. "If we left here now we might make Cananea, Mexico, by Christmas night."

"What are you sayin'?"

"I guess I'm askin' you to come with me, Anna."

Staring down at the gun in his hand, and the abhorrent satchel of money, she shook her head, slowly at first, then more adamantly as her anger mounted. "And what," she began in a tight voice, "do you intend to do about that?"

"It'll buy us a new life, Anna."

"It'll buy us trouble. Trouble I don't want any part of, Steve Burke. I've had a lifetime of that sort of trouble and I don't want any more." She whirled and caught the door, slammed it so hard the impact upset the lid on the coffeepot. It bounced off the stove and hit the floor, then kept rolling until it hit the rung on the chair where Steve had propped his foot.

Dog lifted his head as she stepped over him and dumped the eggs in a bowl with little care if they broke. Then she grabbed up the towel and flung open the oven door.

"Don't ask it of me," she said through her teeth. She slid the over-brown cookies from the oven, dropped them on the table, and stared at Steve. "We could never build happiness on the misfortune of others, and that's what it would be—usin' money someone else had worked and saved hard to earn. I couldn't live with the guilt."

His eyes turned to hard sapphires. "Then what am I supposed to do with it? Fling it down the well?"

"You can turn it in."

He glared at her in disbelief. "And spend the next five years in prison?"

"If you surrender, they might be lenient."

He threw back his head and roared with laughter. "With my history? I'll be lucky if they don't hang me outright."

"Then fling the damned money down the well and be done with it!" she cried.

"There's a thousand dollars here—"

"A thousand miseries! A thousand reasons why we would never stop lookin' over our shoulders. What pleasure would we find in livin' with that?"

Steve closed his eyes briefly and shook his head. "Anna girl, you don't know what you're askin' of me."

She sat down on the bench very near him. "I'll wait for you as long as I must if it means we can go through life without fear of the law."

Steve stared at the gun beneath his hand before his stern eyes came back to hers. "You're askin' me to make a choice between my freedom and you."

"Yes, I guess I am."

"I can't do it, Anna. I can't go back to prison."

"Then I guess that's all to be said for us." Her voice quavered and tears rose to her eyes. Very slowly, she stood and went through the motions of opening the oven, shoving the last tray of cookies inside, then slamming the door so hard that the windows rattled. She refused to face Steve again; instead went about the chore of tidying the already spotless kitchen, scrubbing nonexistent grease spatters, and rewashing dishes that she'd cleaned and dried a half hour before.

Steve left his place at the table and, taking his saddlebags and gun with him, exited the house, closing the door forcefully behind him. Anna stood rooted to the floor, the soapy dishcloth gripped to her breast as she squeezed her eyes closed and fought back the desire to run after him.

She hurled the cloth at the dry sink and marched to her bedroom, fell to her knees, and threw open the lid of a trunk that had belonged to her mother. Beneath a layer of knitted doilies, configurations of intricately knitted snowflake shapes that had once reflected her mother's naive dreams of what love and marriage would bring her, were tissue-wrapped baubles that twinkled and glittered with reflected light.

How many years had the Christmas ornaments lain buried in the musty chest, forgotten, only to flash with life and fire the moment they were touched by light— the way hope had blazed anew in Anna's breast the moment Steve had whispered "Anna girl" in her ear? Even now the memory brought warmth to her cheeks and filled her with a glow that radiated to the tips of her fingers.

She dragged the trunk into the other room and unloaded it, hanging each fragile ornament on the tree, refusing to acknowledge the lump of despair that kept growing in her throat.

The door opened and closed behind her. Anna turned. Steve's hair was windblown, his cheeks red from the frigid wind. With the gun shoved into the waistband of his breeches, his face dark, and his mouth curled in a reckless angle, intensifying the leanness of his cheeks, he looked every bit the desperado. His wounded shoulder sank slightly lower than the other, whether in pain or submission she couldn't tell.

He eased the door closed behind him and strode toward her, stopping so closely that his tall body was pressed against hers and the scent of his skin and the cold filled up her senses until her mind stopped working and the world became a jumble of confusion.

He drew the gun and pressed the barrel almost roughly beneath her chin, then tipped her head back. "You know I could force you to go to Cananea with me," he told her.

"But you won't because you know we could never be happy with that money between us."

"We can never be happy without it. You can't build

somethin' out of nothin', Anna. Without money, there's no hope of startin' over."

"There's us. We start from there."

Lowering the gun, Steve wearily turned away. "Good intentions won't put a roof over your head, Anna, and that's what I intend to do." He picked up a cookie, angled it this way and that so the light through the window made the dusting of sugar glitter against his fingertip. "A woman needs a home—"

"A woman needs the man she loves."

There came a swell of silence in the room, the quiet so intense they could hear the tapping of each snowflake against the windows. Steve carefully replaced the cookie on the tin and raised his eyes to hers. All his life he had waited for someone, anyone, to say that word—love—to him. And now . . .

"What are you sayin'?" he whispered in a broken voice.

"That I love you."

"Don't say that unless you mean it." The words sounded desperate, and he blushed, as angered over his show of weakness as he was desperate to hear her say it again.

Anna sighed. With a slight smile on her lips, she studied the Christmas ornament in her hand, little realizing that she looked like an angel herself with her soft hair spilling around her face. "I love you for what you are—"

"I'm a no-account outlaw."

"You're a man who's been backed into too many corners."

They stared at each other, the tension between them as electric as heat lightning.

She took a long breath and released it. "You got somethin' in you that Billy Joe never had, Steve."

His eyes questioned *What?*

"A conscience," she replied. "I believe in you even if you don't. I believe that you can go straight if you've got a good reason to, and I want to be that reason.

Now put the gun away, come here, and let me prove it."

He set the revolver aside as Anna moved toward him, the ornament still held gently in her palm, which he caught in his hand. He studied the glistening bauble, the reverence with which she held it, and in that moment felt as cherished as the beautiful treasure that seemed to personify the dreams they both held for the future.

"Could you come to love me?" she asked shyly, her green eyes wide and hopeful.

He gently cupped her face in his hand. "Lady, I've dreamed of lovin' you all of my life."

He kissed her, a tentative brush of his mouth on hers, as if the passionate moments that had passed between them before had never existed. He kissed her as if for the first time, his heart thundering and his soul flying, and suddenly the idea of spending the next five years in prison didn't seem so bad after all . . . if it meant sharing an entire lifetime with Anna—of loving her and being loved by her . . .

He removed the ornament from her hand, raised her palm to his mouth, and kissed it. Reverently. Unashamedly. Then he took her in his arms and eased her down, beneath the tree, and showed her, once again, what bliss loving him would bring her.

An hour later they lay sated in each other's arms, right where they had fallen, their entwined image reflecting in the mirrored surfaces of the Christmas ornaments. Anna rested her head on Steve's shoulder, her eyes closed, while Steve stared at the ceiling and allowed his mind to drift to thoughts not of the past but of the future. Until the first rush of frigid wind whipped over them, neither was aware that the front door had suddenly opened.

Dog scrambled to his feet. Anna shoved her dress down over her knees, and Steve sat up. He stared at the dark image silhouetted in the doorway, knowing even before the figure stepped out of the swirling snow and into the room that it was his brother.

Clint Burke's bearded face broke into a grin. "Well, well. Here I expected to find you dead or dyin', li'l brother. Instead I find you sprawled on the floor lookin' for all the world like a man who's just took himself a woman." His eyes cut to Anna. "And a fine-lookin' woman at that."

Anna clutched the front of her dress closed and caught Steve's hand as he stretched to his feet and helped her up. Dread wrung the breath from her as she regarded the intruder, and though she did her best to remind herself that this stranger was Steve's brother, and Steve would never allow him to harm her, one look at the malevolence snapping in his dark eyes told her that Clint Burke was trouble. Big trouble. She'd seen that meanness too many times in Billy Joe's eyes not to recognize it now.

Clint kicked the door shut against the cold, removed his coat and hat, and hung them from pegs on the wall. Dog growled, but Clint ignored him. His eyes were still on Anna, making her flesh crawl and her body shake with distress. She might have been looking at Steve, so closely did they resemble each other. From beneath his black slouch hat, Clint's dark hair tumbled to his shoulders. He wore a spanking-new coat, and beneath it a fancy vest and blue trousers tucked into boots polished to a mirrorlike gleam. His white shirt was snowy, his string tie carefully knotted. No doubt he was the best-dressed outlaw in the territory, and the deadliest. Anna knew a killer when she saw him; this one would have no qualms about murdering a woman.

Clint walked to the stove and poured himself a cup of coffee, turned it up to his mouth, and drank deeply, despite its blistering heat. Then he wrist-wiped the liquid from his lips. All the while he took in the scenario, his gaze shifting from Steve to Anna to the satchel of money on the table. At last he plunked the cup down. "I waited up near Durango Pass for you to show up," he told Steve. "That was the plan if anything went wrong and we got separated . . . 'Course I wasn't countin' on you sitting there like a lame duck waitin' for that driver to shoot you. What happened, Stevie boy? You turn yeller while in prison?"

"Maybe I just turned smart, Clint."

"Meanin'?"

Steve glanced at Anna before moving away. "Maybe I decided at the last minute that our stealin' that money was a mistake."

"A mistake? That wasn't the impression I got when we decided to pull the job."

"You," Steve said, "decided to pull the job."

"I didn't hear you complainin' none. Fact is, you kinda liked the idea of spendin' a few pesos on rotgut and whores." Clint dropped into a chair, rocked back on two legs, and grinned at Anna. " 'Course when you can git it free—"

Steve moved so fast that Clint had little time to react before the chair was kicked from beneath him. Anna screamed and stumbled back as Clint hit the floor with a startled yowl and enough impact to shake the walls. Before he could clear his hair from his eyes, Steve was standing over him, looking dangerous. "You'll keep your mouth shut about Anna, Clint. She saved my life. That's more'n you've ever done. Fact is, now that I think about it, I have to wonder why it is you let me sit there and take that bullet."

Clint's eyes narrowed. "Pa always said you was born with all the looks in the family, but with the brains of a piss ant."

"Pa said a lot of things, most of them wrong."

Shoving aside the chair, Clint climbed to his feet, dusted off his coat, and smoothed his tie. Only then did he look at Steve. "Pa was right about one thing. A man can't wait for the world to take pity on him. A man goes out and takes what he wants."

Anna took advantage of the brothers' antagonism to

move with caution toward the bedroom door, glancing all the while at the rifle propped against the wall. Close. Closer. The men's voices were rising and—

She grabbed for it, screaming as she was shoved aside and the Sharp wrenched from her hand. As she stumbled back into the tree, knocking several of her treasured baubles to the floor where they shattered, she stared in stunned amazement into Steve's dark, angry face.

"What the hell are you doin', you little fool?" he shouted.

Furious, she came to her feet, hands clenched and eyes blazing. "Surely you don't think I'm gonna stand here and allow him to murder me in cold blood!"

"Murder? Clint?" Steve shook his head. "The Burkes may be thieves, Anna, but we aren't killers."

"I know a killer when I see one. I was married to one, remember? That bastard there"—she pointed a shaking finger toward Clint—"has got no scruples!"

With an abrupt laugh, Steve turned away, slung the rifle down on the table, and looked at Clint. His brother stood near the stove, his weight on one hip and his coat tucked snugly behind his holstered gun. Clint returned his study without blinking.

"Damn you," came Anna's voice behind him. "You're goin' with him, aren't you? All that talk about wantin' to start over and put your past behind you was nothin' more than a lot of prattle."

Steve's gaze locked on his brother as he replied, "Nobody said anything about leavin', Anna."

"If he didn't come for you and the money, then what's he doing here?"

"I'm his brother," he said more softly, his gaze never leaving Clint's face, though a nauseating realization was forming in the pit of his stomach and squeezing his chest. He wasn't looking into Clint's eyes but his father's. "Tell her, Clint. Tell her you don't intend to hurt her and that the only reason you're here now is to see to my welfare."

Clint smiled. " 'Course it is. Like pa always said, blood kin always stick together, Stevie boy. Now git your things and we'll get out of here."

There it was, the choice he knew he would be forced to make sooner or later. He could walk out that door now and never look back, keep on riding, perhaps deep into Mexico, and spend the next years of his life looking over his shoulder for the law or he could remain here with Anna and face another prison sentence. Christ, the choice had seemed so much easier to make an hour ago, when there had been only he and Anna locked in each other's embrace.

Anna stepped around him and planted herself before Clint, her defiant chin upthrust and her hands fisted at her sides. "Git out of my house," she said, frost and flint in her voice. "I'm givin' you to the count of three—"

"And what?" he sneered.

Anna spun on her heels to face Steve. "You said you love me. Are you a liar as well as a thief? Well? If you take that money and ride out of here, you're headed for worse trouble. Somewhere there's gonna be another stage and another driver, and next time his bullet will kill you."

"There won't be any more robberies, Anna."

"So you thought when you left prison. That lasted just long enough for you to meet up with him. You said so yourself."

"Shut up," Clint drawled, and without warning, he buried his fingers in her hair and yanked her head back so hard she screamed. The next thing she knew she was flying face-down toward the floor and hit it with a groan before rolling to her knees, grabbing a spiral-backed chair, and shoving it at him. All hell broke loose then. Anna scrambled to her feet, managed to snatch the money satchel off the table, and ran for the back door while Dog let out a ferocious howl and the men's raised voices became incomprehensible.

Anna hit the back steps with a skid, danced in place

on the ice, then struck out in a run, little knowing or caring where she would go in that moment, just realizing she had to do something to bring Steve to his senses.

Seeing Anna plow out the door with the money, Clint let out a furious shout and, shoving Steve away, he followed, giving Dog a swift kick as the hound made a halfhearted lunge at his leg. Then Clint was barreling out the door after Anna, his gun drawn, bringing a roar of warning from Steve, who pursued him. Steve caught his brother no more than half a dozen feet from the house, throwing his weight against him and gasping as they hit the slushy ground. He groaned and grabbed his shoulder, remotely aware that his brother had slithered from beneath him and was shouting in the distance. Then a gun fired and he thought, *Oh, God, please . . .*

Then he was rolling to his knees, sliding in ice and mud, but unable to feel the stinging sleet coating his face and hair and hands as the numbness of shock set in. He saw Anna on the ground; his brother was walking toward her, sliding a little, his gun pointed at the small heap of pale hair and fragile limbs—

Was she dead? Had Clint actually shot her? *Oh, please, God, if there is a God who can truly forgive sinners of their past transgressions, please don't let Clint kill her; I'll do anything, anything—*

Then she raised her head and stared up at Clint, and Steve yelled, "No!" He scrambled to his feet, vaguely aware that the blood staining his shirt from his wound was freezing to his skin. He ran down the path. "Don't shoot! Damn you, Clint, don't shoot!"

Clint looked around. His mouth was pulled back in a smile that turned Steve's blood cold. He saw himself in that instant—the man he would inevitably become if he continued his lawless ways. Breathing heavily, his every breath a blur of steam through his lips, Steve stared into his brother's eyes. "What the hell has happened to you?" he demanded. "The Clint I used to know would never have shot a woman. The brother I used to know stood face to face with our pa if he ever dared to raise a hand against our mother, and tried his best to persuade Pa out of his life of crime. You used to talk about getting out of this life, of starting over if you only had the chance. *What the hell happened to you!*"

The sleet hissed around them, then Clint quietly said, "We all got choices to make, Stevie boy. You make 'em, and live by 'em, and damn the consequences. I tried goin' straight after you went to prison and Pa was hanged. It got me nowhere."

"Maybe you didn't try hard enough." It was Anna, looking up at Clint from the ground, her hair and face and shoulders dusted with ice.

Clint laughed, bent, and retrieved the satchel of money before looking at Steve. "I got what I want right here. Now you're either with me or you ain't, li'l brother. Make up your mind." He slung the bags across his shoulder, holstered his gun, and started back toward the house. Steve watched him go, still stunned by his brother's lack of conscience; he recognized the traits of their father, and realized in that instant that Clint was already a lost man.

Legs planted firmly apart, fists clenched, Steve stared down at Anna while the wet and cold seeped through his clothes, all the way to his bones. He shuddered. Moving slowly, he walked to Anna, went down on his knee, and took her face in his hands. "I've got to know, Anna. Do you love me?"

"Yes."

"And you swear to God Almighty that you'll wait for me?"

She nodded.

He kissed her mouth, then stood. The sleet was falling harder; his brother's image shimmered before him, a vague blur in the distance. He started to walk.

"Steve?" Anna cried behind him. "Steve!"

By the time Steve entered the house, Clint had donned his hat and shrugged on his coat. He was stuff-

ing his pockets full of Anna's cookies, taking little notice that the delicate confections over which she had
worked so diligently were crumbling in his fingers.
Steve glanced around the room, noting again the red
velvet bows, now slightly crumpled, that were displayed with pride. His eye caught on the one-winged
angel peering down at him from the top of the tree,
and he realized just what it had cost Anna to decorate
this old place up for the holidays. She could have kept
the unhappy memories of her childhood buried, but
for him she had chosen to start again, to build on the
future instead of the past.

"Get your things, Stevie boy, and let's get out of
here."

Steve closed the door and reached for the gun he
had earlier placed aside. "I'm not goin', Clint."

Clint looked momentarily surprised, then he
laughed. "That posse'll be here eventually."

"They've been here once already. Anna could have
turned me in, but she didn't. She gave me the chance
to start over, Clint. They'll be back and this time I'll be
waitin' for 'em."

Clint shrugged and tipped his hat lower over his
brow. He reached for the money satchel.

"Leave it," Steve said.

Clint's eyes came back to his. With his fingertips
frozen just above the money bags, he replied with a
cold smile, "You got some idea of keepin' it all for
yourself?"

"I'm not keepin' it, Clint. I'm turnin' it over to the
sheriff."

"You crazy?"

"Maybe. All I know is I don't want to end up like
Pa or Paul . . . or you. At last I have a chance to start
over and I'm gonna take it."

"The path to hell is paved with good intentions,
Steve."

"Least I'll get there with a clean conscience." He
raised the gun. "Now get away from that money."

Clint's eyes flickered toward the navy revolver in Steve's hand. Still, he reached cautiously toward the satchel and picked it up. "Put it away, Steve, and turn your back if you want no part in this."

"Why do I have the gut feelin' that if I turn my back you'll shoot me?"

"Would I do that?"

"Yeah, Clint, I think you would. Now put the money *down*."

"And if I don't?"

"Don't back me into that corner."

Clint considered the money bags, and, for a moment, it appeared as if he would toss the satchel onto the table. Then, with lightning speed, he drew his gun. Steve crouched, hearing the whine of the bullet sing past his ear, his mind exploding with instantaneous disbelief that Clint had truly intended to kill him. He aimed his own gun and fired, watched his brother's body jolt and stumble and fall. By the time the smoke had cleared Anna had shoved open the door behind Steve and thrown herself against him. They stood just inside the doorway, holding one another as the wind drove ice and snow against them.

Then the front door slammed open and Dewayne Crabtree filled the threshold. His bright red beard sported a generous coating of snow, and his eyebrows were white. His Golcher rifle was aimed directly at Steve.

"Thought I heard gunfire." His voice boomed in the small room. Dog crawled out from under the table and, with tail tucked between his legs, ambled over to Anna, who still gripped Steve as if her presence would somehow protect him. Staring harder down his rifle barrel, Dewayne ordered, "Throw down that gun, *amigo*."

Steve bent and placed the revolver on the floor, then kicked it toward Dewayne.

"Anna? You all right?" Dewayne asked.

She nodded, but still she clung to Steve, her head pressed against his shoulder while he held her and stroked her hair. Too soon. Dear God, he would be taken from her too soon. For nightmarish moments she had thought she would lose him to his brother—had known for certain that Clint would either lure him back into a life of crime or kill him. Now the danger was past and here, again, was the awful reality. He must now pay for his crime.

"What in tarnation's been goin' on here, Anna?" Dewayne demanded.

Steve responded. "We're the men who robbed your stage. I'm the one you shot. Anna here . . ." He tipped up her face and smiled into her eyes. "She saved my life . . . in more ways than one."

Dewayne kicked the door closed, barely glancing down at Clint. His eyes were on Anna. "What about this 'un?"

"My brother. He—"

"Was gonna kill Steve," Anna interrupted. "He would have killed me too." She turned to Dewayne, searching her old friend's eyes that watched her with their usual sharp awareness. "Steve wanted to turn himself and the money in."

"And?"

Anna looked up at Steve and smiled.

"Well, I'll be dad-blamed," Dewayne muttered under his breath. Slowly, he lowered the rifle, glanced one last time at Clint's body, and took a visual turn around the house, his eyes registering the tree and the age-tarnished decorations that hadn't seen the light of Christmas day since Anna's mother had died. "Well, I'll be dad-blamed," he repeated.

Steve returned Anna's smile, his own a reflection of the peace and acceptance he felt within himself. "It's gonna be a long five years," he told her, "but it'll be worth it."

She threw herself against him and buried her face in his chest, trying to defy the tears that spilled down her cheeks. Steve kissed the top of her head and laughed. "Be strong for me, Anna girl. Don't let me down now."

At last, Anna pulled herself together, righted her shoulders, and turned to face Dewayne. Steve stepped around her. "I'm ready to go," he said.

A heartbeat passed before Dewayne pulled his attention from Anna's flushed, tear-streaked face. "Go?" he replied. "Go whar?"

"To Nogales."

"Nogales?" He started to grin. "Shoot fire, what would you want to go there for? Fact is, I was just droppin' by to pass on the word to Anna when I heard shots fired. Sheriff Landry and his deputy done gone and got themselves bushwhacked by Injuns up by Apache Pass." Dewayne stooped and retrieved the money satchel from the floor, shook his head at Clint, and tutted.

"What are you sayin'?" Anna, her hands twisted in her skirt, moved hesitantly toward Dewayne as he draped the money bags over his shoulder. "Is—is Frank dead?"

"As a doornail." He guffawed. "Can't say as I'm sorry. That man was as mean as an agitated sidewinder on a windy day. That do leave us a problem, though."

Anna reached for Steve. He gripped her hand reassuringly as Dewayne glanced at Clint.

"What are we gonna do about this mess?" Dewayne finally said.

"I'd appreciate your lettin' me bury him before..." Steve's voice broke as he looked at his brother, then back at Anna. His face said it all, as always, the emotions he felt for her, the regret over having had to kill his brother.

"Before what?" came Dewayne's voice.

"Before we go to Nogales."

"Aw, heck. I don't reckon there's any need for yore goin', mister."

Anna and Steve stared at Dewayne as he tucked the rifle up under his arm and reached for the door.

"I'll let the company know that the man who stole their money is dead. As far as lettin' the law know..."

Dewayne yanked open the door, then braced himself against the cold wind and snow before looking back. He grinned. "There ain't no law in Nogales right now. Fact is, they'll be lookin' for a new sheriff now that Frank's dead. And you know Nogales. A real hell-raisin' town. They'll be needin' a man who's quick with a gun and ain't afraid to challenge evil when he meets it face to face. If you know of anyone fittin' those qualifications, mister, drop by my place in town. We'll see what we can do. Now I reckon I got to ride. Here it is Christmas Eve and I still got a few stops to make."

He disappeared through a flurry of snow.

Anna looked at Steve.

Steve looked at Anna.

Both ran to the door.

Through the curtain of white, they could barely make out the large bulky shape of the stage in the distance, and the man who lithely scrambled up to the driver's seat and took up the reins. "Wait!" Anna cried. Lifting her skirt slightly, she leapt from the house, little noticing that the wind had died; the snow fell thickly but softly upon the silent earth.

"Wait!" she repeated, stopping a fair distance from the coach. Shielding her eyes, she gazed the best she could through the falling flakes, just making out the figure of her old friend as he looked down from his lofty perch and bestowed a smile on her. "Thank you!" she shouted, laughing and crying. "Oh, thank you, Dewayne!"

He threw back his head in laughter, and the great booming sound seemed to echo off the very mountains. With a flick of his wrists the horses took flight. "Merry Christmas!" he shouted, and rolled out of sight.

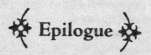

❖ Epilogue ❖

Christmas Evening

ANNA sat at the table with her head in her hands. The food was growing cold and the candles dim. She stared down at the note and reread it for the hundredth time.

Anna. I'll be home for Christmas. Steve.

"Sure you will," she said aloud. "Not only did you steal my old mule to ride off to who knows where, but you took my dog, too. I shoulda known not to trust some no-account outlaw."

She left the table and paced the floor, refusing to look again at the Christmas feast spread out over the table. Since dawn she'd worked her fingers to the bone, determined to make this a Christmas day Steve Burke would never forget. All the while she'd told herself not to worry; Steve would be back. There was some logical reason for his sneaking off in the middle of the night without so much as a fare-thee-well. But the hours had passed. The sun was setting behind the mountains . . . and Anna was alone again on Christmas.

Grabbing her coat and rifle, she shrugged on her wrap as she left the house and plodded through shin-high snow to the barn. She forked hay to the cow and strew corn for the chickens. She glared at Pugnacious, who sat on the plow and eyed her with a partially open beak. "I shoulda stewed you," Anna said. "I shoulda wrung your ornery neck, but I didn't. I was dumb enough to feel sorry for you, to think you might change your foul-tempered ways if I only showed you a little kindness. Even gave you an extra handful of corn. I must be nuts. I'm no judge of chickens *or* men!"

Flinging down the pitchfork, she grabbed her rifle and stormed from the barn, marched back to the house, and slammed the door behind her. That's when she heard the dog barking.

She cocked her head.

There it was again—Dog's bark. This time closer.

Her heart hammering, Anna forced herself to move, to open the front door and stare out through the twilight shadows and falling snow. Dog bounded through the white drifts, ears flopping and tail wagging. Behind him came . . .

She closed her eyes, feeling the emotions rise, bringing the tears she had tried so hard to deny pouring down her cheeks. Steve slid from the mule, then hesitated as he saw Anna in the doorway. She raised her Sharp and pointed it at him.

"What's that for?" he asked.

"Where've you been?"

"Nogales."

"Nogales! What for?"

A slow grin curled his mouth. "It's Christmas, remember? I figured that if a man can't give the woman he loves a present on Christmas day he's not worth much as a man."

Her heart tripped. Slightly lowering the gun barrel, Anna said, "Christmas day's about come and gone, in case you haven't noticed."

"Sorry," he replied sheepishly.

He moved toward the door but was brought to a halt as she yanked back the gun hammer. "Sorry, is it? Is that all you've got to say?"

"I got all the way to Nogales before rememberin' that I don't have any money."

"Oh, Lord . . ." She swallowed. "You didn't—"

"Rob a bank?" Steve's face turned menacing. "Damn it, Anna, is that what you're gonna think every time

I'm out of your sight? Is that any way for a woman to think of her husband?"

"Husband?" Anna lowered the rifle, her gaze locked on Steve's eyes that were regarding her from beneath the brim of his snow-dusted hat. The last streams of sunlight were gradually disappearing as she stepped from the house and sank to her ankles in snow. She moved slowly, hesitantly toward Steve, forgetting the last hours of despair when she'd truly believed that he had deserted her, now recalling only those moments of mindless love in his arms. "Husband?" she repeated softly.

He removed his hat, and his lean, dark face broke out in a smile. Anna stopped a few feet from him, her hands twisted together as she watched his eyes, then his hands as he reached into his pocket.

"As I was sayin'," he began, "I rode all the way to Nogales before realizin' that I had no money to buy you a present."

"Aw," she said, "you didn't have to buy me anything."

"Let me finish. A man needs time to word his proposal right, especially if he hasn't done it before."

Anna smiled. "All right. Go ahead."

"I tried to think of what I could give you—what would mean most to you. A weddin' ring just didn't seem enough, and besides, I didn't have enough money to buy that. So I decided on a job."

"A job? A *real* job?"

"Yeah." He grinned, and, moving to Anna, he took her hand, placed the smooth, cold object in her palm, and closed her fingers around it.

Anna stared down at a sheriff's badge.

"I took an oath on that star," Steve said, "to uphold the law. I intend to do it, Anna, if you'll be my wife."

She clutched it to her breast and gazed up at Steve, his hair glittering with snow, his eyes—oh, those eyes—twinkling with hope. "Yes," she whispered.

He swept her up into his arms and spun her around,

kissed the snow from her face and eyes and mouth. "Merry Christmas, Anna girl," he said as he held her.

"Merry Christmas." She laughed in joy. "Merry Christmas for the rest of our lives!"